# HANGING ON

# HANGING ON

Dean R. Koontz

M. Evans and Company, Inc. NEW YORK, N.Y. 10017

M. Evans and Company titles are distributed in
the United States by the J. B. Lippincott Company,
East Washington Square, Philadelphia, Pa. 19105;
and in Canada by McClelland & Stewart Ltd., 25
Hollinger Road, Toronto 374, Ontario


Library of Congress Catalog Card Number: 73-80168
Manufactured in the United States of America
ISBN 0-87131-118-6
Design by Paula Wiener
1 2 3 4 5 6 7 8 9

For David Williams,
*who made author-editor arguments all unnecessary*
*by being in the right every step of the way.*

# PART ONE

# The First Panzers

## July 10/July 14, 1944

# 1/

Major Kelly was in the latrine, sitting down, his pants around his ankles, when the Stuka dive bombers struck. With good weather, Kelly used the last stall in the narrow, clapboard building, because it was the only cubicle not covered by a roof and was, therefore, considerably less offensive than any of the others. Now, in the late afternoon sunshine, a fresh breeze pouring in over the top, the stall was actually pleasant, a precious retreat from the men, the war, the bridge. Content, patient with his bodily processes, he sat there watching a fat brown spider weave its web in the corner behind the door hinge. The spider, he felt, was an omen; it survived, even flourished, midst stench and decay; and if he, Kelly, only spun his webs as well as the spider did, were as tenacious, he would flourish too, would make it through this damn war in one piece. One *live* piece. He had no desire to make it through the war in one *dead* piece. And that meant spinning tight webs around himself. Shallow philosophy, perhaps, but shallow philosophy was Major Kelly's one great weakness, because it was the only thing that offered hope. Now, mesmerized by the spider, he did not hear the Stukas until they were almost over the latrine. When he *did* hear them, he looked up, shocked, in time to see them sweep by in perfect formation, framed by the four walls of the stall, shining prettily in the sunlight.

As usual, the trio of stubby dive bombers came without the proper Messerschmitt escort, flaunting their invulnerability. They came from the east, buzzing in low over the trees, climbing as they reached the center of the open encampment, getting altitude for a murderous run on the bridge.

The planes passed over in an instant, no longer framed in the open roof of the last stall. A turbulent wind followed them, as did a thunderclap that shook the latrine walls.

Kelly knew he was as safe in the latrine as anywhere else in camp, for the Stukas never attacked anything but the bridge. They never bombed the cheap tin-walled bunker that was shelved into the soft ground near the tree line, and they ignored the heavy machinery building as well as all the construction equipment parked behind it. They ignored the headquarters which was half corrugated sheet tin and half clapboard and would have made a dandy target; and they were oblivious of the hospital bunker cut into the hillside near the river—and of the latrines behind HQ. All they cared about was pulverizing the damn bridge. They passed over it again and again, spitting black eggs from their bellies, flames blossoming beneath them, until the bridge was down. Then they bombed it some more. They transformed the steel beams into twisted, smoldering lumps of slag, unrecognizable and unusable. Then they bombed it some more. It was almost as if the three pilots had been severely traumatized by the bridge during their childhoods, as if each of them had a personal stake in this business, some old grudge to settle.

If he avoided the bridge, then, he would be safe. Intellectually, he was quite aware of this; however, emotionally, Major Kelly was certain that each Stuka attack was directed against him, personally, and that it was only good luck that the pilots got the bridge instead. Somewhere deep in Nazi Germany, some fine old school chum of his had risen to a position of influence and power, some old chum who knew just where Kelly was, and he was running these Stuka flights to have him wiped out as fitting retribution for some slight or other that Kelly had done the old chum years and years ago. That was it. That had to be it. Yet, as often as he considered his school days back in the States, Major Kelly could not recall a single old chum of German extraction who might have returned to the fatherland for the war. He still would not give up on the theory, because it was the only one which made sense; he could not conceive of a war, or any battle in it, that was waged on a purely impersonal basis. At one time, he was sure, Churchill, Stalin, and Roosevelt must have snubbed Hitler at a cocktail party, thereby generating this whole mess.

Now, caught in the latrine at the start of the attack, Major Kelly stood and jerked up his trousers, catching them on an exposed nailhead and ripping out half the backside. He slammed through the dusty latrine door into the open area at the south side of the machinery shed. He was just in time to see the Stukas, four hundred yards upriver, arc high over the bridge and punch out their first ebony bombs. Turning, the seat of his pants flapping, he ran for the bunker by the trees, screaming at the top of his lungs.

Behind, the first bombs hit the bridge. A hot, orange flower blossomed, opened rapidly, ripened, blackened into an ugly ball of thick smoke. The explosion crashed across the encampment with a real physical presence, hammering at Kelly's back.

"No!" he shouted. He stumbled, almost fell. If he fell, he was finished.

More bombs plowed into the steel floor of the bridge, shredded the plating squares, and hurled thousands of sharp, deadly slivers into the smoke-darkened sky. These jagged fragments fell back to earth with a wind-cutting hum that was audible even above the shriek of the Stukas and the shattering explosions of more bombs.

He reached the steps in the earth and went down to the bunker door, grabbed the handle in both hands, and wrenched at it. The door did not open. He tried again, with no more success than before, then fell against it and pounded with one fist. "Hey, in there! Hey!"

The Stukas, circling back from the bridge, came in low over the bunker, engines screaming. They established a sympathetic vibration in his bones. His teeth chattered like castenets. Shuddering violently, he felt himself throwing off his strength, letting the weakness well up. Then the Stukas were gone, leaving behind them a smell of scorched metal and overheated machine oil.

Major Kelly realized, as the Stukas shot out across the trees to make their second approach on the bridge, that no one inside the bunker was going to open up and let him in, even though he was their commanding officer and had always been nice to them. He knew just what they were thinking. They were thinking that if they opened the door, one of the Stukas would put a two-hundred-pound bomb right through it, killing them all. Perhaps that was a paranoid fear, but Major Kelly could understand it; he was at least as paranoid as any of the men hiding down in the bunker.

The Stukas, which had grown almost inaudible at the nadir of their swing-around, now closed in again, their engines winding up from a low whistle through a shrill keening into an enraged scream that made Major Kelly's hair stand right on end.

Kelly ran up the bunker steps to the surface and, screaming again, plunged past the back of the machinery building, past the latrine, and along the riverbank toward the hospital bunker. His legs pumped so hard and so high that he seemed in grave danger of hitting himself in the chest with his own knees.

The Stukas thundered in, lower than before, shattering the air and making the earth under him reverberate.

Kelly knew he was running toward the bridge, and he hated to do that, but the hospital bunker was a hundred and fifty yards closer to the span than the latrines had been, offering the only other underground shelter in the camp. He reached the hospital steps just as the first Stuka let go with its second load of bombs.

The entire length of the bridge jumped up from its moorings, twisted sickeningly against the backdrop of smoke-sheathed trees on the far side of the gorge. The structure tossed away I-beams like a frantic lover throwing off clothes. Long steel planks zoomed above the blanket of smoke, then shot down again, smashing branches to the ground, splitting the dry, baked earth.

Kelly looked away, ran down the hospital steps, and tried the door just as the second Stuka let go with its payload. The bridge gave some more, but the hospital door wouldn't give at all.

Kelly ran back up to the surface, screaming.

The last plane swooped over the gorge. Flames gushed up in its wake, and smoldering pieces of metal rained down around the major, bouncing on his shoes, and leaving scars where they hit.

The Stukas, peeling off at the apex of their bombing climb, turned over on their backs and flew upside down toward the trees, to lead into a third approach.

"Arrogant sons of bitches!" Kelly shouted.

Then he realized he shouldn't antagonize the Stuka pilots, and he shut up. Was it possible that any of them had heard him above the roar of their own planes and above the noise of bridge sections settling violently into the gorge? Unlikely. In fact, impossible. However, you didn't stay alive in this war by taking chances. It was always possible that one or more of the pilots could read lips and that, flying upside down with a perfect view of him, they had discovered the nature of the epithet which he had so thoughtlessly flung at them.

Suddenly, with the planes gone over the trees, he was alone, standing in a low pall of black smoke that rose like flood waters out of the gorge and spread rapidly across the entire camp. Choking, wiping at teary eyes, he began to run again—then stopped cold as he saw that there was nowhere to run *to*. Caught with his pants down in the latrine, he hadn't gotten to either of the bunkers in time to be let in with the other men. Unaccustomed to battle, the technicians and laborers in Kelly's unit of Army engineers had developed only one useful talent for battle conditions: running. Any man in the unit could make it from one end of the camp to the other and into the bunkers so fast he'd have won a medal at any

Olympic track event. Unless, of course, he was confronted with some obstacle—like pants around his ankles, an exposed nail that ripped out the seat of his pants, or the latrine door. Which was what had happened to Kelly to slow him down. And now he was here alone, waiting for the Stukas, doomed.

The smoke rose around him in black columns, rolled menacingly over the C-shaped clearing in which the camp stood, obscuring the HQ building and the machinery shed and the latrines, closing out life and bringing in death. He knew it. *I feel it coming,* he thought. He was doomed. He sneezed as the smoke tickled inside his nostrils, and he wished to hell the Stukas would come back and get it over with. Why were they making him wait so long for it? All they had to do was drop a couple of bombs anywhere nearby, and it would be over. The sooner they did it the better, because he didn't like standing there in that smoke, sneezing and coughing and his mouth full of an oily taste. He was miserable. He wasn't a fighter. He was an engineer. He had hung on as long as he could reasonably hope to; the war had finally defeated him, had foiled his every stratagem, destroyed his every scheme for survival, and he was ready to face up to the awful truth. So where were the Stukas?

As the smoke gradually cleared, leaving only the gorge clouded in ugly vapor, Major Kelly understood that the Stukas weren't coming back. They had done all they needed to do in their first two passes. He wasn't doomed after all, or even injured. He could have remained in the latrine, watching the spider, and saved himself all this effort. But that wasn't the way to hang on, to stay alive. That was taking chances, and only madmen took chances. To stay alive, you moved constantly this way and that, searching for an edge. And now that the Stukas were gone, so was Major Kelly's pessimism. He *would* come out of this in one piece, one *live* piece, and then he would find General Blade—the man who had dropped their unit two hundred and fifty miles behind German lines—and he would kill the son of a bitch.

# 2/

"This is a fairy tale, grand in color but modest in design," Major Kelly said. He stood on the burned grass at the edge of the ruins, a fine gray ash filming his shoes and trousers, his big hands and his shirt, and even his face. Sweat ran down his forehead, streaking the ashes, and fell into his eyes. The acrid fumes that rose from the broken bridge and stirred around his feet added an eerie and inhuman touch to his shallow philosophy. Continuing in the same vein, he said, "None of this is real, Sergeant Coombs. It's all a fairy tale of death; you and I are merely the figments of some Aesop's imagination."

Major Kelly, a dreamer who always hoped to find a whore in every nice girl he met, was given to such fanciful extrapolations rather more often than would have pleased General Blade if that august commanding officer had known.

Sergeant Coombs, short and stumpy, forty-five years old and a career man, was *not* given to fanciful extrapolation, not even in his dreams. He said, "Bullshit!" and walked away.

Major Kelly watched his noncom plod—Sergeant Coombs did not walk like ordinary men—back toward HQ, wondering what he ought to say. Though he was clever at formulating odd bits of philosophy, Kelly had no talent whatsoever for discipline. Sergeant Coombs, canny for all his stumpiness, understood this and took advantage of the major. At last, when the noncom was at the door of the corrugated shed and would shortly be out of reach, Major Kelly shouted, "Bullshit to you, too, Coombs!"

Coombs jerked as if he had been shot, swiftly recovered his composure, opened the shed door, and stepped grandly out of sight.

Below Kelly, in the ravine, the bridge lay in a chaotic heap. Too much smoke obscured the structure for him to get a good look at it; however, as a vagrant breeze occasionally opened holes in the fumes, he did get a few brief glimpses. He didn't like what he saw. Everywhere he saw destruction. That was a word that usually was used in conjunction with another word Major Kelly liked even less: death; death and destruction. Although no one had died on or under the bridge, Major Kelly was deeply disturbed by what the suddenly made and just as suddenly closed holes in the smoke revealed. The bottom of the ravine was strewn with chunks of concrete and jagged lumps of stone, all scorched black and still radiating wavering lines of heat. Trees had been shattered by the explosions and by hurtling lengths of steel. Most of these had not caught fire, but their leaves were blackened and limp, little wrinkled lumps like thousands of huddled bats clinging to the branches. The bridge beams rose out of the rubble at crazy angles, ends broken, twisted by the explosions and by the intense heat, looking like nothing so much as the ribs of some prehistoric monster, the weathered bones of a behemoth.

The holes in the smoke closed again.

Lieutenant David Beame, second in comand of the unit, thrust head and shoulders above the black vapors, as if the stuff were solid and he had broken through with some effort. He spied Kelly and scrambled up the slope, stumbling and falling, cursing, finally gaining the fresh air at the top. He was covered with grime, his face an even black except for white rings around his eyes where he had repeatedly rubbed with his handkerchief. He looked like a vaudeville comedian in blackface, Kelly thought. Wisps of smoke trailed after Beame, soiled ribbons that the breeze caught and twined together and carried away.

"Well, Dave," Kelly said, "what's it like down there?" He really didn't want to know, but it was his place to ask.

"Not so bad as before," Beame said. He was only twenty-six, twelve years younger than Kelly, and he looked like a college student when he was cleaned up. Blond hair, blue eyes, and downy cheeks. He could never understand that it was always as bad as before, that nothing ever improved.

"The bridge piers?"

"Nearside pier is down. I couldn't even locate the struts through the anchorage and down to the pile. All gone. Farside pier's okay, bridge cap in place and the bearings sound. In fact, the farside cantilever arm isn't even bent. The suspended span is gone, of course, but we still have a third of the bridge up."

"Too bad," Major Kelly said.

"Sir?"

It was Major Kelly's duty, as directed by General Blade, to see that this bridge, which spanned a small river and a larger gorge for some nine hundred feet, he kept open. The bridge was presently behind German lines, despite the great advances the Allies had made since Normandy. No one had yet seen any Germans around here, except those in the Stuka dive bombers which had knocked out the damned bridge three times after Kelly's men had rebuilt it. The first time, in its initial existence, the bridge had been destroyed by the British. Now that Allied armored units hoped to cross the gorge at this point, whenever the German Panzer divisions had been turned back and finally overwhelmed, it must be maintained. At least, General Blade thought it must. This was one of his private contingency plans, a pet project. Kelly thought that General Blade had lost his mind, perhaps because of chronic syphilis, and that they were all going to die before any Allied armored units could ever use the bridge. Though Kelly believed these things with a deep and abiding pessimism, he also believed in getting along with his superiors, in not taking chances, in hanging on. Though they were all going to die, there was a slim chance he would last out the war and go home and never have to look at a bridge again. Because this slender thread of hope was there, Major Kelly didn't tell the general what he feared.

Beame, wiping at the grime on his face, still waiting for some sort of explanation, coughed.

"What I meant," Kelly said, "was that I wished they'd taken out the entire bridge."

"Sir?"

"Beame, what is your civilian profession?"

"Civil engineer, sir."

"Beame, if you had no bridge to keep rebuilding here, more than two hundred miles behind German lines, if no one bombed this bridge so that you could repair it, what the hell would you do with yourself?"

Beame scratched his nose, looked around at the clearing, the encircling trees, the smoking gorge. "I don't know, sir. What would I do?"

"You'd go mad," Major Kelly said. He looked at the sky, which was very blue; and he looked at the cantilevered bridge, which was very demolished. He said, "Thank Christ for Stukas."

# 3/

Lieutenant Richard Slade, darker and chubbier than Lieutenant Beame and looking somewhat like a choirboy with a vicious streak, was called The Snot by everyone in the unit except Sergeant Coombs. Slade did not know this, and he would have been enraged if he had heard the nickname. He was a young man with an overdeveloped sense of pride. Now, he came trotting out from HQ to tell Kelly that General Blade was going to call through in fifteen minutes. "The General's aide just placed the alert call in code," Slade said.

Kelly tried to keep his torn trousers out of sight. "That's not supposed to be until tonight." He dreaded talking to the general.

"Nevertheless, he'll be on in . . . about twelve minutes now. I suggest you be there, sir." He pushed his thick, brown hair back from his forehead and surveyed the bridge below. "I imagine we'll be requiring supplies again."

"I imagine so," Kelly said. He wanted to punch Slade in the mouth. Even when Lieutenant Slade used the correct form of address, he imbued the obligatory "sir" with a sarcasm that infuriated the major.

Slade said, "Sir, you'd better make a supplies list before he calls, so you can read it quickly—and so you won't forget anything."

Major Kelly gritted his teeth so hard he almost broke his jawbone. "I know how to handle this, Lieutenant Slade."

"I was only making a helpful suggestion." The lieutenant sounded hurt, though Kelly knew he wasn't. You couldn't hurt Slade, because Slade had a huge, rubber ego that bounced your insults right back at you, quick as a wink.

"Dismissed," Kelly said, though he knew he wasn't a good enough disciplinarian to make the word mean anything. He was tall, lean, well muscled, and hard-looking. He had very black eyebrows and what he fancied was a piercing gaze, and he should have been able to keep a man like Slade in line. But he couldn't. Probably, that was because Slade realized how terror-stricken he was. Being terror-stricken made him less like an officer and more like an enlisted man.

"Will the Major entertain another suggestion?" Slade asked.

Why the hell did he have to talk that way? *Entertain,* for Christ's sake! *Entertain!*

"What is it, Lieutenant?" Kelly attempted to be abrupt, icy, and harsh. That wasn't one of his better roles, however, and Slade seemed to think he was only being stupid.

"We rebuilt the bridge after the British bombed it, and the Stukas showed up to destroy it again," Slade said. He was one for repeating what everyone already knew, as if the fact gained some deep clarity that only his voice could impart to it. "When the Stukas went, we built the bridge a second time. The second flight of Stukas came and knocked the bridge down again. Yesterday, we completed repair of the bridge, and now the third flight of Stukas wiped it out." He looked at Kelly and Beame, waiting for some reaction. He seemed unaware of the fumes that rose from the gorge, and he was the only man present who was dressed in immaculate fatigues.

"So?" Kelly said at last, realizing they would remain there through the night and the following day and even beyond that if he did not prod the lieutenant.

"I believe we have an informer in our midst."

Kelly looked incredulous, but not too incredulous, since Slade just might be right. "Who do you suspect, Slade?"

"Maurice," the lieutenant said, triumphant, grinning, The Snot.

Maurice was the mayor of the only nearby French village, a hamlet of four hundred souls, so small it hadn't been on any of their maps when they were first dropped here behind German lines, following the successful landing at Normandy. For the most part, the townspeople were farmers and laborers; Maurice owned the only grocery and the hardware store, a third of the town's businesses which lined the single main street. Maurice was perhaps sixty years old, drank too much, bathed too little, and bragged that his eldest son was in Brittany working in the FFI—*Forces Françaises de l'Intérieur*—and had renamed his town Eisenhower once the Normandy invasion had acquainted him with that word.

Slade, seeing the disbelief in their faces, said, "I know that's an unpopular notion. I know how much everyone here likes Maurice and how much everyone thinks Maurice has done for us. But you'll remember that I have never fully trusted him, and you'll admit that he has the best opportunity to report to the Germans."

"Surely there isn't a radio in Eisenhower," Kelly said. "And he would need one to make reports. . . ."

"Perhaps it was dropped to them by a German night plane," Slade said. He always had an answer, which was another reason why everyone hated him.

Kelly wiped the soot off his face, looked at the blackened palm of his hand, wiped his hand on the seat of his pants, and jumped when his fingers slid over his own bare ass. Embarrassed, he said, "I can't picture that." He wondered if there were long black finger marks on his behind.

Slade wasn't done. "Why is it that the Stukas have never given our position to any element of the German army? Why haven't they sent ground troops after us, to wipe us out? Why is it that the Stukas bomb the bridge but not our positions? The machines, all our supplies, stand unharmed so we can rebuild the bridge again. Could it be the krauts are playing some sort of game with us?"

"What would their purpose be?" Kelly asked.

Slade frowned. "I haven't worked that out yet, but I will." He looked at his watch, snapped his head up so suddenly he'd have lost his toupee, if he were wearing one, and turned back toward HQ. "General Blade will be coming through in less than four minutes." He trotted away.

Beame, who wasn't given to swearing that much, said, "That fucking little creep gives me the fucking horrors."

"Let's go talk to the general," Major Kelly said.

# 4/

The big, wireless transmitter was a malevolent, hulking monster that always intimidated Major Kelly. It hummed like a swarm of bees, singing some monotonous and evil melody that echoed ghostily behind every voice that came and went over its open channel. Perhaps, if he spoke to someone other than General Blade on the set, it would not seem so monstrous. If he could talk to Betty Grable or Veronica Lake or to his mom, it might seem, instead, like a big old shaggy dog of a radio. But there was only General Blade.

Once they had exchanged call signs, General Blade said, "Blade calling Slade for Kelly." Then he laughed. Finished laughing, he said, "Slade? Blade. This is the Blade and Slade Show, and our first performer today is Major Walter Kelly."

"I can't take it again," Lieutenant Beame said, bolting for the door. It slammed noisily behind him.

"General Blade calling, sir," Lieutenant Slade said. He looked quite serious. He never seemed to see anything odd in the General's insane patter.

Maybe Slade had syph too. Maybe he was already rotten in the center of his brain, crumbling and almost dead.

Kelly sat down in the single metal chair that decorated the radio room, looked around at the rough board walls, the dust, the spider webs, the board floor. The chair was cold against his bare behind, but it wasn't the sole cause of the shivers that coursed through him. He lifted the table mike and said, "They bombed the bridge again, General."

"They bombed *what*?" General Blade asked.

In a number of ways, Kelly thought, Blade and Slade were

similar. The lieutenant was always telling you what you already knew, while Blade was always asking you to repeat what he had already heard. Perhaps Lieutenant Slade was the bastard son of General Blade; perhaps both of them had contracted VD from the same woman: Blade's mistress and Slade's mother.

"They bombed the bridge, sir," Kelly repeated.

"How?" Blade asked.

"With three airplanes and several bombs," Major Kelly said.

"*Three* airplanes, Kelly?"

Kelly said, "They appeared to be airplanes, sir, yes. They had wings and flew. I'm pretty certain they were airplanes, sir."

"Was that sarcasm, Kelly?" the general croaked through the hulking monster on the table before Kelly.

"No, sir. They were all Stukas, sir."

After a long silence, when Kelly was about to ask if he had died in the middle of the Blade and Slade Show, the general said, "If there were three planes, but none of them attacked your buildings, and all of them dropped on the bridge, doesn't that tell you something interesting?"

"Maybe they like us and don't want to hurt us, sir."

The general was silent even longer this time. When he spoke, he spoke gently, as if to a child. "One of their own people is there with you—an informer."

Kelly looked at Slade who smiled and vigorously nodded his thin, pointed head. Keep it up, Kelly thought. Keep shaking your head, and maybe it'll fall off. Maybe the syph will have rotted through your neck, and your head will fall off, so grin and shake your head.

To the microphone, Kelly said, "Informer?"

"How else do you explain their attacking only the bridge? How do you explain their not sending in a ground force to deal with you?" But the general really didn't want any military strategy from Kelly, or any cheap philosophy either. He went on before the major could answer: "Do you fully understand that the whole idea of keeping this bridge open is mine, Kelly? When it proves to have been a wise move, I'll be rewarded for it. But by God, until it does pay off, I have my neck stretched under the ax. Do you think it was easy for me to get you and your men, the construction equipment and materials, flown two hundred and fifty miles behind German lines?"

"No, sir," Kelly said. He remembered that ordeal quite well, even these four long weeks later: the parachute drop, clearing the brush and marking the temporary runway for the first plane full of heavy equipment, the hard work, the tight schedule, the terror. Mostly the terror.

Blade said, "Do you think it's a simple matter to keep this whole maneuver hidden from the more petty officers back here at command, from men who would like nothing better than to pull me down into the mire and climb over me on their way to the top?"

"I can see that it isn't easy for you, sir."

"Damn straight!" The general cleared his throat and paused to take a drink of something. Probably blood.

Choke on it, you pig, Kelly thought.

The general didn't choke. He said, "I want a list of your requirements, to augment whatever's salvageable there. The stuff will be flown in after midnight tonight. I want the bridge back up, no matter what the cost!"

Kelly read off his hastily scribbled list, then said, "Sir, how's the front moving?"

"Gaining ground everywhere!" Blade said.

"Are we still two hundred and thirty miles behind enemy lines, sir?" The last time he had talked to Blade, the front had advanced about twenty miles in their direction.

"Only two hundred miles now," Blade assured him. "In a couple of weeks, you'll be on the right side of the fence."

"Thank you, sir."

"Now, let me have Slade."

The lieutenant took over the chair, pulling it close to the

scarred table on which the radio stood. "Uh . . . Slade here, sir."

"This is Blade, Slade."

"Yes, sir!"

Major Kelly stood behind Slade, watching, hypnotized by the horrible routine he had witnessed countless times these past four weeks.

"Slade, Blade signing off. Another edition of the Blade and Slade Show is over."

"Yes, sir!"

"Christ!" Major Kelly said, bolting for the door.

# 5/

The hospital bunker was an abominable hospital in every respect, but the worst thing about it was the stink, the rich blanket of revolting odors that permeated the place and could not be chased out. The hospital had no windows, being a bunker, and no fresh air. Even with the door wide open, the place constantly stank of burnt flesh, decay, sweat, vomit, and antiseptics. Lily Kain, who nursed the sick and the wounded, said you got used to the smell after a while and didn't even notice it any more. But that notion had no appeal for Major Kelly; he wanted to be aware, always, of the smell of death and corruption. If the hospital ever started to smell nice to him, he knew, his number would be up.

Immediately inside the bunker, a battered table and two rickety chairs stood to one side, the nurses' station. Beyond, ten cots stood in shabby imitation of a genuine hospital ward, five along each wall, a thin gray blanket folded on each, meager comfort against the chill in the subterranean room which gave little evidence of the bright summer day aboveground.

Three low-wattage bulbs strung on a single frayed cord for the length of the rectangular room, powered by the small camp generator, did little to dispel the gloom. The walls seemed draped in a heavy purple fabric of shadows, and the corners were all pitch black. Kelly glanced quickly at those corners when he came in, and he felt as if inhuman creatures lurked there, waiting and licking their scaly lips, and watching with big, demonic eyes.

Cockroaches and fat centipedes scurried along the earthen floor and clung to the rough ceiling, moving in and out of pools of light, silent, cold, many-legged.

Only two patients resided in the hospital bunker when Major Kelly arrived there fresh from bolting the radio room. One of these was Liverwright, who had been wounded in one of the previous bombings, six days ago. He had been bathing in the river when the Stukas made their first pass, and he had taken a three-inch sliver of steel deep in his right thigh. The second patient was Kowalski, the zombie.

Three people attended the patients, though none of them had medical training. General Blade had not been able to kidnap a doctor or a medic for them, as yet.

Lily Kain, the only woman with the unit, was cutting gauze into neat bandage squares when Kelly arrived, her scissors making crisp snipping sounds in the heavy air. Because of the heat aboveground, and because she apparently had reptilian blood, she was wearing one of her skimpy, sequined dancer's costumes, out of which her ass cheeks bulged. She had the kind of ass cheeks that bulged well: pale, firm, beautifully formed, without the hint of a droop. Indeed, everything about Lily Kain was perfectly formed, all five-feet-six of her. She had thick black hair and wide-set black eyes and a freckle-spotted face, little upturned nose, full lips—a wet-dream face. Her breasts were big and incredibly uptilted; they threatened to spill out of her dancer's costume. Her waist was tiny, and her hips almost fleshless, legs long and flawless. She gave Kelly a fierce hard-on.

"Watch your jugs," Kelly said, grabbing her sequined backside. "Watch your jugs, or they'll fall out of your suit."

"You watch them," she said. Her voice was cool, almost a whisper, but with force enough to let a man know she had her own resources. "You're better at watching them than I am."

"How are they?"

"My jugs?"

"No," he said. "I know your jugs are fine. How are the men? Anybody hurt in today's raid?"

"Everyone made it to the bunkers in time," she said. Her pretty face was dotted with sweat, but it hid no deception. She didn't know about Major Kelly's being caught with his pants down in the latrine, and he was not about to tell her. She stopped folding gauze and cocked her right eyebrow. Lily had a way of cocking her right eyebrow that made you think she was going to shoot you with her nose. "I'm worried about Liverwright. Six days, and he can't seem to heal. He may get blood poisoning yet."

"No negativism," Kelly ordered. "This is, after all, just a fairy tale, a fable. We're all figments of some Aesop's imagination, bound to his will."

"I'd like to reduce Blade to a figment of *my* imagination, then cut his balls off," Lily Kain said. Lily Kain, though freckled and pug-nosed and inordinately pretty, was not your average, reserved, quiet American girl.

"I just finished the Blade and Slade Show," he told her. "Supplies will be coming in tonight."

"Parachute—or a landing?" she asked. She looked pitiful, lost and delicate and needful of comforting. Major Kelly wanted to comfort her. He wanted to pat her hand and console her and say, "Now, now." He also wanted to rip her skimpy sequined costume off and split her right there, but he managed to restrain himself.

"They'll land," he said. "The shipment's too heavy for a parachute drop this time."

This pleased Lily Kain. Every time a transport landed, she hoped she could persuade the pilot to take her back to Allied territory. After all, she didn't belong here. Everyone knew that. If anyone forgot it, even for a moment, Lily reminded him.

"I don't belong here," she reminded Kelly.

And she *didn't* belong here, if the truth were known, the only woman in a unit of Army engineers, two hundred miles behind German lines, dressed in a sequined costume out of which her jugs might pop at any moment. General Blade was responsible, in part, for her being there. Though unable to supply the unit with a doctor or a medic, General Blade had managed to divert a USO troop across the front to the unit by the bridge. Certain air corridors were open, not well patrolled by the Germans, and such a thing could be done without too much risk. Still, there was the matter of diverting the troop from somewhere else, from a place where they were expected, and no one could understand how General Blade had managed that. When Major Kelly had observed that obtaining a medic ought to be a cinch after such a coup, the general had accused Kelly of a lack of appreciation for his hard work in getting the USO people there, and had pouted and refused to speak to the major for nearly a week. Anyway, the troop had given them a great show, as such shows went—a juggler, a bad comedian, two singing sisters with buck teeth who called themselves Irma and Imogene, a magician, a mimic whose every imitation sounded like Fred Allen (partly because the mimic himself sounded like Fred Allen), and a dancer—and they'd accepted the unit's invitation to supper and drinks afterward. They had not been aware that they were behind German lines, but they'd been nervous enough to drink heavily. Lily Kain boozed like a man and passed out like one, too. Singing "Over There," the troop boarded the special plane from General Blade's headquarters, leaving much later than they had anticipated. Only after they had gone for an hour did Kelly, Danny Dew, and Lieutenant Beame bring Lily Kain out from the latrine stall where they had hidden her when she passed out.

"I don't belong here," Lily Kain repeated.

"I know," Kelly said. "But—"

"I gave Liverwright the morphine," Nurse Pullit said, interrupting them, smiling and nodding at Kelly. "His hip looks worse than ever."

Nurse Pullit was the second person assigned to the hospital bunker to tend the wounded. Nurse Pullit was actually Private Pullit in drag, and Private Pullit was not a nurse at all. No one could say where Private Pullit had gotten the white uniform he wore, but it looked good on him. He had hemmed the skirt so that it fell just above his dimpled knees, a somewhat daring fashion, and he kept the uniform well starched. He wore a bandanna over his head to conceal his still predominately male hairline, a cheerful scarlet cap that made him look a bit like a Negro mammy. Except he wasn't a Negro. Or a mammy.

When he had first volunteered for hospital duty and had shown up in his uniform, with his legs shaved and his face lightly powdered, the wounded men had attempted to get up and return to their duty stations. Even Private Stoltz whose left leg had been broken in two places and only recently set argued with Major Kelly that he was well enough to return to his post. Stoltz had actually made it up four of the six steps to the bunker's door before he screamed and passed out, bumping back down and badly cutting his forehead on the concrete edge of the last step.

Now, however, the men were grateful that Nurse Pullit had been assigned to their unit as a laborer, for Nurse Pullit proved to be adept at suturing wounds, applying bandages, lancing infections, and offering sympathy. Besides, Pullit's legs really weren't that bad.

"Everything all right, Nurse Pullit?" Major Kelly asked.

"Poor Liverwright," Nurse Pullit said, quietly, casting a

glance back at the man in the first cot against the far wall. Nurse Pullit's lips drew into a bow and made a *tch-tch-tch-ing* noise.

Before he realized quite what he was doing, Major Kelly had put his hand on Nurse Pullit's ass. Rather than insult Nurse Pullit by drawing back, he kept his hand where he had inadvertently put it, though he certainly felt strange.

"Is there anything I can do, anything that you need?"

"We've got good supplies of medicine," Nurse Pullit said, batting her thick lashes over her blue eyes. No. *His* lashes, over *his* eyes. "We could do with a doctor, but that's up to that nasty General Blade. However, there is something I wanted to ask you. . . ."

"Yes?"

"Well," Nurse Pullit said, "Lily has a delightful pair of white pumps in her costume trunk. The heels aren't really that awfully high. I could manage them, even on this dirt floor, and they would add so much to my uniform if I had them."

Major Kelly looked down at the combat boots on Nurse Pullit's feet. "I see your point," he said.

"Then I can have them?"

"Of course."

"Oh, thank you!" Nurse Pullit squealed. "I'm the happiest nurse in the world!"

## 6/

The third person assigned to the hospital bunker was Private Tooley, the pacifist. Private Tooley was six feet tall, weighed a hundred and eighty-five pounds, and had once lifted weights. His arms were like knotted hemp covered with tar, thick and rippled, lumped with muscle. He could do more work than any three men when a bridge needed to be repaired, and he never once complained about the eighteen-hour days a repair job might sometimes require. No one could understand, then, why Private Tooley was a chickenshit pacifist.

Sergeant Coombs, as bewildered about Tooley as everyone else, confronted the private in the HQ rec room one night, over a bottle of Jack Daniels. They had both been sitting in the small, board-walled room, sprawled on benches, backs against the wall, drinking and counting the spiders on the ceiling. The air was hot and thick, the night silence even thicker, and eventually they could not ignore each other any longer. At first, their conversation had been gruff, unconnected, meandering. With more liquor, and once they had all the spiders counted, it got spirited.

"What would you do if someone attacked your grandmother?" Sergeant Coombs wanted to know. "You're a pacifist, so what would you do?"

"Who would want to attack my grandmother?" Tooley had asked.

"Let's say it isn't sexual."

"She isn't rich, either," Tooley said.

"Seriously, suppose you were there, and someone attacked your grandmother with a gun. Would you shoot him first?"

"Do I have a gun too?"

Coombs nodded. "Yes."

"I wouldn't have a gun."

"Why not?"

"I'm a pacifist."

Coombs had reddened, but he said, "Suppose, just for the sake of this discussion, that you had a gun, a real gun." He took a pull of the whiskey, keeping his eyes on Tooley.

"How good am I with the gun?" Tooley asked.

Anticipating a loophole, Coombs said, "You're an excellent shot."

"Then I'd shoot the gun out of his hand."

Coombs took another drink, looked at the spiders, kept his temper in check, and said, "You're a lousy shot."

"You just said I was an excellent shot."

"I take it back."

"If I was a lousy shot, I wouldn't try to kill him," Tooley said. "I wouldn't dare try."

"Oh?"

"Yes. I might hit my grandmother instead."

Coombs stared at the bottle for a long time. When Tooley was about to touch him to see if he had passed out, the sergeant said, "Suppose you were driving a truck on a cliff road, too fast to stop. A little girl suddenly appears on the road, just around a bend. You either hit the little girl or drive over the cliff and kill yourself. You either crush and mangle this beautiful, blue-eyed, curly-headed little child—or you drive over the cliff. What would you do?"

"What happened to the man with the gun?" Tooley asked. "What did he do to my grandmother?"

"Forget him," Coombs said.

"How can I forget him? What if he kills Grandma while I'm out driving this truck?"

"Forget the first example," Coombs said. "Let's pretend you're in that truck. What would you do?"

"I'd blow my horn for the little girl to get out of the way."

"Your horn doesn't work."

"I'd wave and yell at her," Tooley said, raising his voice, almost as if the child were in front of him, as if this bench were the seat of a wildly careening truck.

"She couldn't hear you above the roar of the truck!" Sergeant Coombs said, standing, waving his fists for emphasis.

"Jesus Christ!" Tooley screamed. "How stupid is this kid? If she sees a truck bearing down on her, isn't she going to run for the bank and get out of the way?"

Triumphant, still standing, jumping up and down a little in his excitement, Coombs said, "She's too young to walk."

"Can she *crawl*?"

"No!"

"I'd drive over the cliff!" Tooley shouted. He grabbed the liquor, rocking the entire bench on which he sat, his eyes squinted tightly shut, waiting for the crash.

Coombs said, "Suppose your mother was in the truck with you?"

"My mother?" His eyes snapped open.

"Your mother."

"What the fuck would my mother be doing with me, in a truck, driving along a sheer cliff on a narrow road at sixty miles an hour? Why the hell isn't she back there helping my grandmother who's being attacked by the man with the gun who doesn't want to rape her?"

"I don't know anything about your family," Coombs said. "I only want to see how your chickenshit pacifism gets you out of this one?"

Tooley leaned back, hugging the liquor bottle to his chest. His eyes were white, unblinking. He licked his lips. Tense, thinking furiously, he was still a huge man, but he resembled a child. A frightened child. He said, "I'd slam on the brakes!" He leaned forward, as if hit in the pit of the stomach. "I'd try to stop before I hit the kid!"

"Hah!" Coombs roared.

"Hah?"

"You should hit the kid and save yourself and your mother. What the hell does a stranger mean to you, anyway?"

"But if I braked in time . . . ?"

"Hah! You'd slam on the brakes, going at sixty on a narrow road, send your mother through the windshield and kill her instantly. Bam. Dead. You'd fishtail past the little girl, smash her to jelly, plummet over the damn cliff, and crash through your grandmother's house and kill the old woman and yourself and several innocent bystanders. That's what would happen, and all because of your chickenshit pacifism!"

Tooley huddled into himself even more, stunned at the crisp, awful vision of ultimate catastrophe which he had been given.

"No, Tooley," Coombs had assured him, "it won't work. Pacifism is a wonderful idea, but it just isn't applicable to the real world."

Then he got up and walked out of the rec room, leaving Tooley glued to the bench.

However, Sergeant Coombs didn't manage to make Tooley change his outlook. The private still refused to pack a gun and spent most of his time helping the wounded in the hospital—especially Kowalski, who was the second patient, a regular zombie.

Fresh from talking with Nurse Pullit, Major Kelly walked to the end of the bunker and sat down next to Tooley on a gray cot which was drawn up close to Kowalski's cot. He pointed at the mute figure between the sheets, and he said, "How's your zombie doing today?"

"Same as usual," Tooley said, though he was disturbed by the major's choice of words.

Kowalski was lying quietly, his head heavily bandaged, eyes open, staring at the ceiling. He had collected a piece of bridge support in the back of his head when the British bombed the gorge four weeks ago, and he had not moved or spoken to anyone in all the days since. He stared at the ceiling and dirtied his pants and took food from Tooley which, once he had digested it, he craftily employed to dirty his pants again.

"There's a plane coming in tonight," Kelly told Tooley. He saw a fat centipede skitter along the floor, near the end of the bunker. It gained a shadowed wall and disappeared, probably on its way to the ceiling. He wondered if there were anything clinging to the ceiling just above his own head.

The pacifist looked at the zombie and then at the major, and he said, "Do you think they would take him back where he can get good medical attention?"

"You know what they'd do with him, even if they did agree to take him. They'd open the bay doors and dump him out at twenty thousand feet."

Tooley winced.

Kelly looked around at the patients, back at Nurse Pullit and Lily Kain who were engaged in an animated conversation about the nurse's new pumps. Pullit kept pointing to his combat boots and making odd gestures. "Tooley, I didn't come to the hospital bunker to look in on the patients. I came to see only one person."

Tooley nodded, smiling. "Lily Kain, sir. Gorgeous jugs!"

"Not Lily," Major Kelly said.

Perplexed, Tooley scratched his head. "Nurse Pullit?"

"Not Nurse Pullit. Why would I come to see Nurse Pullit?"

"Nurse Pullit's got pretty good legs," Tooley said.

"Not Nurse Pullit," Major Kelly said. He wiped the back of his neck, which was sweating, and he finally glanced up at the low ceiling. In the dim circle of light from the nearest bulb, there were no centipedes over him.

"Kowalski, sir?"

Kelly looked dumbly at the pacifist. "What about Kowalski?"

"Is that who you came to see, sir?"

Kelly frowned. "No, Tooley. I came to see you."

"*Me*?" Tooley was genuinely surprised and pleased. "Well, this is nice of you, sir. I can't offer much in the way of entertainment, but—"

"Tooley," Kelly said, lowering his voice even further, his words hissing like sandpaper along the concrete ceiling, deadened by the dirt walls, rattling on the corrugated tin, "you're the only one I can trust. I know you wouldn't turn informer and leak information to the krauts, because you don't want to see either side win."

"Through force," Tooley amended. "I want us to win, but I don't really believe in force."

"Exactly," Kelly said. "But someone *has* been leaking information to the krauts, and we have to find out who he is."

Tooley nodded soberly. "You think this informer might have come to me, since I'm an avowed pacifist—might have thought of me as material for a second subversive in the camp."

"That's it."

"He hasn't," Tooley said. "But if he does, I'll let you know right away, sir."

"Thanks, Tooley," Major Kelly said. "I knew I could depend on you, no matter what everyone says about you."

Tooley frowned. "What does everyone say about me?"

"That you're a chickenshit pacifist."

"I'm a pacifist, all right. But where do they get the other part of it, do you think?"

"I wouldn't know," Kelly said. He got up, scanning the ceiling for centipedes, pulling his coller tight around his neck. "Anyway, keep your eyes open for any unusual—incidents."

"Yes, sir."

Kowalski suddenly dirtied his pants.

# 7/

Crickets worked busily in the darkness, telegraphing shrill messages across the flat, open runway area toward the trees which thrust up on all sides. The crickets, Major Kelly was sure, were working for the Germans.

The sky was overcast. The clouds seemed like a roof, lighted from behind by dim moonlight, low and even, stretched across the land between the walls of the forest. Occasionally, heat lightning played along the soft edges of the clouds like the flash of cannon fire.

At the eastern end of the runway which Danny Dew had gouged out with his big D-7 dozer, Major Kelly, Beame, and

Slade waited for the DC-3 cargo plane. They stood close together, breathing like horses that had been run the mile in little more than a minute and a half. They stared toward the far end of the open strip, at the tops of the black trees, heads pushed a bit forward as they tried to catch the first rumble of the plane's engines.

A frog croaked nearby, startling Beame who jumped forward and collided with Kelly, nearly knocking the bigger man down.

"A frog," Slade said. But he didn't sound sure of himself.

The frogs, Major Kelly thought, were in league with the crickets, who were telegraphing messages to the Germans.

Abruptly, silencing the crickets, the sound of the plane's engines came in over the trees, low and steady and growing.

"Move!" Major Kelly said.

To the left and right, enlisted men struck matches, bent down and lighted tiny blue flares at each corner of the runway. They looked like overgrown altar boys at some alien worship. At the far end of the crude strip, another pair of men did the same, briefly lighted by an intense blue glow before they stepped back into the shadows under the trees. Now the pilot had a means of gauging the length and width of the runway. This really wasn't much for the pilot to judge by; he might as well have tried an audio landing with the sputtering of the flares as his only points of reference.

By the same token, the four blue lights weren't much for a random patrol of German night bombers to beam in on, either.

The pilot, Major Kelly knew, would already have begun to scream. He always began to scream when he started losing altitude a mile out over the trees to the west. When he came in sight of the blue flares, he would scream even louder. He said their permanent runway wasn't much better than the temporary affair he had first landed on. He said it was too short, too uneven, and too narrow. He said it wasn't macadamized, that the oil-and-sand surface was extremely treacherous. He said the four blue flares hurt his eyes and interfered with his judgment when he was putting down, even though he had to have the flares or not land at all. Besides, he said, the runway was behind German lines. Even if General Blade did have him by the short hairs, the pilot said, he had no right to send him and his plane and his crew behind German lines. He said this again and again, until Major Kelly went to great lengths to avoid him. The pilot had to shout about this to Major Kelly, because the general had forbidden him to tell anyone else that he had been behind enemy lines.

"What do you want to be behind enemy lines for?" the pilot would shout at Kelly, his face red, his hands fisted in the pockets of his flight jacket.

"I don't want to be here," Kelly would say.

"But here you are."

"On orders," Kelly would say.

"That's your excuse," the pilot would say.

There was really no reasoning with the pilot, because he was consumed with terror the entire time he was at the clearing.

Now, by the south side of the HQ building, twelve enlisted men waited to unload the materials which would, when combined with sweat, remake the bridge. All of the enlisted men were as nervous as the pilot, but none of them was screaming. The first time the pilot had brought the big plane in, the enlisted men had screamed right along with him, bent double, faces bright with blood, mouths open wide, eyes watering, screaming and screaming. But Sergeant Coombs had been infuriated by this display of cowardice. He had punished them the following day with KP duty and a severe calisthenics session. Because they feared Sergeant Coombs more than they feared the Germans, the men were forced to express this nervousness in less obvious ways. They stood by the HQ building, in the shadows, snapping their fingers, popping their knuckles, grinding their teeth, slapping their sides, clicking their tongues. One of them was kicking the side of the corrugated tin wall as if he did not believe it were real, as if he were testing it. The enlisted men, more aware of their mortality than the officers, were always afraid that the krauts would catch the cargo plane on radar, would follow it and bomb the shit out of the runway and the camp. The Stukas were friendly. The Stukas, for some reason, only wanted the bridge. But a flight of German night planes couldn't be counted on to limit its objectives. So the enlisted men sweated out each landing and each take-off, suffering from the same terminal disease that afflicted Beame: hope. They didn't understand that nothing improved, that it wasn't any use sweating out anything. Whatever would happen would happen. Then, when it did happen, *that* was the time to sweat.

The cargo plane's engines grew even louder now, tantalizingly near, though the plane remained beyond the patch of open sky that the surrounding woods permitted them.

"It's close," Slade said.

Suddenly, the big aircraft was there. It came in so low over the pines that Kelly had difficulty separating it from the black trees. It carried only two running lights, one on each wing tip, and it seemed more like some gigantic bird of prey than like a machine.

"Here comes the plane," Slade said, though everyone had already seen it. Nothing ever improved. Not even the lieutenant.

"He isn't putting it down fast enough," Lieutenant Beame said. He thought: Christ, it's going to plow right through us, knock us down like three bowling pins at the end of an alley.

The DC-3 slanted in fast, correcting.

"Not enough," Kelly said.

The pilot had not cut back. The props churned as thunderously as when the craft had slipped in over the trees.

"What the hell's he doing?" Lieutenant Slade demanded.

The big plane roared toward them, a prehistoric behemoth bellowing a mindless battle cry. Its tires were still off the rugged, oiled strip. The tiny running lights on its wings seemed, to Kelly, to swell until they were gigantic searchlights.

"Run!" Beame shouted. But he couldn't run. He could only stand there, hypnotized by the onrushing plane, blinking at the half-seen blur of the whirling props.

The pilot gave up on it. The craft rose sharply, tilting dangerously toward the dark earth, swooped over the three men and the trees behind them, racketing away across the forest.

"He's going to try again," Lieutenant Slade told them.

Able to run now that it wasn't necessary, Beame turned and loped into the trees, bent and vomited on a patch of wild daisies.

The moment the DC-3 had passed over them, all the fear went out of Major Kelly. Temporarily, at least. He had watched the plane plunging toward them, and he had been sure that he would die in seconds. The whole situation had that ironic touch which was so much a part of the war: surviving the Stukas and the Germans, he would now be slaughtered accidentally by his own people. When he wasn't, when he realized that the plane had passed over and left him unhurt, he chose to take his safety as an omen. If he had not been killed that time, he would not be killed the next. The pilot would put his ship down, and everything would go as planned. He would survive. For tonight, anyway. Maybe he would be blown to bits the first thing in the morning, but for the remainder of the night, he could rest easy.

The engine noise of the DC-3 faded, moving around them, then grew in volume again as the pilot made his second approach.

"Here he comes again," Slade said, unnecessarily.

Beame, back from vomiting on the daisies, said, "God."

The transport came into sight again, over the trees. It slanted in much more quickly than it had before. In fact, it angled too sharply, touched the runway at too high a speed, bounced. Tires squealed. The walls of the forest threw back echoes that sounded like anguished human cries. The aircraft shuddered, touched again, bounced again. The third time down, it stayed down. Its engines, thumping like a hundred hammers slamming into a block of wood, cut back, whined down, stopped with a suddenness that left them all deaf.

The silence of the night rushed in like collapsing walls of cotton, and they were too stunned to hear anything at all. Gradually, they began to perceive the crickets once more, the frogs, the breeze in the trees, the pounding of their own hearts.

"She's down," Slade said.

Even if they hadn't been watching, they would have known the plane was down, for in the cricket-punctuated night, they could now hear the pilot screaming. At some point during the flight from the west, he had cranked open a vent window, and now his arm was hanging out that window, and he was beating on the side of the plane. The sheet metal boomed like a drum, counterpoint to the pilot's unmelodic wailing.

Lieutenant Beame ran to the flare on the right, threw sand on it, and watched it sputter out. I would have gone out as easily, he thought, if the pilot had muffed that first try. I would have blinked out like a damped flare. He turned quickly and walked to the second spot of blue light, unwilling to carry that train of thought any further. He threw sand on this flare and looked toward the far end of the strip where someone else was just smothering the flares down there.

Above the runway, though he was still screaming, the pilot put out the running lights on the wings of the DC-3.

"There go the men to unload the plane," Lieutenant Slade said.

Beame squinted, but he could not see them. He had been night-blinded by the flares.

"Oh, God," Lieutenant Slade said, his voice breathy. "Isn't it all so inspiring?"

# 8/

Lily Kain's high heels went *tock-tock-tock* on the wooden landing steps as she climbed up the hatchway in the hull of the cargo plane. She went inside, into darkness, her footsteps echoing from metal walls. Hunched over to keep from hitting her head on the low ceiling, and careful not to touch the loops of poorly insulated wire which drooped from their overhead moorings, she went forward to the cockpit and leaned inside.

"Hello there!" she said, trying to be cheery and sexy.

"Hello," the copilot said, turning around in his sweat-stained flight seat. He was a tall, thin kid from Texas with an Adam's apple that made him look like he'd swallowed a whole orange and got it stuck in his throat.

Lily ignored him. He was too young and ineffectual to help her. She turned all her charm on the pilot, who had just stopped screaming, and she said, "Hello there!"

"Hello, Lily," the pilot said. His voice was hoarse.

"That's a nice costume you're wearing," the kid from Texas said. He gulped wetly, as if the orange had come unstuck.

During the day, when the heat baked the earth and the trees stood limp and parched, Lily Kain wore a dancer's costume, even though the men had begun to call her Miss Cock Tease. She couldn't understand why they were upset by her near nudity; after all, *they* walked around shirtless, all bronze and hairy. Didn't they understand that all those lovely, bunched and sunbrowned muscles made *her* horny? Sometimes she wanted to grab one of them and throw him down and rip off his khaki slacks and rape him. The only thing that gave her pause was the knowledge that, in the Army, rape was a crime punishable by ten years to life imprisonment. That would make her anywhere from thirty-four to – when she got out. It just wasn't worth it, not for a transitory thrill.

In the evenings, if it was cool, she wore one of Major Kelly's work uniforms which she and Nurse Pullit had cut down to size and resewn by hand. Lily's street clothes had been carried off with the rest of her USO troop, and she had been left behind with nothing more than a trunkful of scanty costumes. At least the work uniform afforded her a means of modesty whenever the mood struck her. It seldom struck her. Modesty just wasn't worth it.

When the transport plane landed this night, the air was chill, and it was a night for the work uniform and for modesty. However, Lily was wearing a pale-white velvet dancer's costume when she went to see the pilot. It was cut high along her hips, revealing all of her long legs, and it was cut so tight through the crotch that she knew she'd never be able to have children once she got out of it. She didn't want any children, of course. Raised a Roman Catholic, part of a large family, she had sworn off having her own kids when she'd been fifteen. One night, sitting at the family table, she'd looked around at all those shining Irish faces, then looked at her washed-out mother and her dried-up father, and sworn off pregnancy. Pregnancy was the most vicious disease imaginable. Now, she actually welcomed the murderously tight fit of her dancer's costume. It was tight in the top, too, so that her ample jugs were like tortured balloons that might squeak free and fly away. The costume had no back whatsoever. It was cut to her dimpled ass and gave a hint of backside cleavage. She might as well have been nude. That was the idea.

"Why don't you come outside?" Lily asked the pilot as she watched him watch her jugs. "We'll go for a walk."

"I don't feel like it," the pilot said, watching her crotch

now, his fine eyes desperately searching for a stray, curling pubic hair.

He always refused to get out of his plane when he landed. He told the men in Kelly's unit that he had been given a vision in a dream, and that this vision had warned him not to get out of his plane when he landed supplies there. In the dream, the pilot had seen FDR and Truman sitting on matched commodes with their faces wreathed in golden light. In unison, speaking as sweetly as angels, they had warned the pilot with this: "If you ever leave your plane at Kelly's camp, your life won't be worth a fart." Then they farted in unison, for emphasis. When Lieutenant Slade first heard about the pilot's vision, he said, "Inspiring!"

"Oh, come on," Lily said, holding a hand out to the pilot.

"No." He was adamant. He had suddenly abandoned his pubic-hair search and had focused on the bulkhead beside her.

Abandoning all pretense, as she always had to, Lily said, "Take me with you, please!"

"You know we can't, Lily," the pilot said. Though he was looking at the wall, he was seeing Lily in his mind's eye. He began to sweat.

"Why can't you?" she asked, pouting her full lips.

"Officially, you aren't here."

She twisted slightly, leaning against a steel strut that reinforced the cabin walls against major flak damage. She was lighted exotically by the green and amber scope bulbs on the control panels, and she looked very good. Long legs, perfectly curved. Firm thighs. Hips just wide enough. No waist at all. Swelling breasts, jammed up, nipples almost peeking over velvet cups. Face half in shadow, full lips parted with a promise of more than just a kiss. She looked tremendous.

"You look tremendous," the pilot said, still staring intently at the wall. "But that won't do you any good. You aren't here; no one's here." But he looked back at her jugs, now, as if *they* were here. "This place is two hundred miles behind German lines, and the high command hasn't ordered anyone in here yet. Therefore, there isn't anyone in here. Yet. And I can't bring back someone who wasn't here to begin with." When he was done with his speech, he was breathing heavily, and he was looking at her jugs more longingly than ever.

"You can't deny your senses," Lily said.

"Yes, I can," the pilot said.

"If I'm not here, who are you talking to?"

The pilot was silent awhile, thinking about that. The sounds of the ground crew unloading the big transport through both its bay and cargo doors were audible but somehow removed from his reality, a distant background noise that reminded the pilot of carnival workers setting up tents and stands and rides in the fairgrounds near the house where he lived as a child. He would have liked to think about that some more, except he remembered where he was and was too terrified to think about anything but death.

"Who are you talking to if I'm not here?" Lily asked again.

"A figment of my imagination," the pilot said.

"Major Kelly's already used that one," she said.

"What?"

"Never mind." She thought a moment. "If there isn't anyone here, who are these supplies for?"

"What supplies?" the pilot asked. He was gripping the edges of his battered flight seat with both hands, fighting off an urge to rise up and rip her clothes off and fuck her through the floor of the plane. His face was sheathed in sweat.

Lily sighed. "If you're not behind German lines, where are you?"

The pilot smiled and relaxed a bit. "Iowa City, Iowa."

"What?"

"I can see the cornfields from here," the pilot said, looking out of the windscreen at the cornfields.

Lily followed his gaze but could see nothing other than darkness and a few men carrying heavy crates of supplies. A small collapsible loading crane trundled toward the transport's cargo doors. But no cornfields.

"You're crazy," she said.

"No. I see fields of corn, endless fields, tall and green."

Lily stepped forward and touched the pilot's cheek as he stared out through the windscreen, and she jumped in surprise as he nearly leaped out of his flight seat. He smiled nervously and tried to pull away. He was pudgy and red-faced and in need of a shave; even when he wasn't terrified, he would have looked rather ordinary and unappealing. Still, she said, "I think I could get to like you."

"What's there to like?" he asked. "A knot of nerves, spastic colon, stomach ulcers . . . nothing. . . ."

"Still, I could," she said. She bent closer to him, her jugs right in front of his face now. She was willing to tell the pilot anything to convince him to take her back to Allied territory. Actually, she found him revolting; however, telling him these fantasies didn't hurt anything. "We could have lots of good times."

The pilot took a thermos from a pouch on his seat, opened it, and poured himself a cup of steaming coffee. He did all this slowly, deliberately, as if he were trying to give himself time to gather his wits and meet the challenge she presented. His hands shook so badly that the coffee kept slopping over the rim of the cup. He said, "I'm sorry, Lily, but you don't arouse me at all."

"Don't I?"

"Not at all."

Suddenly, Lily could see only a bleak future. She could see another week here at the camp, another week of waiting for the inevitable flight of Stukas, another week of wondering if she would go home as a corpse or as a girl with a brilliant theatrical career ahead of her. Those were the only two possibilities, because she couldn't see any way she could go home as a *corpse* with a brilliant theatrical career ahead of her. She realized that she would have to go further than before, would have to pressure the pilot more than ever.

"So you might as well go," he said, slopping coffee all over his hand.

She reached behind, found the zipper on her velvet costume, tugged it down and peeled to the waist. Her large, fine breasts fell forward, a symphony of jiggling flesh, the dark nipples high on the top of their matched upward thrusts, hard and prominent.

"Gosh," the kid from Texas said. He squirmed in his seat, making the cracked leather squeak.

Lily ignored him. She had to ignore him. For one thing, he couldn't help her get out of the camp. For another, if she paid him any attention at all, he'd lose his head and take her while her back was turned.

The pilot watched her jugs. He seemed hypnotized. When he began to speak, he sounded far away, as if repeating something he'd memorized in church but had never really believed. "I am not aroused by you, because General Blade wouldn't like it if I were aroused by you and brought you back. You'd go around telling everyone about Kelly and this camp and the general's contingency plan, and you'd get the general in all sorts of trouble."

She moved slightly as she shook her head, and her breasts shivered deliciously, the nipples swelling, the cleavage touched with a blush. "No, I wouldn't do that. I wouldn't tell a soul. What would happen—you and I would have lots of fun. That's all that would happen."

"Gosh," the Texan said, still squirming. "Gosh."

The pilot licked his lips. He was shaking like a train on a bad track, close to derailment. Half the coffee in his cup was gone now, though he had not drunk any of it. "I know you better than that," he said. "I've heard you curse the general, and I know what you'd do. The general wouldn't want you to come back. Whatever the general wants, I want. There's a war going on. In a war, the little people only survive if they do what the big people tell them to do.

I'm a little people. The general is a big people. The general doesn't want me to be aroused by you, and therefore I'm not aroused."

Lily slipped out of her costume altogether.

The Texan sucked in his breath and almost choked.

"You've got an erection," Lily told the pilot.

"I haven't." He was shaking so badly now that his coffee cup was empty. The controls in front of him gleamed wetly; steam rose off them.

Lily dropped one hand to the juncture of her thighs and performed a magic trick in which one of her fingers disappeared. "Yes, you have."

The pilot looked down at his lap, at the telltale, arrow-headed bulge in his slacks.

Lily was running both hands up and down her body now, cupping her fine breasts, now her buttocks, caressing her thighs, almost encircling her waist.

The pilot opened his thermos bottle and dumped the whole batch of steaming coffee into his lap. He winced, bit his lip until blood came, but did not move otherwise.

"It didn't work," Lily said.

The pilot looked at his lap. He was still erect. "Damn," he said. By now, he had bitten his lip so hard that blood gleamed on his chin. His clothes were sodden with perspiration, and his hair lay in lank, damp strands across his dripping forehead. "I want what the general wants."

"You'll run out of coffee sooner or later," Lily said.

"No, I won't," the pilot said. "I brought three thermos bottles." He showed her the other two. "I want what the general wants," he repeated.

She stared him straight in the eye for a long minute, then sighed. She stopped caressing herself and picked up her costume. "I guess you're telling the truth."

"I am."

"It's sad," she said.

She turned and started out of the cockpit.

"Wait a minute, Lily!" the Texan said.

She turned, breasts slapping together, flushed green by the control lights. "What is it?"

His Adam's apple bobbled up and down. "I—Well, I don't care what the general wants."

"Yeah," she said. "But you aren't the pilot."

"I could be—one day soon."

"Hey!" the pilot said. "What's that supposed to mean?"

The Texan shrugged. "You might take a flak fragment in the neck." He smiled at Lily, as if he were anticipating that development with pleasure.

"If it happens," Lilly said, "*then* we'll talk."

She went back through the plane, down the narrow corridor in the center of the fuselage, toward the hatchway where she had come in. She stopped only once, to slip back into her velvet costume and pull up the zipper.

Outside, on her way back to the hospital bunker, she began to think about the only two words that mattered: death and sex. Deep down in every man or woman's mind, those were the two words that really counted for anything, two animal urges or conditions of the species which drove you relentlessly through life. You tried to avoid death for as long as possible, while grabbing all the sex you could get. Ordinarily, built as she was and uninhibited as she was, she would be able to function well in a world governed by those drives. But the war had turned everything around. She had sex to offer, and that was how she could avoid death. But the only way the pilot could avoid death was to refuse sex. The irresistible force and the immovable object. Two deer, they were, with antlers locked and no way to escape.

"Nice night, isn't it?" an enlisted man asked when she passed him on her way to the bunker.

"Fuck off!" she said.

He stopped as if he'd walked into a wall. "Jesus!"

Sulking, she went down the hospital bunker steps, calling for Nurse Pullit. She needed a shoulder to cry on.

# 9/

Three days after the bridge was bombed out, it was nearing completion once again, straight and true, spanning the gorge and the river in the middle of the gorge and the unsalvageable ruins of the previous bridges that the Stukas had destroyed. This speed was not particularly amazing, since Major Kelly was commanding a trained crew of construction workers and some of the best Army engineers in the war. In fact, their progress with the bridge was amazingly *slow*. After all, with the guiding help of the Army engineers, only twelve thousand American and Canadian workers had built the monumental Alcan Highway from Dawson Creek, British Columbia, to Fairbanks, Alaska: 1,671 miles of roadway completed in only eight months, when it was clear that the Japanese were operating in the Aleutians and that such a highway was desperately necessary for North America's defense. In the Pacific theater, the Army engineers had cleaned out the demolished ruins of old bridges and had spanned jungle rivers with portable Bailey bridges in mere hours. Later in the war, when the Ludendorff Bridge would be damaged under Nazi attack and eventually fall apart carrying Allied traffic, Army engineers would replace the span in less than half a day, though it was 1,068 feet long. Therefore, Major Kelly's unit was actually ponderously slow in replacing the ruined bridge by their camp. There was a reason for this. So long as the bridge was unable to bear traffic, no Stuka flight would be dispatched to bomb it, and they would be able to count on some peace and quiet. Once the bridge was up again, however, they'd have to sit around on tenterhooks, waiting for the dive bombers. The longer they took to rebuild the bridge, then, the better.

In fact, Major Kelly would have liked to take about a month or six weeks to rebuild the bridge. The only thing that kept him from taking that long was the realization that General Blade would order Lieutenant Slade to kill him and assume command.

As the bridge neared completion, Major Kelly and Lieutenant Beame inspected the bearings on the new bridge cap after the nearside canitlever arm had been fastened down on shore and to the pier. All that remained, when their inspection was completed, was the anchoring of the suspended span between the two cantilevers. While they were still beneath the bridge, clinging to the concrete supports by means of belts and mortared chain handholds, soaking up the cool shadows while they worked, Sergeant Coombs came to the edge of the river and yelled down at them.

"The Frog's here!" he yelled.

That was Sergeant Coomb's way of saying that Maurice, the mayor of the only French village nearby, had come to see the major. Sergeant Coombs had few friends among the peoples of other races and religions. The sergeant didn't particularly care. As he often said to Slade when they spent an evening together reading over the Army field manual, "There was a rich kid in my hometown who had a black governess, a big ugly woman. Parents thought it was classy to have a nigger tending their kid. Worse than that, she wasn't a citizen of the States. She was French. A frog nigger. Or a nigger frog, whichever way you see it. Top that off with the fact she was a Catholic. A mick frog nigger. Or a nigger mick frog. Or a frog nigger mick. Whichever." When Lieutenant Slade would ask what had happened, as he always did, the sergeant would cluck his tongue and finish the story. "The mick nigger frog was with them twenty years. The kid grew up, got drunk, raped a girl, and slit her throat. Got electrocuted. The kid's old man started taking up with whores, gave his wife the clap, and had nearly everything taken from him in the divorce settlement. The wife started betting the horses and running with young jockies and lost most of what she took off the husband. If they hadn't hired that nigger, where might they be today?"

"The Frog's here!" the sergeant shouted again.

"I heard, I heard!" Major Kelly said, scrambling up the ravine, dust rising in clouds behind him, stones kicking out from under his feet and falling down on top of Beame who tried to keep up with him.

"I am not a frog," Maurice said, stepping into sight a dozen paces from Coombs. "People are not animals—except, perhaps, to the Nazis. One should never refer to human beings with the names of animals. It is degrading. I refrain, after all, from calling Sergeant Coombs a pig."

Sergeant Coombs colored a pink, hamlike shade, and turned and stomped back to the corrugated shed where he tended the construction machines that he loved. He didn't salute Major Kelly or request his commanding officer's leave. He did, however, say, "Bullshit."

Major Kelly shook Maurice's hand, marveling as always at the inordinate greasiness of Maurice's complexion. The man's round chin was like a large, oiled bearing. His cheeks were slick. His nose was beaded with oil in the creases and shined overall. His hair was combed straight back, pasted to his round head by a heavy coat of clear lubrication. Fortunately, Major Kelly thought, Sergeant Coombs had not yet called Maurice a *greasy* frog.

"What brings you here today, Maurice?" Kelly asked. But he knew what brought Maurice there: the possibility of a profit. The possibility of a profit motivated Maurice like food or sex or liquor or success motivated other men.

Quite to the point, Maurice said, "I would like to have your backhoe. The Cat, you know which I mean?" He wiped his greasy hands on his baggy trousers and looked past the major at the heavy, camouflage-painted piece of equipment.

Major Kelly shook his head sadly. "You know we can't permit Army property to be used for a civilian project."

"You misunderstand, Major!" Maurice said. "I do not wish to borrow the backhoe. *Au contraire!* I wish to own it."

"You want to buy the backhoe?"

"No, no, no."

"You want me to give it to you? Just give you The Cat?"

"That's right, Major."

Major Kelly wished that Maurice didn't speak English so well, that the channels of communication between them were severely limited. It was dangerous to be able to communicate with the old son of a bitch. Just past the turn of the century, when he was seventeen, Maurice had immigrated to America where he'd remained until just after the First World War. He had returned to France because, as he told the major, there was a greater chance of his making a fortune there. He had not done badly in the States, and he hoped to use his capital to invest, cheaply, in the shattered motherland and then grow along with her as she was restored. He'd done well, though not so well as he had thought he would. In France again, he found that his countrymen were not enamored of Americans, not in the least, and that they distrusted any Frenchman who had once gone to live with the Yanks. Still, he had made and lost and remade and relost fortunes. Right now, he was trying to make a fortune by screwing Major Kelly to the wall. He tried this about once a week. He hadn't failed yet to get what he wanted.

"I suppose," Major Kelly said, "that there's a good reason why I should just give you the machine."

"An excellent reason," Maurice agreed, wiping a hand over his white, greasy hair. His fingers were greasy too.

"Information to sell?"

Maurice nodded. "Information that will save your lives," he said, grandly. Maurice could be grand, when he wanted. Even with his hair all slicked back and his face greasy, he could be grand.

"You exaggerate, surely."

"Never."

"What's the nature of this information?"

Maurice looked meaningfully at the backhoe and arched one bushy eyebrow.

"You can't expect me to give you the machine without knowing what I'm getting in return," Major Kelly said. "That's not nice, not nice at all. I am always nice to my men and nice to you—so why is everyone nasty with me?"

Maurice nodded sadly, sympathizing with the major, but he would still not say what the information was that he had to sell.

Major Kelly turned and pointed at the camouflaged backhoe which sat on the edge of the riverbank, by the bridge entrance, digging-claw up and bent, mud crusted on its teeth. "Do you know what that piece of equipment costs? Do you realize how important it is to my mission here?"

*"Quelque chose."*

"It is *not* a trifle," Kelly said.

Maurice pulled at his greasy nose and sighed, *"Coûte que coûte*—it will not save your lives."

Major Kelly watched the little frog carefully, and he finally decided he had to trust him. He couldn't risk ignoring the bastard, in case he really did have something vital to say. Maurice was just the sort to let them die in order to teach them a lesson.

"So?" Maurice asked.

"All right. You can have the damn thing. But not until you've told me what you came to tell me."

"I must have the backhoe first," Maurice insisted.

The Frenchman jammed both hands into his baggy trouser pockets and looked at the earth, suddenly so still that he appeared to have turned into a column of stone. The illusion was so convincing that Major Kelly felt a solid hammer blow to Maurice's head would crack him into thousands of shards. Kelly had to fight off an urge to go looking for a construction mallet. He knew Maurice would stand this way until he got what he wanted or was refused it outright. And, in the meantime, death was bearing down on them in some form the major couldn't guess.

Kelly sighed. "Okay."

"Excuse me?"

"You can have The Cat."

Maurice smiled. "You won't regret this."

"I better not," Kelly said, trying to sound fierce.

Maurice turned toward a copse of pines that stood two hundred yards along the riverbank, waved both hands in some prearranged signal. Two young men stepped out of the shadows under the trees and started walking toward Kelly and the frog. "A couple of village boys," Maurice explained. "They will take the backhoe away."

"They know how to drive it?"

"Yes."

The boys, both between sixteen and twenty, went directly to The Cat and began exploring it, until they felt secure. They both climbed aboard and turned to look at Maurice.

He ordered them to start it.

They did, let it idle.

"I suppose you'll want gasoline, too," Kelly said.

"*Cela va sans dire,*" Maurice said, grinning.

"Beame," Kelly said, "bring five ten-gallon cans of gasoline from the camp stores and lash them to The Cat."

"Yes, sir," Beame said. He was unhappy with the order.

"He's a good boy," Maurice said, watching Beame hurry off toward the machinery shed.

Kelly didn't answer that. "Maurice," he said, "you are not an ordinary man. You are something else, you are—"

"*Dégagé?*" Maurice asked.

Struggling with his college French, Major Kelly looked for an epithet he wanted. "*Chevalier d'industrie.*"

Maurice actually bristled. He stood stiffly, face twisted, his greasy hair trying to stand straight up on his neck, his eyes blazing. "You call me a swindler?"

Realizing he had gone too far, reminding himself that he

had never been very good at maintaining discipline, the major said, "That was not how I meant it. I meant—'One who lives by his wits.' "

Maurice unbristled. "Thank you, Major," he said. "I am honored to be so considered by a man I respect as much as I respect you."

As Beame delivered the cans of gasoline to the two young men on the backhoe, Kelly said, "Now, what information has cost me so dearly?"

Maurice was suddenly nervous. "A Panzer unit is moving towards the front, complete with an armored supply convoy and approximately a thousand infantrymen."

Major Kelly wiped at his nose. Looking at Maurice, he had begun to feel that his own nose was bedecked with bright pearls of grease. His nose was dry. That was a relief. "I don't really see that this is worth a backhoe, Maurice."

"The Panzers are coming on this road," Maurice said.

"*This* road?" Kelly looked southward, across the river, unwilling to accept the possibility that he would have to blow up his own bridge to keep the German tanks from crossing over to the camp.

"You did not hear me right," Maurice said, as if reading the other man's thoughts. "The Panzers are coming *to* the front. They will be coming up behind you, from the northeast, from *this* side."

Kelly turned away from the river and looked across the clearing to the trees, the single break in them where the dusty road came through. No military traffic had yet used this road, not since they had been here. They were in the backlands, in an unimportant part of France. Now, all of that had changed. "Oh, God. We're all dead."

"Not necessarily," Maurice said.

Kelly thought of the huge, lumbering Panzer tanks, the supply trucks, the thousand German infantrymen, all moving through this camp, across this bridge, and he couldn't see any way they weren't going to be made dead. "We haven't any mortar or artillery. We aren't a fighting unit. The only thing we have to protect ourselves are our rifles and grenades. How many Panzers did you say?"

"Twelve."

"We're dead."

"Not necessarily," Maurice repeated. "There are things I could rent you, bits and pieces, certain machines that have come into my possession. . . ."

"Artillery?"

"No," Maurice said.

"What, then?"

"German jeeps, uniforms, a German truck."

Kelly thought about it. "You have these things, really?"

"Yes."

"How?"

"*Grâce à Dieu.*"

Major Kelly was certain God hadn't delivered the German equipment to Maurice, but he didn't feel like arguing about that just now. "I don't see what these things will do to help us," he said.

"With little trouble," Maurice said, "you could make the Germans think that this is a camp of theirs."

"Masquerade as Germans?"

"Exactly."

"But none of us is fluent in German!" Kelly said. "The moment we have to speak to one of them—"

"You will have to talk to no one," Maurice said. "The Germans will not stop. Their orders are to rush, and they are wasting no time in reaching the front. They will pass through here with little more than a nod to you."

"The Stuka pilots know we're not German, and they must have reported us to *someone,*" Kelly said. "They bomb us all the time. If the Stuka pilots know, the Panzer commanders are going to know, too."

"Possibly not," Maurice said. "In Germany, the air force tells the army nothing, for all the services are fiefdoms and jealously guard their own secrets."

"It won't work."

"What else can you do?" Maurice asked.
Kelly thought about it some more. "Nothing."
"Then let us hurry. The Panzers will be here tonight."

# 10/

Lieutenant Slade tugged at his Nazi uniform where the tightly buttoned jacket fit much too snugly over his hips. He would have liked to ask Nurse Pullit to help him let out the seams of the jacket so that he would not look so hippy and fat, but there'd been no time. "I don't like this plan one bit," he said. Thinking of his career, he said, "And I want my opinion to go down in the record right now, this minute." He looked at Major Kelly who wore a black SS uniform complete with silver skulls and a sheathed dagger at the waist. Lieutenant David Beame wore an excellently fitting oberleutnant's uniform and looked dashing. The major and Beame were so resplendent, in fact, one might have thought they were on their way to a dance. It was a good thing there wasn't any dance, though, because Slade would have been embarrassed for any woman—aside from Lily Kain whom he considered nothing more than a cheap hussie—to see him in his tight uniform. "I think what we're doing is all wrong," The Snot said. "It's degrading and unpatriotic—and it definitely smacks of cowardice." He could not understand why both *their* uniforms should fit so well, while his was tight across the hips. Had they planned this? Had the rest of them got together and made certain that his uniform would fit too snugly across the hips and therefore make him seem ludicrous and silly? Maurice would not be above that. It was quite within Maurice's abilities to purposefully supply

Slade with an ill-fitting uniform, making him the brunt of private and public jokes. "What we should do," Lieutenant Slade said, "is make a stand. I'm not saying we would win. But we could deal them a hard blow, and perhaps a decisive blow. We would have the advantage of surprise. And even if that wasn't enough, if we lost, we'd still all make our mark in the history of this war." Another thing that bothered Slade was the fact that his uniform was that of a *private* in the German army. If he had to wear a German uniform, it seemed only proper that he should have one of a rank at least equal to his own. Major Kelly, after all, was wearing a lieutenant-general's uniform, and Beame was dressed as an officer. It was degrading to be sitting here in the backseat of the jeep, wearing a tight uniform several ranks below his own. He wanted to cry. He just wanted to cry.

Kelly and Beame didn't want to cry. They wanted to scream and run. Instead, they watched the convoy of German vehicles move slowly down from the highlands toward the clearing, the camp, and the bridge.

Only one road entered the clearing. It came from the northeast, a rudely paved lane that dropped out of the foothills and slanted gradually into the flat land around the river. From where they sat, they could see for more than a mile along that road, to the top of one of the hills where it fell away, out of sight. In the darkness, the lane was studded with what appeared to be an endless stream of headlights. The first of these vehicles was no more than a quarter of a mile away from them, just entering the flat land a thousand yards ahead of the big Panzers. In a couple of minutes, it would be here. Soon after, the mammoth tanks would pass them close enough to be touched. Already, at a few minutes past eleven o'clock, fully an hour ahead of when Maurice had said to expect them, the heavy pounding of tank-tread trembled the earth. The roar of the massive engines, still so distant, was beginning to make conversation almost impossible.

Still, Lieutenant Slade managed to talk. He said, "You

know we can't hope to fool them, anyway. Kraut uniforms and an armored kraut jeep don't make us krauts. They'll spot us right off."

He looked behind them at the silent, dark buildings. All of the American-made machinery was drawn back in among the trees behind the main bunker, out of sight. A row of German transports, holed and rickety but sound enough to the eye, in the dark, flanked the machinery shed. None of the other men in the unit was visible, though they were hidden everywhere, armed and ready to fight if this ruse should fail and the night should end in violence.

But they were acting like cowards, the lot of them, Slade thought. They were unwilling to face the enemy directly, and they actually would not do so unless they had no other choice. What would their girl friends say about them if they could see them now? What would Slade's own mother say? Slade's mother was a very patriotic woman, an Army wife, and an avid collector of war stories, both fictional and factual. Slade's mother believed in heroism. Her husband had been a hero as had been her father and her grandfather. Slade's mother insisted, when he was first sent to Europe, that Slade become a hero himself, even if he had to be wounded or die in the process. To be wounded was preferable to dying, of course, because if he died he could not beguile her with stories about Over There. It would be just terrible if Slade's mother's friends had sons who became heroes, while Slade remained undistinguished in battle. How humiliating that would be for Slade's mother. After all, she had done so much for him, and he could hardly pay her back with humiliation and degradation. And he could hardly let himself be killed before he had a chance to tell her a couple of good stories about heroism. So, if he had to die fighting the goddamned krauts, why couldn't he die in his own uniform? How would his mother ever explain this to her friends? She could bear it, she told him, if he died in some heroic way—but how could she bear the news that he had died in a jerry uniform? And a jerry *private's* uniform! She wouldn't be able to handle it. She'd crack up.

"The least we can do," The Snot said, making a final effort to sway them over to his point of view, "is blow up the bridge so the Panzers can't make it to the front."

Neither Kelly nor Beame replied. Kelly merely nodded up the road where, abruptly, a motorcycle and its sidecar were silhouetted against the oncoming convoy lights. They were not yet to the clearing, but coming fast.

The Snot took out his revolver and checked to be certain it was loaded. How would his mother ever explain to her friends about her son in a German uniform and trying to kill the enemy with an unloaded gun? It was loaded. The Snot hoped he would have to use it.

The cyclist stopped his machine twenty feet from the bridge, and both the German soldiers stared at Kelly, Beame, and Slade. They were fair-skinned and young, athletic men who looked too hard and knowledgeable for their age. They did not seem to be suspicious, merely curious.

Kelly smiled and waved. The noise of the oncoming tanks was too loud for his voice to carry across the hundred yards to the soldiers.

The man in the sidecar got out. A rifle was slung over his shoulder, black with black leather straps, polished. He was more than six feet tall, further elevated by the well-heeled boots, his pot helmet worn back off his forehead in a relaxed fashion. He bent close to the cyclist and said something which made the other man laugh.

Good, Kelly thought, they're laughing.

Suspicious men don't laugh, Beame thought, relieved.

Are they laughing at me? Slade wondered.

The cyclist changed gears and drove away, across the bridge, leaving his companion alone.

It was German routine to station a sentry at the approach to a bridge before the Panzers began to cross it, and it was also German routine for the sentry to inspect the nearside bridge for concealed explosives prior to taking up his post. This man didn't bother with that, apparently because he thought the bridge was already under German control. Instead, he walked across the road, onto the grass, coming directly toward the jeep where Kelly, Beame, and Slade sat. Great. He wanted to chat.

"Go away," Beame said, under his breath.

But the sentry did not go away. He came on, smiling, waiting until he got close enough to speak over the thunder of the Panzers that were rushing down on them. He was even larger than he'd first appeared, a husky young brute who would know how to take care of himself in almost any situation. He was handsome in a robotlike sense, his face all hard lines, his hair yellow-white, eyes gleaming blue-green like the eyes of a deer, a perfect specimen of the Master Race. His teeth were even and white.

Behind the sentry, Sergeant Coombs rose from the slope by the bridge. Bent over almost double, he ran lightly over the grass, just out of the bright lights of the approaching tanks. Sergeant Coombs was not handsome, tall, or athletic. He was not blond, blue-eyed, or possessed of good teeth. Nevertheless, Major Kelly was certain which would die tonight. Not Coombs. Never Coombs.

The German, intent on reaching the men in the jeep, didn't hear the sergeant coming.

"No," Beame said.

Sergeant Coombs drove the knife into the soldier's back, slipped it in between two ribs, and thrust it brutally upwards, probing for the heart.

The soldier screamed.

Even with the Panzers so near, Kelly heard the cry.

Coombs pulled the blade out and watched the German go down on his knees. He had not hit the heart. The soldier was alive and trying to shrug his rifle off his shoulder. He jerked about clumsily, gasping desperately for breath, much too slow to save himself. His face had gone even whiter, his eyes round and blank.

Coombs stepped forward and put his knee in the middle of the soldier's back, encircled his neck with one burly arm, jerked his head up. The German's face turned involuntarily toward the sky, exposing a vulnerable white throat. Kelly thought he could see the pulse beating rapidly in the kid's taut jugular. Then Coombs's big right hand moved. The blade gleamed for an instant, and the strained flesh parted quickly and deeply, ear to ear. For a brief moment, the smooth, grinning second mouth fell open in a leer–then filled up with blood which looked more black than red in that dim light. Filling, the wound then gushed.

The soldier let go of the rifle and reached up to touch the spurting wound. His fingers hooked into the gash, blood spilling down his hand, and then let go with the sudden realization of what they had touched.

"Go away," Beame said again. But this time he was not sure to whom he spoke: to the dead soldier, to Coombs, to himself, or not to any *person,* but to a thing, a power?

The soldier was trying to walk on his knees. He was bleeding like a pig at the slaughter, already dead but unwilling to give up. He waddled forward a foot or two, dragging Coombs with him, his head still upturned, his glazed eyes seeking his killer. Then, abruptly, he fell forward on his face, his head half off his shoulders.

# 11/

Sergeant Coombs, the only man not frozen into immobility by the murder, slid his bloody hands under the German's armpits and dragged him backwards to the riverbank, over the edge and down under the shadowed bridgeworks. The scorched grass where the brief struggle had taken place was marred by two long, parallel tracks which had been cut by the dead man's boot heels. And there was blood, of course. Pools of it. Still, the trail was unremarkable. The blood looked like oil, machine oil or maybe grease. No one would notice.

Kelly turned and looked back along the road, as much to get his eyes off the blood and his thoughts off the dead soldier as to see what was happening behind them.

The first of the convoy vehicles lumbered like stolid elephants through the archway of giant pines. They lurched, hesitated, then came on, engines grinding like thousands of badly cast gears: *grrrrr-rrr-rrrrr.* And then they were in the C-shaped clearing where the camp lay. From now on, anything could happen. In seconds, the Panzers' headlights high on the knobbed turrets would sweep across the bridge: up the slight incline of the approach, over the framing beams, onto the deck. . . . And they would reveal the lack of a sentry. When that happened, the jerries would have to know that something was wrong. They would slow down. They would stop.

When they stopped, everyone would die.

If a couple of shells were fired at the jeep, Major Kelly thought, he and Beame and Slade would be so much jelly decorated with steel slivers and sparkling bits of glass. Pretty but not functional. The only way to hang on was to stay functional.

Kelly looked anxiously at the point along the ravine where Coombs had disappeared with the corpse. What was taking them so long down there?

"Maybe I could take up guard by the bridge," Beame suggested.

Kelly shook his head. "You're dressed as an oberleutnant, and they'd wonder what you were doing at a private's post."

"We can't just sit here—"

"We *have* to just sit here," Kelly said.

Beame said, "Slade's dressed as a private. He could take

up the sentry's post without making the krauts suspicious."

Major Kelly wiped a film of perspiration from his face and thought about that: was there any chance of Slade getting killed? If there were, he'd send The Snot out right now. At least *something* good would come of this crisis. Thinking about it, though, he realized Slade would fumble his role and expose them. He'd have to keep the lieutenant in the jeep, out of trouble.

Where were the men under the bridge? This was their job. They'd had time to strip the German soldier, time for one of them—

"There!" Beame exclaimed, pointing.

Danny Dew, the dozer operator, climbed over the edge of the riverbank, dressed in the dead man's uniform. It was a perfect fit, and the rent made by Sergeant Coombs's knife was not visible. Indeed, Danny Dew looked as if he had been born in that uniform, as if he had goose-stepped out of his mother's womb, had saluted the doctor with a stiff arm, and had run the nurse through with his bayonet. He was a marvelous German soldier, muscular and stiff, his head held straight and proud, eyes cold and malevolent as he took up his position by the bridge. The only problem, so far as Major Kelly could see, was that Danny Dew was a Negro, a colored person, so dark that he hinted of blue.

Ordinarily, a Negro wouldn't be assigned to a white unit in the American Army, because there were separate colored regiments. The Army practiced rigid but quiet segregation. The only reason that Danny Dew was in Major Kelly's unit was because he was a damn fine D-7 operator—and the only one available for immediate and quiet transfer to beef up their unit for this crazy mission behind German lines.

"Maybe he was the only one of Coombs's men who'd fit into that uniform," Beame said.

As the first tank lights splashed across them, Major Kelly looked at Danny Dew's shining black face, his wide white grin. He groaned aloud. He bashed his head against the steering wheel, over and over. That felt so good he didn't want to stop. It made him pleasantly dizzy and caused a sweet, melodic buzzing in his ears which drowned out the roar of the tanks.

"Danny Drew certainly doesn't look Aryan," Lieutenant Slade said, telling everyone what was already known.

At the bridge, Danny Dew stood stiffly beside the eastern bridge frame, the rifle held across his chest.

"Here comes the first of them," Slade said.

Everyone had already seen the first vehicle. Even Major Kelly had stopped bashing his head on the steering wheel long enough to look at the first vehicle.

An armored car led the procession, traveling nearly as fast as the motorcycle. Its head lamps struck Danny Dew like a spotlight zeroing in on a star stage performer. The car passed him, jolted across the first floor beam, lights bobbling wildly, and kept on going across the bridge. At the other end, it slammed down onto the roadbed again and disappeared around the bend two hundred yards beyond the river, hidden from them now by a rise in the land and the thickening forest. It had never even slowed down.

"Luck," Major Kelly said.

"God's on our side," Slade said.

"Here comes another," Beame said.

The second armored car was coming fast, though not nearly so fast as the one before it. This driver seemed less sure of himself than his predecessor had been; he was hunched over the wheel, fighting the ruts and the hump in the center of the pavement where the lane had hoved up like a hog's back. He would be too busy with the unresponsive steering of the cumbersome vehicle to take much notice of Dew. However, the five other Germans with him would have more time to look around.

They glanced at Kelly, Beame and Slade as they went by, then looked ahead at Danny Dew.

"Here it comes," Kelly said.

The car hit a rut, bounced high, slewed sideways, and nearly went off the road. The driver fought, kept control, plunged through the entrance to the bridge and accelerated. In a few moments, he was gone, and still Dew stood at the bridge.

Beame closed his eyes and let his head fall forward with relief. He sucked cool night air into his lungs, then reluctantly raised his head and looked eastward, toward the convoy.

The third armored car came much more slowly than either of the first two. It carried four Germans in addition to the driver, and it weaved uncertainly from one side of the lane to the other. Battered, splattered with mud, it had obviously seen better days. The left rear fender sported a six-inch shell hole. The windshield was cracked and yellowed.

"Why's he coming so slow?" Slade asked.

"Is something wrong with him?" Beame asked. "I can't hear the sound of his engine with the tanks and all; is he breaking down?"

Kelly said nothing. He knew, if he opened his mouth, he would scream.

The armored car passed them, the engine making a peculiar grinding noise. An inordinate cloud of exhaust fumes trailed them. A minute later, they thumped over the bridge approach, slid through the entrance in what seemed to be slow motion, and went across without stopping.

Major Kelly still didn't feel good about Danny Dew standing out there pretending his eyes were blue and his hair yellow, because the Panzers were next. All twelve of them. In each of the Panzers, the captain of the tank stood in the hatch on the top of the turret, watching the way ahead, sometimes calling orders down to the driver in his forward cubbyhole. The driver, in each case, had only a slit to see through and was too busy with navigation to pay attention to a sentry. But the tank commander, topside, would have Danny Dew fixed in his sight for long, long seconds. A minute or more.

"We're all dead," Major Kelly said. He began beating his head against the steering wheel once more.

"You're beating your head against the steering wheel," Slade said.

Kelly beat even harder.

"No SS officer ever loses control like that," Slade said.

For once, Slade was right about something. Kelly stopped beating his head against the wheel and contented himself with gripping the wheel in both hands and trying to break it loose of the steering column.

"Better be careful about that," David Beame said, nodding at Kelly's whitened knuckles. "If you break it off, Maurice will assess you for it."

That was true enough. But he had to do *something*, and he couldn't very well climb into the back seat and pulp Lieutenant Slade's face, as he wanted to do. One of the tank commanders would surely notice a scene like that and become too curious.

The first Panzer approached the bridge. One moment it was a black shape behind bright head lamps. Then it loomed out of the darkness, its great tread clattering on the Tarmac roadbed. It brought with it an odor of hot metal, oil, and dust.

"So big," Beame said.

Kelly squeezed the wheel.

The tank commander, a tall, fine-boned Aryan, stood in the turret, hatless, his shirt open at the throat revealing fine yellow hairs that gleamed in the reflection of the head lamps. He scanned the men in the jeep, peered menacingly at Major Kelly—but more at the much-feared SS death's-head on his cap than at Kelly's face—then looked imperiously away.

What *were* these men? Kelly wondered. Where did these legions of hard, fair-faced Aryan supermen come from? Surely, not all the German people were like these; they could not all be so icily handsome, so withdrawn and cold and lifeless. Was Hitler creating these in his basement, through some arcane magic?

The tank commander was watching Danny Dew. His hands were braced on opposite sides of the turret hatch, to keep him steady, and he was staring straight ahead at the sentry.

The steel tread clattered up the incline.

"He's seen Dew," Kelly said.

The long barrel of the tank's biggest gun nearly scraped the horizontal part of the entrance frame before the giant machine tipped onto the bridge floor and nosed down a bit. A moment later, it was roaring away, toward the far bank of the river. The tank commander had not seen anything out of the ordinary, after all.

"I don't believe it!"

Slade said, "He didn't even notice Danny Dew is a nigger."

The second tank ground toward the bridge. The commander nodded to Dew abstractedly as he guided his machine through the end posts and away toward the other shore. It reached the other side and soon disappeared around the bend.

"Still ten to go," Beame said.

Slade said, "Take my word for it. Before this is over, we're going to have to fight them."

One by one, the next ten Panzer tanks, fully prepared for battle, driven by some of the most dedicated and steely-nerved army technicians in the world, captained by officers who were among the best of the German military class, passed over the bridge without hesitation. A few of the tank commanders nodded at Dew. Most ignored him.

"Here come the trucks," Slade said as the trucks came into sight behind the last of the rumbling Panzers.

According to Maurice, there were thirty trucks, each carrying more than thirty men in addition to the driver and the officer up front. They were not nearly so large as the tanks. They would be able to streak through the bridge posts without any anxious moments, and each driver would have time to give Danny Dew a quick but thorough looking over.

The first truck hit the graded bridge approach at forty miles an hour, closing the gap between itself and the last tank which was already at the far side of the gorge. It bounced badly in the ruts; the soldiers in the back looked grim as they sat on metal benches and gripped the side slats to keep from falling to the floor. The truck jolted onto the bridge and growled away, followed closely by another and another and still another of the transports.

"This is too much," Kelly said. "Our luck will change."

It didn't. None of those drivers, turning glassy blue eyes on Danny Dew as they went by, saw anything amiss. Not just then, anyway. Perhaps later they would think of it. Five years from now, one of these dumb krauts would sit up in bed in the middle of the night and say to a startled wife: "That sentry was a *Neger*, for God's sake!" Now, though, all the trucks went past without incident.

Behind the last of the trucks, separated from the transports by fifty yards, was the first of the two motorcycles that wrapped up the procession. It passed with a noisy clatter. Immediately after it was by, Danny Dew stepped back and away from the edge of the bridge, rolled over the top of the riverbank and out of sight of the final cyclist. It was in this last sidecar that he would ride away—if he were really a German sentry.

Now came the worst part.

"This is the worst part," Slade said.

Usually, according to Maurice, the last cycle picked up the sentry. Now and again, however, if the sentry felt like a bit of relief from the windy ride of the sidecar, he would flag down one of the last transports and climb into the back of the truck. Kelly was hoping the man on the last cycle would go on if he saw no sentry waiting, sure that his man had joined the troops in the back of one of the transports. Also, since this was apparently a German camp, the cyclist wouldn't see how anything could have gone wrong. And he wouldn't take the time to stop and search for his man, because he wouldn't want to fall too far behind the main body of the convoy, not in a foreign country where—quite often—

the peasants had been known to play some bloody tricks on their conquerors.

The situation was further complicated by the fact that they could not risk a shot now that they had gotten this far without being discovered. They couldn't kill the cyclist yet, if he became inquisitive. The last of the convoy was still in sight, the roar of the tanks far ahead. The night had gotten just still enough to allow a shot to carry to the men in the open backs of the last couple of transports still on the bridge.

The motorcycle slowed.

"He's stopping," Beame said. His voice sounded like that of a frog only partly turned back into a prince.

The motorcyclist slowed even more.

He looked them over as if they were on display and he was thinking of buying one of them. He scanned the bridge, searching for the sentry he was supposed to pick up, then he looked at them again, having come even with their jeep.

He was young, even younger than the soldier Sergeant Coombs had killed, with his helmet flat down in place and his body girdled up in black leather belts. He looked sharp, not easily fooled, like a farm kid who had found a new sophistication in his uniform and was trying to live down what he considered shamefully simple origins. A long-snouted machine pistol was holstered on his hip, and a completely unnecessary bandolier of ammunition wound around his chest.

He stopped his cycle altogether.

Thinking fast, Kelly grinned and waved him on, pointing after the convoy to indicate that the sentry had already left.

The rider hesitated.

"Go away," Beame whispered.

The cyclist finally lifted one hand off his bars to wave back, then accelerated and went on his way.

For about ten feet.

Then Lieutenant Slade shot him in the back of the head.

# 12/

The cyclist fell into the handlebars, recoiled lifelessly, and began to slide sideways in a graceless heap.

Unguided now, the heavy motorcycle jolted out of a shallow rain furrow and swung erratically toward the bridge abutment. It was made more stable by the sidecar than it would have been with only its own two wheels, but still its single head lamp made crazy, jiggling patterns on the night.

As the dead soldier tipped into the sidecar which the bridge sentry would have occupied, Slade's second shot took him through the shoulder and passed straight into the gasoline tank under him. There was a flat, contained explosion hardly louder than either of the shots. Flames engulfed the machine and the dead man as the whole bright bundle crashed headlong into the concrete bridge support.

Major Kelly stood up in the jeep and drew his own gun, as did Lieutenant Beame. Slade, standing up in the back seat, already had his pistol out, of course, and he was jabbering about his success in nailing the kraut. Neither Kelly nor Beame said anything. They watched the retreating trucks, waiting for one of them to pull up and disgorge German infantrymen. Then it would be all over. At least, Major Kelly thought, Slade would get it. The whole thing might be worth dying for if Slade were killed too.

The last of the transports had already come down on the roadway on the far side of the gorge and was making for the bend which would put it out of sight. The first motorcycle was close behind it. Surely, either the two soldiers in the motorcycle or the men sitting in the last of the open-end trucks would see the fire, begin to wonder. . . .

But the Germans kept moving away, rounded the bend, were gone. A minute went by. Two minutes. Five. When the Germans had not returned in ten minutes, Major Kelly knew they never would. By the time they saw the last motorcyclist was missing, they wouldn't know where to look for him. Amazing.

Lieutenant Slade watched the smoldering motorcycle and the shapeless body sprawled within it. He smiled. "One more jerry that won't be shooting up American boys."

"Why?" Beame asked.

"Because he's dead," Slade said, perplexed by the question.

"Why did you kill him?" Beame amplified.

"What would my mother have said if I'd let them all go?" Slade asked.

"Who?"

"My mother!"

"How would your mother ever find out, if you had let him go?"

"She has connections, sources," Slade said, looking down at himself. "You'd be surprised at my mother's sources." He tugged at the hem of his jacket. "I shouldn't have had to wear this silly uniform. Look at my hips. My hips look ridiculous in this uniform." He looked at the dead German in the middle of the road, a black lump in a wreath of gray smoke. "*His* uniform fit him well enough."

# 13/

The sentry's corpse was startlingly white. It lay on its back by the edge of the river, one hand on the middle of its chest as if it were feeling for its own heartbeat. The skin was snowy, unnaturally white, almost phosphorescent. The body hair was too light to be seen. The dead man looked like a big, molded doll, all of painted rubber: long rubber legs, rubber arms, a thick rubber penis now horribly limp and curled over two rubber, felt-furred testicles. In the light of Kelly's torch, there were only two spots of color—the incredible blue eyes, and the red-black blood on the upper torso which had poured out when Coombs had slit the sentry's throat.

That could be me, Kelly thought. Someday, it will be.

He turned away, shifting the beam of his torch, and came upon Danny Dew who was standing directly under the bridge. Leaving the corpse behind, trying to forget it, he went over to the Negro. "That was amazing," he said.

"What?" Danny Dew asked. He was stripping out of the German uniform. His powerful black body gleamed with perspiration; droplets of sweat clung to the tightly curled black hairs on his chest, like jewels sewn into his skin. He looked like an oiled harem guard. Except that he wasn't a eunuch.

"That none of the Germans noticed you weren't—weren't Aryan," Kelly said. "That was fantastic."

Danny Dew laughed, showing lots of white teeth. Were they really white, Major Kelly wondered, or were they only bright by comparison with Dew's dark face? That was one of the great mysteries that had haunted white Americans for as long as Major Kelly could remember. His mother had always said their teeth were not clean and white, but only appeared to be, because the rest of them was "painted so dark." Major Kelly remembered hours spent in discussions of Negro dental conditions, the family gathered around the kitchen table like a group of psychic gypsies discussing the netherworld. Even this near, even though Danny Dew was a close companion and had been for months, Major Kelly could not be sure about his teeth.

Danny Dew said, "I pretended I was white."

"Pretended?"

"Well, I was the only one down here big enough to look good in that uniform, so I had to do something, didn't I? So I directed myself at those jerrys, and I *thought* white."

"But you still *looked* colored."

"To you. I wasn't directing myself at you. Anyway, looks don't matter. It's all in how you think."

"Even if you were thinking white, you looked colored," Kelly insisted.

"If you can't accept it, forget it," Danny Dew said, tossing off the last of the German uniform and picking up his own pants. "But it's all in the head, Massah Kelly, all in de ole head."

Kelly leaned back against the hard edge of a bridge support and said, "I can't accept that, no. If all a man had to do to become someone different was to *think* himself different, there wouldn't be a war. Each of us could be a German, Japanese, Britisher. . . . No one would want to fight anyone else any longer."

Danny Dew buckled his belt and pulled up his fly, struggled into his shirt which stuck to his sweat-slicked chest. "That's why I wish other people would start using their heads, like me," he told Kelly. "If everyone just pretended more, we could get out of this crappy place."

# 14/

At four in the morning, only a few of the men in the camp were asleep. Six enlisted men were sitting in the woods immediately south of the camp, drinking cheap whiskey out of tin cups and singing songs over the graves of the two dead Germans. They weren't really mourning the dead men. But they couldn't just throw them in the ground and walk away. If the tables were turned, they would want someone to drink and sing over their graves, at the very least. They got very drunk, and they ran out of songs to sing.

In the shabby rec room of the HQ building, about twenty men sat on the benches and in the café chairs Maurice had provided for a price. They drank more cheap whiskey out of more tin cups. They didn't sing, though. They just sat there, drinking, not looking at each other, as if there were a religious service in progress.

Under the earth, in the main bunker, ten other men were playing poker at a pair of battered wooden tables. No one was enjoying the game, but no one wanted to call it off. If they called it off, there was nothing else to do but think. No one wanted to think.

Other men wandered about the camp, going nowhere, trying not to run into anyone. These were the ones who couldn't play poker. They *had* to think.

At four in the morning, Major Kelly was in the rec room. He was talking to General Blade, who had just put through an emergency call on the big wireless set. "You've got an emergency, Major," the general said.

Lieutenant Slade, standing at Kelly's shoulder, stiffened. Maybe he would get to be in a battle, after all.

"Sir?" Kelly said.

"A unit of Panzer tanks, armored cars and infantry trucks are on the way toward you. They ought to be crossing the bridge in a few hours."

"Twelve Panzers, sir?" Major Kelly asked.

General Blade was unsettled by the major's inside knowledge. "How could you know that?"

"They passed over the bridge three or four hours ago," Kelly told him. Then he told him the rest of it, except for the account of Slade's gun work. He wasn't trying to protect Slade, not at all. But he was afraid that, if he told Blade about the dead cyclist, the general would recommend Slade for a medal or something, and then The Snot would become unbearable.

"Well," General Blade said, "I'm glad to see you've got such good relationships with the locals—that you've cultivated them as informers."

"Yes, sir," Kelly said. He saw that Lieutenant Slade was fidgeting about, debating whether to insist that Kelly mention the backhoe which they had lost in the bargaining with Maurice. He was probably also trying to think how to let the general know about him killing the cyclist. Kelly placed a finger to his lips to warn Slade off.

Still, the lieutenant said, "Aren't you going to tell him about the backhoe?"

Slade was close enough to the microphone for it to pick up what he had said. General Blade had heard. "Backhoe?"

"You little shit," Kelly said.

"What was that?" the general asked.

"Not you, sir," Kelly said.

"What's this about a backhoe?"

"We lost it, sir," Slade said, loud enough to be heard.

"Lost it?" the General asked.

Major Kelly pulled his revolver from his holster and leveled it at the middle of Lieutenant Slade's face. "You know what this will do to your face?" Kelly asked.

Slade nodded, swallowed hard.

"I'll put one right up your nostril," Kelly promised.

"A backhoe?" General Blade asked. "Up my nostril? Kelly—"

"It's all right, sir," Kelly interrupted. "I was talking to Lieutenant Slade."

"What's going on there, Kelly?"

"Slade's drunk," Kelly said. "Too much celebrating after the Germans went by."

The General was surprised. "I didn't think he was that sort—to drink so much."

"It happens, occasionally," Kelly said.

Lieutenant Slade colored, opened his mouth to speak. Kelly thrust the revolver close to his face, shutting him up.

"One more thing, Major," General Blade said. "I've also been informed that the Nazi high command is considering switching a Panzer division from the Russian front and moving it westward within a week or so. That would mean a convoy of eighty tanks or so, supply trucks, truck-mounted 88 mm antiaircraft guns, quite a string. Naturally, if they *are* dispatched and use the route that'll take them over your bridge, they're going to camp there with you for the night. It would take half a day, anyway, to put that big a force across the bridge."

"Camp with us, sir?"

"If they come that route," Blade said.

"But, sir—"

"Don't worry about them," Blade said. "They'll probably never be dispatched, and even if they are they'll come west on some other highway."

Kelly nodded, then realized the general couldn't hear a nod. "Yes, sir. I won't worry, sir." He cleared his throat and said, "Sir, how is the front moving these days?"

"Better. Better. You're only a hundred and ninety miles behind lines now."

"But that's only ten miles less than—"

"I know how happy this makes you," General Blade interrupted. "Now, I have to be going, Kelly. I'm glad you squeaked past the first unit of Panzers, damn glad. I wanted you to know about the possibility of that big division being sent your way in a week or so; I wanted you to have time to plan for it, if it comes."

"Plan? Plan? How can I plan for—"

"It's probably never going to come near you," Blade said. "But you can't be too careful these days, the way things are. Good luck, Major. I will be in touch, and I'll expect you to keep that bridge open, sir!"

Major Kelly stared at the hissing microphone and returned it to Slade as if tranced by it. "Eighty tanks? Antiaircraft guns mounted on trucks? Infantry? Supplies? Staying overnight? Slade, we can't fool the Germans for an entire night!"

"Like the general said," Slade observed, "they'll probably never be sent, or if they are they won't come this route." Secretly, he wished they would come this route, so that there would be one great big fucking battle with lots of heroism and derring-do. To Kelly, because he knew it was what Kelly wanted to hear, he said, "We're in for a change of luck. I feel it."

Kelly frowned. For all the time he spent reading the Army field manual, Slade was as naive as everyone else. Didn't he know nothing ever improved, not a whit?

# 15/

Things had to improve, Lieutenant Slade thought. The camp was in a very bad way: hiding, choosing to deceive the Germans rather than fight them openly. Major Kelly was a coward. Lieutenant Beame was a coward. All the men were cowards. Something had to change. Someone had to show the men that all was not lost; they could still accomplish something in this war. Someone had to take the reins and be tough with these sons of bitches, make them shape up, put a little guts in their bellies. So far as Slade could see, he was the only one to do it.

He would have to kill Major Kelly.

Once Kelly was dead, Lieutenant Beame would gladly abdicate his role as the new commander of the unit, and General Blade would put Slade in charge. *Then,* things would improve.

An hour after the general's call, Lieutenant Slade stood in

his tiny blanket-partitioned quarters in the main HQ building, fashioning the mask he would wear when he killed Major Kelly. He couldn't very well kill him openly even if Kelly *was* a coward. Therefore, he had cut two holes for his eyes in the burlap potato sack which he had filched from the food stores down at the main bunker. He looked at the mask and wondered if he should cut a slit for his mouth. If he wanted to talk with the mask on, he would need a slit where his mouth was. Otherwise, his voice would be muffled. On the other hand, he didn't have anything to say to Major Kelly. He just wanted to kill him. He wasn't going to lecture him first. Okay. No other holes.

He pulled the sack open and slipped it over his head, tugged it around until the holes were directly in front of his eyes. He could breathe well enough, though the bag made the air smell like dirt and potatoes. Bending stiffly, he looked at himself in a small, cracked mirror which he had laid on his cot. Not bad. Not bad at all. Sinister. Frightening. He would give Kelly a real scare before he put a few bullets in the bastard's gut, a real scare indeed.

He took the sack off his head, folded it and tucked it in his trousers, inside his undershorts. He didn't want anyone accidentally uncovering the bag and remembering it later, after Kelly had been killed by a mysterious man in a mask.

The only thing he had to worry about now was when to do it. Tonight? No. Not yet. Give Kelly more time to show his cowardliness. It might even be a good idea to put it off as much as a week. Then, when he did kill the son of a bitch, General Blade would be even more disposed to treating the matter lightly. General Blade would see what a coward Kelly was, and he would be pleased to have Richard Slade in charge of the camp.

Smiling, Slade put the cracked mirror under his cot. He lay down and picked up the Army field manual from the pasteboard trunk at the head of the bed, and he started to read by the shimmering yellow light of the single, tiny electric bulb.

# 16/

The next morning, after Maurice reclaimed the equipment he had rented to them, The Snot said, "This conclusively proves that Maurice is in league with the krauts." He looked at Major Kelly, then at Beame, and he did not seem to understand that they wanted to beat his face to a pulp. Even the pacifist, Tooley, had confessed that, at times, even *he* wanted to beat The Snot's face to a pulp. Slade continued, "If we accept that we have a traitor in the unit, our morale will decline. But if we look outside our ranks for the culprit, our morale can be maintained and our field of suspects narrowed. And Maurice stands head-and-shoulders above all other suspects. He has access to German equipment . . . and you certainly don't believe those stories he told you about partisan work, about stealing the German equipment, laying ambushes for German patrols on other highways! How'd he really get those things? Hmmm?" Slade took their silences to mean they were speechless, utterly unable to imagine how Maurice had *really* gotten hold of those things. He said, "Suppose he was consorting with the Germans, selling them information in return for trucks, uniforms, and artillery? And then he was renting these same things to us in return for the backhoe and—and whatever else he could get, maybe the dozer the next time. Suppose that's what he's doing. You see, of course, what he has in mind, what his eventual goal is." Again, he interpreted their silence as sheer stupidity. He smirked, actually smirked, and said, "Maurice is establishing a small army of his own: trucks, artillery, construction equipment, guns, and uniforms. You mark my words. When he feels he has enough strength, he's going to declare Eisenhower a separate, free French nation!"

Major Kelly and Lieutenant Beame walked away from The Snot. They went to the bridge and stood looking it over, each afraid that he could not control his urge to pulp Slade's face.

Slade mistook their retreat for a concession to his point and their lack of response for a weakness of will that made it impossible for them to act. He called after them: "When the time is ripe, that village will secede from the rest of France! And when the war is over, they'll discover that backhoe and whatever else Maurice has of ours, and they'll say the United States of America urged the village to secede, that we meddled in the internal affairs of our great ally, France. It will be a black day for America's foreign image!"

Even down by the river, where the water sloshed over the rocks and pieces of bomb-blasted bridgework, Kelly and Beame could hear the lieutenant shouting. The major wished a few Stukas would make a bombing pass. On Slade. If he just knew who the traitor was, who was reporting to the Nazis every time the bridge was rebuilt, he would try to arrange just that, a bombing run on Slade. He'd station Slade at some lonely point, far away from the camp and the bridge, and then he would get the krauts to run a bombing mission on him: three Stukas. He would use four blue runway flares to mark Slade's position. If that worked well, then he'd try it with Coombs. And, most definitely, three Stukas with full loads. This would have to be a very final sort of operation, because he didn't want to risk a badly botched bombing and end up with another Kowalski on his hands.

# PART TWO

# Worsening Conditions

## July 15/July 17, 1944

# 1/

Sitting at the desk in his office in the HQ building, Major Kelly dipped his fingers into a tin bowl full of mud, smeared the thick slop on his head. It was cool and soft, but it stank. He massaged the gunk into his scalp in lazy circles, then scooped more of it from the bowl and repeated the process until his head was capped in a hardening layer of wet, black soil.

Major Kelly had been plagued by a widow's peak ever since he was a teen-ager and he had never once thought that it was in any way becoming to him. His mother said it was becoming to him and that it made him look sophisticated. So far as Major Kelly was concerned, it only made him look old and bald. He didn't want to be old or bald, and so he was always anxious to find some medication or process which would restore the hair around his widow's peak and make him look young again. He had tried massages and salves, greases and tonics, internal and external vitamins, less sex, more sex, less sleep, more sleep, sleeping with a bed cap, sleeping without a bed cap, washing his hair every day, washing it only twice a month, eating lots of carrots, eating lots of eggs, beer shampoos, standing on his head, prayer. Nothing worked. Now, Sergeant Coombs had mentioned the mud treatment, and Major Kelly was trying that.

He was desperate. Ever since they'd been dropped behind German lines, his hair had been falling out faster than it usually did, and his widow's peak was widening and deepening. In fact, he now had a widow's promontory, flanked by two enormous bays of baldness. If he didn't stop the erosion soon, he'd have a widow's island, encircled by gleaming skin, and then no one would love him any more. No one loved a bald man. Was Mussolini loved?

Ever since General Blade had called on the wireless more than a day ago and Major Kelly had learned of the possibility of the Panzer division moving his way, his hair had been falling out at an unprecendented and alarming rate of speed, like snow or autumn leaves. It fell out in clumps, in several twisted strands at a time, fell out when he combed his hair, when he scratched his scalp, when he turned his head too fast, when he nodded. He was even afraid to *think,* for fear his hair would fall out.

Major Kelly couldn't tolerate the prospect of baldness. He had known too many bald men—his Uncle Milton, a grade school teacher named Coolidge, a high school chemistry teacher, Father Boyle, and Sergeant Masterson in basic training—and he knew how cruel well-haired men could be when they talked about the baldies behind their backs. Chrome dome, skinhead, glass bean, bone head . . . The nasty names were limitless. Major Kelly refused to be known as Chrome Dome or anything similar. He'd rather die first.

Of course, he might. The odds on his living through this were damn slight, after all. If that Panzer division, complete with supply trucks and ack-ack guns and infantrymen, moved toward the bridge and stayed by it overnight, then Major Kelly wouldn't live long enough to have to endure any cruel nicknames. And *that* was exactly why his hair was falling out. He was worrying too much about the Panzer division, and his hair was falling out—and it was all a vicious circle.

He put more mud on his head. It stank.

He was still putting mud on his head ten minutes later when Nurse Pullit wobbled into his quarters wearing Lily Kain's high-heeled white pumps. Nurse Pullit was also wearing what was intended to be a beatific smile—which didn't look as good on the nurse as the pumps did. In fact, Major Kelly thought the smile was a leer, and he was immediately defensive.

"You've got to come to the hospital!" Pullit squealed. Pullit's red bandanna had slipped back, revealing a still predominately male hairline. "It's a real miracle! A real miracle!"

"What is?" Major Kelly asked, peering into his shaving mirror to see how stupid he looked with mud all over his head. He looked very stupid.

"Kowalski!" Nurse Pullit said, oblivious of the mud.

"Is he dead?" Kelly asked.

Pullit frowned, looking at Kelly's face in the mirror. "I said it was a real miracle!"

"Then he *is* dead?"

"No," Pullit said. "He's come around, and he's talking!"

Major Kelly looked up from the mirror, turned, and stared at Nurse Pullit. "Your bandanna's askew."

Pullit reached up and tugged it into place and smiled sweetly. Pullit could look exceptionally sweet, at times. "What about Kowalski?"

"He's talking, is he? What's he saying?"

Nurse Pullit pulled on a bee-stung lip. "We're not exactly sure about that. It's—it's strange. Tooley says you ought to come and hear it right away."

"He does, huh?"

"Yes, sir. He sent me to fetch you."

Reluctantly, Kelly got to his feet. A drop of warm mud slid down his forehead, down the length of his nose and hung there like a decoration. He followed Nurse Pullit to the hospital bunker, across the dried grass and dusty clearing, staying ten paces behind where he could admire the excellent slimness of the nurse's legs. The white pumps had done well by those legs. All that could improve on them now was a pair of stockings. Perhaps he could bribe the pilot of the supply plane and have some nylons flown in for the nurse. Pullit would appreciate. . . .

He suddenly remembered who Nurse Pullit was: Private Pullit. He decided that, if in a moment of weakness he ever ordered and received those nylons, the best thing to do would be to use a pair of them to strangle himself.

In the hospital bunker where the three dim bulbs cast eerie shadows on the rough plaster walls, where the centipedes ran and water dripped steadily in the black corners, Kowalski was sitting up in bed, his eyes opened wide, his mouth loose. Liverwright, currently the only other patient in the bunker, was standing at the foot of the mad Pole's bed, holding his swollen hip, having temporarily forgotten his own pain, engrossed in the miracle of Kowalski. Lily Kain and Private Tooley flanked the Pole, bent towards him as if he were a wise man whose every word was priceless.

"Sir," Tooley said, looking sideways at Kelly, "you've got mud all over your head."

"I know," Kelly said. "I know." He looked down at the Pole. "What's this bag of shit been saying?" As he spoke, he scanned the ceiling for any nearby centipedes. He did not know why he feared centipedes so much, but he did. Maybe he was afraid that, if they fell on his head, they would kick around and tear out even more of his hair.

Obligingly, though he only addressed the air, Kowalski began to speak. Spittle collected at the corners of his mouth, dribbled down his chin. His lips were like two large, inflated rubber tubes glistening with oil. "Stuka bomber . . . in darkness . . . a power glide . . . concealed approach . . . people on the bridge . . . many people . . . bridge. . . ."

Then Kowalski was silent once more. No one else dared speak, and when the silence was thick enough to cut, Kowalski cut it with a fart.

Lily looked up, lips puckered. Her freckles stood out like flecks of cinnamon on the soft golden tissue of a fresh-baked roll. Kelly wanted to eat her up. "What does he mean?" she asked.

"It almost sounds like a warning," Tooley said. "As if he were just looking into the future, as if he wants to warn us."

"He's raving," Kelly said. "It's nothing more than that."

He felt a new trickle of mud run down his nose, and he wiped it away as inconspicuously as possible.

"But if he's really—"

"First of all, no one ever goes out on the bridge," Kelly said. "You know that. So there couldn't be, as he said, many people on the bridge. The reason no one ever goes out on the bridge is because everyone's afraid of getting bombed." As Tooley tried to speak, the major waved him down and went on: "And the Stukas wouldn't make a special night mission of it. They always come in the daylight."

"If you're sure," Tooley said.

"You can take my word for it," Kelly said.

Kowalski fell back against his pillows, returning to his dumb trance, and crapped on the sheets.

## 2/

On that night's edition of the Blade and Slade Show, the general told them they would probably come through this war without a single casualty in their unit—aside, of course, from Kowalski. And you never could tell when Kowalski might spontaneously reject the sliver of steel in his brain, thereby insuring complete recovery. That was what the general expected, he confided in Major Kelly: spontaneous rejection. He told the major that people were all the time spontaneously rejecting arthritis and cancer and other dread diseases. There were hundreds upon thousands of cases of spontaneous rejection in medical histories. Why shouldn't Kowalski, then, spontaneously reject his brain damage? If he could see his way clear in this matter, the general said,

Kowalski would be doing the general a great service. He would, by spontaneously rejecting that sliver of steel, be vindicating the general's policy in this matter. With Kowalski cured in such a fashion, rescued from certain death, then none of them would die behind enemy lines, because this would be a good omen, a sign, a portent, an assurance. Again, the general promised the major that none of them would die in this war, for they were his favorite men, his own.

"Yes, sir," Major Kelly said.

"I love you guys," General Blade said, choking a little on the line—either because it was a bald-faced lie, or because he actually had deceived himself into thinking he loved them.

"Yes, sir," Major Kelly said.

"Kelly, if that Panzer division actually gets sent your way, if you have to fight those Nazi bastards, I want you to know one important thing. The men who die fighting to keep that bridge erect will not be dying uselessly. They will be dying for a cause, for Truth and Freedom. They will all be long remembered in the American history books and, no doubt, in the hearts of *all* mankind."

When Major Kelly delicately observed the discrepancy between the general's earlier assurances and his second speech about dying for a cause, the general said the Blade and Slade Show was over for another night.

They were one hundred and eighty-six miles behind German lines.

# 3/

Several hours later, Major Kelly crawled up from the bottom to the top of the hospital bunker steps and looked out at the few unlighted buildings, the silent machines, and the flat black open spaces of the camp. "It's okay," he whispered. "There's no one around."

Lily appeared at his side, crouching on the steps. She was wearing her made-over fatigues, no shoes. "Are you sure?"

Kelly grimaced. "I'm sure."

"Are you *really* sure?"

"For Christ's sake," he said, feeling like a fool, "why don't you look for yourself?"

Lily moved up one more step and peeked out at the camp. It was dark and quiet, oddly like a motion-picture studio lot when the filming was done for the day. She tilted her head to one side, listening for footsteps, conversation, laughter. . . . Nothing. "I guess it's okay."

"Of course it is."

"We better go before someone comes along."

Kelly took her hand, helped her up, and ran with her along the riverbank toward the slope by the bridge.

When Major Kelly had the urge to put it to Lily Kain—and, naturally, when Lily Kain was of the mind to have it put to her—he could not satisfy his desires in his own quarters. Major Kelly's quarters were in the HQ building, because the major had decided early to set a good example for his men by refusing to sleep in the bunker by the trees. The men did not know that the major's rejection of the bunker was more paranoid in nature than it was heroic. He feared being buried alive in the bunkers while he slept more than he feared being blasted to bits if the Germans should drop a bomb on the HQ structure. Therefore, he slept well and still managed to look like a hero to the men. Unfortunately for the major's love life, Sergeant Coombs and Lieutenant Slade also made their bunks in the HQ building, separated from the major's quarters by nothing more than a series of blankets strung on wire. If Kelly and Lily attempted to satisfy their desires in Kelly's quarters, Lieutenant Slade was certain to report them to General Blade, who might very well order the major castrated. Or worse. After all, this was *fornication.* Besides, the general wanted all the major's energies to be put into the maintenance of the bridge. Kelly also feared that Sergeant Coombs, in a position to watch and listen, might discover that the major was less of a cocksman than himself, and would thereafter be more difficult to discipline.

Lily, of course, slept in the hospital bunker, as did Nurse Pullit and Private Tooley. Kelly had considered the possibilities of the hospital as a temporary den of iniquity. If they pilfered the drug supply, they could put Liverwright or any other patient to sleep, and they wouldn't have to worry about Kowalski observing their love rites. Private Tooley would most likely be generous enough to take a long walk if Kelly threatened to beat his head in. After all, Tooley was a pacifist. But that left Nurse Pullit, and Kelly didn't think for a minute that Nurse Pullit would leave. He thought Nurse Pullit would want to stay. He was afraid Nurse Pullit would say, "Put it to me, too!"

Despite Pullit's genuinely lovely gams, Kelly didn't want to put it to anyone but Lily Kain.

The other bunker was always in use by men who slept there. The rec room, which was the mess hall, which was half of the rickety HQ building, was never without a few men playing cards, bullshitting, or arguing. That left the great out-of-doors.

When they had first searched for a secluded place for their amorous activities, Major Kelly and Lily Kain had chosen the slopes of the ravine beneath the bridge. It seemed certain to be the most private place available. No one ever went near the bridge, because no one could ever be sure when the krauts would bomb it again. Once the bridge had been rebuilt, it was taboo. And, though making love under the bridge meant that they courted instant death from a Stuka attack, they went back again and again. What was instant death, after all, compared to a brief moment of orgasmic pleasure?

Besides, they only went under the bridge at night, when the Stukas never attacked, when they could forget their fear and indulge their senses. Sex, Kelly had long ago concluded, was essential if a man were to hang on. If a man couldn't fuck now and then, he'd start taking chances, lose his grip. You can't hang on if your grip is gone.

Sex was as important to survival as was cowardice.

That night, two days after the Panzers, Major Kelly and Lily Kain went down the green slopes—which were actually mostly brown and burnt and all muddied by the tracks of dozers and other equipment, but which appeared nonetheless Elysian to them in their rutting heat—went under the bridge to a patch of generally undisturbed grass by the edge of the oiled, burbling, light-flecked river. There, with little time for the niceties of civilized romance, the major undressed her and lowered her to the grass, preparatory to putting it to her.

Overhead, on the bridge floor, there were sounds like autumn leaves rustled by the wind—or like a gentle rain pattering out of the open heavens. It was good background music for their performance.

Now and then during the day when the major caught a glimpse of Lily Kain in her dancer's costume as she was on her way to or from the mess hall, he would comment to Lieutenant Beame, his right-hand man, on the fine structure of the woman. He would say, under his breath because he actually was breathless, "She has one of the finest bodies I've ever seen!"

Beame was a virgin, though he thought no one knew he was. He believed that his best defense against discovery and ridicule was cool indifference, since he thought the world's greatest lovers were really rather coolly indifferent except when they were in bed. Beame would say, "Oh, well, a body is a body."

"Tits," Major Kelly would say. "She has the finest pair of tits I've ever seen, big and round and pointing right at the sky."

"Tits are tits," Beame would say.

"And those legs! Sleek, trim—longest legs I've ever seen!"

And Beame would say, "Legs are legs."

One day when he felt like teasing Beame, Kelly had gone his usual horny litany, then added, "She has the sexiest thumbs I've ever seen!"

And Beame had said, "Thumbs are thumbs." Then he had realized what he'd said. He blushed. "Yeah," he had added, "she *does* have nice thumbs."

And she had a nice body, too. It was all breasts and hips and firm buttocks and legs. Very little waist. Right now, Major Kelly didn't care about her mind or her personality, her religion, politics, or even about her moderately bad breath. He only cared about her wonderful body. He lay beside her, kissing her forehead, her eyes, her pert nose, then her lips, sucking on her tongue until he thought he might swallow it. He took handfuls of her jugs which she offered him with a graceful arching of her back, and he pondered the engineering miracle of those breasts. They *were* engineering miracles. He should know: he was an engineer. He tested those jugs for solidity and texture, squeezing and releasing them, massaging them with his fingertips and palms. He swept his hands up their undersides to gauge their thrust, took the big hard nipples between thumb and forefinger and gently turned them this way and that, making them even larger. A miracle. Two miracles, perfectly matched. He caressed and bounced and licked those miracles until he felt he was ready to explode with an infusion of divine power.

Overhead, the pattering sound ceased and was replaced by the soughing of the wind.

Major Kelly let the wind help build the atmosphere of sweet sensuality, and when he felt that it had been built high enough, he took off his own fatigues. He seemed to be moving through syrup, undressing so slowly that he would never finally be unfettered and able to achieve penetration. A man on a slow-motion film, he peeled off his shirt and, an eternity later, pulled off his shoes and then his trousers. It was, he thought, like that old mathematical riddle: if a chair is ten feet from the wall, and if you keep moving it half the distance to the wall, how many moves will it take until the chair is touching the wall? The answer, of course, is that the chair will never be touching the wall. It will get closer and closer through an infinite number of moves but can never, theoretically, be finally *there*. Right now, as he pulled off his shorts, Kelly thought that he was the chair while Lily was the wall. They were never going to get together.

And then he was nude and between her legs. He lifted her buttocks, another pair of engineering miracles, and guided himself into her, all the way, moaning in the back of his throat as she moaned in the back of hers.

The gentle breezes above were punctuated by hard, regular gulping sounds, like something thick and wet being dropped down a pipe, sounds that did not belong here in the midst of romance. As these gulping noises increased, grew louder and more frequent and finally dominated the night, Major Kelly broke his embrace of Lily Kain with a wet, mournful sucking noise of rudely disengaged organs. He got to his feet and, utterly unashamed of his own nakedness, walked out of the shadow of the bridge floor, and looked up at the twenty or thirty men who were lying on the bridge and hanging over the edge watching the action.

"We can forget the patter of feet," Kelly said, "and pretend it's only leaves rustling."

None of the men replied. They just hung up there, wide-eyed, looking down at him and stealing quick glances at Lily Kain.

"And we have agreed to imagine that the breathing is the sigh of the wind." He spread his arms imploringly. "But I can't deal with that sound. Is someone up there eating peanuts?"

Lieutenant Beame was eating peanuts. He grinned sheepishly.

Half a dozen of the other men, without saying a word, picked him up, took him to the end of the bridge, and beat the shit out of him. When they came back and stretched out again, the major returned to Lily Kain.

"Idiots," she said.

"It was only the leaves," he said.

"Morons."

"Gentle breezes."

"I suppose," she said.

Lily had been sitting up, waiting for him to come back. Now, she lay down again, parted her thighs which were another pair of engineering miracles.

That was all Kelly needed to put him back in the mood. He walked forward on his knees, slipped his hands under her, lifted her, and got into her again as smoothly as a greased piston into a firing chamber. He thrust several times as she moved up against him, and when they were firmly joined, he rolled her over, holding her against him, until he was lying on his back and she had the dominant position.

Above them, many breezes worked across the bridge floor.

Lily began to bounce up and down on him. It was the most miraculous thing Kelly had ever seen. Her two big jugs worked round and round, slapped together, rose and fell, jiggled, quivered, swung, *bounced.* In the wash of yellow moonlight, those gyrating globes became more than twin miracles. They transcended the mere miraculous. They were a divine experience, a fundamental spiritual vision that stunned him and left him gasping.

"Oh, God! Oh, God!" one of the breezes said, above.

Kelly ignored it. He raised his head and nipped at her jugs, took part of one of them between his lips and nearly suffocated himself in flesh.

Lily was climbing toward her brink, sliding up and down on him, her head thrown back, mouth open. She made little sounds in her throat. Little obscene sounds.

As he felt her reaching her crest, Kelly thrust up, jamming hard into her, trying to finish with her. He knew that he would never again endure such incredible pleasure. He was sure of it. Of course, he was sure of it every time that he had her, was convinced in every instance that this was the ultimate and final joy; but now, his certainty was nonetheless complete for its familiarity. He could not conceive of anything to match this. He could not imagine another bout of this wet, hot, soft, nibbling, licking, jiggling, sucking, bouncing, sliding, slipping, thrusting, exploding excitement. Wide-eyed and breathless at the sight of her, he rushed both of them toward completion. "Soon, soon, soon, soon," he mumbled ardently into her right breast.

But it was just not their night. As Major Kelly felt himself swept toward the brink, as he redoubled his efforts so that he might reach his end with hers, the Stukas bombed the bridge.

# 4/

The hospital bunker was full of wounded men. Nurse Pullit was holding cold compresses against the back of Private Angelli's neck, while Angelli bent forward and let his nose drip blood into a rag. Tooley was treating a man for minor burns of the right arm, and a dozen men waited for treatment. All ten cots were occupied, and four men sat on the damp floor with their backs against the wall, cradling their arms or legs or whatever was hit.

Fortunately, the attack had first been directed against the farside pier. The men lying on the bridge floor staring over the edge at Major Kelly and Lily Kain on the grass below had time to jump up and run before, on a second pass, the Stukas placed two hundred-pounders exactly where they had been. Their wounds, for the most part, were minor: scrapes, cuts, weeping lesions, nosebleeds from the concussion, second-degree burns from being too near the outward-roiling flash of an explosion, twisted ankles, pulled muscles.

"You should all be thankful you're alive!" Major Kelly told them as he paced back and forth in the crowded bunker. He was trying to keep up company morale. He recognized that company morale was constantly hitting new lows, and he felt he had to do something to check this dangerous slide into utter dejection, depression, and apathy. The only problem was that his own heart wasn't in it. *His* morale kept hitting new lows, too, and he just could not think of any way to improve things. Except to harangue the men. "You should be thankful you're alive!" he repeated, grinning fiercely to show them how thankful he was.

The wounded men stared at him. Soot-smeared, blood-dappled, eyes white and wide, hair greasy and twisted in knots, clothes filthy and tattered, they did not seem cheered at all. One of them, when Kelly's back was turned, muttered, "Shallow philosophy." But that was the only response.

"What's a nosebleed?" Kelly asked them. "What's a little cut on the arm or a burn?" He waited for an answer. When no one said anything, he answered himself: "It's nothing! Nothing at all. The important thing is to be alive!"

One of the men started crying.

Kelly tried to talk some more, but the crying drowned him out. He walked down the row to the fifth cot on the left. "Liverwright? What is the matter, Liverwright?"

Liverwright was sitting on the edge of the cot, leaning to one side to take the weight off his swollen hip. Tears streamed down his face, and his mouth quivered unprettily.

"Liverwright? What is it?"

"The important thing is to be alive, just like you told us," the wounded man said.

Kelly smiled uncertainly. "Yes. That's right."

"But I'm dying," Liverwright said. He was crying harder than ever, sobbing, his voice distorted as he tried to cry and breathe and talk at the same time.

"You aren't dying," Kelly said. He didn't sound convincing.

"Yes, I am," Liverwright said. "I'm dying, and I can't even die in peace. Now, all these men are moved in here. Everyone's rushing around. There's too much noise. And you're standing there shouting at us like—like General Blade."

Liverwright had been the radio operator on alternate nights, before he took the piece of steel in the hip. He knew Blade. Even so, Major Kelly thought Liverwright must be delirious. "Me? Like Blade?"

Liverwright sniffed and wiped halfheartedly at his running nose. "Here we are in the worst trouble of our lives—and you're telling us we never had it so good. Half of us are wounded—and you're telling us it's nothing. Most of us will never get home again—and you're telling us we should take it easy, relax, count our blessings." Liverwright blew his nose without benefit of handkerchief, wiped his sticky fingers on his shirt. "I always thought you were different. I thought you weren't like other officers. But down deep, you have the potential."

Kelly was stunned by the accusations. All he could say was, "What potential?"

"To be another Blade," Liverwright said. "You could be another General Blade." He began to bawl again. His whole body shook, and he rocked back and forth on the edge of the cot, nearly tipping it over.

"Me?" Kelly asked, incredulous.

"I'm dying, and you're talking at me like General Blade. I can't take it. I can't."

Suddenly, not really aware of what he was doing, Kelly reached down and took hold of Liverwright's shirt. He lifted the wounded man clear off his cot, held him up as if he were an airy ball of rags. He pulled Liverwright against him, until only an inch or two separated their faces. "Don't you ever say anything like that." His voice was tight, issued through clenched teeth. His face was red, and he was sweating more than the heat could account for. "Don't you ever call me anything like that. Blade, the rest of them like Blade, on both sides of this fucking war, aren't a whole hell of a lot different. They're the throwbacks, the brutes, the cavemen. Don't you goddamned ever call me something like that!" He dropped Liverwright back on his cot, without regard for the man's hip.

Liverwright blew his nose again, wiped at his eyes. "Am I dying?" he asked.

"Probably," Kelly said. "We all are, bit by bit."

Liverwright smiled slightly. "Okay," he said. "Okay."

Nauseous, ashamed of himself, Major Kelly went up front where Lily and Nurse Pullit were treating the last of the wounded.

Amazingly enough, the major and Lily Kain had escaped injury, though they had been directly under the bridge when the Stukas glided in. Lily told Nurse Pullit all about their escape as the two of them treated the wounded. "He was lying there, flat on his back, shoved right up in me. You know?"

Nurse Pullit giggled.

"Even if the Stukas hadn't glided in, we probably wouldn't have heard them any sooner. Anyway, when the first bombs hit the far side of the bridge, he got his hands and feet under him and started off."

"With you on top?" Nurse Pullit asked.

Lily explained how it was. Kelly, his back still parallel to the earth, Lily still screwed on tight, had pushed up and scuttled along the riverbank like a crab. Two minutes later, when they were a quarter of a mile downriver from the bridge, he was still lodged firmly inside of her, and she had climaxed at least half a dozen times. It had been like riding a horse with a dildo strapped to the saddle. She wanted to try it again, Lily told Nurse Pullit, but she thought it might be best to wait until the bridge was likely to be bombed again. After all, the fear of death was what had given the major the energy to perform these acrobatics.

When Kelly came up front, after the confrontation with Liverwright, Nurse Pullit said, "I heard all about it!"

"It wasn't like she said," Kelly told the nurse.

"He doesn't remember," Lily said.

She and Nurse Pullit giggled.

So far as Kelly was concerned, Lily's story was fantasy. One moment, he was under the bridge watching it come apart over him; the next moment, he was a quarter of a mile downriver, by the water's edge. He couldn't figure out how he got there, and he refused to believe the grotesque picture Lily painted. He chose, instead, to believe that he had pretended to be out from under the bridge—and therefore *was* out from under it, just as Danny Dew had pretended to be white.

"Just like riding a horse with a dildo," Lily Kain said, shaking her head and laughing.

Major Kelly couldn't take any more of that. He turned away from them and walked to the far end of the bunker. As he passed Liverwright, he said, "You're dying." Liverwright seemed pleased by his honesty.

Private Tooley, who was stationed at that end of the bunker, washing out scrapes and cuts which his new batch of patients had sustained, said, "If you'd heeded Kowalski's warning, you wouldn't have been under the bridge in the first place."

"Who in the hell would ever think Kowalski knew what he was talking about?" Major Kelly asked, turning to look at the mad Pole who lay quietly in his cot, staring at nothing. "Kowalski is a zombie, a bag of shit. He can't even feed himself any more. How in the hell was I to know that this dumb bag of shit would be right?"

Private Tooley daubed some grit out of a sliced forearm, then sent the man to the front of the bunker where Lily and Nurse Pullit were dispensing antiseptics and applying bandages. He said, "I wish you wouldn't call him names like that."

"What should I call him, then?"

"Private Kowalski," Private Tooley said. "That's his name."

Major Kelly shook his head. "No. That isn't the Private Kowalski that I knew. The Private Kowalski that I knew always laughed a lot. Has this bag of shit laughed recently?"

"No, but–"

"The Private Kowalski I knew liked to play cards and used to bitch a blue streak when he lost. Has this man tried to get up a poker game since he was brought here, or has he cursed you out?"

"Of course not, but–"

"Then this isn't Private Kowalski," Major Kelly said. "This is nothing more than a bag of shit. The sooner you accept that, the better you're going to feel. A bag of shit doesn't die. You don't have to be sorry for it."

"Next time," Tooley said, trying to change the subject, "you better listen to him."

"Next time, let's hope there's more to his ravings—like dates and times. What good is an oracle who can't give dates and times?"

Private Kowalski belched.

"There!" Tooley said.

"There *what?*"

"He's improving."

"How so?"

"He belched."

"The only thing a belch is an improvement over is a fart," Major Kelly said.

"But it *is* an improvement."

Major Kelly shook his head. His head felt as if it were going to fall off. He could not allow that. His headache was bad enough now. "You will never learn, Tooley. Things don't get better. They just don't. They stay the same way, or they get worse. Kowalski is a bag of crap, and he'll only get worse. If you want to hang on, accept that. Otherwise, you'll never make it."

"I'll make it."

Kowalski belched. Then he farted. Then he relieved himself on the clean sheets.

"A relapse," Tooley said. "But only temporary."

Major Kelly got out of there. He turned so fast he stumbled into Private Angelli who was no longer suffering from a bloody nose and who was now seeking treatment for his abraded shoulder. He weaved past Angelli, did not even look at Liverwright. At the front of the bunker, Lily Kain and Nurse Pullit were still giggling, so he avoided them as well. He pushed through the bunker door and collided with Sergeant Coombs.

"I was looking for you," Coombs said. He was huffing like a bull, and his eyes were maniacally alight. It was obvious that the sergeant would have liked to add something to his statement, something like: "I was looking for you, Diarrhea Head." However, he restrained himself.

That surprised Major Kelly, because he was not accustomed to the sergeant restraining himself. Apparently, even Coombs could be affected by disaster and the brief but fierce presence of death.

"And I was coming to find you," the major said. "I want the men on the job fast. That wreckage has to be cleared, salvage made, and the reconstruction begun by dawn. I want you to check the men in the hospital and be sure there's no malingering; if a man's fit to work, I want him out there working. We're not going to dawdle around this time. If there is really going to be a Panzer division sent this way, I don't want them to show up and find a pile of ruins where the bridge should be. I don't want them angry, and I don't want them having to linger on this side of the gorge. Is this clear?"

"It's clear," Sergeant Coombs said. He thought: you coward. He wanted to stand and fight the krauts for a change, even if they would be putting handguns against tanks. "Something I want to show you, first," he said, cryptically, turning and stomping up the steps.

Major Kelly followed him topside where the fire in the brush around the bridge had not yet been fully doused and strange orange lights played on the darkness, adding an unmistakable Halloween feeling. They walked east along the river to the latrines, which had taken a direct hit from a misplaced two-hundred-pounder. Most of the structure was shredded, with the undamaged walls leaning precariously.

"Was anyone inside?" Major Kelly asked. The nausea he had experienced in the hospital bunker returned to him now.

"No," Coombs said. "But look at this!" He led Kelly to the line of earth-moving machines which were parked in the vicinity of the outhouses.

"They don't look damaged to me," Kelly said.

"None of the machines were touched," Coombs said.

"Well, then?"

"But they were covered with crap," Coombs said. He held up his big hissing Coleman lantern as if searching for an honest man. "What a cleaning-up job this is going to be. Christ!"

On closer examination, employing his olfactory sense as well as his eyes, the major saw that what appeared to be mud was not actually mud at all. It really did look like mud from a distance, great gouts of mud sprayed across the windscreens, splashed liberally on the mighty steel flanks, packed around the controls, crusted in the deep tread of the oversized tires. But it was not mud. The sergeant was right about one thing: if Major Kelly had ever seen shit, this was it.

Coombs lowered his lantern and said, "Now let's hear the bit about Aesop, about how all of this is just a fairy tale, grand in color but modest in design."

Major Kelly said nothing.

"Well?" Coombs asked. He held the lantern higher, to give them a better view of the crap-covered vehicles. "What kind of fairy tales, I'd like to know, are full of crap?"

"All of them," Kelly said, "I thought you understood that."

# 5/

The following day was the hottest they had endured since they'd been dropped behind enemy lines. The thermometer registered over ninety degrees. The sun was high, hard, and merciless, baking the earth and the men who moved upon it. The whispering trees were quiet now, lifeless, rubbery growths that threw warm shadows into the gorge and across the fringes of the camp. The river continued to flow, but it was syrupy, a flood of brown molasses surging sluggishly over rocks and between the high banks.

In the gorge, Kelly's men worked despite the heat, wrestling with the steel beams that never wanted to go where they were supposed to go. The men cursed the beams, each other, the sun, the still air, Germans, and being born.

Private Vito Angelli, whose bloody nose Nurse Pullit had treated last night, worked on the near side, wielding a pegging mallet against the newly placed bridge plates, tightening connections which Private Joe Bob Wilson tempered with a gasoline hand torch. Angelli slammed the mallet in a slow, easy rhythm designed to accomplish the most work with the least effort. Each blow rang across the camp like the tolling of a flat bell, punctuating the other men's curses.

At the other end of the bridge, Privates Hoskins and Malzberg were working hard to line up and secure the couplings between the farside pier and its cantilever arm. They were in charge of a dozen men, and they were the only two in the detail with preliminary engineering training, but they were hefting the wooden wedges and driving the hammers as hard as anyone. This surprised the men working with them, for no one had ever seen Hoskins or Malzberg work. Between them, the two men controlled all the gambling in Kelly's camp: poker games, blackjack, craps, bets on the hour of the next Stuka attack, penny pitching, *everything*. Hoskins and Malzberg were natural con men. They were the only men in the entire unit who had thought to bring cards and dice along when the unit had been flown behind German lines, and both of them acted as if this were the only contribution they should have to make for the rest of the war. However, now that Kelly had warned them about the possibility of more Panzers coming this way, they were as desperate as the other men to get the bridge repaired. If the bridge weren't in shape when the Panzers came, and if the Nazis had to stay by the bridge all night and everyone in Kelly's camp was killed, that would put quite a crimp in their rake-off from the games.

In the gorge, the cement mixers rattled as some of the strongest men in camp turned them by hand. Saws scraped through damaged planking, cutting new boards for braces and flooring. Stoically, the men worked. Fearfully, too.

As Major Kelly paraded back and forth from one crisis point to another, he saw that, as usual, the most valuable worker was Danny Dew whose expertise with the big D-7 dozer made the whole thing possible. Because of Dew, the unit put the bridge in place in a record, for them, twenty-six hours.

As Coombs often said, "Even if he's a nigger, and he is, he can handle that machine like a man should handle a woman."

Sergeant Coombs was always the first to admit that a black man could be good at something. He didn't like them, he said, but he was willing to give them their due. Once when some of the men went to Eisenhower, the village, to a dance that Maurice had arranged, all the young village girls wanted to dance with Danny Dew. "All them niggers," Coombs observed, "have a natural rhythm." Later, when the men discovered some of the village girls were not averse to a well-presented proposition, Danny Dew seemed always to be disappearing with one or another. "That's a darkie," Sergeant Coombs told Slade. "They have puds like elephant trunks and always ready. It's a primitive trait that's been refined out of white men." When the men played softball, they all wanted Danny Dew on their team, because he was the best player. "Natural for his kind," Coombs said. "They're all good at sports, because of their primitive muscles. Our primitive muscles atrophied when our brains got bigger, but them niggers still have primitive muscles." Even when Danny Dew won a pot in poker, Coombs looked for hereditary explanations. "Never play poker with a nigger," he told Slade. "That natural rhythm of theirs tells them when good luck's coming, when to bet heavy and when light. They have a natural instinct for gambling. A nigger can have a fantastic hand and not show it. Natural poker faces. Too dumb to get excited about the right things."

But the thing Danny Dew did best was operate the D-7 dozer. He could plow up ruins, stack them neatly, and not bend the pieces which had survived the bombing and might be used again. All the hot day, he sat high in his dozer seat, shirtless, ebony muscles gleaming with sweat. He waved at Kelly now and then, and he talked constantly to the D-7 as if it were alive.

The machine was his virility symbol.

Kelly was fascinated by Danny Dew's relationship with the dozer, because he'd never thought a black man needed a virility symbol. White men bought fast cars or owned guns, built huge and phallic homes and amassed fortunes. But a colored man needed no symbol of his manhood. His manhood was formidable enough to speak for itself. Yet here was Danny Dew with a virility symbol he could not do without. In the morning, he washed the dozer in the river, oiled it, greased and polished it. In the afternoon, he raced it back and forth across the field for fifteen minutes, because he was afraid it would come to feel unwanted unless it was used every day. In the evening, he slept on its wide tread, on a bundle of folded blankets, forsaking his cot in the main bunker. At odd moments, he amorously caressed the wheel, the clutches, the seat, the backrest. . . .

If you asked—few ever did—he explained in detail about the hydraulic steering clutches, the forward reverse lever which allowed you to drive in all speeds front and back, the booster springs . . . the stressed blade . . . the four mammoth cylinders!

One night when they had been drinking, Kelly asked Danny Dew why he needed a virility symbol. And Dew said, "Because of my balls."

"Your balls?" Kelly had asked.

"My testicles," Danny said glumly.

"They're gone?"

"No. I've got them."

"Well?"

"They're not normal. My testicles are abnormal."

"Abnormal?" Kelly asked, incredulous.

Danny took a drink of whiskey. "It's been the curse of my life, Kelly. I feel silly. And feeling silly makes me feel inadequate—and so I need the dozer."

Kelly hesitated, drank. Then, "What's wrong with your—balls?"

"They're silly."

Major Kelly's face felt fuzzy. He wiped at imaginary cobwebs. "Yes, but *how* are they silly?"

Danny was exasperated. He waved his arm for emphasis. "Silly! They just are, that's all. They're laughable."

"Has anyone ever laughed at them?" Kelly asked.

"Everybody who's seen them." Danny looked suicidal.

"Even the girls in Eisenhower?" Kelly asked, recalling how easily Danny had gotten the girls there.

"Even them." Danny took a drink and let whiskey run out the corner of his mouth. He didn't seem to know he was losing it.

Kelly poured another drink. He was only using the whiskey as an excuse not to ask what, finally, he *had* to ask. "Could I see your funny testicles?" When Danny sighed, Kelly said, "I don't want to touch them."

"Sure, sure," Danny said, as resigned as a weak woman submitting to a powerful rapist.

"You don't think this is an odd request?" Kelly asked anxiously.

"No," Dew said. "Everyone wants to see them when they hear how damn funny they are." He stood, unzipped his pants with considerable fumbling effort, reached inside, cupped himself, and revealed his cock and balls.

"What's funny about them?" Kelly asked.

"Come on," Danny said. "I can see you want to laugh. I'm used to it."

"They're perfectly ordinary," Kelly said. He looked closely, because he wanted a good laugh, needed a good laugh, but he couldn't find anything funny about them.

"Don't be sarcastic. Go ahead and laugh, but don't make it any worse."

"Really, Dan, there isn't—"

"Shit," Danny Dew said. "You're smirking behind that frown. You think you'll make me let down my defenses—and *then* you'll laugh at me. I know you sadists. Come on, now. Everyone laughs. No one's ever sympathetic."

"Nothing to be sympathetic about," Kelly said. "You have ordinary—"

"There!" Dew said, pointing and grinning. "That's better! Laugh. Go on, don't worry, laugh your head off. That's the way!"

Kelly looked around the blanket-walled room. Only the two of them were there, and neither of them was laughing. "I'm not laughing," he said.

"That's it!" Danny went on. He slapped the table, grinning and nodding his head. "Laugh it up. I told you they were funny!"

"But—"

"Well, now, try to be decent about it," Danny Dew said, no longer grinning. "You don't have to laugh *that* hard. You'll make yourself sick if you keep it up, for Christ's sake. Now, stop it!"

"Who's laughing?" Kelly wanted to know. He wasn't laughing at all.

"Stop it, you bastard!" Danny said. "Come *on*, Kelly!" He put his balls away and zipped his fly, stepped back against the blanket. "I'm going to leave if you don't stop. You ought to be ashamed. Do you laugh at cripples and blind men?" He lifted the blanket flap. "You get hold of yourself. I'll expect an apology." He left.

To the empty room, Kelly said, "But I wasn't laughing, Danny."

It was a shame, the major thought later, that Danny Dew —who could think himself into being anyone else in the world—could not pretend himself another set of balls if he thought his own were funny. Not even Danny Dew, who could became a white man at will, not even Danny could escape everything.

So thanks to Danny Dew, the bridge was completed at two o'clock in the morning, twenty-six hours after the unit set to work on it. The last of the men staggered out of the ravine like the dead returning from hell. They had worked a sweltering day and a muggy night, and they could hardly see where they were going. Most of them trudged back to the main bunker, but no one wanted to sleep underground. They fell down in the grass and looked at each other and mumbled about the heat and fell asleep. A few men could not sleep, at first. They had been driven to the limits of their endurance, and they had come around the bend of exhaustion to a sort of manic insomnia. But in an hour, lulled by the snores of their fellows, they too slept.

A score of men went to the rec room where there was ice for cold drinks that Maurice supplied. Privates Hoskins and Malzberg were trying to start a poker game in the rec room, even though they were almost too tired to shuffle the cards. The men slumped on the benches and floor and looked at Hoskins and Malzberg as if they were insane. Actually, they were.

Hoskins sat at a scarred table talking to the men. "You worked hard," he told them. "You deserve a little fun, an interesting game."

Malzberg, the tallest in the unit, stood in the middle of the room and spread his arms despairingly. "We're doomed anyway," he said, in a rumbling voice full of the sadness of ages. "We've no chance. We're all dead men. We can't afford to throw away our last precious hours of life in sleep."

By the time he'd finished, all the men in the room had fallen asleep.

"Blackjack?" Hoskins asked.

Malzberg sat down, dwarfing the table. "Deal," he said.

Fifteen minutes later, even they were asleep.

# 6/

"Kelly, wake up."

The major snorted, blinked, opened his eyes and looked directly into Private Tooley's flashlight. "Turn that thing off!"

Tooley turned it off, blinding both of them. They were only inches away from each other, but it was like being sealed up in two separate cans side by side on a grocery shelf. Talking from his can, the pacifist said, "I have something to tell you."

Kelly sat up on his cot, felt the canvas shift under him and the spindly frame twist with his weight. He smacked his lips. "What time is it?"

"Four in the morning."

"What morning?" Kelly asked.

"I know you just got to sleep," Tooley said. "So did I. But this is important. Kowalski just sat up in bed and warned me about another raid. He was shouting so loud he woke me."

Kelly tried to think who Kowalski was, but he couldn't get his mind functioning. The room was too hot. His undershorts were pasted to him with sweat, and even the cot canvas was damp and slippery. "Another air attack?"

"Yes, sir," Tooley said. "His exact words were: 'Rising sun, bombs in the trees, bridge kaput.' " Tooley shifted as his haunches stiffened, wiped sweat out of his eyes. "Did you hear me, sir?"

Major Kelly remembered who Kowalski was. He said, "Tooley, the Germans haven't had time to learn that the bridge is back up. And if they're judging by our past record, they won't come around again for a couple of days. No informer in this unit could have passed the word to the krauts in so short a time."

"Sir—"

Kelly kept his eyes closed, trying not to wake up any more than he had to. Besides, he was afraid that if he opened his eyes again, Tooley would flick on the flashlight and shatter his corneas. "Don't pay any attention to a bag of shit like Kowalski. Look, the rising sun is the symbol of Japan, not Germany. I don't think the Japs could have diverted a bomber to the middle of Europe just to attack our little bridge, eh? Not likely, eh? Eh? Look, Tooley, what you do, you go back to the hospital and go to sleep. And if Kowalski starts blabbing again, you smother him with a pillow."

"But Major Kelly, I—"

"That's an order," Kelly said.

He listened as, reluctantly, Tooley got up and lifted the blanket and went away. Then he lay there, trying to imagine that the heat was not heat at all, but a snug blanket draped across him and that he was twelve and back home and sleeping in his attic room and that it was winter and snow was falling and his blanket kept him warm, very warm, against the cold. . . . In a few minutes, he fell asleep as the frogs and crickets, cavorting in the snow, croaked and chirruped secret messages all the way around the world to Germany.

In the morning as dawn lined the horizons, after the frogs had gone to bed and the crickets had been silenced by the growing dew, in the first orange rays of the elevating sun, Major Kelly was awakened by the shrieking approach of a bomber. A big one. Coming in low.

Kelly leaped out of bed, wearing only his damp shorts and an expression of admirably controlled terror in the face of a familiar intolerable persecution. He grabbed his service revolver from the top of the pasteboard trunk and plunged through the khaki-colored Army blanket and out the door of the HQ building.

The day was far too bright, even at dawn. The sunlight put a flat glare across the mist that lay over the camp and made the French countryside seem like a stage setting under the brutal beams of a score of huge kliegs. He raised an arm to shield his eyes, and he saw the plane. It was a B-17, highlighted by the new sun. It swooped over the camp, straight for the bridge.

"One of ours!" Slade shouted. He had stumbled out of the HQ building in the major's wake and now stood at his left side. He was, as usual, a vocal repeater of visual events.

"Why didn't I listen to Kowalski?" Kelly asked.

Slade gave him a curious look.

The B-17 let go at the bridge with two bombs that slid straight for the span's deck like Indian arrows for cavalry targets. All of this was out of place, unfitted to the peaceful morning, the slightly chilled air, and the sun like an open oven door in a country kitchen. Still, as the big plane turned up on the other side of the gorge, the bridge leaped up in a spray of steel, wood, cable, and concrete. A flash of light made the day seem less bright by comparison, and the roar of the explosion brought the sky falling down. The twisted beams, miraculous in flight, glittered prettily and fell back in a chiming heap. The flash of the explosion gave way to smoke which rolled out of the gorge and devoured the edge of the camp.

"Our own plane," Kelly said. He was numb.

The B-17 came back, loosed six bombs. Two fell over the northeast edge of the woods, two over the open space between the main bunker and the HQ, and two over the bridge approach.

When Kelly saw the second two released, he shouted, "Christ! He's after everything!" He put his head down and ran for the hospital bunker, though he knew it was useless.

The two bombs released over the woods angled down and slammed into the earth directly between the main bunker and the HQ. The blast made Kelly scream. He glanced sideways as he ran, saw a wall of earth rising skyward and pouring across the space between the buildings like a brown wave of lava.

The second pair of bombs, which had been dropped over this now devastated area, exploded in twin balls of searing, white flame at the southwest corner of the HQ building, not far from where Kelly and Slade had been standing. Flames spewed out in all directions. The earth convulsed, showering heavy clumps of ground in all directions. Aflame, the west wall of HQ buckled inwards, then popped out again and tore loose of the other three partitions. It fell to the earth with a sound like a slammed door. The three standing walls shuddered violently.

The two bombs let loose over the bridge approach sailed toward the center of the span. They passed either side of it and exploded below, in the ravine. More flames. The ground near the gorge heaved and rolled and settled reluctantly.

Dazed men streamed out of the rec room which now had only three walls. They had been awakened by the attack, startled to see their room open around them like a packing crate, and they had yet to figure out exactly what was going on.

Major Kelly reached the head of the hospital steps and looked up at the B-17 which was circling around for another run at the camp. Far above it, in the morning sky, a trio of Allied fighter planes which acted as its escort went around in lazy little circles, waiting for big brother to finish and come back to them.

Slade hurried up, panting. His face was flushed, but he looked more excited than frightened. "What can we do?"

Kelly ran down the steps and tried the bunker door. Locked. He really hadn't expected anything else.

The B-17 came back. It roared in lower than before and let go at the HQ building again.

The missiles overshot and blew a huge chunk out of the riverbank. Shrapnel and dirt cascaded over six or seven men who had run the wrong way after coming out of the rec room.

Major Kelly thought he heard someone screaming in pain, but he could not be sure.

"We have to *do* something!" Slade insisted.

Major Kelly watched the bomber circle again. The damn pilot wasn't done with them. Any pilot with a grain of sense would have cut out by now; this asshole had to be some patriotic, gung-ho promotion seeker with no real sense of his own mortality.

Slade grabbed the major's arm. "Listen to me! We have to stop them, for Christ's sake!"

Kelly pushed the lieutenant away and shouted at the men who were still too dazed to get away from the HQ building. "Over here! Run, you idiots! Move! Run! Get away from there!"

Slade grabbed him again, using both hands this time and digging in hard with his fingers, molding a grip in Kelly's bare arm as if the major were made of clay. "What are you going to do? You cowardly son of a bitch, what are you going to do?"

Kelly drew back his free arm and struck Slade across the face, harder than he had ever hit a man before. When the lieutenant fell back, stunned, Kelly grabbed him with a fierceness far worse than Slade's had been a moment ago. Kelly's eyes were so wide open they appeared on the verge of falling out; his mouth was a twisted, thin-lipped hole in his face; his nostrils flared like those of an animal. "What *can* I do, you fucking little creep? Did Blade give me artillery? Did Blade give me antiaircraft weapons? What am I supposed to do with nothing? Can I fight a fucking B-17 with a bulldozer and pegging mallets? Use your fucking brain, Slade!" Then he let go of him, because they were both knocked off their feet by two more explosions.

Kelly rolled to the bottom of the hospital bunker steps and smacked his head against the bunker door. Cursing, he crawled back to the top to see what had been hit.

The bridge. It made a tortured, metallic squeal the same pitch as the squeal inside Kelly's head and collapsed into the gorge with an almost practiced grace.

Slade was standing on top of the hospital bunker, holding his service revolver in both hands and shooting at the bomber. Kelly had lost his own gun somewhere, but he didn't feel like hunting it just now. He watched Slade fire all his chambers at the plane, to no effect.

While the lieutenant was reloading, the B-17 climbed skyward to join its escort, and the four United States Air Force planes streaked westward, out of sight, back toward the safety of Allied territory.

Up near the HQ building where the bombs had torn away a large piece of the riverbank, someone was screaming. It was a monotonous scream, rising and falling and rising and falling again in a predictable pattern. Kelly walked that way, though he didn't want to. He passed a smoking crater that smelled like rotten eggs, passed the charred wall of the rec room which was still smoldering a little, and he came to three men who were lying on the ground midst pieces of bomb casings, fragments of limestone, and clods of earth.

He knelt beside the first. Private Hoskins. "You okay?"

Hoskins's eyes fluttered, opened. He looked at Kelly, got it sorted out remarkably fast, reached out for support and sat up. He was twenty-eight years old, a small-town boy from upper New York State—but right now Hoskins looked a hundred, and as if he had seen everything bad there was to see. His nose was bleeding across his lips, wet ribbons of some gay disguise. Most of his clothes had been torn off by the blast. Otherwise, he seemed to be in good shape.

"Can you walk?" Kelly asked.

"I think so."

Kelly helped him to his feet. "Go see Pullit and Kain."

Hoskins, the gambler, nodded. He walked off toward the hospital bunker, weaving a bit, as if a pair of roulette wheels were strapped to his shoulders.

The second man lying on the ground was Private Osgood

from Nashville, Tennessee. Kelly did not know him well. He would never know him well. Osgood was dead, pierced by twenty or more pieces of shrapnel, bleeding from the face and neck and chest, from the stomach and the legs, a voodoo doll that had gotten into the hands of a witch with a real grudge to settle.

Kelly walked closer to the ravine where the third man lay on his side, holding his stomach with both hands. It was Private Peter Danielson, Petey for short. He was the unit's foremost drinker and hell raiser. Kelly had reprimanded him on three separate occasions when Danielson had pissed in Sergeant Coombs's office window, all over Coombs's desk and papers.

"Petey?" Kelly asked, kneeling beside the man.

Danielson's scream died into a low sobbing, and he focused his watery eyes on the major.

"Where are you hurt?" Kelly asked.

Danielson tried to speak. Blood oozed from the corner of his mouth and dribbled down his chin, thick as syrup.

"Your stomach, Petey?"

Danielson blinked and slowly nodded his head. He jerked as his bladder gave out and his trousers darkened with urine. Tears came to his eyes, fat and clear; they ran down his round cheeks and mixed with the blood on his chin.

"Can I look?" Kelly asked.

Danielson shuddered and managed to speak. "Nothing to see. Okay." His teeth and tongue were bright with blood.

"If I could look, maybe I could keep it from hurting," Kelly said.

Danielson started to scream again, that same monotonous ululation. His mouth was wide open, all red inside, and bloody foam bubbled at both nostrils.

Slade had come up beside Kelly while the major was talking to Petey Danielson. "What's wrong with him?"

Kelly didn't answer him. He took hold of the screaming man's hands, which were cold. He was prepared to pry Danielson's hands away from his stomach, but the wounded man surrendered with surprising weakness. Then, with nothing to hold in its place, his stomach fell away from him. It just bulged out through his shredded shirt in a shapeless, awful mass. Undigested food, blood, intestines, feces, and the walls of his stomach flopped onto the ground in a slithering, glistening mass.

Danielson screamed and screamed.

"Christ," Slade said.

Major Kelly looked at Danielson's insides, trying to pretend them out of the way, trying to pretend Danielson back to health. He couldn't do it. He stood up, trying not to be sick. He turned to Slade in the jerky way of an automaton in a big department-store Christmas display, and he took the loaded revolver out of Slade's hand.

Danielson was curled up on himself now, trying to stuff his ruined intestines back through the neat slit the shrapnel had made in him. He was screaming and crying and apologizing to someone.

Major Kelly aimed the revolver at Danielson's chest but found that he was shaking too badly to make a good shot. He planted his feet farther apart and gripped the gun with both hands as he had seen Slade doing when the B-17 was over them. He shot Danielson four times in the chest, until the man was dead.

He gave the gun back to Slade.

He walked away, holding his hands over his ears, trying to block out Petey Danielson's scream which he imagined he could still hear like a siren cutting across the smoking campsite.

In his quarters, Kelly put on new shorts and a dirty pair of khaki slacks. He took his bottle of Jack Daniels out of the pasteboard trunk and took several long pulls straight from the neck. Although he wouldn't have believed he could be functional so soon, though he wouldn't have thought he could push Danielson out of his mind so quickly, Kelly was ready to listen to Lieutenant Beame half an hour later when Beame came in to report on the condition of the bridge.

"Both piers are undamaged," Beame said. "But we'll have to repair the entire floor and superstructure. All in all, not so bad."

"We'll have to get on it right away," Kelly said. "The Panzers must be on the way."

Beame didn't understand.

Kelly said, "We were hit by one of our own bombers. That means the Panzer division is on its way west and the brass wants to deny it the use of this bridge."

Beame didn't like that. "No. It can't be."

"There's no other reason for them to risk a B-17 and its escort on such a limited target. We're all doomed."

# 7/

The HQ building had not been damaged, except for the fallen wall. In a few hours, even that was in place and all was as it had been in that corner of the camp. The radio room was undisturbed, and the wireless hummed menacingly.

Major Kelly wanted to call the general to order supplies and ask about the big Panzer division, but he could not do that. The wireless communications link between the camp and Blade was decidedly one-way; only the general could initiate a conversation. So far, this had been fine with Kelly. Now, however, once the men had been set to cleaning up the debris and there was nothing to do, the major's mind dwelt on too many unpleasant possibilities which a single call to the general could have confirmed or negated. Probably confirmed. The worst would happen. The B-17 had bombed the bridge because the Panzers were on their way.

Still, until he got word for sure on tonight's Blade and Slade Show, Kelly would have to occupy his time in some manner that would take his mind off these other things. He decided he might as well return to the problem of the camp informer. Operation Traitor Hunt would keep him busy and, perhaps, gain him some respect from Slade and Coombs.

He sat behind a plank table-desk just inside the door of the mess hall, toying with a dagger. For the first time since they'd been dropped behind enemy lines, he was wearing his uniform. He felt it was only proper, while carrying on an interrogation, to wear his uniform and to toy with the dagger, thereby instilling a combination of respect and fear in the men he questioned, insuring their cooperation. Also, he wore his uniform because it gave him an excuse to wear a hat which covered the worst of his widening bald spots and prevented the interrogation subjects from laughing at him and making cruel jokes. The only trouble was that he perspired heavily, leaving the uniform wrinkled and streaked with sweat. And he had twice cut himself while toying with the dagger.

"Next!" Kelly called.

Lieutenant Slade opened the door and escorted the next man inside: Danny Dew, who had just taken a break from his D-7 work in the gorge. Danny sat on the hot seat, leaned back, clasped his hands behind his head and smiled. "What's the hubbub?" he asked, flashing white-white teeth.

"Wipe that smile off your face, soldier," Major Kelly said.

But he was no good at discipline, and he knew Danny Dew too well to throw the least bit of fear into him. Danny Dew looked sideways at Slade and grinned, as if they all shared some private joke.

"That's better," Major Kelly said, refusing to acknowledge that the smile was still there. He leaned forward on the table, pointing the dagger at Danny Dew. "Corporal Dew, have you any idea why we're questioning every man in this unit?"

Danny grinned at him. "No, Massah Kelly."

"Because," Major Kelly said, "there is a traitor among us, and we are going to find out who he is before he has another opportunity to report us to the German Air Force or to—any other German force."

"Wonderful, wonderful!" Danny Dew said.

Kelly nodded. "I will tell you what I've told every man so far, Dew: I want to trust you, but I can't. For all our sakes, I've got to assume that you could be the kraut agent. There's no way I can actually find out for sure, short of torturing you, and that is impractical. Therefore, I want to say this, Dew: if you are a kraut agent, and if you don't tell me now and let me find out on my own, later, I will have you executed without trial."

Dew smiled. "Ain't nothin' in my ole head, Massah Kelly."

"Christ," Kelly said. "If you insist on doing that bit, can't you at least get it right? Not 'head'—'haid'!"

"Ain't nothin' in my ole haid, Massah Kelly!"

Kelly toyed with his dagger awhile. "Execution without trial," he said again. "But that isn't all, Dew. Before I have you killed, I'll assign you to the radio room where you will be tied to a chair and forced to listen to every one of General Blade's calls."

Danny Dew stopped smiling.

"Furthermore," Major Kelly said, warming to the routine again, "I will order the shortwave channels kept open at periodic intervals so that you will have to listen to other transmissions of other officers like General Blade, wherever and whenever we can locate them."

Danny Dew looked distinctly ill. He had taken his hands from behind his head and clasped them between his knees. He was hunched forward as if he were going to be sick on the floor.

"And when you're screamingly insane, then we'll kill you." Kelly waved the dagger to emphasize the point. "Now, are you the damned traitor, the kraut informer?"

"No, sir!" Dew said.

Kelly smiled. He softened his tone of voice and tried to

look sincere. "Actually, I wouldn't turn you in, even if I learned you were a traitor. You understand that? I wouldn't interfere with your work. It's just that I want to know, you see. I'd promise not to get in the way of your traitoring, so long as you stopped trying to fool me. Do you get my meaning?"

"Yes, sir. But I'm not the traitor."

Kelly sighed. "Dismissed."

Shaken, wondering if he were still under suspicion, Danny Dew got up and left the interrogation room.

Lieutenant Slade brought in the next man, who wasn't a man at all. It was Lily Kain. She was wearing a skimpy, sequined dancer's costume out of which her jugs might pop at any moment. She sashayed across the interrogation room and sat down in the chair in front of Major Kelly, crossed her gorgeous legs, and folded her hands in her lap. She grinned at Kelly and licked her lips and winked.

"First," Kelly said, "you've got to understand that this is serious business, Miss Kain!" To forcefully underline this statement, the major raised the dagger and, as he finished the sentence, drove the wicked point of it into the top of his plank table-desk. He also drove the point of it through the edge of his left hand. "That's okay," he said. He smiled at Lily and Slade to let them see how okay it was. "This is all a fairy tale anyway, a figment of some Aesop's imagination. None of it is real." However, the blood was real enough.

# 8/

When General Blade called at nine o'clock that night, he listened to Kelly's report on the B-17 attack, then got right to the bad news. "The German high command has ordered those Panzers and all attendant companies westward. According to our sources, Kelly, they'll be coming your way."

Although he had been expecting this for days, Kelly was speechless. His hands shook. He felt cold and weary. "When, sir?"

"They'll be moving out from a staging area near Stuttgart the day after tomorrow, taking as direct a land route as possible. Twice they'll leave the regular highways for shorter secondary roads that will take them through the back country where Allied reconnaissance won't be likely to spot them. That's maybe a-hundred-eighty miles from your position, as the crow flies—two hundred and sixty miles by road. Considering the size of this deployment, they'll be lucky to make your camp in four or five days. So you'll have guests in about a week, Kelly."

The major brushed nervously at his face. "How many guests, sir?"

"Not easy to say," Blade said. "According to our sources inside Germany, this isn't a neat division. It's an amalgam of broken Panzer brigades that escaped the disaster in Russia—and some of the new tanks fresh from Hitler's underground factories near München. There will also be a detail of SS overseers to watch that the *Wehrmacht* fights according to Hitler's orders. So you have maybe ninety Panzers—"

"Ninety!"

Blade went on as if he had not heard. "Approximately fifteen armored cars, ten self-propelled howitzers, four Jagdpanthers—that's the tank-hunting tank the krauts have—nine heavy-transport trucks carrying well-anchored 88-mm ack-ack guns to provide defense against air attacks on the convoy. Then there are two big flatbed transports with high-range aerial searchlights to pick out targets for the 88s, forty-odd trucks carrying fifteen hundred infantrymen to secure what objectives the Panzers overwhelm, and an undisclosed number of motorcycle escorts and message men."

"Has anyone there estimated the length of time they'll need to get across the bridge, sir? It's a narrow bridge, awfully narrow."

"Twelve hours," Blade said. "Or more."

Kelly swallowed hard. "Maybe we could tear down this bridge and build a wider one before they get here. We could do it if you'd get us the materials—"

"Wouldn't do much good," Blade said. "That convoy isn't going to drive straight through. They'll need a rest about the time they get to you. Even if the bridge were wider, they'd stay overnight."

"Why don't we bomb the convoy, sir?" Major Kelly asked.

"It would be a high-risk proposition," Blade said, "taking a squadron of bombers that far behind enemy lines to hit a well-guarded convoy."

"Yes, but—"

"Command already decided to let them come ahead until they're in our territory where we have the advantage. We can take them out much easier and with fewer field casualties if they're closer to the front. Since your bridge was bombed this morning, I guess Command also decided to slow them down until a good defense can be readied. Otherwise, I can't tell you much."

"How far behind the lines are we?" Kelly asked.

"Only one hundred and sixty-two miles, Kelly!"

"I don't suppose there's any chance that the front will have moved this far by the time the Panzers get here?"

"You never can tell," Blade said. That meant no.

"Sir, what can we do?"

"I've given considerable thought to your problem," Blade said. "Is it possible to use the ruse you employed with the first Panzer unit?"

"No," Kelly said, though it pained him to say it. "That was a small force that passed in half an hour. But this division, this big convoy is going to stay the night. We'd never make them believe we were Germans, sir, especially when none of us speaks the language." He felt hollow inside, eaten out by termites. In a moment, he'd fall down in a heap of dust. "Is it possible for us to be airlifted out of here, sir?"

"No," Blade said. "That bridge must be kept open after the Panzers are across, so our own people can use it if the front suddenly breaks eastward."

"If we're dead, we can't keep it open, sir." This seemed like an inescapable truth to Kelly, an argument so sound it would knock Blade off his chair.

It didn't knock him off his chair. "I have faith in your ingenuity, Kelly," General Blade said. "I'm sure you'll pull through this with some clever plan or other." He cleared his throat, or perhaps he snarled at someone in his office, and he said, "Now, what supplies do you need? I think I can have them flown into you before dawn."

Five minutes later, the Blade and Slade Show was over.

Shortly before midnight, Major Kelly sat in his quarters and put mud on his head. His heart really wasn't in the treatment tonight. If they were all going to be killed a week from now, what did it matter if he was bald or hairy? Nevertheless, he smoothed the muck all over his head. By worrying about his hair, perhaps he was making a rebuff to death. Perhaps, in this simple ceremony, he was actually taking a courageous stand. Or maybe he just didn't have the guts to face up to what was coming.

He was interrupted in the midst of these unpleasant thoughts and in the middle of his pate ministrations by Maurice and two tough-looking French kids who were about sixteen years old and deadly as sharks. His hair slicked back and glimmering in the dull light, his face shiny, grease beaded in the folds around his nose, wearing his customary baggy pants and dirty checkered shirt, smiling that dangerous smile that meant he smelled a profit, Maurice sat down on the end of Kelly's cot and said, "*Bon soir*!"

Kelly, sitting at his table-desk with a headful of mud, reluctantly nodded at the bootleg bottle of Jack Daniels that stood out in plain sight. When Maurice smiled for an answer, Kelly poured him a drink in a battered tin cup. Maurice tossed this off in one swallow.

"What can I do for you, Maurice?" Kelly asked, wiping his muddy left hand on a damp towel.

Maurice ignored the major's strange cap. "You have hurt your hand!" He pointed at the bandage under the mud on Kelly's left hand.

"It's nothing. A minor knife wound."

Maurice push his glass forward, brushed a fat mosquito off his forehead, and raised his greasy white eyebrows in surprise. "Hand-to-hand combat, Major? I've had no report of Germans in the area, not in our backwater!"

"No Germans," Kelly agreed.

Maurice accepted a second slug of whiskey as graciously as if it had been freely offered, but he did not drink it. He was perplexed, trying to figure out where his complex information-gathering network could have failed. "Then how do you say—mutiny?"

"No mutiny," Kelly said.

"Who cut you, then, *bon ami*?"

Kelly recalled the interrogation of Lily Kain when he had run himself through, and he couldn't see how he could explain that. "I stabbed myself."

"Suicide!" Maurice said, clutching his chest. "You musn't think it!"

"Not suicide," Kelly said. "If I'd wanted to kill myself, I wouldn't have used a knife—and I wouldn't have stabbed my *hand,* Maurice."

"Where would you have stabbed?" Maurice asked, leaning forward. He was clearly interested.

"Perhaps my neck," Kelly said.

"Ah. Yes. Quick."

But Kelly didn't want to talk about the knife wound any more. He couldn't explain it and, besides, the longer they sat there the more conspicuous his headful of mud seemed to become. Hoping to get rid of the Frenchman quickly, he said, "What brings you here tonight, eh?"

"Trouble," the old man said.

The hard, young sharks with him nodded gloomily like a couple of mutes accidentally signed on for a Greek chorus.

Kelly sipped his whiskey. It tasted awful. It didn't *really* taste awful, he knew, but his subjective sense of taste had been badly thrown off by Maurice's sudden and unwelcome appearance.

Maurice said, "When my friends face trouble, I face it with them."

"And I'm facing trouble?"

Maurice nodded gravely. "You, your men, bad trouble."

Because he was feeling perverse, because the drying mud made his scalp itch, because he felt foolish, and chiefly because he didn't think even Maurice could get him out of the coming debacle, Kelly didn't respond as Maurice expected. "No trouble here," he said.

"You toy with me," Maurice said.

"No. No trouble."

"*Credat Judaeus Apella.*"

"It's true."

Maurice tossed off his whiskey. "You know as well as I that a major Nazi Panzer division is coming. It's far larger than the one we hoaxed."

"True enough," Kelly said. He squashed a mosquito that was burrowing in the mud on his head, poured himself more whiskey even if it did taste horrible.

"And you don't call this trouble?"

The sharks raised their eyebrows, looked at each other for Kelly's benefit.

"No," Kelly said. "You call it trouble when there's a chance of your escaping it. Words like trouble, danger, risk—all imply safe options. There is no way out of this. Therefore, it is no longer trouble; it is merely fate. We have a bad case of fate, but no trouble."

"There is one flaw in your reasoning," Maurice said. He was smug as he poured a third glass of whiskey, his heavy lips tight, as if he had just sampled a fine vintage wine or had delivered a particularly special *bon mot.*

Kelly watched the greasy frog carefully. What was in Maurice's crafty mind? What did the old man have to gain here, now? "What's the flaw?"

"There is a way out," Maurice said.

"Can't be."

"Is."

"Can't be."

"Is."

"Tell me about it," Kelly said, tossing back his whiskey. "Better yet, I'll tell you about it, because you've got to be thinking some of the same things I've thought myself. First, you're going to suggest that my men and I take our machines and withdraw into the woods, hide out for the duration of the Germans' crossing. But that won't work. Even if we could eliminate every sign of the camp, we couldn't get the big machines deep enough into the woods to hide them. Someone would stumble upon them; we'd be found out and killed in an hour. You might also suggest my men and I level the camp and move into Eisenhower where we could hide until the Panzers are by. That won't work either. Moving the machines would churn up the road through your village and leave us wide open to any other German patrols on another route. Besides, and most importantly, the Nazis are bound to run at least a minimal search of your town. There is no way we could conceal seventy-odd men and all these big machines against even a cursory inspection. Lastly, you might think we could hide out in the woods and abandon our machines to be destroyed by the Germans. But if we did that, General Blade would abandon *us*, and then we'd be as good as dead—stranded here behind German lines."

"I'm aware of all that," Maurice said.

"But there's still a way?" Major Kelly, against all his better judgment, allowed himself a bit of hope, the terminal disease. He couldn't help himself.

"Yes. A way out," Maurice said.

His sixteen-year-old sharks nodded soberly.

Having forgotten the mud on his head, treacherous hope kindled, Major Kelly leaned toward The Frog. "How much will this cost us?"

"Considerable," Maurice said.

"I was afraid of that."

"However, you will receive a great deal in return—you will live."

Kelly gave himself another dribble of whiskey, though he could not afford to drink much more. Already, he was seeing two of everything, including two of Maurice. He did not want to get drunk enough to see three of everything, because the pair of Maurices was already more than he could stand. "Specifics. What do you want in return for whatever help you give me?"

Maurice held up a hand for patience. "First let me explain how you can save yourselves. After that, the price will not seem so bad."

"Go ahead." He drank his dribble of whiskey.

Maurice put down his glass, got up, stiff and serious even in his baggy trousers. "You will not move any of your equipment or attempt to conceal your presence. Not even the big D-7 must be driven away. Instead, you will build a town on this sight, a town designed to shield all of your heavy machinery and your men from the Nazis."

Kelly butted the heel of his palm against his head to clear

his ear and hear better. Chunks of dried mud rained down around him. "Build a town?"

"Exactly," Maurice said. He smiled, warmed by his own suggestion. "You will build a French village here and hide your massive machines in the specially designed buildings. Clever, eh?"

"Impossible," Kelly said. "You don't throw up a building in a few hours. And we'd have to—construct a whole town before the Germans got here."

"You *do* throw up the building in a few hours," Maurice said. "*If* you do not intend to live in it for very long."

"That's another problem. Who will live in this town?" Was he hearing Maurice right? Did he have mud in his ears? He checked. No mud.

"I will supply half the population of my village. With your men, they will make a convincing citizenry."

"My men don't speak French. They'll be found out immediately."

"I've considered that," Maurice said. He poured himself a last whiskey. "The one institution the Nazis have been careful not to tamper with extensively is the Roman Catholic Church. Hitler respects the Church's worldwide power if not its philosophy. Himmler himself is a Catholic. Therefore, our fake town will be a religious community, a retreat for priests and nuns and selected members of the laity. It will be built around a convent. And we will tell the Nazis that, in this convent, the deaf and dumb are taught simple skills. Your men will be the poor afflicted peasants, while the women from my village have already volunteered to be the nuns. It is quite simple, really."

"More simple yet," Kelly said, "why not build the convent in Eisenhower? We could conceal the machines and my men inside of it and not have to build a whole damned village."

"No good," Maurice said. "According to my resources, the man in charge of this Panzer convoy is General Adolph

Rotenhausen. He was in the first waves of shock troops to overwhelm France. He passed through my town then, out on the main highway. He made his headquarters in my house four nights running during the invasion of France. He knows Eisenhower has no convent. And he knows that, in the midst of this awful war, no new convent could possibly be built, for lack of supplies."

"But if he knows your town," Kelly said, "he must know that no other village exists here, in this clearing."

Maurice shook his head. "Rotenhausen's Panzers invaded and departed France on the same highway, that which passes through my village eight miles south of here. Perhaps follow-up troops came down this old back road. But no Panzers. In those days, they did not have to use unlikely routes to avoid air attack. There was no resistance to them at that time."

"Still . . . build a whole town? Madness!"

"The alternatives are unworkable. And while Eisenhower is not built to conceal your machines, a town of your own making *would* be so built."

"We can't build a village in a week," Kelly insisted.

"I've heard that the Army engineers can do the impossible."

"Not in a week. Not with the bridge to rebuild as well."

Maurice waved his hand as if to say this was taken care of. "I will detail workers from my village to augment your labor supply."

"Unskilled labor. It's—"

"Remember that your town must last only one brief night! And the convent alone will house your machines—and be beyond suspicion."

They listened to the crickets chirrup outside the corrugated walls. The same insects would probably sing on his grave, Kelly knew. Above their chorus, he imagined the clatter of Panzer-tread, the stamp of marching feet, ack-ack guns, submachine guns. . . . He knew it was hopeless, knew they were doomed. Yet he had to play along. A character in a fairy tale must play his role regardless of the certainty of the outcome. Otherwise, the disaster might be even worse than that which the script, the story, called for.

"We'll have to talk about this some more, though it won't work."

"But it *will* work," Maurice said. The sharks smiled. "It will."

"Never. But let me wash this mud off my head. Then we'll talk about it some more and pretend we think it really *could* work."

# PART THREE

# The Village

## July 18/July 21, 1944

# 1 / JULY 18

At dawn, Kelly, Beame, and Slade stood by the bridge ruins, watching the road on the far side of the gorge where it disappeared around the hillside.

"They aren't coming," Slade said.

"Give them a chance," Beame said. "The sun's hardly up."

A dirty mist lay in the gorge, roiled over the river. Snakes of mist slithered up the bank and danced restlessly before them, touched by golden morning light. Behind, to the east, the sun had risen below the tree line. Hot, orange Halloween light like the glow from a jack-o'-lantern's mouth flushed between the black tree trunks where the forest was thin, and it filled the east entrance to the clearing.

"They aren't coming," Slade said. He was delighted by the plan, because it made the major look like an idiot. And coward. It gave Slade justification for murdering the dumb bastard and taking command of the unit. He giggled.

"Look!" Beame shouted, suddenly excited.

On the other side of the gorge, an odd procession filed around the bend in the road, making for the place where the bridge had stood. Maurice lead the parade, dressed in another—or maybe the same—checkered shirt and pair of baggy pants. Behind him were middle-aged men with their sleeves rolled to their elbows—and older but evidently vigorous grandfathers with their sleeves rolled up too. Only a few teenage boys were included, for most young men were off fighting the war. But there *were* many strong young girls and determined matrons in their long scrub dresses, hair tied back from their faces. They carried hoes, rakes, shovels, picks. The men pushed creaking wooden wheelbarrows or carried precious tools.

"How many?" Beame asked when the head of the procession reached the gorge and the tail had not yet shown itself.

"We were promised a hundred to start with," Major Kelly said.

Maurice found a way down the gorge wall, using some of the old bridge's underworks for support. His people followed him, carefully picking their way across the river, stepping from one unsteady mound of rubble to the next. The men with the wheelbarrows lifted these above their heads, and they looked like canoeists fording shallow water.

Beame grinned fiercely. "I believe we might just pull it off!"

"You do?" Kelly asked.

"I don't," Slade said, giggling.

"For once," Kelly said, "I have to agree with Lieutenant Slade."

Two hours later, Lieutenant Beame was down in the ravine with Danny Dew, surveying the wreckage which yesterday's B-17 attack had produced. The two bridge piers were still standing, stone and concrete phallic symbols, but the steel and wooden superstructure and the bridge flooring had collapsed into the gorge. Much of the planking was smashed, charred, or splintered beyond repair, though several large sections like the sides of gigantic packing crates were salvageable. Likewise, some of the steel support beams, cables, angle braces, couplings, and drawing braces had survived and could be used again if Danny Dew were only careful not to crush them when he started through here with his D-7 dozer.

"Over there!" Beame shouted, pointing at a jumble of bridge parts.

"I see it!" Dew shouted. "Ten-foot brace! Looks undamaged!"

They were forced to shout because of the din in the gorge. For one thing, the buckled plating on which they stood was the cap of a heap of refuse which was blocking the middle of the river. The water, diverted into two narrow streams by this barrier, gushed past them in a twin-tailed roar of white spume.

"Is that a coupling?" Beame shouted.

Dew squinted. "Yeah! And a good one!"

Added to the roar of the water were the sounds of fifty French men and women who were doing preliminary salvage that was best completed before the dozer came through. Hammers, wrenches, drills, shovels, and torches sang against the background of the moving river. And, worse, the French jabbered like a cageful of blackbirds. They were jabbering so loudly that when Beame tried to hear himself think, he failed. They jabbered at the Americans who were giving them directions in a tongue they could not understand, and they jabbered at one another, and many of them jabbered to themselves if no one else was nearby.

"I don't see anything more!" Beame shouted.

"Me either," Dew said. "I'll get the dozer." He scrambled down the shifting pile of junk, leaped the narrow divide of shooting water, and came down on both feet on the shore. Very athletic. Beame had always heard that Negroes were good athletes, but Danny Dew was the first proof he had seen. He watched Dew climb the steeply sloped ravine wall and go over the top without effort.

That was when he saw the girl.

She was standing at the crest of the slope, fifty yards from where Dew went over the top. She was watching the workers, the gentle morning sun full on her.

She was the most beautiful girl Beame had ever seen. She looked no older than twenty-one or -two, perhaps only seventeen. Though it was difficult to judge her height from this angle, he thought she must be tall for such a slender girl, maybe five-seven. Her complexion was Mediterranean, dark and smoky. Great masses of black hair cascaded around her face and fell to the sharp points of her widely spaced breasts. All this took Beame's breath away. He was affected by the way she stood: shoulders back, head up, exuding grace, a serene and almost Madonnalike figure.

Though Beame was no womanizer, he knew he had to meet her.

He went down the rubble heap too fast, lost his footing. He tottered and fell into the spume, flailing. He swallowed a mouthful of water, tried to spit it out, swallowed more. He was drowning. He felt himself swept around the rubble. He banged into a steel girder, shoved desperately away, scrambled for the surface, realized that he did not know where the surface was. Then, abruptly, he was in calmer water. He bobbed up, sputtering, shook his head, swam a few strokes to the shore, and crawled out, amazed that he was still alive.

The girl had not gone away. She was up there, watching him now.

Had she been anyone else, he would have run away and hidden until she was gone. But she was the most beautiful girl he had ever seen. Wiping his hands down his sodden trouser legs to press the water out of them, he surreptitiously checked to be sure his fly was closed. It was. He started up the slope.

He did not make it to the top as easily as Danny Dew had done. He slipped and fell twice. His wet clothes took on a patina of mud, and his face was smeared with long brown streaks of topsoil. What did the girl think? She had seen Danny Dew come off the rubble, across the water, and up the hill as if he were walking across a room—and now she saw Beame floundering like the first legged fish that crawled out of a prehistoric sea. He felt like an ass.

But she was smiling. And it was not a cruel smile.

Beame waved and started towards her. The closer he got, the more he saw how beautiful she was. By the time he was standing in front of her, he was numb, speechless in the aura of her radiant beauty. Her hair was really black, not just dark brown. Her complexion was Spanish and flawless, her eyes as large as olives and as black as her hair. Her nose was small, fine-boned, exquisitely arched. Her smile was wide and warm. Her teeth were square and white, her lips two ribbons tied in a sensuous bow.

"Hello," he said, clearing his throat. "My name's David Beame."

"Nathalie," she said.

"What?" He thought she had told him, in French, to get lost. Or worse.

"That's my name," she said. "Nathalie."

"You speak English," he said, relieved that she had not been insulting him. "I'm pleased to meet you, Nathalie." She was *gorgeous.*

She was flattered by his ill-concealed admiration. She blushed. Beame was happy he had flattered her. He knew he was blushing too, and he wiped his face with one hand, never realizing his hand was muddy.

"How is it you speak English?" he asked.

"Father taught me."

"And who is your father?"

"Maurice," she said.

Could this be true? Could greasy, conniving Maurice Jobert give half the seed to make a girl like this? "I've never seen you before. You weren't at the village dance a couple of weeks ago."

"I had a summer cold. Papa made me stay in bed until the fever broke." She cocked her head and looked at him. "You are staring—so intently."

Startled, Beame wiped a hand across his face to cover another blush.

"You're getting mud all over your nose," she said, putting one finger to his face, taking it away, showing him the mud.

"Oh," Beame said, feeling like an ass. He wiped his muddy nose with his muddy hand. Realizing his error, he used his shirttail next. But that was even muddier than his hands. Suddenly, he wished that he had drowned when he fell into the river.

"Are you nervous?" Nathalie asked.

"Me? No. Why should I be nervous?"

"Father says you are all scared of dying. Father says you are the only soldiers he's ever seen who are aware of their own mortality." She smiled. Just gorgeous. "He likes doing business with you, because you have no illusions."

"You mean it's *good* that we're nervous?" Beame asked, surprised.

"Oh, yes. Very good."

"Well," Beame said, "I'm *very* nervous." He let her see how his hands were shaking. "At times, I'm so terrified I'm not functional. I haven't had a good night's sleep since we landed here." When she nodded sympathetically, Beame could not let go of the subject. "I have awful nightmares. I can't eat. I pick at my food and get indigestion, and the worst gas. . . . I've been constipated for three weeks. If I could have one good shit, I think—" He realized what he was saying, and he wanted to leap off the edge of the ravine.

She looked down at the workers again, embarrassed for him. She presented Beame with a lovely profile which soothed him and made him feel like less of an ass. Indeed, he felt as if he had been transformed into a spirit by the white heat rolling off her. If she turned and touched him, her hand would go straight through.

After a long silence, he heard himself say, "You're beautiful."

She looked at him timidly, blushing again. "Thank you."

Beame's heart rose. She was just what he had thought she was! A flower, an innocent, a girl-woman as precious as anything he had ever wanted. And if he just did not start talking about his constipation again, he might be able to win her.

# 2/

Sergeant Emil Hagendorf had a voice like a 78 rpm phonograph record playing on a turntable forever moving at 60 rpm, and he always sounded morose. "You don't know what it's like," he said, morosely.

Major Kelly sat down on one of the rec room chairs. "What what's like?"

"Chaos," Hagendorf said. His pasty face grew paler at the word.

"I *live* in chaos," Kelly said.

But the major knew his own ability to cope with the chaotic did not help Hagendorf. Before the war, Emil, the unit's chief surveyor, had developed a comfortable philosophy of life. He believed there was a precise order and pattern to everything in the universe. He thought he could look dispassionately at *anything*—religion, sex, politics, money—survey it as he would a roadbed, stake it out, and eventually understand it. He had lived by his philosophy, a man of order and routine. He rose at the same hour each morning, neither smoked nor drank, and took a woman only as often as his system demanded one. He planned his future as carefully as he surveyed land, and he was able to cope with whatever came along. Drafted, he went through basic training with high marks, was quickly promoted, seemed at home in the Army. Then, when he was behind the lines with the unit for one week, he became a sloppy, inefficient, falling-down drunkard. And Major Kelly had not been able to rehabilitate him.

"You've got to stop drinking," Kelly told the chief surveyor when he confronted him in the rec room that morning.

Hagendorf picked up his bottle of wine and went over to the dart board that was nailed to the rec room wall. "See this? It's divided into all these little sections." He pointed to each of the sections on the board, which took a while. "Throw a dart here, you get five points . . . or here, you get ten. Or a hundred, here. I once thought life was neat and compartmentalized like that."

"Life isn't like that," Kelly said.

"I know, now." Hagendorf took a long swallow of wine, his whiskered neck moving as he drank, sweat beading on his white face. "My whole philosophy—gone. My sense of direction, fundamental beliefs—destroyed by General Blade. And you."

"What's that got to do with drinking too much?" Kelly asked.

"You'd drink yourself to death, too, if your philosophy of life was suddenly proven wrong."

"No. I'd find something else to believe in."

Hagendorf shuddered. "That's chaos. What *do* you believe, by the way?"

"That this is all a fairy tale, grand in color but modest in design. You and I are figments of some Aesop's imagination."

"That's the worst philosophy I've ever heard." He clutched his wine bottle in both hands. "It's illogical. A good philosophy must be based on logical precepts, on valid proofs. How can you prove we're figments of a cosmic imagination?"

"I don't have time to argue with you, Emil," Kelly said, his voice rising on each word, until there was a hysteria in it which matched Hagendorf's hysteria. "The Panzers are coming! We have a whole village to build in just six days!" Red-faced, trembling, he unrolled a tube of onionskin paper and flattened it on the table, used a pair of metal ashtrays to hold down the ends. "I have a job for you, Emil."

"Job?" Hagendorf looked skeptically at the paper.

Briefly, Kelly explained how they were going to hoax the Germans with the fake town. He tapped the paper. "I've done a preliminary blueprint of the town we'll build. You'll mark off the streets and lots."

Hagendorf blanched. "You can't ask that of me!" His face was soft, soggy, pale as a fish belly. "Surveying again—I'll get a taste of how it used to be. I'll crack up!"

"I've been fair, Emil. You haven't had to work in weeks. Beame and I have done the bridge surveying, but that's simple stuff. I need *you* for this." He pointed at the wine. "And no drinking until you're finished with the job."

"You're killing me." Hagendorf came over and looked at the plans.

"We already have the road that comes from the east and crosses the bridge." Kelly traced this with his finger. "We're going to need two more streets paralleling that road—here and here. Then we need two crossing streets that go north-south. Finally, I want a sort of service road running all around the village, at the edge of the woods."

"This is going to take a lot of time," Hagendorf said.

"You have today," Kelly said.

"Impossible!"

"Hagendorf, we have six days. Only six days! Every minute I waste arguing with you, the Panzers get closer. You understand me?"

"Can't do it without wine," Hagendorf said, finishing his wine.

"You have to. I don't want this marked out by a drunk. You've become a real wino, Emil. You don't know when to stop."

"Untrue! I've cut back. I've only had one bottle so far today."

"Jesus, Emil, it's only an hour since dawn. You call that 'cutting back,' do you?"

"You're going to destroy me," Hagendorf said. His round shoulders slumped more than usual, and he appeared to age before Kelly's eyes.

"Nonsense," Kelly said. "Now, *move!* Let's get down to

the machinery shed. Your men are waiting. We've dusted off your theodolite and other tools. Hurry, Hagendorf! Six days will be gone before you know it."

"My theodolite," Hagendorf said, dreamily. His mind spiraled back to more pleasant times when the world could be measured and *known.* Abruptly, he dropped his wine bottle and started to cry. "You really are destroying me, sir. I warn you! I warn you!"

Fifteen minutes later, as Kelly stood by the shed watching Hagendorf stagger away with his assistants, Private Vito Angelli—the Angel from Los Angeles as Pullit had begun to call him—came along with his French work crew. They all jabbered at once, laughed, and gesticulated furiously, as if they were on stage and required to exaggerate each gesture to communicate with the people in the back rows. Angelli stopped them at an enormous bomb crater north of the machinery shed.

Kelly hurried over and clapped Angelli on the shoulder. "Going okay?"

Angelli was thin, dark, all stringy muscles, intense eyes, and white teeth. "We've filled in all the other craters below the bridge road."

Angelli could not speak French, and none of the workers could speak Italian or English. Therefore, Angelli used a lot of gestures and smiled a great deal, and said, "Eh? Eh?" When dealing with his relatives who had come to the States from the old country and who often spoke a different dialect of Italian than he did, he had learned the best way to be understood was to punctuate everything with numerous *ehs.* It never failed. No matter what you said, if you framed it with a couple of *ehs* you could topple any language barrier.

Angelli turned to the workers, clapped his hands. "One more hole to fill, eh? Eh? Quick job, eh? But big job gets done *pòco a pòco,* eh?"

The Frenchmen laughed and went to work. They all had shovels, and they energetically attacked the ring of blast-thrown soil, scooping it back into the crater from which it had come.

"Faster!" Kelly said. They seemed to be working in slow motion. "Angelli, tell them to shovel faster. We've got only six days!"

"But they *are* shoveling fast," Angelli said.

"Faster, faster, faster!" Kelly demanded. When Angelli gave the order and the Frenchmen complied, the major said, "You've got excellent rapport here. If all the men could work with the French as well as you do, we might come close to building the town before the Germans get here."

Angelli grinned. "Then you think we'll do it, sir?"

"Never," Kelly said. "I said we'd come *closer* to doing it if we had your rapport with these people."

"Do not be so negative, *bon ami*." Maurice appeared out of nowhere at Kelly's elbow. "The work goes well. You will have a new bridge tonight, with my people helping. Your chief surveyor has begun to mark off the streets and lots. My wonderful people have cleared away random brush and have filled in the bomb craters. We've come so far in so few hours!"

Kelly looked at the bundle of papers Maurice was carrying. Ignoring The Frog's optimism, he said, "Those the forms?"

"Ready for signatures," Maurice said, handing them over.

Reluctantly, Kelly took them. "The men won't like this."

"Oh, but they will!" Maurice said. "They are sure to see what a real bargain I am giving them. Americans love bargains."

Private Angelli looked warily at the forms. "Why won't we like those? What are they?"

"Credit contracts," Maurice said. "Nothing sinister."

Angelli was perplexed. "Credit contracts?" he asked, squinting at the bundle.

"One for each man in the unit," Maurice said. He thumped the middle of his checkered shirt. "Made out by hand, written by me or members of my immediate family, very official."

"Credit contracts?" Angelli repeated.

"Let me explain," Kelly said, wearily.

# 3/

Sergeant Coombs was operating the small cargo shuttler when Major Kelly found him. He had been trundling the more compact construction materials from the storage dump by the runway to the men at the bridge, and though it was now well past noon, he had not taken a single rest break. He was sweaty and dirty. His back ached, his arms ached, and his knuckles were skinned and sore. He had stoved his left thumb but had kept on working while it swelled to half again its normal size. He was in no mood for Major Kelly. Only his great respect for the rules and regulations regarding the responsibilities of rank kept him from being completely uncooperative.

"I have something for you to sign," Major Kelly said.

Major Kelly had spent all morning running around the camp getting the men to sign various papers which he carried in a folder under his arm. He was not dirty or sweaty. Coombs knew that Kelly didn't have an aching back or aching arms or a stoved thumb. He regarded the proffered document scornfully and said, "What is it?"

"Nothing much," Kelly said, evasively. "Just sign it, and I'll stop bothering you."

Sergeant Coombs looked at the pile of matériel he had yet to transfer to the bridge, scratched the back of his sunburned neck, and was tempted to sign the damn thing, whatever it was, just to be rid of Kelly. He was still on the shuttler seat, with crates stacked on the forked platform before him. He could sign and be on his way again. But something in Kelly's manner, a sort of phony good humor, warned Coombs. "What is it?" he repeated.

"Just *sign* it. Quick, now. I've got to get every man's signature if I'm going to keep Maurice's help. And I need Maurice's help. Every minute counts in this, Sergeant. So *sign.*"

"I won't sign anything that I don't know what it is," Combs said.

Kelly's smile faded. "Well, look, you know how much help Maurice has been, bringing in all these workers."

"Frogs," Coombs said.

"Yes, perhaps they are. But the fact remains that we need them. And in the days ahead, Maurice will be doing even more for us. And you can't expect him to do it all out of the goodness of his heart. Maurice wants to make a profit from it. That should be something every red-blooded American can understand. We Americans believe in the profit system, free enterprise. That's one of the things we're fighting for."

"What about this paper?" Coombs asked. For such a stumpy man, he was damned difficult to fool.

Major Kelly was distinctly uncomfortable now. He could not stop thinking about the Panzers. While he was standing here with Coombs, how much closer had the Germans come? Too much closer. . . . Kelly looked nervously at the stack of crates beside the shuttler, at the sky, at the ground, everywhere but at Coombs. "Maurice wants to be paid for his help. Naturally, we're the only ones who can pay him. So what Maurice wants from us—he wants two hundred bucks from every man in camp."

"I don't have it," Coombs said.

Kelly shook his head in agreement and frustration. "Who does? But Maurice understands how things are with us. We're paid in scrip when the DC-3 comes in from Blade's HQ, but most of us lose it to Hoskins or Malzberg in a day or two, at best. Maurice understands, and he does not want to be at all unreasonable. He's willing to extend us credit, provided we sign these forms he's given me. You pay fifty dollars now, the other one-fifty over the next six months."

Coombs was suspicious. "Six months?"

"That's right."

"We'll be gone in six months."

Kelly shrugged. "Maybe he's banking on the war not being over that fast."

Coombs would not swallow that. "There's something you're not telling me."

Kelly sighed, thinking about the Panzers, about the minutes melting away. "You're right. You see, this paper you're to sign . . . well, it's an admission of collaboration with the Nazis."

Coombs looked at Kelly as if the major were a stone that had come suddenly to life before his eyes. He could not believe what he was hearing. "Admit I collaborated with the krauts, even if I didn't?"

Kelly smiled nervously. "Maurice has written a different confession for each of us." He looked down at the paper in his hand and quickly scanned the neat paragraphs of precise, handwritten English. "Yours states that you sabotaged the equipment which you were assigned to maintain, that you interfered with the building of the bridge."

Coombs did not know what to say.

"You can see where Maurice might feel he has to use such an extreme credit contract," Kelly said. He liked to call the paper a credit contract rather than a forged confession or something equally distasteful. "This kind of document would guarantee his money even if we were transferred out of here before we paid him in full. None of us would want his contract turned over to Allied military officials."

"What did you confess?" Coombs asked.

"Transmitting information to the Nazis via our wireless set." He forced the rumpled paper into Coombs hand, gave him a stubby yellow pencil. "Just sign the damn thing, Sergeant. Time is our greatest enemy."

"I won't sign." Coombs's jaw was set, and his pulse pounded visibly at neck and temples.

"Sergeant, you *must*. I've got more than forty men to sign

up yet. If one refuses, others will too. And the deal with Maurice will fall through. . . . You'll die with the rest of us!" He was trying to scare the sergeant, and he scared himself in the process.

"I'm not afraid to fight," Coombs said.

Exasperated, Kelly watched Coombs try to hand back the confession. He refused to touch it. He swatted Coombs's hand as if trying to push back more than the paper—as if he were fighting off the inevitable death rushing down on them. Couldn't Coombs see that one man's pride or stubbornness could kill them all? After a full minute of this thrust and counterthrust, with the credit contract getting pretty badly mutilated, Kelly leaned toward Coombs. "What the fuck rank are you?" he screamed.

Coombs looked at him as if he were witless. "Sergeant."

"And I am a major, right?" Kelly drew himself up to his full height. "Sergeant, as your commanding officer, I *order* you to sign that paper and give me fifty dollars. *Now.*"

Coombs's face drained of color as he realized his dilemma. He was in a spot where he had to go against one of the two moral principles that made him tick. He either had to refuse an order from a legitimate superior—or cooperate with this coward and become, in effect, a coward himself. For a long moment he sat on the shuttler, swaying back and forth as if buffeted by two gale force winds. Then, leaning quickly forward and holding the confession against one of the packing crates on the forked cargo platform, he signed his name. His need for order, for a sense of rank, for rules and regulations, had won out over his loathing of cowardice.

"Fifty dollars," Kelly said, taking the signed document.

As the sergeant handed over the money, something else occurred to him. "This isn't all Maurice is getting, is it?"

Kelly was uncomfortable again. He was anxious to be off, signing up the other men. Precious minutes were being wasted! Besides, he was a bit ashamed of this business. Sometimes, he was shocked at the immoral things life forced him to do. . . . "Maurice gets a few other little things," Kelly admitted. "Like your cargo shuttler . . . the camp generator when we leave. . . ."

Coombs was distressed. "What else?"

"Only one other thing," Kelly assured him. "A tollbooth."

Coombs could not make any sense out of that. He scratched the back of his neck, spat in the dust, taking as long as possible to respond. He knew Kelly and some of the others thought he was stupid. He was not really stupid at all, just taciturn and grumpy. For the life of him, though, he could not see what the major was talking about, and he was forced to look stupid. "Tollbooth?"

"After the Panzers pass through and we're safe," Kelly said, "we're going to build a tollbooth on the other side of the gorge, in the road just before the bridge. It'll have a pole across the road and everything. Maurice's people will work there, bring extra money into Eisenhower."

"Oh." Compared to an operator like The Frog, Coombs supposed he *was* stupid.

"As soon as you pay Maurice the rest, he gives back your contract. Thanks for your cooperation, Sergeant." Kelly turned and ran back toward the HQ building where several men were hurriedly reviewing the construction plans in the shade by the rec room door.

Lieutenant Beame was one of them. However, he was standing pretty much by himself, thirty feet from the knot of men.

Major Kelly went straight to him, because he liked to get each man alone when he was selling the idea of the credit contract. He knew it would be dangerous to let them group together when he delivered his spiel. It had to be a one-to-one relationship in which he could employ what little talent for discipline he possessed. He had to be able to concentrate on one man in order to overwhelm his victim with his practiced patter and with dire predictions of what the Panzers would do to them if they did not get this damned village built in just six days.

"Got something for you to sign," Kelly said, giving Beame the paper.

"Oh?"

All the while that Kelly explained the fine points of the credit contract to Lieutenant Beame, the lieutenant stared over Kelly's shoulder at nothing in particular, a silly smirk on his face. When Kelly asked him to sign the paper, Beame took the pencil and scrawled his name in sloppily looping letters. He was still grinning drunkenly. He gave Kelly the scrip without quibbling, and his expression remained eerily mongoloid.

"What's the matter?" Kelly asked. "What are you grinning about?"

Beame hesitated. Then: "I met a girl."

"I don't understand," Kelly said.

"The most beautiful girl I've ever seen." Beame almost drooled.

"Who?"

Beame told him. "I asked her to come back this evening for a romantic dinner. Maybe you can meet her then."

"In the mess hall?" Kelly asked.

The mess hall, which was the rec room, was anything but romantic. And the food Sergeant Tuttle served them was hardly the stuff of a lover's supper. Sergeant Tuttle was camp cook. He had not been a cook in civilian life, but a sanitation worker in Philadelphia.

"Not the mess hall," Beame said. "I've bought some groceries from Tuttle, and I'm going to cook the supper myself. We'll eat down under that stand of pines along the riverbank." Beame looked at Kelly, but Kelly was strangely unable to catch the lieutenant's eyes. It was as if Beame were looking through him at some vaguely perceived paradise.

"Are you in love?" Kelly asked.

Beame's grin became sloppy. "I guess maybe I am."

"That's foolish," Kelly warned him. "Love is a form of

hope, and hope is a terminal disease. You get in love with someone, you become careless. Your mind wanders. Next thing you know, you collect a two-hundred-pound bomb down the back of your shirt. Love is deadly. Just fuck her and forget the love part."

"Whatever you say," Beame said. Unmistakably, though, the lieutenant had not heard a word the major said.

Kelly was about to press the point, in hopes of saving Beame before it was too late, when Lieutenant Slade arrived with *his* form. "You get one of these?" he asked Kelly, shoving a yellow paper into the major's hand. He gave one to Beame, who did not even glance at it.

"What's this?" Kelly asked, giving Slade a suspicious look.

"It's a questionnaire," Slade said. He had an armful of them.

Kelly read the headline across the top: WHO IS THE TRAITOR?

"We all know there's a traitor in camp," Slade said. "Someone keeps telling the German air force when the bridge is rebuilt so they can bomb it again right away. Last night, when I called General Blade and after you gave him our supplies order, I asked him to have this questionnaire printed and delivered when the DC-3 came in. He thought it was a good idea." Slade pointed to the list of questions and blanks where the answers were to go. "Just fill these in. You don't have to sign your name or anything. There's a response box nailed to the wall outside the rec room, and it's unmonitored. When you have this ready, deposit it in the box."

Kelly looked at the paper. The first question was: "Right off, are you the traitor, and would you like to confess if we guarantee you a light punishment?"

"See how it works?" Slade asked. "Even if we don't obtain a confession, I will be able to analyze these forms and find out who our informer is." He smiled, immensely pleased with himself. "Statistical analysis. That's all it is, Major."

Kelly opened his mouth to tell Slade that he was an idiot,

then thought better of it. He read the second question from the sheet: "Have you noticed anyone in the unit behaving strangely lately?"

"*That* one ought to get a response," Slade said, nodding his head emphatically. He belonged in an asylum.

With this credit contract business, Major Kelly could not afford to make any new enemies or antagonize old ones. Therefore, he told Slade that the questionnaire was a marvelous idea. "Here, now you take one of my forms," he said, giving The Snot his credit contract.

Slade looked at it with as much suspicion as Kelly had shown while studying the questionnaire. "What is this?"

"A credit contract," Kelly said. Using the stature of his rank, the weight of his command, the force of his personality, and the mesmeric quality of his gaze, he tried to make Lieutenant Slade sign the paper and pass over the fifty dollars in scrip.

"I won't sign this paper," Slade said, when Kelly was done. "And I am not going to give you or Maurice fifty dollars in scrip." He did not seem to be particularly angry. Indeed, he was grinning at the major. "This is craziness, you know. Opting for this cowardly plan in the first place—then asking your men to hock their reputations to pay for it. This is more than I ever hoped for. You have gone way too far this time."

"Minute by minute, the eventual arrival of the Panzers becomes more of a reality, a nearer threat," Major Kelly said. He was beginning the argument which, in his own mind, was the most forceful one in favor of hocking their reputations and anything else on which Maurice wanted to take a lien. "If we tried to fight off a force as large as this Germany convoy—"

"Are you ordering me to sign this?" Slade interrupted, rattling the credit contract in Kelly's face.

The major considered it for a moment. He had successfully pulled that stunt with Coombs. However, though they were much alike on the surface, Coombs and Slade were utterly different underneath. What worked on one might only bring a stiffer resistance from the other. "I can't order you to do anything like that," Kelly said.

"Damn right," Slade said. He dropped his credit contract, turned away from them, and hurried over to the men by the rec room door.

"You're in for trouble now," Beame said.

Kelly watched as Slade conferred with the men standing in the shadows. He was gesturing with one hand, clutching his questionnaires against his chest with the other. He kept pointing at Kelly.

"Sowing dissension," Beame said.

Most of the men laughed at Slade and walked away from him. But a few, a sizable minority, remained and listened. They might have thought that Slade was an ass, but they nonetheless shared his philosophy. The seed of rebellion was dormant in them, but susceptible to water and gentle cultivation.

"He's telling them not to sign your paper," Beame said. "They have to sign."

"I thought you couldn't make it an order?"

"I can't," Kelly admitted. "But if too many of them refuse and we can't get up the money that Maurice wants, the whole deal will fall through. The people from Eisenhower won't help us. We won't be able to build the town by ourselves. We won't be able to hide from the Germans. We'll all die."

In the next hour, fifteen men refused to sign credit contracts.

# 4/

In the flickering campfire light under the copse of pines by the river, Nathalie was even more beautiful than she had been the first time Beame saw her. Her black hair, like that of an Egyptian princess, blended with the night. Her face was a mixture of sensuous shadows and warm brown tones where the firelight caught it. Images of flame flashed in her eyes. She smiled enigmatically as a sphinx as they sat side-by-side on the ground and watched their dinner cook.

She was near enough to touch, but he did not touch her. Sitting with her legs drawn up beneath her, leaning against the trunk of a pine, wearing a simple sleeveless white dress that was cinched at the waist by a red ribbon, she looked too fragile to survive the lightest embrace.

Beame leaned forward and looked into the pan suspended above the fire. "Done," he said. "I hope it's good." He put a thick slice of dark bread in the center of each mess tin, ladled the main course over the bread. Steam rose from it.

"What is this called?" Nathalie asked.

He handed her a mess tin. "Shit on a shingle," he said, without thinking.

"*Pardonnez-moi?*"

"I mean . . . that's what it's called in the mess hall," Beame said. "Uh . . . out here it's creamed dried beef."

"Ah," she said, cutting into the soggy bread with her fork. She tasted one morsel. "Mmmmm."

"You like it?"

"It is very good."

He looked at his own serving, tasted it, found it *was* good.

"That's funny. I must have had this a thousand times, and I always hated it."

After they were finished, they had red wine, which was her contribution to the evening.

"I've never had wine from a tin cup," Beame said.

"It would taste the same from crystal."

"I guess it would." He wanted to kiss her, but he knew that was improper this early in their friendship. Besides, if he kissed her he would probably faint and miss the rest of what promised to be a fine evening.

They watched the fire slowly dying, and they sipped wine. As the fire darkened, Beame's head lightened. He was able to forget the bridge, the Nazis, everything. In the weeks the unit had been here, this was the only time he had felt at ease. "More wine?" he asked, when he came to the bottom of his cup.

She swallowed the last of hers. "Yes, please."

When they settled back again, cups replenished, he was conscious of the silence, of his inability to engage her in trivial conversation. "You may have noticed my—"

"*Mauvaise honte?*" Her voice was husky and pleasant.

"What's that?"

"Bashfulness," she said. "But I like it."

"You do?"

She nodded, looked away from him. She sipped her wine; it glistened like a candy glaze on her lips.

A few minutes later, he said, "Say something in French. Just anything. I like the sound of it."

She thought a moment, one long finger held to the corner of her mouth as if she were hushing him. "*Je ne connais pas la dame avec qui vous avez parlé.*"

The words flowed over Beame, mellowing him. "What does that mean?"

"It means—I do not know the lady with whom you spoke," she said.

French was a fantastic language, Beame thought. That

was such an ordinary sentence in English but so poetic in her tongue.

"Well?" she asked.

Eyes closed, lolling against a tree, Beame said, "What?"

"Won't you tell me who the woman was?"

Beame opened his eyes. "What woman?"

She met his eyes forthrightly. "This afternoon, just after you invited me to dinner, a woman came up from that bunker and called to you. We said our goodbyes, and you went to talk with her."

"Oh, that was Lily Kain." He explained how Lily happened to be in the unit.

"She's lovely," Nathalie said.

"She is?"

"Don't tell me you have not noticed. I suppose she has many suitors."

"Lily?" Beame asked. "Oh, no. She and Major Kelly have a thing going."

"I see," she said, brightening somewhat. She drained her cup and handed it to him. "May I have more wine?"

When he filled her cup and returned it, their fingers touched. The contact was more electric than he would have expected. Sitting beside her again, watching the fire, he realized he had forgotten how beautiful she was. Now he was once more slightly breathless.

She did not sit back against the tree, but knelt, using her calves for a chair. She held the wine in both hands and was very still. In time, she said, "The frogs are singing."

"I always thought they just croaked," Beame said. But when he listened, the frogs did seem to be singing. "You're right." In the faint-orange ember glow, he suddenly saw her nipples against the tight bodice of her dress. . . . He looked quickly away, ashamed of himself for staring even as long as he had.

She sipped her wine. He sensed that she was staring at him, but he could not look up. He was a mess of confused emotions inside; his previous serenity had strangely vanished. "Say something else in French, will you?" he asked.

She looked around at the trees, at the half-seen needled branches overhead. She stared at the fire and listened solemnly to the singing frogs. "*Je pense que cela doit être la plus belle place du monde.*"

"That's lovely. What does it mean?"

She smiled. "I believe that this must be the most beautiful place in the world." She saw Beame's perplexity. "Don't you think it is?"

"It's *nice,*" he said, unconvinced.

"But you can't think of it without thinking of the war," she said.

"Yeah. I guess, otherwise, I might agree." His eyes traveled to her breasts, then rose guiltily again. He realized, suddenly, that she had seen him look at her so covetously. Their eyes met, they both blushed, and they looked away from each other.

"Tell me about America," Nathalie said, a while later.

"Hasn't your father told you about it?" Beame asked, his voice thick and barely recognizable.

Before Nathalie could reply, her father replied for her. "I most certainly have told her about America," he said, stalking like a brontosaurus out of the trees and into the small clearing. He threw an exaggerated shadow in the campfire light. "And I have also told her to avoid all soldiers no matter if they are German, American, or French."

Nathalie came quickly to her feet. "Father, you must not think—"

"I will think what I wish," Maurice said, scowling at them. He no longer looked like a fat, greasy old man. The strength born of years of hard labor was evident in the powerful shoulders and in the hard lines of his face. He looked capable of tearing Beame into tiny, bloody pieces.

"We were only talking," the lieutenant said, also rising.

"Why did you not ask my permission?"

"To *talk*?" Beame asked. He glanced at Nathalie. She was staring at the ground, biting her lip. "Look, Mr. Jobert, it was just a nice little dinner—"

Maurice advanced another step, cutting the lieutenant short with one wave of his right hand. The campfire illuminated the lower half of his face but left his eyes and forehead mostly in shadows, giving him a demonic appearance. "Just a nice little dinner? What of the wine?"

Beame looked guiltily at the bottle which rested against a tree trunk. "The wine—"

"I provided the wine, father," Nathalie said.

"That makes it much worse," Maurice said. "Alone at night, drinking with a soldier—*at your own instigation!*"

"He's not like other soldiers," she said, a bit of fire in her now. "He is a very nice—"

"All soldiers are alike," Maurice insisted. "American, British, French, German, whatever. They have one thing in mind. One thing only. Now, girl, you come with me. We're returning to the village."

Beame was helpless. He watched as Maurice led the girl out of the woods, out of sight, out of the lieutenant's life. "I didn't even touch her," he told the darkness where Maurice had been.

The darkness did not respond.

"I wish I *had* touched her," Beame said.

The roof had been taken off the main bunker at the south end of the clearing, and preparations made for erecting one of the fake buildings over this ready-made basement. As a result, the men who had been sleeping there were dispossessed. And for the first time since the unit had been dropped at the bridge, the tents had been broken out and set up. They were lined in a haphazard way, the rows wandering, intersecting randomly—more the work of a troop of inept first-year boy scouts than that of a trained Army group.

Major Kelly walked briskly along one of the tent aisles, followed by twenty men. He had personally chosen each of his escorts, and he had made certain that they all had four things in common: each was big and muscular; each was mean; each was rowdy; and each one had signed his credit contract.

They stopped before a tent which looked like all the others that stretched away in the darkness, and Kelly used a flashlight to consult the chart he had prepared before sundown. "This is Armento's tent," he told the men with him. Armento had been one of the nineteen bastards who had *not* signed their credit contracts. Smiling grimly, Kelly leaned down, pulled back the flap, and shouted, "Up and out of there, Private Armento!"

Armento had worked hard all day on the preparations for the construction of the village, and he was sleeping sound as a stone when Kelly called him. Shocked by this intrusion into his deserved rest, he nearly knocked the tent down when he scrambled out of it. "What? What? What?" he asked Kelly and the men behind Kelly. He rubbed his eyes. "What?"

"Sorry," Kelly said. "Emergency. Got to requisition your tent."

And he *was* sorry to have to use pressure tactics on Armento and the other holdouts who had not signed their confessions. He felt like a monster, an insensitive creep, another General Blade. But he had no choice. The Panzers were coming. Death was coming. There was nothing else to do.

Five of the men behind the major, all bigger than Armento, knocked down the tent and rolled it up. Before Armento could ask any questions, Kelly led his husky escorts down the aisle to the next victim.

By now, everyone was out of his tent. Most of the men were grinning, because they knew what was up. Only nineteen of them were bewildered. . . .

Kelly was directing the tearing down of the eighth tent,

embarrassedly parrying all questions, when Lieutenant Slade arrived. Slade was furious. "You are harassing the men who stood with me, the men who wouldn't sign those insane credit contracts." Slade shook a finger in Kelly's face.

"Not at all," Kelly said, feeling like a heel. "The hospital staff says we're short of bandage materials. If we suffer another Stuka attack, the shortage could be a matter of life and death. So we're confiscating a few of the tents to cut them into strip bandages." He felt ill, and he hated himself.

"*Canvas* bandages? Ridiculous! If you're *not* harassing these men who stood with me," Slade said, "why are you demolishing only *their* tents?"

"Are we?" Kelly feigned surprise. He consulted his chart. "Why, we just picked the names out of a hat." Into which, of course, they had only put the names of the men who had not signed their contracts.

Lieutenant Slade followed them, ranting impotently as the tents came down. As they were folding up the eighteenth square of canvas, he planted himself in front of Kelly. "You aren't going to rip down *my* tent. You won't bully *me* into signing away my good name!"

"I'm not bullying anyone," Kelly said, wishing it were true. "Besides, your name wasn't drawn from the hat. We aren't confiscating *your* tent. *You* will be snug and warm and dry tonight." Kelly looked at the sky, pointed at the thick gray thunderhead clouds rushing westward. "Sure does look like rain before morning." He was conscious of all the other men looking skyward with him. "These other fellows whose names were drawn at random from a hat will have to put up with a soaking, I'm afraid. But we couldn't make it any fairer. . . ." Any unfairer. Kelly sighed. "We have to remember there's a war going on, and that some of us must make sacrifices. At least we don't have to put everyone out in the rain, eh? *You* needn't worry, Lieutenant."

Slade saw the full implications of what the major had said. He grimaced. "Very cunning, sir. But you are not going to divide and conquer us. We aren't going to put our lives and futures in the hands of a man like Maurice, no matter what you do to us."

"I admire your strong character," Kelly said.

Ten minutes later, the eighteen tents had been stacked in a corner of the hospital bunker. They made quite a mound.

Lily Kain put her arm around Kelly's waist and detained him at the bunker door as he was leaving. "You really think it will work?"

"Work?" Kelly asked. "Never. Oh, this and a few other things I have planned might get them to sign their credit contracts. But that won't mean very much in the end. We're all going to die. We just have to go through this charade now to keep the fairy tale moving. You know?"

"Don't start with that fairy tale shit," Lily said.

"Can't help it. Puts things in perspective. Keeps me alive."

A can opener of lightning took the lid off the night, and thunder rumbled like an escaping vacuum. Rain bounced on the steps, spattered on their faces, ran into the hospital bunker behind them.

Kelly smiled, happy that the men were now almost certain to sign their contracts. Then he frowned, depressed by the realization that he had been forced into becoming a somewhat ruthless manipulator of people.

Well . . . anything to hang on.

# 5 / JULY 19

Shortly after dawn, two men came to see Major Kelly in his quarters. They were both wet, shivering, pale, water-wrinkled, and defeated even though the rain had stopped falling half an hour ago. Kelly was slipping into clean, dry fatigues when they rapped on his blanket wall. "Help you fellows?" he asked, peering around a woolen corner. He smiled warmly.

Two minutes later, only *seventeen* men had refused to sign the credit contracts.

*It's working!* Kelly thought, when they had gone. But then he remembered that the Panzers would arrive in little more than four and a half days. Right now, he should be engaged in the serious planning which was essential to the early stages of the construction of the fake village. The bridge was up, the preliminary work done, and now he ought to be plunging into the main project. Instead, he was wasting time and energy trying to trick the holdouts into signing their damned confessions. If he was achieving his lesser goal, he was also losing the chance to attain the greater one. He might eventually get every man to sign his contract—but by then he would have wasted so much time that they could never build the village before the Germans arrived. . . .

Nevertheless, he was the first in line for breakfast at the mess hall, because he wanted to have a front row seat for the morning's carefully planned drama. "Looks delicious," Kelly told Sergeant Tuttle when the cook ladled hot cereal into his mess tin.

Tuttle leaned across the steaming kettle. "I don't like doing this," he whispered.

"We need Maurice's help," Kelly whispered back at him. "Without it, we all die. These bastards have to be *made* to sign."

"I know," Tuttle said, looking back at the line of impatient men.

"Two more came across. Kasabian and Pike. You can treat them like you normally would," Kelly said.

"But the others—"

"You know what to do with the others."

Kelly got the rest of his breakfast and sat down at one of the crude tables. He toyed with his cereal, but his attention was riveted on the men in the breakfast line who had not cooperated in the matter of the credit contracts.

Private Armento was the tenth man in line, first of the troublemakers to reach Tuttle. The cook looked over Armento's shoulder, silently pleading with Kelly. The major turned his thumbs down. Reluctantly, Tuttle "misjudged" the position of Armento's plate and poured a ladle of hot cereal all over his hands.

Quite a lot of commotion followed.

Then, Private Aaron Lange, another holdout who was immediately behind Armento, got the hot-cereal treatment when he held out *his* tin. When he and Armento finished dancing around the room and blowing on their reddened fingers, they came over to Major Kelly and signed their credit contracts.

"I'm glad you men have finally seen where your best interests lie," Kelly told them, putting their contracts with the others that had been signed.

All morning, one by one, the holdouts began to see the same light which Armento and Lange had seen. Private Garnett put his signature on his contract after he tripped and fell with his second full mess tin. He had also tripped and fallen with the first. Private John Flounders signed up when, after waiting in the serving line for twenty minutes, he discovered that, curiously, Sergeant Tuttle ran out of hot cereal just before Flounders was to be given his. When the morning's work assignments were read and Private Paul Akers learned he had been assigned to that detail which would shovel out the old latrine ditch and carry the stinking contents into the woods, Akers came around to Kelly's way of thinking. Private Vinney, who was also assigned to the latrine job, lasted for less than five minutes before throwing away his shovel and signing up. And three other men stayed with it until they were accidentally bumped into that vile trench by two workmen who were trying to jostle past them with a heavy length of pine planking. . . .

At 9:15 that same morning, Kelly went over to the hospital bunker and waved the completed forms at Lily Kain. "When they ask for their tents back, you can tell them we found a crate of bandage materials that we'd overlooked. Tell them we won't have to cut up their tents after all."

"They signed?" she asked.

"All but Slade."

"But will Maurice be willing to overlook Slade?"

"Sure," Kelly said. "If I sign a second confession and guarantee to pay Slade's two hundred bucks, why should Maurice be upset?"

"You'd do that?" she asked.

"Do I have any choice?"

"I guess not." She brightened, smiled, puffed out her wonderful chest. "Well! Now that this is settled, everything should run pretty smoothly."

"No," Kelly said. "This is only a reprieve. We have Maurice's help now, but that won't matter. Something worse will come up. We'll be delayed a few more minutes or hours. We can never get this finished in time. We're all doomed."

In the next two hours, the race against time was begun in earnest. All over camp, projects were launched. Thanks to Angelli's ability to cross all language barriers, the Americans and the French worked fairly well together. Ditchlike foundations for the walls of the fake buildings were marked and cut. A few outhouses were framed and erected. In the midst of all this, Danny Dew roared around the clearing on his virility symbol, scraping out the streets which Hagendorf had surveyed yesterday.

The demolition of the HQ building was quick and dangerous. Headquarters had to come down, because it was obviously a temporary structure and military in origin. It would not have fooled the Germans for a minute. Therefore, after breakfast, the shortwave radio and the furniture were moved out of HQ, and a crew of workmen dismantled the corrugated metal roof. An hour later, the roof was gone, and the walls began to fall, slamming the earth like a series of angrily closed doors, casting up obfuscating clouds of dust.

Armed with hammers and pry-bars, goaded on by Major Kelly—"Faster, faster, faster, for Christ's sake!"—Maurice's laborers swarmed over the thin partitions. They separated metal from wood, tore one plank from the next, stacked the materials where they could later be used in the construction of the village.

The Frenchmen, Kelly thought, were like Eskimos stripping the carcass of a huge old walrus, leaving behind them nothing of value.

It was a pleasant thought, and he was still thinking it when Tooley came running over from the machinery shed waving his arms and shouting. "Major Kelly! Major Kelly, why did you put Hagendorf in the box, sir?"

"Hagendorf?" Kelly knew it was a bad idea to ask for an explanation. He sensed another crisis that would waste precious minutes. But he also knew that if he ran away, Tooley would only run after him. "Hagendorf? In the box?"

"Yes, sir. In the box, sir."

"What box?"

"In the machinery shed, sir. Don't you remember which box you put him in?"

"I didn't put him in any box," Kelly said, feeling not unlike a character in a Lewis Carroll fantasy.

Tooley wiped his broad face with one hand, pressed the hand on his shirt, and left a huge wet palm print. "We were clearing out the machinery shed so it can be knocked down. The last thing we came to was this big crate Sergeant Coombs has been meaning to convert into a tool chest for several weeks. The crate was supposed to be empty; but Hagendorf was inside. With maybe twenty bottles of wine. He's naked and drunk, and he insists you put him in the box." While he talked, Tooley unbuttoned his shirt and took it off. His thick weight-lifter's torso was shiny with sweat and alive with muscles.

"I didn't put Hagendorf in the box," Kelly said.

"We didn't force him out, because we didn't know why you put him there."

"I didn't put him there."

"We didn't want to interfere in whatever you were doing. We thought maybe you put Hagendorf in there to guard the box."

"Hagendorf isn't guarding the box," Kelly said, wiping sweat from his own face.

"That's what I said. I said you must have put him in the box for some other reason." Tooley spat on the dry earth.

"I didn't put Hagendorf anywhere," Kelly said.

"Hagendorf says you did."

"Let's go talk to Emil about this," Kelly said.

Thirty French men and women and a dozen of Kelly's men were clustered in the late morning sunshine outside the open machinery shed door. The noise and stench of perspiration were unendurable. Kelly and Tooley pushed through the crowd into the cool, dark, empty, and comparatively quiet interior which had been gutted for demolition. "Why aren't these people working?" Kelly asked.

Tooley shrugged. "They're Angelli's people, and they aren't worth a damn when he's not egging them on. Of course, he's up at the hospital bunker."

Kelly stopped just inside the door. "Is Vito hurt?" He hoped not. Angelli was essential. No one could handle the Frenchmen like he could. Besides Maurice, he was their only real contact with the French.

"It's not that," Tooley said. "He's okay. He's just up there romancing Nurse Pullit."

"*Romancing* Nurse Pullit?" Kelly was not certain he had heard right.

"Well sure. The nurse *is* attractive. Sooner or later, someone was bound to fall for her."

"*Fall* for her?" He felt as if he were Tooley's echo. "Not that too!"

The pacifist did not seem to see anything strange in the Angelli-Pullit romance. "There's the box," he said, pointing across the room. "Hadn't we better get Hagendorf out of it?"

The only thing remaining in the large, main room of the

shed, besides Sergeant Coombs and Lieutenant Beame, was an unpainted crate near the far wall. It was eight feet long, four deep, and four wide. It looked like a natural pine coffin. Standing at the foot of it, Coombs might have been a mourner. A disgruntled and angry mourner. "Hagendorf won't get out of this box you put him in," Coombs said, as Kelly approached.

"He's not in there to guard it," Tooley told Coombs.

"Then why'd you put him in there?" Coombs asked Kelly.

"I didn't put him in there." Kelly reached the crate and peered inside.

Hagendorf, the chief surveyor, was lying in the box on a bed of his own clothes, naked as the day he was born. If he had been born. Kelly was not sure about that. Naked, pale, chubby, Hagendorf looked more like something which had been hatched. "You put me in here," he told Kelly.

Kelly looked at the two dozen wine bottles which surrounded the surveyor. More than half were empty. "You got wine from Maurice, and now you're drunk, Emil."

"This is my coffin," Hagendorf said. "You put me in it. You made me get out my theodolite and survey your crazy village. You're the one who gave me a glimpse of the order and purpose I once knew and can never know again." Hagendorf's voice had grown quavery. Now, he started to cry. "You destroyed me. You put me in this coffin—you and no one else."

"Get out of the box," Kelly said. "It's heavy enough without you in it."

"I'm dead," Hagendorf said. "I can't get out."

Kelly sighed, look at the others. "Let's get him out of there."

"No you don't!" Hagendorf screamed as they reached in for him. He spread his legs, braced his knees against the side of the box, his feet against the bottom. There was a supporting frame holding the sides of the crate together, and the surveyor gripped this with fingers like chitinous claws.

Though Coombs pulled at his legs, Tooley at his left arm, Beame at his right arm, and Kelly at his head, all of them grunting and putting their backs into it, Hagendorf would not be moved. He was the most tenacious corpse they had ever seen.

"Look here, Emil," Major Kelly said, letting go of Hagendorf's head and wiping the chief surveyor's spittle off his hand, "we don't have time to fool with you. The goddamned Panzers are coming, Emil. We have a whole town to build before they get here. This shed has to come down and fast. This site has to be made ready for another building. These walls have to be torn up so we can reuse the wood and metal. Now, you come out of that fucking box, or I won't be responsible for what happens to you."

Hagendorf began to blubber again, and when he spoke his voice was, once more, the 78 rpm record played at an eternal 60 rpm. "I'm dead and rotting. . . . What more can happen?" He held on to his coffin, his soft pudgy body now lumpy with muscles that had not been flexed near the surface of Hagendorf's body for as long as ten years.

Kelly picked up an empty wine bottle, and held it like a club. "Emil . . ."

"You destroyed me," Hagendorf said, tears running down his face.

"No violence, please," Tooley said, rubbing his hands together as he watched the scene leading inevitably to spilled blood.

"I'm sorry, Emil," Kelly said. He swung the bottle at Hagendorf's head.

The surveyor jerked out of the way. The bottle missed him, shattered on the side of the crate.

"Hold him down," Kelly told the others.

Coombs grabbed the surveyor's legs, while Beame stood across the box from Kelly and pressed down on Hagendorf's chest. Tooley wanted no part of it.

Kelly picked up another bottle and raised it over Hagendorf's head. "We haven't any time to waste, Emil. But I'll try to make this just a tap," he said when he saw Hagendorf was watching him intently through a veil of tears.

Then he swung the bottle.

Hagendorf let go of the box, grabbed Beame and pulled him in as a shield. The bottle smashed on Beame's golden head, spraying glass and dark wine.

"Ugh," Beame said, and passed out. Blood trickled out of his scalp.

"You killed Beame," Tooley said, stunned, hugging himself.

"It's just a tiny cut," Kelly said. "I didn't swing hard enough to kill him."

Coombs was disgusted. "Now you've got two of them in there."

Kelly considered the crate for a while. "Maybe we could get a bunch of men in here and carry the box out with Hagendorf still inside."

"With Hagendorf and *Beame* inside," Tooley said. He had stopped hugging himself, but he looked at Beame out of the corner of his eye as if he remained unconvinced that the lieutenant was alive.

Kelly saw that getting Beame out of the box was going to be every bit as difficult as getting Emil Hagendorf out of the box, because Hagendorf was holding tightly to Beame to shield himself from further violence. Kelly could almost hear the clatter of Panzer tread, louder by the second. . . . "We'll get a dozen men—"

"No," Coombs said. "If we lift that box and Hagendorf starts jumping up and down or rocking in it, we'll fall with it. Someone'll break a leg. Or worse."

"Worse—like Beame," Tooley said.

"Beame's okay," Kelly said. He ignored the two of them and searched desperately for a solution. He could not leave the crate here and order the shed's demolition, for Hagendorf would probably be killed by collapsing walls. Major Kelly did not want to kill anyone. Petey Danielson had been enough. . . . "I've got it!" he said, suddenly turning from the crate and crossing the musty room to the doorway where the workers stood in the sunlight and squinted curiously at him. He located one of his own men, Private Lyle Fark, and spoke to him for a minute or two.

Fark was a tall, angular Tennessean, all bone and gristle, with a surprisingly gentle face as fine as water-carved, sun-bleached sandstone. He nodded vigorously as Kelly talked, then turned and disappeared through the press of jabbering villagers.

"What's that cocksucking bastard up to now?" Coombs wanted to know.

"I've always sort of liked Fark," Tooley said.

"Not Fark. Kelly."

"Oh, you're right about *him*!" Hagendorf cried from inside the crate. He had pulled the unconscious lieutenant over him like a coverlet, and he peered up at Coombs from the hollow of Beame's right armpit. "Kelly's a bastard. He—"

"Oh, shut the fuck up," Sergeant Coombs said.

A few minutes later, Private Fark pushed back through the crowd and handed something to Kelly. The major took it, nodded, came back across the room. He walked straight up to the crate, holding a small object in one hand which was pressed flat against his thigh. He looked at Hagendorf who was still peeking at the world through the curious perspective of Beame's armpit. "Last chance."

"You put me in here!" Hagendorf cried. "You did it!"

Kelly sighed. He picked up a wine bottle, raised it, faked a swing.

Hagendorf rolled the hapless lieutenant into the blow—and unwittingly bared one of his own pale, hammy, naked thighs.

Raising the object Fark had fetched for him and which Tooley and Coombs now saw to be a hypodermic syringe from the hospital, Kelly plunged it into the surveyor's thigh just as he checked the downswing of the empty bottle and spared the unconscious Beame another wound.

Hagendorf screamed, tried to throw off Beame. He scrabbled at the sides of the box, desperate to get up. The needle broke in his flesh. It dangled from his leg, focal point of a spreading circle of blood. In seconds, Hagendorf was fast asleep.

Private Tooley shook his head admiringly. "You'd make a good pacifist. That was very clever. That puts an end to the Hagendorf crisis."

Kelly looked down at the chalky, chubby man who was half-concealed by Lieutenant Beame. "Maybe not. If Hagendorf has gone over the edge—and if he hates me as much as he seems to, maybe he deliberately did a bad surveying job for the village. Maybe he sabotaged it."

"Hagendorf wouldn't do that," Tooley said.

"Hagendorf is crazy," Kelly said, dropping the ruined syringe. It *clinked* when it hit the packed-earth floor. "He was driven crazy by his own sanity. Before he came into the Army, he was too sane for his own good. His sanity drove him out of his mind. He saw everything in blacks and whites. When it came time for him to test his philosophy, Hagendorf could either be wholly sane or wholly insane. He was *already* wholly sane. So he had to become wholly insane." He looked at Tooley and Coombs and saw that they did not understand a word of it. They were looking at him as if he were wholly insane. "Hagendorf is a crazy wino," Kelly said, simplifying it for them. "He'll do anything. I'll have to check up on the work he finished yesterday before we go on with too much more of the building."

On his way out of the shed, Kelly looked at his watch. How much time had he wasted with Hagendorf? Twenty minutes? Half an hour? Too much.

Suffering from a severe headache, traces of blood still crusted in his yellow hair, Lieutenant Beame went straight from the hospital bunker to the secluded knoll in the woods where he and Nathalie had secretly planned to have lunch together. He was very circumspect about leaving the camp, and he was sure no one saw him go. He crept cautiously through the woods, took a circuitous route to the knoll through blackberry brambles and treacherous ground vines.

Natalie was waiting for him.

But so was her father.

"You are scum!" Maurice said, advancing on Beame as the lieutenant backed off the knoll and into the trees again. "My daughter will not be brought to ruin by a quick-handed soldier. Do you understand?"

"Yes, sir," Beame said, backing into an oak tree. "But—"

"She will be courted openly, not behind my back. And she will not be made a fool of by some carousing GI. Need I say more?" He loomed over Beame, his big belly perfect for intimidating anyone he could back against a wall.

"Father—" Nathalie began, behind the old man.

"Do not interrupt your father," Maurice said, without turning back to her. He pushed at Beame with his belly, crushing the lieutenant against the oak.

"Sir," Beame said, "you don't seem to realize—"

"I do not wish to become violent," Maurice said. "But I can if I must." As example, he clenched his fist and thumped Beame once, on top of the head, right on the spot where the bottle had broken. "Understand?"

Through tears, Beame said, "Uh . . . yeah. Yes, sir."

Maurice turned away from him. "Come on, my dear," he told the girl, in French. "And in the future you must respect your father more."

Major Kelly ate lunch while riding around on the D-7 dozer with Danny Dew. He had to stand up, wedged between the open dash and the roll-bar behind Dew's chair—which was a tight fit and only crucial inches from the churning tread. That made for a messy lunch, but not merely because the dozer shimmied and bounced so much. It was messy chiefly because Kelly was eating a stewed-tomato sandwich.

"Is that a stewed-tomato sandwich?" Danny asked when Kelly climbed on the dozer, holding the oversized sandwich in one hand. Red juice and slimy seeds dripped from Kelly's fingers, ran down his wrist and under his cuff.

"Yeah," Kelly said. "Because of my hair." He bit the sandwich, and juice sprayed all over his face.

"A stewed-tomato sandwich is good for your hair?" Dew asked.

"No. It's not good for my hair. But it isn't bad, either. It's neutral. It's meat that's bad for hair growth, you see."

"Meat?" Dew asked.

"Meat. So I eat vegetable sandwiches." He took another bite. "Can we get going? I want to see the whole camp. I want to be certain that Hagendorf designed the streets the way I laid them out. I don't trust the crazy drunken bastard."

Dew started the D-7, taking his eyes from Major Kelly's disgusting repast only with the greatest effort.

They roared away from the riverbank and circled the camp on the service road that edged the forest. Clouds of dust sprayed up behind them; and because the dozer could not proceed with any real speed, the dust often caught up with them, swept past, bringing temporary blindness and laying a soft, golden-brown patina over them, a sheath which darkened Kelly and lightened Danny Dew.

Already, Danny had finished most of the work on the streets. With the dozer's monstrous blade barely scraping the surface, he had smoothed the land which Kelly had charted and which Hagendorf had staked. He had plowed off four inches of topsoil, then rolled back and forth over the streets to compact and harden the well-aerated earth which lay beneath the sod. This made the fake village's streets lower than its houses, conveyed an impression of much use, years of wear.

"Looks pretty good, doesn't it?" Danny Dew shouted above the engine noise.

"Not good enough!" Kelly shouted.

"Looks like we're going to build a village in four days, doesn't it?"

"No," Kelly said. "Never."

The major was not the least bit pleased by any of the pleasant things he saw. The streets had been marked off just as he had planned them. All that remained to be done to them was the removal of the ridges of dirt which the plow had built up on both sides of the street, and the smoothing out of the dozer's tread imprints from the hard dry earth.

Already, half the convent's foundation was up: a low stone wall that was to be the base for the enormous building. Last night, there had been no stones here, just the shallow trench in which the wall would be erected. Now, two sides of the convent's square underpinning—each a-hundred-twenty feet long—were up, and the other two sections had been started at trench bottom. Well before the Germans arrived, the convent would stand complete, looming on the north side of the bridge road, in the heart of town. Ideally, the entire convent would be of stone. But they had neither the time nor the cement to put up anything so elaborate. As is was, the mortar between the fieldstones had been poorly portioned out; and the stones had been so hastily laid that, to the professional eye, they looked like the obvious short-term hodgepodge they were. Fortunately, none of the Germans would be architects. The size of the convent, the forbidding design, would convince them that it was as real inside as out. But inside, of course, there would be nothing at all. Except the big machines.

"We sure will fox them!" Danny Dew shouted, grinning, looking a little bit like Stepin Fetchit.

"Not for a minute," Kelly said.

The dozer rumbled down the bridge road, moving slowly eastward.

Across the road from the convent, a work crew had dug

sixteen postholes, filled them with concrete, and anchored one four-by-six pine beam in each pit. These thrust up in a rectangular pattern, rustic columns with nothing to support. They were joined at the ground by flanking beams to help brace them. This afternoon, perpendicular beams would be fitted at the top to support the floor of the second story. The walls would go up tomorrow, both exterior and interior, and the finishing touches could be applied even while the roof was going on. This was to be the only fully built structure in the church-oriented town, the only one with a second level *inside* as well as out, the only one that might fool a carpenter or architect—for it was, if they had any say in it, where the German commander would make his temporary headquarters for the bridge crossing. It was the rectory.

Danny slowed the D-7 as they passed a group of men who were working diligently on another house, one of the many nuns' residences. All of the buildings—aside from the rectory and the church—would be built with more speed than craft on bare wooden platforms. They would have no insides at all. Walking into one would be like walking from one side of a stage setting to the other. In an exceptionally high wind, some of these hollow, flimsy structures might move around like sailing ships on water. With that disasterous prospect in mind, Major Kelly had ordered that nearly all the platform houses would be one story high, which made the village look odd but only slightly out of character.

"You think Hagendorf did it right?" Danny shouted.

"It looks that way," Kelly said. "But we haven't heard the last of Emil. He's still a troublemaker."

As they turned off the bridge road into the service road by the woods, heading back for the southern end of camp, Lieutenant Slade ran in front of them, waving his arms like a railroad signalman. Danny shifted down, braked, the tread clattering and squealing. The dozer stopped five feet in front of The Snot.

"I've seen enough for now!" Kelly shouted. "I'll get off here and see what Slade wants!"

What Slade wanted, Kelly soon discovered, was to complain. "I want to complain," he said as soon as the dozer was far enough away to make conversation possible.

"Well, well," Kelly said. He did not enjoy listening to his men's complaints, though that was one of his functions as commanding officer. He must listen, sympathize, advise. . . . It was unfair. *He* had no one to whom he could deliver his complaints. This was the worst thing about the war: his helplessness. "Well, well," he repeated, wishing Slade would drop dead.

"Nobody's filled out my traitor questionnaire," Slade said. More than ever, he looked like a wicked choirboy. "*You* didn't even answer it. It's the worst thing that's ever happened to me." He seemed caught between rage and tears. So he just sulked.

Kelly slapped his clothes, brushing off the chalky dust that made him look a bit like Boris Karloff as The Mummy. "That must be an exaggeration. This—"

"Is the worst thing that's ever happened to me," Slade insisted, his mouth drawn so far down at the corners that his lips seemed in danger of catching under his chin. "It's proof the men don't respect me."

Major Kelly was surprised by Slade's tone. It was full of human anguish, suffering, and sensitivity which Kelly had thought a pig like Slade would be incapable of. Incredibly, he felt a surge of compassion for the lieutenant. "Nonsense, Slade. The men *do* respect you."

"No, they don't."

"Sure, they do."

"No," Slade said. "Behind my back, they call me The Snot." Shining tears hung at the corners of Slade's eyes.

"Nobody calls you that."

"Sure, they do."

"Well, maybe they do," Kelly said. "But they mean it affectionately."

"You're lying," Slade said, wiping his nose with his sleeve.

"If they cared about me, respected me, they would have returned their questionnaires."

Kelly suddenly realized that he knew nothing about the lieutenant. Though they had been together in Britain before D-Day, had surely exchanged past histories, the major could remember none of that. All he could remember about Slade was what he had discovered after they were dropped behind German lines. . . . Furthermore, this eerie gap in his memory was not precipitated by his loathing of the man. Indeed, he realized he could not remember anything basic and personal about *any* of his men. Why? Why should he have forgotten all that was good to know about them—while retaining only the knowledge of their foibles and insanities? But he knew . . . It was not good to be intimate with war buddies. You could not afford to make friends. Making friends, you lost them. . . . You had to know their foibles and neuroses, because you had to know how to protect yourself from them. Judging from the behavior of the men since the unit had been parachuted in here weeks ago, they too had come to understand the joys and benefits of friendlessness. They had escaped from the responsibilities of friendship, escaped into drinking, gambling, insanity.

"What will I tell General Blade?" Slade asked, snuffling. "I'll be humiliated!"

The trickle of compassion Kelly had begun to feel when Slade cried now swelled into a torrent. He put his arm around Slade's shoulder and began to walk with him along the service road, in the shadows of the pines and sycamores. "I'll talk to the men, Richard." It was wise to have no friends to lose to the war, but Kelly now saw there was a point where isolation and distrust was more damaging than valuable. "I'll make sure they fill out their forms."

"Would you?" Slade asked, nearly quivering with pleasure.

Kelly smiled. "Richard, we have got to be more open with each other. Any time you have a complaint, you come right to me with it. Don't let it fester." They went past a group of workers who were taking a twenty-minute lunch break, and

Kelly gave them the thumbs-up sign. They looked at him as if he were an institutional case, but he failed to notice. He was brimming with camaraderie and compassion. "It's time we tried to *know* each other, Richard."

"I *do* have another complaint," Slade admitted. "You want to hear it?"

"Of course! Don't let it fester!"

They left the service road and walked down the street that was parallel to the bridge road. Workmen were erecting several skinny outhouses and laying the platforms for nunneries and for a deaf-mute school.

"Well," Slade said, "I think we should stop trying to hide from the Germans."

"Oh?"

"We should stand and fight," Slade said. He was encouraged by Kelly's attitude, by the major's arm around his shoulders. "It's cowardly to hide." Maybe Kelly had come to his senses and would act like an adult. Maybe there was no longer any need to kill him and assume command. "We should fortify the clearing and blast the hell out of those krauts. We have handguns. Maurice could supply a mortar or two."

"A mortar or two."

"I'm aware we'd all be killed," Slade said. "But think of the history we'll make! They'll know all about us back in the States! We'll be heroes!"

Kelly stopped walking and dropped his arm from Slade's shoulder.

Slade stopped a couple of paces ahead of the major. "Right, sir? Isn't it sick and cowardly to hide? Shouldn't we fight like men? Don't you agree?"

Kelly sucked in a deep breath. "You're an asshole, Slade," he shouted, his voice growing louder by the word. "You're an idiotic, simpleminded emotional and mental wreck!" He could not imagine how he could have forgotten the Slade who had shot that German soldier in the back of the head, or the Slade who thought war was glorious, or the Slade who read the Army field manual for relaxation. "You're insane, Slade! You're a monomaniac, a fiend, a myth-enthralled child, a monster!"

"I thought you wanted to be friendly," Slade said, his face ashen.

"Fuck friendliness!" Kelly roared.

"You were going to be warm and understanding."

"Fuck warmth and understanding!" the major screamed, spittle flecking his chin. He stomped his foot as if he had just squashed those virtues under his heel. "I *want* to be cold, hostile, isolated! I don't want to hear your fucking complaints. You're a creep, Slade. Everybody loathes you!"

"I'll get you for this," Slade said. "So help me—"

"You're an imbecile, Slade!" Kelly screamed, red in the face now.

Slade turned and ran, arms out in front of him like a comic-book character fleeing a grisly, risen corpse. The workmen stopped working to watch him go.

"And another thing!" Kelly shouted, doubled over as if suffering cramps. "No more messing around with that questionnaire! We don't have time for that shit! We have four days! Four days, and we need every minute of it for serious business!"

Slade scrambled over a slight rise, then down the riverbank, out of sight. He was probably just going to sulk in a patch of cat-o'-nine-tails. Dreamer that he was, Kelly hoped Slade intended to drown himself.

Drained, Kelly turned abruptly and walked into Angelli and Pullit. Without a word of apology, emptied of words now, the major pushed past them. A dozen long strides later, he stopped, turned, suddenly conscious of the anomaly he had just seen. Pullit and Angelli were walking hand-in-hand. Kelly remembered what Tooley had said: Angelli was romancing the nurse; he had fallen for her. . . .

"Private Angelli!" he called. When the loving couple turned, Kelly said, "Come here, Private." He hoped he sounded stern.

Vito and the nurse exchanged a few brief words. He kissed the nurse on the cheek, and Pullit hurried off toward the hospital bunker.

"Yes, sir?" Angelli asked, walking back to the major. He was not wearing a shirt. His slim, brown torso was sweat-slicked—and decorated with what seemed to be a fresh tattoo: two letters, N and P. They were done in blue and red, and they were *so fresh* that the swelling had not yet gone down.

Kelly looked sideways at Angelli, as if he were ready to turn and run if the private made a wrong move. "Uh . . . what's this about you and Nurse Pullit being . . . well . . . having a—romance?"

"Isn't she perfect?" Angelli asked, grinning winningly.

Kelly winced. "She's not a she. She's a he. Angelli, what is going on here?"

"I think I love her," Angelli said, as if he had not heard Kelly's news. Or did not believe it.

"Pullit is a *him*," Kelly insisted. "Look, this is—sick. Vito, I know that some of the men have gotten strange since the pressure was put on, but this is too much. It's too far. You have to get over this."

"I'll never get over her," Angelli said, dreamily, smiling just the way that Beame had smiled when talking about Nathalie Jobert.

"Vito, we have four days or so to build this town. That means we need full and enthusiastic cooperation between us and the French. There are only three people who can generate that cooperation: Maurice, me, and you. I need you to keep the largest French work crew on the ball. And this morning, you weren't with them. You were romancing—Pullit."

Angelli was hard-muscled, scrappy, not at all in line with Major Kelly's picture of a pervert. Yet he sighed and said, "I wish I could speak French. It's the language of love. . . ."

Major Kelly backed up a few feet. "Look here, Vito. I'm *ordering* you to stay away from Nurse Pullit. You will be severely punished, maybe even court-martialed, if you go near the nurse."

Angelli's face fell. He touched the swollen letters on his chest. "But I might lose her if I'm not persistent."

"Good," Kelly said. "Now, get back to your work crew. For Christ's sake, man, the Germans moved ten miles closer while you two were strolling around, holding hands, mooning over each other! Move your ass!"

The labor strike came at four o'clock that afternoon.

Major Kelly was up in the framing beams of what would soon be the second level of the rectory, inspecting the joists and the angle braces. Most of the men around him were his own, for this job required nearly all skilled labor. He was not, therefore, immediately aware of the cessation of work noises in the rest of the camp.

Lyle Fark brought the news. "Major!" he called from the bridge road in front of the would-be rectory. "Major Kelly!"

Kelly crawled along the grid of wooden beams and looked down at Fark. "What is it, Private?"

The Tennessean was unnaturally agitated. "You've got to come down. That Maurice is losing his mind. He's called a labor strike!"

Kelly just leaned out over the skeleton of the rectory and stared at Fark, unmoving, unable to speak.

"Do you understand, sir?" Fark shuffled his feet. Dust rose around him.

"A strike," Kelly said. "A work stoppage."

"Yes, sir. He says his people aren't getting paid enough."

"My people are not getting paid enough," Maurice said.

He had gathered all one hundred French workers at the bridge. They were climbing onto the three flatbed German trucks which they now used to shuttle to and from Eisenhower. They were jabbering and laughing.

"They've taken everything we've got. You've milked us

dry already!" Kelly said, pulling on a pair of imaginary udders.

"Not at all," Maurice said. "You still have a great deal which my people could use." He made a long face. "I have just realized how much you and your men have, and how little you are paying my poor people to save your skins. It seems I must now reopen negotiations if work on the village is to continue."

"But what can you *want*?" Kelly asked. He was ready to give up anything, even the clothes on his back. "I'll even save my shit and package it as manure," he told The Frog. "Anything!" That imaginary thunder of Panzer-tread grew even louder, the thump of marching feet close behind. . . .

"If you can't see what is left for you to pay us with," Maurice said, scratching his hairy, bloated stomach which peeped out between halves of his shirt, "then perhaps you need some time to think." He turned toward the trucks, then back to the major. "And there is one other thing. Besides an increase in pay for my people, I want you to obtain for me a written guarantee from this Lieutenant Beame of yours. I want him to swear in writing that he will not attempt to court my daughter." Maurice hunched his shoulders and balled his fists at his sides. "I will not have my daughter used by a soldier."

As the last of the Frenchmen got onto the trucks, Kelly said. "This is ridiculous. Look, can't you wait until we can talk–"

Maurice was adamant. "I do not believe you will negotiate in good faith until you realize I am serious about this work stoppage."

"You're wrong!" Kelly declared, throwing his hands up. "I'll negotiate in the very best of faith. I'll do anything! You can have my teeth for piano keys!"

"I do not want your teeth," Maurice said. "You have much more to offer."

"But *what*?" Kelly asked. "You've got two hundred bucks from each of us. And you're going to get a tollbooth–"

"The very fact that you cannot imagine what to give us is proof that you will not bargain seriously at this time," The Frog said, turning, walking away, climbing into the cab of the first truck.

The three vehicles started up. Smoke plumed from the tail pipes.

As the first truck started for the bridge, Nathalie Jobert jumped off the bed of the last one and ran the few steps to Kelly. She grabbed his hands and held them tightly. "*Monsieur,* please do not hate my people because of my father. Do not even hate him. He is more bluff than fight. He will be back tomorrow, and he will help you build your village if you'll only give him the bulldozer and the shortwave radio. That is all he wants. In fact, he will not even hold out for that written guarantee from David."

"He can have the shortwave radio," Kelly said. "But I don't see how I can give him the dozer. That's Danny Dew's virility symbol, and he won't take kindly to my giving it away. You know, I *need* Danny. I can't finish the village without him."

"But the dozer and radio are all that will satisfy my father, Major." She let go of his hands and returned to the last truck, which was waiting for her. She jumped onto the the bed, sat with her long legs dangling over the lowered tailgate.

"Anything but the dozer," Kelly said.

She shook her head. Her black hair spread out like a silk fan, folded up. "I wish I could help. But that is all my father would take."

The truck started away. It entered the bridge. Crossed the bridge. Went around the bend on the other side. Out of sight.

# 6/

"We should send a commando squad into Eisenhower tonight and kill that crazy frog bastard," Sergeant Coombs said.

Major Kelly ignored the sergeant's suggestion.

Instead, he gave the men a pep talk. And he tried to flog them into accomplishing their own work *and* that of the Frenchmen now on strike. He doubled job assignments. Mind racing feverishly, he looked for and found and implemented all tolerable shortcuts in their construction procedures. He cut the supper break down to fifteen minutes. He stalked from one end of the clearing to the other, doing his Patton imitation: badgering, cajoling, screaming, shaking his fist in the faces of the goldbrickers, joshing, berating, threatening. . . .

"If we don't get our little religious community built before the Germans get here, we're finished," Kelly told them. "They have rifles, pistols, automatic pistols, cannons, ack-ack guns, grenades, submachine guns, mortar, flamethrowers, tanks. . . . They'll grind us into fish meal. Any of you want to be be made into fish meal? Huh? Any of you?"

None of the men wanted to be ground into fish meal. They worked hard, then harder, and finally hardest.

A three-man search party went looking for Lieutenant Beame when Kelly learned that the junior officer had not shown up at his work assignment after lunch. Beame was supposed to be guiding the blueprinting and initial construction of the church tower, a job only he or Kelly was qualified to do. But he was missing, and his men were idle. . . . Half an hour after they set out, the searchers came back with the lieutenant. They had located him on a grassy knoll in the woods where he had been lying on his back, looking at the sky and daydreaming.

"What's the *matter* with you?" Kelly demanded of Beame. "You're the only man here besides me who can do this sort of planning. You're the only other full engineer. I *need* you, Beame. You can't go wandering off into the woods—"

"I can't stop thinking about her," Beame said. "Nothing else matters except her. And he won't let me see her. . . ." He looked like a sad clown.

"Who?" Kelly asked. "Who's he and who's she?"

"Maurice is he. Nathalie is she. I love her, but he won't let me near her."

"Love can get you killed," Kelly told him. "I order you to stop loving her. Get on the ball, Beame! Don't desert me now."

Kelly also had to keep an eye on Angelli, who kept trying to sneak away to see Nurse Pullit. Vito was one of the few men quick and limber enough to slip around on high beam frames, troubleshooting connections and looking for flaws in supports and braces. He was vital, even when there were no Frenchmen for him to oversee. And now when their chances were evaporating like water in a teakettle, he was playing the love-sick schoolboy. Even when he *was* working, Vito was, like Beame, in such a state of longing that he could accomplish only a third of the work he should have done.

When night came, they worked on, though they ordinarily would have stopped and called it quits until dawn. There was not much that could be done in complete darkness. If they used enough lanterns to throw sufficient light on their work, they risked becoming targets for Allied and German planes. Tonight, they compromised. Kelly allowed the use of half the lanterns they needed—which provided just enough light to attract the dreaded bombers but not enough to permit efficient labor.

Finally, at 10:30, Tooley came to see the major. The pacifist was pale, sweaty, filthy, exhausted. His ropy muscles did not look so formidable as they always had before. His thick neck seemed to be made of rubber and was supporting his head with difficulty. "Let them stop, Major! For God's sake, be merciful!"

"The Germans are coming. We can't stop. We're dead if we do!"

Tooley shook his head. It was almost more effort than he could endure. "They're so tired and terrified of attracting night planes that they aren't getting anything done, anyway. And if you expect them to achieve anything tomorrow, you have to let them rest tonight."

Kelly knew the pacifist was right. "Dammit!" He sighed. "Okay. It's all useless anyway. It's a fairy tale. It can't be real. Tell them to knock off. We couldn't finish it in time even if they worked twenty-four hours a day."

By eleven o'clock, the camp was dark and still. Rushing silently westward, marshmallow mountains of cumulus clouds obscured the moon and stars. The shadows had all run together in one inky pool. A few tent flaps rustled in the variable wind which had sprung up halfheartedly from the east, and the crickets chirruped softly and intermittently in the nearby woods.

Neither the wind nor the crickets was sufficient to rouse the men. Those not yet asleep soon would be, when weariness became greater than fear.

The roof was off the main bunker, and none of the men could see much sense in sleeping in a roofless bunker. It would be like wearing a bulletproof vest made of cardboard, or like wearing cotton galoshes in a rainstorm, or like dating your own sister. Therefore, they had put up the tents, most of them precisely large enough to accommodate two men in complete discomfort, though a few—like Major Kelly's—were spacious. Because they were temporary and did not deserve much planning time, the tent rows were haphazardly drawn, an intriguing maze that confused and confounded everyone. The pegs were makeshift and poorly wedged, while the taut guide ropes made a treacherous tangle in the darkness. Still, the tents were better than the roofless bunker. As Kelly had said, "As long as you can't see the sky, you can pretend that you're shielded by sheets of steel. You can pretend the tent is made of heavy armor. You can trick yourself into sleeping better."

But Major Kelly was one of the few men who was unable to trick himself into sleeping better. Or at all. He lay in his tent, in the diffused orange light of a single, oily candle, and he worried about everything: the Germans, Hagendorf, the Germans, Lieutenant Beame, the Germans, the romance between Angelli and Pullit, the strike and the possibility that he would have to give away Dew's bulldozer, the Germans. . . .

Suddenly, Private Tooley, breathing like a spent horse, poked his head through the unsecured tent flaps and cried, "Major!"

Kelly sat straight up, smacking his head into a tent pole.

"It's awful!" Tooley gasped.

"What? What?" Kelly rubbed his head and stumbled to his feet.

"Kowalski just made another prediction. It's horrible!"

"You broke in here to tell me about that bag of shit?" Kelly asked, incredulous.

"He's been right before," Tooley said. "In fact, he's never been wrong."

Major Kelly was worried in spite of himself. "What's he saying now?"

"Come quick and see!" Tooley said, dropping the flaps and disappearing.

"Tooley!" Kelly pushed out of the tent, looked around. The pacifist was twenty yards away, running towards the hospital bunker. "Damn!" Kelly said.

Two minutes later, he stumbled down the hospital's uneven, earthen steps, breathing like a horse that had been in the same race as Tooley. He struck his shoulder on the door frame, staggered inside. The lights were dimmer and the stench twice as bad as he remembered them. A veritable flock of centipedes scattered in front of him. He shivered, went down the aisle to the end of the bunker where Pullit, Lily, Liverwright, and Tooley stood by the mad Pole's bed.

Kowalski was rigid, eyes wide and tongue lolling. He had a fat, pale tongue, utterly disgusting. He was sitting in a steaming puddle of his own urine, and he looked curiously as if he belonged there.

"What's he saying?" Kelly asked, wheezily.

As if on cue, Kowalski said: "Too little time . . . no time . . . less than we need . . . never build town . . . never . . . too little time . . . less than we think. . . ."

"He means the Panzers," Lily said. Her face was drawn and fearful—and sexy.

"If we don't have time to build the fake town," Tooley said, "there will be bloodshed." Despite his muscles, Tooley sounded like a frail spinster facing a gang of undiscriminating rapists. "What are you going to do about it, Major?"

"He means the strike will slow us down," Kelly said. "We already know that."

"He's talking about something else," Tooley said. "Something worse than the strike. Something that *has not yet happened.*"

"Even if he is," Kelly said, "what can I do? He hasn't given me enough to go on. *Why* don't we have enough time? *What* terrible disaster is pending?"

Tooley looked at the zombie, patted his head. "Tell us more, Kowalski."

Kowalski was silent.

"He's already warned us," Lily said. "He hasn't anything more to say."

Refuting her, Kowalski leaned toward Lily and said, "Cu. . . ."

"Yes?" she asked.

Everyone leaned closer, listening intently. The walls seemed to recede; the dreariness was replaced by a sense of the cosmic, a spiritual mood that was undeniable and hinted of forces beyond the ken of man. The lights were no longer dim, merely mysterious. The centipedes were forgotten. They listened to the wise man's words as if the fate of the world hinged on his pronouncements.

"Cu . . . cu . . ." Kowalski's eyes were fever-bright. His tongue moved obscenely between his cracked lips as he tried to finish what he wanted to say. "Cu . . ."

"He's got something big to say," the pacifist insisted. "I know he does."

"Cu . . . cu . . . cu . . ."

"He's almost got it!" Tooley fisted his hands, arms bulging as he pulled for Kowalski.

Major Kelly felt, all of a moment, in the midst of a miracle, some fundamental religious experience which he would treasure the memory of for the rest of his days. He had not been so choked up and teary since he had seen Margaret Sullavan in *Back Street.*

Watching Lily, Kowalski rocked back and forth. His tongue fluttered. His eyes blinked so rapidly it seemed the lashes would give him flight. "Cu . . . Cu . . ."

Lily held her hands out to him, encouraged him as one might encourage a baby who was walking toward his mother for the first time. "Don't give up, poor dear," she cooed. "Tell us. Try, Kowalski. Tell us, poor baby."

"Cu . . . cu . . . *cunt*!" Kowalski squealed, lunging for her. He ripped open her khaki shirt and pawed her bare breasts. He gibbered with delight.

Pullit screamed.

Liverwright was immobilized by the sight of Lily's jugs.

Still screaming, Pullit ran for the bunker door, red bandanna trailing behind. "Help! Help, someone!"

Going to Lily's rescue, Kelly stumbled on a cot brace, staggered, and fell heavily onto the makeshift bed. The cot collapsed.

Kowalski rolled into the major, and for an instant their faces touched nose-to-nose. Kowalski's eyes were wide and bloodshot, but possessed a certain lucidity which Kelly had not seen there for long days. *"Cunt, cunt, cunt!"* he screamed. Then, like a door closing, the semirationality left his eyes, and a bottomless stupidity returned. Drool ran out of the left corner of his mouth and down his chin.

Private Tooley grabbed the major by the scruff of the neck and hoisted him to his feet. "You okay, sir?"

Kelly nodded dumbly, brushing at his clothes.

"What do you think?" Tooley asked.

"About Kowalski? Shoot him. Put him out of his misery."

Tooley was hurt. "No! I think he's getting much better."

"Sure he is," Kelly said. "Sure he is."

Although he thought Kowalski should be put out of his misery, Major Kelly was worried about the zombie's prediction. They could not withstand another crisis. Even if they settled the labor strike, they had little chance of getting the village built in time. If one more problem arose. . . .

"You don't look sleepy," Lily said, taking his arm as he reached the bunker door. "I'm not sleepy either. Why don't we take a walk together?"

They walked to the woods, then to the knoll where Beame had expected to meet Nathalie for lunch. And then, of course, they stopped walking and undressed and made love. Even as worried as he was, Kelly was ready for Lily Kain.

When they were finished, they lay side-by-side in the grass and stared at the clouds overhead. Stars popped out between bands of mist, then disappeared once more. "You're a gem," Kelly told her. "You're the only woman I've ever known who hasn't the slightest reservation about having it put to her."

"Nonsense," she said. "Every girl wants to have it put to her."

"You're wrong," he said, squeezing her hand.

"I can't believe that. Every woman wants to have it put to her. It's fun!"

"Well . . . most women probably do want to have it put to them, but they won't admit it," Kelly said.

"Then how do they ever get it put to them?"

"Reluctantly. They protest, repeatedly refuse—give in reluctantly."

"What a waste of time," Lily said.

"And when they've had it put to them, when it's over, they cry and say how ashamed they are. Or pretend they didn't enjoy it."

"I *always* enjoy it," Lily said.

"I know," Kelly said.

Before they had become lovers, when she masturbated at night, her moans and cries roused the camp. Every man in the unit was enthralled by her performance, listening intently to the symphony of garbled noises until, by her crescendo, she was leading an orchestra of self-abusers. And now, of course, there were the regular shows beneath the bridge. . . .

Kelly put his arms around her. And though his terror did not go away, it dwindled for the next fifteen minutes and was almost forgotten as they moved together a second time.

Afterwards, he slept. And he dreamed. Usually, the dreams were about Petey Danielson: vivid, colorful replays of the man's guts falling out onto the dry earth. . . .

When he woke, trying to scream, Lily was there beside him. She smoothed his wet brow with one hand and cooed softly to him. "It's okay. It was just a bad dream, darling." Her warm flank was pressed against him, and the full weight of one large breast fell against his chest. She kept on smoothing his brow until his heartbeat slowed considerably and his dry mouth grew moist.

"How long was I asleep?"

"Maybe an hour," she said.

He started to sit up, but she pressed him back down. "We ought to be getting back," he said.

"Let's sleep out here tonight. The mosquitoes have gone. It's cool."

When he thought about getting dressed and walking back to his tent and undressing again for the night, he said, "Okay."

She snuggled up against him and kissed his ear. "I love you, Kelly."

"Don't say that."

"It's true."

"It's crazy. Love can be deadly. When you're in love, you go around in a daze. You stop being careful. You get killed. Don't be in love with me."

"You're in love with me, too," she said.

He closed his eyes, let the sounds of the forest settle over him like a fog: wind in branches, grasses rustling, crickets, toads, the scurrying sound of squirrels. . . . "Forget the love part. Let's just fuck and forget the love part, huh? Otherwise, we're dead."

"Go to sleep." She smoothed his forehead like Florence Nightingale in an old textbook drawing he had once seen. Except Florence Nightingale had not been nude.

"Promise you won't love me," he insisted.

"Go to sleep.

"Promise."

"Okay, okay! I promise not to love you."

He sighed happily. "Good. I don't want to die yet." He drifted toward sleep for a few minutes, then stirred, suddenly worried. "The Panzers! We—"

"Go to sleep, darling," she said. "Tomorrow's time enough to worry about the Germans. Remember, I don't love you."

"Not at all?"

"Not at all."

He tumbled into sleep again, dreaming of bombs which exploded like pastel clouds of chalk dust: green, yellow, blue, and purple. Men fell down dead, gushing pastel blood. The cries of the dying were muted and soft like the calls of giant pastel jungle-birds.

Except for Lily who comforted him and kissed him each time he woke, everything about the night was horrible. And now there were only four days left in which to build the village.

# 7 / JULY 20

The French workers returned to the clearing at noon, six hours after they were scheduled to arrive.

"Why waste six hours?" Kelly asked Lyle Fark when the private brought the news. "Why not return when they were supposed to, so we could negotiate and get this damn strike over with?"

"Psychology," Fark said. "Maurice wants you desperate before he sits down to bargain with you."

Maurice entered Kelly's tent five minutes later, mopping at his face with the tail of his checkered shirt. His enormous, round stomach was exposed, pale as a large honeydew melon, hairy as a coconut, the navel large and deep. "Your Private Fark met me at the bridge," he told Kelly. "He says you are prepared to negotiate."

The tent was large enough to contain a small table and two straight-backed chairs. Major Kelly was behind the table. He pointed to the chair in front of it. "Sit down. Let's talk business."

"*Certainement, mon ami,*" Maurice said, sitting where Kelly had pointed.

"You were supposed to be here at dawn," the major said, trying to be as reasonable as he could. He wanted to pick up the table and break it over the mayor's head. But he knew that would not facilitate an end to the labor strike.

"You have worked my people so hard," Maurice said, shrugging. "They were in need of a long night's sleep."

Kelly bit his lip until he thought blood would come, but he managed to keep his hands off Maurice's throat. "What do you want?"

Maurice frowned. "You have not yet thought of anything to offer?"

"The shortwave radio," Kelly said. "You want it?"

Maurice brightened, wiped sweat from his face. "It would be of great benefit to my community, cut off as we are from so much of France."

"It's yours," Kelly said.

"*Merci.* But it is not enough."

The major gritted his teeth and spoke through them, sounding like Humphrey Bogart. "What else? The D-7 dozer?"

"Ah," Maurice said. "That would be fine."

"This isn't easy, Maurice. You know the dozer is Danny Dew's virility symbol, his own way of hanging on in this chaos."

Maurice shrugged. "He will adapt."

Major Kelly had spent all morning wondering if Danny Dew would adapt. And he had been certain the black bastard would not. Danny depended on that big machine too much; he would not let it go without a fight.

"I need Dew," Kelly told Maurice. "I can't risk making an enemy of him. Without him, we'll never get the village done. There are jobs only the dozer can accomplish—and only under Danny's hand. So, we're going to have to keep this a secret. Not a word of this transaction can get back to Danny."

"One day, it must," Maurice said. "When the dozer leaves this clearing."

"That's my one condition," Kelly said. "You can't take possession of the dozer until we can con a new one out of General Blade—then, if Danny still won't give the old one up, you can have the replacement. It will be a better machine, anyway."

"And if you can't get another bulldozer from Blade?" Maurice asked.

"I will. I'll tell him this one's already been ruined."

Maurice thought about it awhile.

Kelly looked at his watch. The minute-hand seemed to sweep around the dial as if it were marking off seconds.

At last, Maurice said, "I am not an unreasonable man, Major."

Kelly gritted his teeth so hard he almost broke his jaws.

"I will be satisfied with this arrangement, if you write it out in the form of an ironclad contract which I have spent most of the night drafting." The Frog took a long sheet of paper out of his trousers and put it on the table.

"I'll sign anything," Kelly said.

"And what about the written guarantee from your Lieutenant Beame?" Maurice asked, leaning conspiratorially over the table.

Kelly felt that he owed Nathalie Jobert a favor. She had told him what her father would settle for, and she might give additional help in the future. "I am afraid that cannot be obtained," Kelly said. "He is adamant. And I can't rightly order him to sign. This thing between Beame and your daughter is a private affair and should not come between you and me."

Maurice scowled.

"*You* must compromise now," Kelly said. "I've come more than halfway."

"You are right," Maurice said. He struck the table with one hand. "I accept your offer. The strike is ended."

"And Danny must not learn about the dozer. It is essential we keep that a secret."

"We will try," Maurice said, drawing a tiny cross over his heart.

Kelly pushed his chair back from the table and stood up. His head brushed the canvas ceiling, and horseflies rose noisily from the outer surface. "In all honesty, I have to say that I am making this deal only because most of my men still think we can build the town in time to fool the krauts."

"And you don't believe we can, *mon ami*?"

"There never was much of a chance," Kelly said, edging around the table. "And now that you've wasted nearly a whole working day with this strike of yours, there's no chance at all."

"You are quite wrong." Maurice rubbed his pudgy hands together. "*C'est vrai,*" he added, seeing Kelly's skepticism. "I would not have called the strike without first finding some way to make up for the lost time. We will be done with your false town ahead of schedule, my friend. All thanks to the miracle of prefabrication."

"Prefabrication?" Kelly asked. He wrinkled his nose, partly in an expression of bewilderment and partly because Maurice Jobert was sweaty and smelly. "I don't understand."

"You will!" Maurice said. He went to the entranceway, and lifted a canvas flap. "Be at the bridge in one hour, and you will understand perfectly." He chuckled madly and winked at the major.

At 1:20 that afternoon, Maurice returned from Eisenhower with the first truckload of pieced-up barn walls. They were standing on edge in the back of a board-sided German cargo truck, each panel twelve feet high and twenty feet long—which was precisely the size of a wall of one of the single-story platform houses that comprised a sizable portion of the fake village.

The striking workers had not slept away the morning, after all. Instead, they had scouted barns, sheds, stables, and outbuildings which were firmly constructed, dismantling some of these and cutting them into maneuverable sections. They had taken only tightly joined panels that could pass as the walls of houses and churches. A passable exterior was all that mattered, for the insides of the fake houses would not be plastered or finished in any way. And after cutting up a barn, they had enough walls for seven or eight single-story platform buildings. A stable might build half a convent. A milk house could be sawed up and put back together as a two-story nuns' residence.

"It will save an incredible amount of time," Maurice told Kelly as the major inspected the walls stacked in the back of the truck. "One of the most time-consuming jobs is putting the siding on the buildings. Now, we can nail it up in huge pieces."

Kelly was not so sure. "No matter how well built a barn is, the wall is only a single thickness of wood. Some of the boards are not going to meet perfectly. Light will escape through them. Anyone looking at a fake house, made from these panels, will see light showing through the slats and know that it's a phony."

"Then no one must light a lantern inside any house but the rectory—and the church," Maurice said. "Your men must pass the night in darkness."

"They haven't much choice," Kelly said.

Though the individual partitions were heavy, there was plenty of sweaty, dirty, grunting, fear-driven manpower to cope with them. Twenty men wrestled each monstrous twelve-by-twenty wall from the bed of the German truck, and balanced it between them with considerable shouting and staggering back and forth.

"For God's sake don't drop it!" Private Fark screamed, as he took the front position on one of the walls. "It'll kill us if we lose control!"

With sunbrowned muscles bulging and sweat running in salty streams, with grunting and cursing that would have embarrassed many of the hard-working Frenchwomen if they had understood it, the walls were moved from the truck and toted to various platform houses which were now framed but not yet sided. The walls were balanced precariously against the frames of the platform houses, again by sheer muscle power, and the carpenters went to work nailing the panels to the beams which had been waiting since yesterday. Twenty long nails across the top, one every foot, then the same ratio down both sides, hammers smacking loudly, a chorus of blows echoing across the camp. When the straining, sweat-slimed men let go of the wall, the carpenters scurried along the base, praying that the thing would not rip loose and collapse on them, and they nailed that edge down as well. Then, while Maurice went for another load and while the majority of the husky laborers went to other tasks—of which there were many—the carpenters resecured the walls, pounding in again as many nails, one exactly between each pair they had already placed. At the corners of the building, where the prefabricated panels often did not meet in perfect eye-pleasing harmony—and where, in fact, there was sometimes as much as a two-inch gap despite the cut-to-order nature of the materials—the carpenters nailed up vertical finishing boards from foundation to eaves; these ran perpendicular to the horizontally slatted ex-barn-walls and provided the one-story structures with a surprisingly well-constructed appearance.

"And appearances are all that matter," Major Kelly told Lieutenant Beame as they inspected the first prefabricated building to be finished. "The krauts won't be going into any of these places. Just the rectory. Maybe the church, if any of them are Catholics."

"But the church and the rectory will be *real*," Beame said. "So we'll be safe. We'll pull if off."

"Never." It was the most positive reply Kelly had in him.

And yet the afternoon went fairly well, so far as the other men were concerned. A great deal was accomplished. The ten-foot-square entrance foyer of the convent—into which the Germans might venture, though no farther—was framed and walled, even though the convent's larger outer walls had not yet been thrown up. A few outhouses were completed and roofed. "You call yourselves members of the Army engineers?" Kelly screamed at his men. "It takes you two hours to build a goddamned shithouse? Faster! Faster, damn you!" The rectory walls crept toward a nonexistent second-story roof, these not prefabricated but crafted with care; and between the porch posts the floor of the rectory's veranda took shape, and the stoop in front of it and the steps leading down from the stoop and the sturdy banisters on both sides of the steps. "Three and a half days!" Kelly screamed at the men working the rectory job. "That's all you have. Not a month!" The town's small church, built on low stone walls similar to those that would give the convent the air of permanence it needed, was framed from foyer to auditorium to sanctuary to sacristy, complete with an eighteen-foot bell tower in which there would not be any bell. Hopefully, the Germans would not notice this omission, arriving as they were in darkness and leaving in the early morning light. A few picket fences were set up around small lawns. And off the street behind the convent, four men worked hard on an old-fashioned stone well complete with its peaked roof, winch bar—but no bucket attached. An isolated religious community would have a few open wells. But who was to say these must function after so many years? This was a dry well. Principally, it was a dry well because the distance between the top of the well wall and the bottom of the pit was six feet, and half of that aboveground. This well could never draw water. But it looked as if it once had. And appearances, as Kelly kept telling his men, were all that mattered. Throughout the afternoon, then, the fake community went as the stone well went: smoothly, steadily, with much sweating, cursing, scraped hands, torn fingernails, cuts, bruises, tortured muscles, suspected hernias, known hernias, and exhaustion. Very little of what they built could be used, but it all looked as if it had been lived in for decades.

Therefore, Kelly should have been happy.

But he distrusted happiness. He forced himself to scowl all through the long, hot afternoon.

He was still scowling at suppertime. He stood by the mess tent at the southern end of the camp, eating a boiled-potato sandwich (with mustard) and scowling at the other men who were hastily consuming creamed chipped beef on toast and cling peaches. He ruined many good appetites.

"Why are you so depressed?" Lyle Fark asked. "Those prefab walls are doing the trick. The work is coming along well."

Before the major could tell Fark about Kowalski's latest prediction, they were interrupted by Lieutenant Slade. Shouting and waving, Slade ran along the tent row, leaping gracelessly over guide ropes and pegs, dodging the men who were sitting before their tents eating supper. The men tried to trip Slade, but he was too quick and watchful for them to succeed. He stopped at the mess tent and unconsciously saluted Major Kelly. "Urgent message, sir! Call from General Blade!"

"Blade's on the radio now?" Kelly asked, around a mouthful of bread and boiled potatoes.

"It's about the Panzers," Slade said.

Kelly paled. "What about the Panzers?"

"I don't know," Slade said. "That's what the general wants to talk about."

Slade appeared to be sincere. Kelly had not overlooked the possibility that Slade was engaged in some elaborate hoax designed to make a fool of his superior officer. Slade would want to get even for yesterday, for the things that the major had shouted at him. But right now, Slade was sincere. He seemed to have forgotten, for the moment, that he hated Kelly. His awe of General Blade was not faked; that old syphilitic bastard must really be on the shortwave set.

Kelly dropped his mess tin and ran. None of the men in front of the tents tried to trip him, but they worked hard to get Slade who ran close behind. Again, they failed.

Since the HQ building had been torn down to make way for the fake community, the radio was being sheltered in Slade's tent, the only tent other than Major Kelly's which was roomy enough to hold the monster and the square wooden table on which it stood. Major Kelly stooped and entered the gloomy canvas room. The place smelled of wet straw and a few dozen mice. Since neither seemed to be present, Kelly supposed that both odors were endemic to the lieutenant. Wrinkling his nose, he went quickly to the radio and picked up the microphone just as Slade entered the tent behind him.

"Kelly here, sir," the major said, voice heavy with dread.

"Kelly?" Blade asked, unnecessarily.

"Yes, sir."

"How's my favorite major?"

Kelly frowned. "I don't know, sir. How is he?"

"Who is this?" General Blade asked, suddenly suspicious.

"This is Major Kelly," Major Kelly said.

"Well, then . . . how's my favorite major?" Blade asked again.

Kelly hesitated. "Is that a riddle, sir?"

"Is *what* a riddle?"

Kelly decided that if it were not a riddle, it was a joke. He was expected to repeat the straight line, and then Blade would give him the punch line. He sighed and said, "How is your favorite major, sir?"

"That's what I asked *you*," General Blade said, somewhat gruffly.

Kelly wiped at his face with one palsied hand. "Sir, I'm confused. I don't know anyone under your command except my own men. I don't know your favorite major and I can't—"

"You're beginning to confuse me," General Blade said. "Let's just talk about the Panzers, okay?"

Swallowing hard, Kelly nodded at the microphone.

"Okay?" Blade asked.

Kelly nodded.

"Kelly?"

Kelly nodded vigorously.

"Is that okay? Kelly, are you there?"

"Yes, sir."

"Did you come up with any plans to use against them?" the General asked.

Kelly suddenly realized that the General did not know about the fake town. He had called three nights ago, a few hours before Maurice came to the major with this plan for hoaxing the Germans, and he had not called back since. "We have a plan," Kelly admitted. But he knew there was no way to explain the fake village to Blade, not in a few minutes and not over the radio and not when they were both confused. So he lied. "Same as before. We'll masquerade as Germans."

"I suggested that a few nights ago," Blade said.

"We're taking your advice, sir." Blade had apparently forgotten all of the faults with the masquerade plan, which Kelly had detailed in their last conversation. Syphilitic old men probably could not retain anything when their brains had finally decayed to the consistency of cold oatmeal.

"Well," Blade said, "what I called to tell you won't come as bad news—not now that you're prepared for the krauts." He took a sip of coffee or blood. "Kelly, you won't have to sit on pins and needles for three more days, waiting for the Panzers. Our original information was faulty. They left the staging area at Stuttgart two days early. So they'll reach you around midnight on the twenty-first, two days earlier than we thought."

Kowalski had been right again.

"Tomorrow night, sir?"

"That's right, Kelly."

For the next few minutes, they talked about Panzers. The general described the size and quality of the force, though nothing had changed in that regard since he had described it a few nights ago. They were still dead. Doomed. Mincemeat.

"Will you be able to handle them?" Blade asked.

"Sure." All he wanted now was to get Blade off the air, stop wasting time.

"I hope so," the general said. "I don't want my favorite major to be hurt."

Kelly could not understand what in the hell the general's favorite major had to do with any of this. Who was this bastard Blade loved so much? Then Kelly decided that the average syphilitic old man could not always be expected to make sense. "Nothing will happen to him, sir. Your favorite major will come through this war unscathed. I'm sure of it."

"That's the kind of talk I like to hear!" Blade said. "Well . . . I'll be getting back to you in a couple of days, once this is over. Good luck, Kelly!"

"Thank you, sir."

Kelly put the microphone down. It brought him nothing but static now, a sound oddly like that you could hear when you held a seashell to your ear: distant, forlorn, empty, as lonely as old age. He switched it off.

"Well," Slade said, "this puts a new light on the case, doesn't it?"

Kelly said nothing.

"We'll never finish the town before midnight tomorrow," Slade said, a titter barely muffled behind one hand. "We'll have to fight the krauts."

"No," Kelly said. Fighting meant violence. Violence meant death. "We aren't taking any chances. We have to hang on, even if there isn't any hope, even if we *dare not* hope. I keep thinking . . . Hansel and Gretel may crawl into the oven, but they don't get burned, you know? And Jack only suffered bruises when he fell down the beanstalk. I don't know. . . . All I do know is that we can't take any initiative. We just play our roles, no matter how crazy they get. So . . . Maurice will have to supply us with fifty more workers—a crew to cut up barn walls in and around Eisenhower and deliver them to us while the other hundred workers are committed solely to the job in the clearing. The new crew can start cutting walls tonight. We'll work later, until eleven or twelve, by lanterns. We have to play our parts."

"This is disgusting!" Slade stamped his foot petulantly. "Cowardly! What will people think of us Stateside? What will history say? What will mother say?"

Kelly left the stinking tent and went to see Maurice about the additional workmen.

# 8 / JULY 21

At 2:00 in the morning, Lieutenant Slade quietly pushed back the tent flaps and stepped outside. He looked at the summer sky. The moon peeked from between fast-moving gray clouds that appeared to be packing into a single seamless bank as they rolled westward. The soft flicker of heat lightning pulsed behind the overcast. There would be no rain tonight. The air was warm, but not moist. The light wind was as dry as sand. However, when these clouds collided with those cold, moisture-laden thunderheads sailing in from the sea, rain would fall in bucketfuls. That would be farther west, toward the Atlantic. Tonight, in this part of France, the sky would remain overcast, but there would be no rain.

Good, Slade thought. The deeper the darkness and the fewer the obstacles it otherwise imposed, the better weather it was for assassination.

Slade looked up and down the twisting, cluttered tent row. No lights showed. No one moved. The silence was profound. In the darkness, even when a piece of the moon threw pale light into the clearing, the tents looked like concrete rather than canvas shelters; they resembled the sharply angled humps of an antitank defense perimeter.

The men were sound asleep, except for those patrolling the bridge road a mile to the east and a mile to the west of the camp as an early warning system to guard against any surprise enemy movement on that highway.

And except for Lieutenant Slade, of course. The assassin.

Slade stepped quietly across the dusty footpath to the

tents which faced his own, and squeezed between two of them without alerting the men who were sleeping inside. He walked away from the tents and the woods behind them, heading north toward the bridge. His ultimate destination was Major Kelly's tent, where he would cautiously peel open the flaps, take out his revolver, and blow the major's head off. However, in case someone *had* been watching him, some snooping son of a bitch peering out a crack between tent flaps, Slade walked in the opposite direction from Kelly's tent, until he was certain that the darkness would have finally concealed him from any unknown observer. Then he stopped and looked at the low sky, catching his breath, trying to still his booming heart.

Now was the time.

Slade unbuckled his trousers, and took his potato-sack mask out of his undershorts. He had kept it there ever since he had fashioned it eight days ago. He had developed a rather severe rash on his testicles and stomach from continuous abrasive contact with the burlap, but he did not care. All that mattered was that no one had yet seen the mask—and no one *would* see it in connection with Lieutenant Richard Slade. Only Kelly would see it and know who was behind it. Then the bastard would die.

Now was the time.

Slade pulled the scratchy mask over his head. He buckled his trousers and took the heavy black revolver from his pocket. His hands trembled. To steady his nerves, he opened his mouth and sucked in a deep breath. He nearly choked on a mouthful of burlap. He spat it out, coughed, sneezed, and began to wonder if this was really a good idea.

But, yes, it was essential that he go through with it. If the unit was to organize and fight the Germans, that organization had to begin right away. There was no time for equivocation; Major Kelly must die. Slade must blow his head off and assume command. Tonight.

Now was the time.

He started for the eastern edge of the camp where he

could follow the trees southward until he was behind Kelly's tent.

But he kept bumping into things. In less than ten steps, he bumped into a lumber pile. He recoiled from that only to bump into the blade of the D-7 dozer a moment later. Ten feet beyond the dozer, he walked into the collapsible loading crane and gave himself a knot on the forehead. Trying to be more careful, he walked with his hands out in front of him like a blind man feeling his way—and he fell into the seven-foot-deep main bunker from which the roof had been stripped two days ago. Work on the fake structure which would stand on the bunker had been postponed in favor of other projects, but in his blood lust Slade had forgotten about that. It was almost as if he were *trying* to walk into things. He *wasn't* trying to walk into things, of course. It was just damned difficult to see where he was going in the dark with a burlap bag over his head.

Getting painfully to his feet, surprised that he had broken no bones, he stuck his revolver in his pocket, and pulled himself out of the abandoned bunker. His shoulder ached; his head ached; he had twisted his ankle. Yet he would not give up. Outside again, on his hands and knees, he tugged the mask into place and looked around.

The tent site was silent. He could not recall if he had cried out when the ground dropped from under him. But even if he had, he had apparently not been loud enough to wake any of the men. Good. Now was the time.

Once more, he hobbled toward the eastern arm of the forest.

Petey Danielson was in the dream, sitting in a mystic, cross-legged pose, his glistening intestines spilled all over his lap. He dug his hands into them, trying to stuff his guts back into his torso. . . .

Finally, Kelly woke, gagging, sweaty, his hands fisted. In a few minutes, when he retained only a vague impression of the nightmare, he became aware of a pressure in his bladder. Because he felt as if Danielson's spirit were lingering within the tent, he decided fresh air and a good piss were exactly what he needed. He got up and went outside.

The best way to get around while wearing a burlap bag over your head, Slade discovered, was to crawl on your hands and knees. He had learned this valuable lesson after walking into three trees. By the time he reached the corner of the clearing where the southern and eastern arms of the forest met, he was shuffling along quite nicely on all fours, making good time.

Slade figured he was wearing holes in his trousers, but he did not care. He cared only about blood. Kelly's blood.

In five minutes, he stopped directly behind Kelly's tent, his back to the woods. He knelt there, surveyed the camp, found it as quiet and still as it had been when he started his journey. A thrill of murderous anticipation coursed through him.

Now was the time.

He got to his feet, and as he did he heard movement behind him in the trees. Before he was fully erect and could turn to face the danger, Major Kelly collided with him, and they both fell down. Hard.

Falling, Kelly was surprised to see, by the weak light of the moon, that he had walked into a man wearing a potato sack over his head.

The man in the sack was so surprised he screamed.

"What the hell—" Kelly got shakily to his feet.

When he fell, the man in the bag had been trapped between Kelly and the trees. Now, he pushed up, whirled away from Kelly, and ran. He crashed headlong into a baby oak, staggered backwards, stunned by the collision.

"Hey!" Kelly said, his balance regained.

The man in the bag recoiled from the sound of the major's voice and plunged deeper into the woods. Flailing at the bushes on all sides, he tripped on a tangle of vines and fell into a cluster of milkweed plants.

"You there!" Kelly shouted.

Stumbling to his feet, slapping at his own face as if he were angry with himself, the man started to run again. He got five feet before he took a low hanging pine branch across the neck and very nearly killed himself.

"I don't understand," Kelly said.

Coughing horribly, the man in the bag pushed past the offending tree. In a few steps, he hit a thrusting outcropping of waterworn limestone and went head over heels down a small hill, out of sight.

Major Kelly stood there for several minutes, listening to the man smash and batter his way with brutal and self-destructive force farther into the barely yielding forest. Eventually, the noises grew faint, fainter still, and faded away altogether.

Confused, Kelly returned to his tent and stretched out on his sleeping bag. But he could not sleep now.

The Germans were drawing nearer by the minute, and already there were too many of his men with severe neuroses that required him to waste precious time away from the construction of the fake village. There was Angelli mooning after Nurse Pullit, and Beame daydreaming about a girl he could not have, and Hagendorf drunk and unpredictable . . . and now there was this striking new direction which Lieutenant Slade's madness had taken, this running around in the middle of the night wearing an old potato sack over his head. . . . He had known, watching the man in the bag nearly kill himself in the woods, that it was Slade. But knowing did not help. He still could not explain this new streak in the lieutenant's psychosis. All it could mean was more trouble.

And they already had more trouble than they could handle.

# 9/

Major Kelly spent all morning running from one end of the clearing to the other, checking up on the work crews and solving construction problems with a rapidity and cleverness he had never known he possessed. Nothing could stump him. It was exhilarating—and it was killing him.

Half the engineering problems should have gone to Beame, but the lieutenant was not functioning at his best level. He probably would not be all right again until he found a way to bypass Maurice and get to Nathalie. The girl really *was* a gorgeous little piece, Kelly thought. But how could Beame let her good looks get between him and the job at hand? Didn't he realize that death was staring them in the face and preparing to bite their heads off?

Most everyone else realized this. With the midnight deadline swiftly approaching, the other men worked harder and faster than they had ever worked in their lives. The camp, the slowly fleshing skeleton of the fake village, hummed with fear and dread. The brutal sun cut through the clouds and made the earth sizzle, but not even that could burn away the cold sweat on the backs of their necks. Beame was about the only goldbricker today.

Besides Angelli, of course. Vito was *supposed* to be working on the crisis that had arisen with the village school. The two-story building, which was framed completely and walled on three sides, had begun to sway slightly in the wind and threatened to collapse now that it was nearly done. Angelli should have been exploring the beams in the school roof—which only he could do quickly and surely—and should have been directing his workers toward the trouble spots he found. Instead, Angelli was up at the hospital bunker romancing Nurse Pullit. As a result, his French work crew stood idle. And the men waiting to finish the siding job on the school were also put behind schedule.

Kelly ran the whole way to the hospital, cursing Angelli's neuroses and his romantic Italian blood. When he came through the bunker door, he saw the lovebirds pressed into the corner on his right. They were giggling. Vito was trying to unhook Nurse Pullit's bra through the thin, silky fabric of her uniform.

"*Vito*!"

Angelli jumped back and dropped his hands from Pullit, looked as shamefaced as a small boy caught at the cookie jar. Nurse Pullit blushed and made a show of straightening the rumpled white dress.

"You come with me," Kelly said, turning and stalking out of the bunker. When he had Angelli outside, marching him back to the school, he said, "This has *got* to stop."

The private scratched the tattoo on his chest.

"The Panzers are coming, Angelli!" Kelly shouted, spraying spittle all over the private's face. "We've no time for this sort of thing!"

"I can't be away from her for more than a few minutes at a time," Angelli said. "I can't bear it for longer."

Kelly was enraged. "Pullit is not a woman! Get that through your head!"

"She's the kind of woman I always wanted to marry," Angelli said, as if he had not heard the major. "She's witty, vivacious, and yet shy. I'd never be ashamed to introduce her as my wife."

Kelly frowned. "Vito—"

"Don't get the idea I'm only interested in her mind and personality," Vito said, nudging Kelly in the ribs as they walked toward the school. "She has fantastic legs, a nice round ass, beautiful big jugs—"

"That's just one of Lily's bras. Those aren't real jugs. Those—"

"And she has such a lovely face," Angelli said. He sighed.

"Angelli," Kelly said, with proper gravity, "you haven't—"

"I certainly haven't!" Angelli said, scandalized by the suggestion. "It isn't that I haven't *wanted* to. She *does* excite me. But she's a virgin, and I just could not take advantage. . . . Well, I know you just caught me trying to take off her bra, but that wasn't anything serious. I wouldn't have pressured her into going the whole way. Mostly, we've just held hands. She's too innocent a woman for me to—"

Kelly put a new strength in his voice. "Nurse Pullit is not a woman. She—"

"She's almost a saint," Angelli said. "I know, sir. She is not an ordinary woman. Not at all. She's a living saint!"

Kelly gave up on Angelli. There was no reasoning with the private just now. They reached the school building, which was still swaying in the wind, and Kelly said, "I'm not going to try to explain to you the truth about Pullit. I just want you to find the trouble with this building and get it fixed. *Now!* Fast, Angelli. And if you run back to the hospital before you're done, I'll shoot your balls off. You won't be any good to Pullit or anyone else, ever." Wasting precious minutes. . . .

The afternoon was both good and bad. Five new outhouses were built. But Sergeant Coombs got into a fight with a French worker. The roof and porch roof were added to the rectory. But a truck hauling prefabricated walls had engine trouble, and its shipment was delayed an hour. The church took shape, and the pews—borrowed from a chapel outside of Eisenhower—fit in perfectly. But Coombs got into a fight with another Frenchman and tipped over a mixer of precious concrete.

Major Kelly shrugged off the good reports and brooded about each scrap of bad news.

At six o'clock, as the afternoon gave way to evening, he was brooding about the concrete which Sergeant Coombs had spilled. He stood at the top of the convent steps, watching the workers swarm over the church and the rectory across the street. Men came to him with problems which he quickly solved. Occasionally, he looked eastward to see if Angelli was still guiding his French work crew.

He was watching Vito when Danny Dew drove the D-7 onto the bridge road and roared down through the center of town, throwing up a wake of yellow dust. Dew stopped in front of the convent. He left the dozer running, jumped off, and came up the steps two at a time.

"What's wrong?" Kelly asked.

If a black man could look pale and drawn, Danny Dew was pale and drawn. His eyes were wide, glazed with fear. "Major . . . there's a rumor going around. . . ." He was unable to put his fear into words.

"Danny? What's wrong?"

Dew leaned against the railing and shuddered, wiped the back of one hand across his mouth. "There's a rumor going around that you traded the D-7—for more help from Maurice."

"Well," Major Kelly lied, "it's *only* a rumor, Danny. I didn't do any such thing. I know what the dozer means to you."

"I got to have the D-7," Danny said. "Nobody can take that away from me, Kelly. I'd die. I'd wither up and die."

Kelly patted Dew's shoulder. "I know, Danny. I wouldn't pull something like that. Besides, we *need* the dozer. I couldn't afford to give it away." He was a bit surprised at how smoothly the lies came out, how sincere he sounded.

Danny began to regain control of himself. The shakes grew less severe, and some of the terror left his eyes. "You serious?"

"Danny, you know I would never—"

In the same instant, both men heard the change in the sound of the dozer's engine. It was no longer just idling. They turned as one and looked down the convent steps.

Emil Hagendorf sat in the driver's chair, holding down on

the brake pedal while he pumped the accelerator. The big machine rocked and groaned beneath him. He laughed, waved at Kelly and Dew.

"Stop him!" Kelly shouted, leaping down the steps.

Emil let up on the brakes.

The bulldozer lurched forward. The steel track seemed to spin for a moment, kicking up dust and chunks of macadam.

Major Kelly jumped from the fourth step and landed feet-first on the wide band of tread. He waved his arms, trying desperately to maintain his balance. The dozer was moving even as he reached it, and he was dragged forward like a man on a horizontal escalator belt.

"Emil, stop!" he shouted.

Hagendorf looked over at him and laughed.

Kelly backpedaled, trying to keep from being tossed in front of the dozer and chewed into tiny pieces. His feet slipped on the knobbed tread as it flashed under his feet. He felt as if he were walking across a spinning sheet of ice in the center of a pitching sea.

Pulling the wheel hard to the right, Hagendorf took the dozer off the bridge road. Under the engine noise, there was no longer the clatter of steel meeting a paved surface.

Kelly did not look up to see where they were going. All of his attention was concentrated on the grinding, steel caterpillar belts. He stretched out, grabbed the roll-bar which rose behind Hagendorf, and pulled himself onto the dozer frame, away from the deadly tread.

"Welcome aboard!" Hagendorf shouted.

He was drunk.

Holding onto the roll-bar, Kelly wedged himself into the same meager niche he had occupied while inspecting the village with Danny Dew a couple of days ago. He bent down and screamed in the chief surveyor's ear. "Stop this thing, damn you!"

Hagendorf giggled. "Maybe that will stop us," he said, taking one hand from the vibrating steering wheel long enough to point to something ahead of them.

Kelly followed the extended finger. "*Hagendorf, no!*"

An instant later, the dozer plowed into the side of one of the single-story platform houses. The place came apart like a paper construction. The wood broke, splintered, gave way. They surged through the wall. The platform cracked and came apart under them, fodder for the ferocious tread. They drove the whole way across the room as the roof dipped slowly toward them, then crashed out through the opposite wall in a shower of pine planking, nails, and heavy beams.

Hagendorf was laughing like hell. A splinter had caught him on the left cheek bad enough to let a steady stream of blood course down his face and drip off his chin. Otherwise, he appeared unscathed.

Major Kelly did not know if he had been hurt himself, and he did not look to see. "Emil, you'll kill yourself!" he screamed.

"You killed me already!" the surveyor yelled. "You and your chaos!"

"You'll kill *me*!"

"Jump."

"Emil, we *need* this machine."

"And *I* need a sense of order!"

The dozer slammed straight into an outhouse. It started to climb the board wall, but then the building went down. Kelly was almost flung out of his niche. The dozer dropped squarely back onto its tread, rattling his teeth. With his left hand, he got a tighter grip on the roll-bar, squeezing it so hard that his knucklebones looked as if they would pop through his skin. The narrow outhouse crumpled into useless pieces as they drove over it.

Hagendorf angled sharply toward the river.

Toward the ravine.

He pushed down on the accelerator.

"No!" Kelly screamed.

The major let go of the roll-bar and threw himself at the chief surveyor, tore Hagendorf's right hand from the steering wheel, punched and gouged the pudgy man until he had climbed atop him. Hagendorf was sitting on the driver's chair, facing front; and Kelly was sitting on Hagendorf, facing the other way, looking directly into the smaller man's bloodshot eyes. The major used his elbow to chop at Hagendorf's left arm until the surveyor finally let go of the wheel altogether.

Unguided, the D-7 roared toward the ravine, straight for the steepest part of the bank.

Kelly hated to be brutal, but he knew the situation called for extreme measures. He punched Hagendorf's face again and again. Blood streamed out of the smaller man's nose.

Hagendorf kept trying to reach around the major and grab the untended steering wheel. He did not trade blow for blow, but concentrated only on regaining control of the bulldozer.

"Give up, dammit!" Kelly shouted.

The chief surveyor would not give up. Even though Kelly had him pinned to the seat, he struggled forward, blinking back tears and blowing bloody bubbles out of both nostrils.

Behind him, Kelly knew, the ravine was drawing closer. Any moment, they might plunge over the edge. . . .

He punched Hagendorf in the mouth. And again. The pudgy man's lips split open. In an impossible, curious slow motion, a single tooth slid out of Hagendorf's mouth, rolled over his ruined lower lip. It came to rest on his round chin, pasted there by a sticky film of blood.

"Please, Emil! Please, give up!"

Hagendorf shook his head. No.

The dozer jolted over something. For a second, Kelly was sure they had plummeted over the ravine wall. Then the dozer rumbled on.

The major struck Hagendorf again, battering him around the ears now. And, at last, the chief surveyor slumped back against the brace behind the seat, unconscious.

*Thank God. Thank you, Emil.*

Kelly reached behind and grabbed the wheel. Using

that to steady himself, he managed to turn around and—at the same time—keep the unconscious man from sliding off the dozer. When he had the wheel in both hands, he used his buttocks to pin the surveyor in place, then looked up.

The ravine was no more than ten yards away.

He stomped on the brake pedal.

Trying to rear up, the bulldozer lurched like a wounded horse in a bad cowboy movie and almost threw them off.

Kelly held on for both of them. He wheeled the machine away from the gorge and braked again.

They came to a shuddering, clanking halt parallel to the drop-off, two feet from the edge of the precipice. Below, the river gushed between its banks, dark and somewhat evil now that the angle of the sun denied it light.

Kelly looked once at the foaming water and the jagged rocks, looked once at the twenty-four inches of earth which separated him from death—then promptly turned his attention elsewhere. He looked back the way they had come, saw the ruined platform house and the demolished outhouse. Both would have to be rebuilt. . . . Neither was a particularly difficult piece of work, yet he felt this was the last setback they could endure. Each minute counted—but thanks to Emil Hagendorf's wild ride, each minute would not count for enough.

Kelly looked at his watch. Almost seven o'clock. The Germans would be here in five hours. Maybe sooner.

It could not be done.

Nevertheless, you had to *pretend* you were going to hang on, even if you were a character in a fairy tale about death. If you stopped pretending, you were sure to die.

He climbed down from the dozer, already composing a list of jobs that might be speeded up in order to obtain workers for the rebuilding of the two structures which Hagendorf had knocked down.

"My big D!" Danny Dew shouted, running toward the dozer. "My big D was hurt!"

Major Kelly ignored Dew. He walked back toward the platform house which Emil Hagendorf had driven through. It was a jumble of broken beams and splintered boards.

Two dozen of his own men and forty or fifty Frenchmen had gathered at the wreckage and were spiritedly discussing Hagendorf's wild ride. Now, they crowded around Kelly, jabbering excitedly.

The major gave them the cold eye, then the tight lips, then the very serious frown—all to no avail. Finally, he just screamed at the top his voice, "*Shut up! Shut up!*" When the laughing and jabbering ceased, he said, "What in the name of God are you idiots doing here? Why aren't you *working?* Why are you wasting time? What are you laughing about? This is serious!" He felt as if his insides were all rising into his skull and would soon explode out of the top of his head. And he was almost looking forward to that. "We have less than five goddamned hours! Move your asses! *I'll kill any son of a bitch who isn't back to work in one minute!*"

There must have been something particularly ferocious in his voice. Although he was known as a man with no talent for discipline, the workers stared at him for a brief moment, then turned and ran.

Too soon, the sunset came in a glorious splash of orange and red. The red deepened into purple.

Night fell. Kelly could almost hear the crash.

It was 9:30 before any workers were available for the reconstruction of the platform house and the outhouse which Hagendorf had knocked down. Even then, Kelly could find only four of his own men and six Frenchmen who had finished their other chores.

By ten o'clock, the damaged platform was patched enough to support the crude framework for the one-story house. Twenty minutes later, that frame was in place, except for the roof beams.

"We'll make it!" Lyle Fark told Kelly.

"No, we won't."

"We only need another hour, at most. We'll be done half

an hour before the Germans arrive—plenty of time left to change into our French clothes and hide these fatigues."

"What if the Panzers get here early?" Major Kelly asked.

While Fark and the other men hammered more frantically than ever, Kelly rounded up eleven more workers who had completed their job assignments. They were weary, sore, stiff, bruised, and full of complaints. Nevertheless, they worked on the reconstruction of the damaged building.

The road to the east remained deserted. But the Panzers could not be more than a few miles away.

Occasionally, Major Kelly imagined that he could hear the great machines and the clattering steel treads. . . . "Faster! Faster, faster!" he urged whenever the ghostly tanks rumbled in the back of his mind. "Faster!"

But it was a command his men had heard too often in the last few days. It no longer registered with them, had no effect. Besides, they were already working as fast as they possibly could.

At ten minutes of eleven, Lyle Fark said, "The roof's almost done. We have to put the windows in, then clean up the place. But we can do it. I told you we could do it."

Kelly shrugged. "It doesn't matter. We're all dead anyway. The krauts will see through this in ten minutes. Or less."

A window frame was raised to a precut hole in the prefabricated wall, nailed into place.

"You keep saying we haven't a chance," Fark said. "If you really believe that we're doomed to fail—why have you worked us so hard to get the village done?"

"What else was there to do?" Kelly asked.

# 10/

Major Kelly thought he looked like a genuine priest. He was wearing sturdy, well-kept black shoes with extra-thick wartime rubber soles and heels. His black trousers were worn but dignified, cut full in the legs and generously cuffed. An almost perfect match for the pants, his black cotton suit jacket was worn at the elbows but was otherwise quite impressive. The vest and clerical collar had been made especially for him, sewn by a woman in Eisenhower, and did most to confirm his image. A black felt hat with a shiny black ribbon band covered his balding head; it was creased and looked fairly old, but it was clearly not the hat of a laborer or farmer. The hat was a size too large for him and came down almost to the tops of his ears, but that only made him look more genuine: a backwoods priest, a man not much of this world.

Yesterday, Kelly had laughed at Maurice's suggestion that he play the town's ranking priest. "My French isn't good enough," Kelly had said.

"At one time," Maurice admitted, "it would not have passed. But in the weeks you have been here, you have recalled your schoolboy French and have learned even more. Naturally, your French would not impress one of my countrymen. He would spot you for a foreigner. But it will sound fine to General Rotenhausen, because his own command of the language is far worse than yours."

"And if one of the other krauts speaks French?"

"Several might," Maurice said. "But none will be fluent in it. Only the German military's elite officers are well enough educated to speak it fluently. And none of them will be in a convoy moving toward the front."

"I don't know. . . ."

Maurice was adamant. "I cannot pretend to be the priest, because Rotenhausen knows me. He knows this is not my village and that I am no holy man. I must not even show my face so long as he is here. And which other of my people would you trust in such a crucial, sensitive role?"

"None," Kelly admitted, glumly.

"Whoever plays the town priest must be able to soothe Rotenhausen and the other German officers. He must make them believe at once that they face no danger in this place, and he must do everything to dissuade them from holding a a building-to-building search before they settle in for the night. I believe you can do all of this," Maurice had said. "As head of the parish and chief resident of the rectory, you will be at the center of the German command the whole night long, where you can discover and eliminate any potential danger to your men."

Reluctantly, Kelly had agreed that he would be the priest. But he had been sure that they were all doomed.

Now, at 11:05 on the night of July 21, shortly before the German force was scheduled to arrive, Kelly looked into the streaked mirror which hung on the wall of the town priest's bedroom, and he decided there was at least a minute chance he would pass. He *did* look pious and religious. And when he spoke in French, to his reflection, he could hardly believe that he had not always been like this: a man of God. Just so the Germans didn't ask for a blessing or a Mass, or even a table grace.

He turned away from the mirror and surveyed the second-floor back bedchamber of the only fully completed house in the entire village. The room was not large, but comfortable. The walls were roughly plastered, white and pleasant except for finger smudges near the door and by the head of the bed, the signs of use which Kelly's men had so meticulously applied only a few hours ago. The bed was full size, the mattress sagging in the middle, framed with a brass headboard and brass posts at the foot. Beside the bed stood a squat nightstand with a chipped enamel knob on its shallow drawer. On the stand was a washbasin and a walnut-encased heirloom clock. The big mahogany dresser stood by the room's only window, the streaked mirror rising from the back of it. The window was tightly covered by a blackout blind which had been taped to the sill. On the wall by the door, a crucifix hung over a religious calendar. The room was simple, neat, lived in.

Too bad, Kelly thought, that the whole village was not this carefully structured and detailed. But that was wishful thinking. Hell, he could even now hear hammers hammering and saws sawing as the workers tried frantically to get the last of the fake houses in shape.

Kelly stepped into the hall and let the bedroom door remain ajar. He went past the other three upstairs rooms, all larger than the one he had left but otherwise identical. At the head of the stairs, he stood in the center of a handwoven rag rug and looked at the rectory altar: two crucifixes, a small plaster statue of the Virgin, a red satin cloth with white lace trim covering the slim pine table on which all these artifacts stood. It was an excellent touch. He even crossed himself, though he was an atheist.

The steps squeaked realistically as he went down to the first floor. Considerable effort had been expended to get the proper noise into them.

The banister along which his hand slid during his descent was worn with use, the grain sharply raised by decades of unconscious polishing. Like all the furniture in the house, the banister came from Eisenhower. Maurice had uprooted it—and other paraphernalia—from his own home, where it had been for sixty years. As payment for this extra service, The Frog wanted nothing more than every item in the unit's possession which he had not already obtained: Sergeant Tuttle's field kitchen and all the cooking utensils; the men's personal revolvers; the tents. . . . Major Kelly had been relieved by the reasonableness of this demand, and he had readily agreed. He had been certain that, at the very least, half a dozen of his men would have to be contracted to Maurice as indentured servants for the rest of their natural lives.

Downstairs, there were more white walls, handmade rugs, religious pictures, and crucifixes. The front room off the porch contained several comfortable chairs, a bench sofa with scattered cushions, a knickknack stand full of more religious articles, a stool by the only window—the glass for which had come from Eisenhower—and a fireplace with logs and tools stacked on the hearth.

The dining room-study combination was half the size of the front room, dark and cloistered. The two narrow windows were covered with blackout blinds as were the windows elsewhere in the house, and the floor was covered by a deep maroon carpet. The furniture was heavy, and there was too much of it. The air here was stuffy. It reminded Kelly of a funeral parlor. Lately, though, *everything* reminded him of funeral parlors.

The downstairs bedroom was small and neat, quite like his room upstairs, except that the bed was not brass. Quite out of character for a priest, he suddenly wondered if he would ever get to put it to Lily Kain on a brass bed.

The kitchen, behind the dining room and bedroom, was large and airy, full of heavy old cabinets, a worktable, and a second dining table with four high-backed chairs.

Kelly walked over to the porcelain sink, which had also come from Maurice's house in Eisenhower, and he worked the handle of the green iron pump. On the sixth stroke, water gushed into the sink.

"Fantastic!" Lieutenant Beame said. He was dressed in coarse gray trousers and shirt with green suspenders and a dirty brown fedora worn back on his head. He was playing a deaf-mute tonight. It was a ludicrous thought. "How can you get water out of a pump when there isn't any well for it to be drawn from?" Beame had not been assigned to the building of the rectory.

"We put a six-foot pit directly under the sink," Kelly explained, watching the last of the short burst of water as it swirled down the drain. The drain fed into a second pit so that the dirty water would not mix with the clean. "Then we lined the pit with concrete, put a tin lid on top, and ran the pump line into the pit."

"And filled the pit with clean river-water," Beame said, smiling appreciatively at Kelly's ingenuity. "But what if *all* the Germans want to wash up? Is there enough water in this pit to draw baths for a dozen officers?"

"No," Kelly said. "But we constructed a crawl space under the house so a man could keep check on the water supply and add to it as it's depleted."

"Who?"

"Lyle Fark's handling that."

"Good man," Beame said. He looked around the kitchen, nodding happily. "We're going to fool them. I know we are, sir."

Beame seemed almost normal. He certainly was not indulging in a lover's daydream right now. "What's happened to you?" Kelly asked. "Did you decide to forget about Nathalie?"

Beame frowned. "No. But I've realized that this hoax isn't going to work unless we put our hearts into it. And if the hoax doesn't work, I'm dead. And if I'm dead, I can't *ever* have Nathalie."

"Wonderful!" Major Kelly said, clapping his hands in delight. "Now you're talking sense. You sound just like me."

"And we *will* fool the krauts," Beame said. "I feel it in my bones."

"I'd feel better if you felt it in your brain," Kelly said.

"We *will* fool them."

"*If* we can maneuver General Rotenhausen into choosing the rectory for his headquarters," Kelly said.

"We can do that."

"And *if* we can keep the Germans from looking into any of the other buildings except the finished ones—rectory, church, convent foyer, village store. . . ."

"You'll do it, sir. You'll outfox them."

Kelly hoped the lieutenant was right. If a German went into one of the other buildings, then the whole scheme would come crashing down around their heads. If the Church's immunity from search and seizure did not protect them tonight, nothing would. And Kelly would never get to put it to Lily Kain on a brass bed. Or on anything at all. "I don't think we have a chance, Beame."

"I pray we do," Beame said. "I pray to God you're wrong."

"Don't pray," Kelly said, running a finger around his tight clerical collar. "I'm an atheist."

"This is no time to be an atheist," Beame said, leaning on the kitchen table.

"It's the *best* time to be an atheist," Kelly said. "If you pray, you get the idea someone's listening. When you get the idea someone's listening, you get the idea someone cares. And when you think someone cares, you're soon sure that your prayers will be answered. And when you think God is going to answer your prayers, you get careless. And some kraut blows your head off."

While Major Kelly was putting on his ecclesiastical suit and while the men were finishing the last few jobs that would make the false community complete, Lieutenant Slade secreted himself in a dense clump of underbrush on the edge of the forest. He settled down to wait for the Panzers. He was not supposed to be in this place at this time. According to Kelly's master plan, he should be spending the night with three other men in one of the false houses. But Slade was not going to play their game anymore. He had plans of his own. . . .

As he lay there, his thoughts drifted and, though he did

not want to think about it, went inevitably to the disastrous assassination attempt he had made on Kelly just last night.

Christ, what a mess!

When he had collided with the major, his heart had nearly stopped. Then, in his frenzy to escape unidentified, he had crashed headlong into that oak, sustaining one of the four worst injuries of the night. Turning from the tree, certain that Kelly was reaching for him, he had taken only a few steps when his ankles caught in a ropy vine, and he fell full length into those milkweed plants. Several swollen pods had burst, spewing thousands of sticky seeds all of which were topped by puffs of airy cotton for the wind to catch and blow away. By the time he had stumbled erect, the milkweed fluff had sheathed his head, filling the eye holes in the potato sack, and totally blinding him. Panicked, he slapped at the stuff, not fully aware of what it was. Behind him, Kelly shouted, so Slade ran again. And that damned branch had slammed across his throat and nearly knocked him to his knees. That was the second of the four worst blows. He felt as if he were being throttled: his ears rang; his tongue popped out of his mouth; and his eyes watered like hydrants. That might even have put an end to his flight if Kelly had not shouted again and reminded him of his danger. Pushing away from the tree—well, he had fallen over that treacherous projection of limestone and rolled down that hill into the blackberry bushes, where he had become tangled in thorny vines. He imagined he heard Kelly again, and he pulled loose of the brambles, turned, and ran. He went some distance before he fell into a lovely half-acre pond in a moody sylvan setting. . . . Sodden, shivering, spitting mud and pond scum, he got up and banged his head into an overhanging limestone shelf. That was the third of his four worst injuries of the night. When he eventually crawled out onto the shore, he was so relieved to be done running, so shattered, prostrate, demoralized, and out of gear that he flung himself flat on his back—and cracked his head on a stone as large as a pony. That was the fourth of his four worst injuries. After that, things got better. In two hours, he reckoned his way out of the forest and back to his tent. There, stripping out of his muddy, bloody, shredded clothes, dropping his disheveled burlap mask into one of his boots, he collapsed on his cot and slept like a dead man.

This morning, upon waking, he had destroyed the burlap mask.

He realized now that he had been thinking like a coward. He should not hide behind a mask when he murdered the major. The act should be open and straightforward. Later, when he won his medals, no one would be able to say he had been devious. He was not just a modern Brutus. He was a hero!

Furthermore, Slade now realized that murdering Kelly yesterday would have been strategically foolish and premature. He had no guarantee that the other men in the unit would fall in behind him and fight the krauts once the major was out of the way. Most of these bastards were as cowardly as Kelly was. They would have inisted on finishing the fake community and trying the hoax without Kelly.

A mosquito buzzed around Slade's head. He crushed it against his cheek, and wiped his bloodied hand on a patch of thick grass.

Out in the phony village, someone risked another lantern in order to have light to work by.

Slade leaned back against a tree trunk and thought about his *new* plan. It was much better than the old plan. . . . He would wait here in the woods until the Germans had settled in for the night. If they didn't see through the hoax at once, he would bide his time until they had posted guards and gone to sleep. Then he would come out of the woods and thoroughly reconnoiter the village. He would learn the position of each sentry, the placement of the main body of troops. He would formulate a plan of attack. And only when that was done would he murder Major Kelly. Then, when the men saw that their situation was desperate, when they had no choice but to strike at the krauts as he ordered—or let him strike alone and less efficiently—they would fall into line. A commando team would slip into the rectory and slit the officers' throats while they slept. Next, they would quietly remove all the sentries. And next . . . well, anything could happen then. But whatever happened, they would be real heroes.

"We'll fool them," Beame insisted. He pointed at the sink, pumps, and cabinets. "Who'd ever suspect this was all thrown together in four days?"

Father Picard, nee Major Walter Kelly, shrugged. He walked over to the kitchen hallway. "I'm giving the town one last inspection. Want to come?" He hoped Beame did not want to come, for the lieutenant's optimism made him uneasy.

"Sure," Beame said.

"It's almost eleven-thirty. The Germans will be here soon. Let's go."

Beame extinguished the kerosene lamp on the table by the front door.

Outside, they crossed the porch, went down the four steps to the brief lawn, which, much abused during the construction, was the least convincing thing about the rectory. The night was muggy and overcast. The crickets were silent.

The rectory stood on the corner of the bridge road and B Street. B Street was one of the two north-south lanes Danny Dew had made with his D-7 dozer, and it was the farthest east of the two. A Street, sister to B, also paralleled the river but was one block closer to the bridge. The two-lane bridge road had become their main street, and diagonally across it from the rectory stood the enormous, three-story, weathered gray convent. To the west side of the house, across the narrow B Street, was the quaint little town church.

Kelly and Beame stood in the middle of the bridge road and looked east toward the break in the trees where the tanks would pass within the hour. The village continued one block in that direction. On the north side as one looked eastward, there were four single-story houses with meager lawns between them, church-owned homes for deaf-mutes. All of the houses were the same inside—hollow, gutted, phony—but differentiated externally by minor details: the size of the porches, condition of the paint, shape of the windows. Though the houses were the same in their dimensions, and though all of their windows were made lightless by identical sets of blackout blinds, they *did* look like separately conceived and constructed dwellings. On the south side of the block, there was only the rectory, rectory lawn, and an outhouse tucked in between two big elms.

The village extended two blocks to the west along the bridge road. The whole north side of the first block beyond the rectory was occupied by the massive convent and its board-fenced yard. Across the street from the convent, again commanding a full block, was the church and churchyard. Then, over beyond A Street and the river, there were a couple of houses and the village store.

Kelly switched on his flashlight and walked north on B Street.

"It looks so *real*, doesn't it?" Beame asked, awestricken.

"Pray the krauts think so," Major Kelly said.

"I thought you told me not to pray."

"That's right," Kelly said. "I almost forgot."

B Street ran only two blocks north-south, half the length of its sister, A Street. The northern block, above the bridge road, was faced with a sixty-foot barrackslike nunnery and a stone well on the east, and with the convent and convent yard fence on the west. Everything was nice and tidy.

From B, they entered Y Street. This was the northernmost of the town's three east-west roads, parallel to the bridge road. It ran one block east, with nothing but two church-owned houses on each side, their outhouses, scattered elms. Across Y Street, facing the mouth of B, stood a fake two-story house in ill-repair.

"Why didn't you give the streets French names?" Beame

asked. "Won't the Germans think it's odd—naming streets after letters of the alphabet?"

Kelly sighed, tugged at his collar. "The letters are for our benefit in a crisis. The krauts won't expect a town this small to have formal street names."

Turning west, they followed Y Street towards the river. On their left was the convent. On the right, there was only open lawn until they reached a two-story fake house at the end of the block. This one was also poorly maintained. Actually, every two-story structure in the village was ugly and decaying—except for the rectory. They did not want Rotenhausen to take a fancy to some building which had no floors inside and no inner walls or furniture. . . . The rectory had to outshine all the others, make a quick and obvious impression.

The second block of Y ended at A Street, which was four blocks long and ran north-south. The first block contained a nunnery and two houses. Kelly shined the flashlight over these, then turned south.

"One thing bothers me," Beame said.

"What's that?"

"Why hasn't the bridge been bombed since we put it up?"

"Well . . . the Allies think they've already knocked it out with that B-17," Major Kelly said. "And the Stukas won't touch it now that they know the *Wehrmacht* wants to use it."

Beame frowned. "If the German air force knows the *Wehrmacht* wants to use the bridge and is cooperating by not bombing us—won't it also have told the convoy to expect to find us here?"

"Maybe not," Kelly said. "There's something *strange* about the Stuka attacks."

"Strange, sir?"

"Remember," Kelly said, "they never bombed *us*, just the bridge. And they always knew when we'd rebuilt it. I don't know what's going on here, but it isn't all jake."

"Jake who?" Beame asked.

"Jake nobody. Just jake."

"He doesn't have a last name?" Beame asked, puzzled.

"*Jake* is an expression," Major Kelly said. "I meant that everything about those Stukas is somehow not right. It's all false."

"Oh," Beame said. "I see. It's not jake."

"Just like General Blade isn't all jake," Kelly said. "At first, I thought he sent us here because he was senile. Lately, I've realized there's got to be more to it than that. I don't know what, though. I wish I did."

The next block of A Street contained a stone well, a sixty-by-forty-foot school for the deaf and, on the east, the fourth wall of the convent yard fence which several workmen were still nailing in place.

And then they reached the bridge road again. To the east was the church and rectory. One block to the west was the bridge. Only three structures fronted the bridge road on that last block: two houses and the church-owned store in which the products and handicrafts of the deaf-mutes were sold to tourists and those in nearby villages. The store was fully completed and stocked with quilts, canned goods, jewelry, clothing, carpentry, and other items which had been taken from Eisenhower and which would be foisted on the Germans as produce of the deaf-mutes if any krauts wandered into the place.

The third block of A, the first south of the bridge road, was faced by two one-story houses on the west. Beneath the first of these was the hospital bunker in which Tooley, Kowalski, Liverwright, and Emil Hagendorf would pass the tense night. Hagendorf would pass the tense night as a prisoner. They had purchased a great deal of wine from Maurice to keep Hagendorf drunk and docile.

On the other side of the block was the churchyard. It was dark and quiet. Kelly could see half a dozen rounded tombstones and the vague outlines of others lying in the deeper shadows. Altogether, Maurice had provided forty-five grave markers which he had borrowed from church and family plots in and around Eisenhower. These had all been set in fresh concrete, over nonexistent graves. More than anything else that had been done, these gave the town a past, an illusion of age and endurance. When Kelly directed the flashlight beam in among them, the sandstone and granite markers gleamed and rose up in chalky skirts from the pools of blue-black shadows on the ground.

The final block of A Street, the southwest corner of the town, held platform houses, sheds, and outhouses. Kelly played his light back there, and he suddenly thought that he and Beame seemed like two watchmen examining a movie lot on their late rounds. They went no farther south.

Z Street was the third east-west lane, south of and parallel to the bridge road and the northernmost Y Street. Z was two blocks long, like Y. On its south side rose a school for normal and deaf-mute children, a stone well, several platform houses built together over what had once been the unit's main bunker. On the north side of Z, the churchyard occupied the first block. The second block contained an open-air shrine to the Virgin Mary, complete with statue and encircling flagstone walkway. Then came three single-story dwellings, all shabby, all with broken-down porches, one with a slightly sagging roof.

"I've been thinking about Blade," Beame said, stopping in the middle of the street. "About his not being all jake. Do you think his being involved in the black market has anything to do with our being sent here?"

Kelly stopped and turned. "Blade's in the black market? How do you know?"

"I don't *know*," the lieutenant said. "But when we were in Britain waiting for D-Day, I heard rumors. I got friendly with junior officers on Blade's staff."

"And they said he dealt in the black market?"

"Implied. They *implied* it."

Kelly thought about that a moment, then shrugged. "I didn't think Blade was smart enough to play that game. But even if he is, what could that have to do with our being sent here?"

"Nothing, I guess. It was just a thought."

They turned from Z into B Street, into the only block they had not yet inspected. On their left was the churchyard and church. On the right was a one-story house with a ratty front lawn, a fence running eastward, and then the rectory and the rectory lawn.

"Back to Square One," Kelly said.

Kelly was impressed with himself and his men, even if all of this *had* been for nothing, even if they *were* doomed. In little more than four days, they had constructed the shells of twenty-five single-story and three two-story houses. They had built one two-story house complete: the rectory. The thirty-foot convent walls had been nailed up, as had the high board fence that surrounded that whole block, and the convent's entrance foyer had been fully finished to provide a place for the German general to pay his respects if he should take it in his head to do so. The shells of two large schools and two nunneries had been thrown up. The church had been built in full, except for the bell tower, which had no stairs or bell . . . and except for the pews which had been borrowed from a country church near Eisenhower. The forty-by-twenty-foot town store had been finished inside and out. They had built another house which Hagendorf had bulldozed to the ground. In addition, they had put up three stone wells, eighteen sheds, twenty-eight outhouses. . . . There were three stables tucked near the woods, horses in each. In some ways, of course, the town was atypical of a French country village. There were no barns in sight, for one thing. And there were no structures made completely of stone. But this *was*, after all, supposed to be mainly a Catholic retreat, a church facility; the Germans could not expect it to look like just any other town. All in all, the accomplishment was enormous, and the patina of reality just thick enough to hoax the Germans. Though, naturally, the Germans would not be hoaxed. They would see through it sometime before dawn. They would kill everyone. Even though he knew he was dead, Major Kelly, alias Father Picard, was impressed with himself and his men.

"It's perfect," Beame said.

"So long as no one goes inside an unfinished building. If anyone does—"

He stopped in midsentence as a sixteen-year-old French boy, Maurice's nephew, roared out of the night on a stolen German motorcycle. The boy came down the bridge road from the east, past the fake houses, his hair streaming in the wind. He had been standing watch on the road, and now there was no doubt what he was shouting above the cycle's chattering engine. "They come! Germans! They come!"

Someone screamed in terror.

Only after the scream died away did Kelly realize it was his own. Get hold of yourself, he thought. It's a fairy tale. Face up to your role. There isn't anything else for you to do.

# 11/

The German convoy's advance motorcycle escort shot out of the trees to the east, doing better than forty miles an hour, heading straight for Major Kelly and the people behind him. It slewed to the right in a puff of dust and gravel, turned broadside in the road, and came to a tire-scorching stop in a cloud of blue smoke. The young *Wehrmacht* soldier driving the cycle and the second man in the sidecar looked stupidly at each other, brows beetled under their pot helmets. They slowly examined the houses and the crowd of French villagers, priests, and nuns which filled the lane only twenty feet ahead.

Kelly almost began to pray, cracked his knuckles instead.

A few of Kelly's people waved. Most remained still and silent, uncommitted to this violent presence.

The soldier in the sidecar pulled a map from between his legs, unfolded it in the light of a hand torch which the driver held for him. A few lanterns burned by the church and rectory, but not enough to help the two Germans. The soldier traced their route with one thick finger on the map, talking to the cyclist as he did so. The driver nodded impatiently and pointed to the crowd in front of them as if to say that the senses could not be denied and the map, therefore, must be all wrong. There *was* a town by the river, despite what the cartographers had drawn.

We're dead, Kelly thought. One of them will be unable to believe the map makers were wrong. That's the German way. Believe the printed word before you believe what the eye shows. . . .

Suddenly, behind the motorcycle, dwarfing it and the houses on the north side of the bridge road, a Panzer jerked forward from the deep forest shadows like a prehistoric saw-toothed reptile smashing its way out of an egg. The wicked black muzzle hole came first, a round mouth in the vaguely illuminated neck of the barrel, a death-spitting orifice that riveted every man's eye. Then came the churning treads, great clattering, banging bands of pitted, bluntly bladed steel that ripped up the broken macadam roadbed and tossed it out behind in fist-sized chunks. Heavy, downsloped tread fenders, thickly coated with mud, shielded most of the tracks from sight but did nothing to soften the terrifying sound of them. The brutally insistent parallel treads snapped and crunched the ground beneath them as a beast might grind up a man's fragile bones in its teeth. Abruptly, the entire tank hove into view: an armadillolike bow with a dragon's middle and stern, scaly and muddy, covered with curious protuberances, green-gray, scarred. The side-hung head lamps had been fitted with blackout caps, permitting only a thin slot of light to lance out from the bottom half of the lenses; the effect was that of a dragon with its eyes slitted while cautiously stalking prey.

Behind the first behemoth came a second. It broke through the trees, growling close at the tail of the leader, eyes slitted too, adding to the cacophony of tread and engines.

As Kelly's eyes adjusted to the scene, he could make out a long line of narrow, blackout headlights stretching to the top of the eastward rise and out of sight. We're all dead, Kelly thought. Mashed. Crushed. All destroyed.

The first Panzer slowed down. Its whirling tracks stuttered noisily. The heavy-duty engines screamed down the musical scale and settled into a deep-throated, unmusical rumble as the tank halted with much shuddering and rattling behind the two soldiers on the motorcycle. Thin white smoke rose lazily from the well-meshed gears inside the tread band, drifted eastward.

Behind the first tank, the second tank stopped as well, rocking back and forth for a few seconds as its frame worked against its tracks. Along the sloping highway, out to the undefined crest of the dark hillside, the rest of the convoy came to a standstill.

Major Kelly, or Father Picard as he must now be, was out in front of the other villagers by a full yard. He looked up at the shelved front of the Panzer and wondered what in hell he was doing here. They were all dead. Crushed. Mashed. And worse. Why in the name of the God he didn't believe in —why had they not run away?

And then he remembered why. They were behind German lines. There was nowhere for them to run.

On the rectory steps, Lieutenant Beame looked from the tanks to the convent where Nathalie was standing in a nun's habit. He was suddenly, incredibly terrified of losing her. Why had he let Maurice put him off? Why hadn't he knocked that fat old frog on his ass and taken Nathalie? Why hadn't he reacted to Maurice like a man? This was the perfect woman. Nathalie was what he had always dreamed about—and more. They were perfect for each other both spiritually and, he was somehow certain, sexually. He wanted her more than he had ever wanted the other women of his dreams—Betty Grable, Veronica Lake, Lana Turner, Marlene Dietrich, Dorothy Lamour, Ann Sheridan, Rita Hayworth, Hedy Lamarr, Jane Russell, Esther Williams, Greta Garbo, Katharine Hepburn, Ginger Rogers, Mae West, Barbara Stanwyck, cute little Mary Astor, the Andrews Sisters whom he had wanted to assault all at the same time, Bonita Granville, Gene Tierney. . . . Nathalie was more desirable than all of those women put together. And now he had lost her. His optimism had vanished in the face of the German power; and he felt certain that he would never see the sun rise.

Standing on the convent steps in her nun's habit, Lily Kain reacted to the Panzers much as Beame had done. She imagined that she could smell death in the muggy night air. She wished Kelly could have found the time to put it to her today. Maybe the sight of these huge war machines would have been easier to take if she had had it put to her recently. Sighing, she raised both hands and waved at the Germans in order to keep from throwing up her nun's habit and diddling herself.

The officer commanding the first Panzer, General Adolph Rotenhausen, clambered out of the hatch and down the side of his tank, stood for a moment on the muddy tread fender. He was a tall, whiplike man, not an ounce overweight. His face was square and harsh, though the features were in no way brutish. There was aristocracy in his heritage; it showed in his carriage and in his thin-lipped smile. His hair was cut close to his head, a white-blond cap that caught the light from the scattered lanterns and gleamed with it. He jumped from the fender and walked swiftly toward Major Kelly.

# PART FOUR

# Deception

## Midnight—Dawn / July 22, 1944

# 1/

When he led them down to the front room after inspecting the second floor, General Rotenhausen stood with his back to the fireplace, his hands folded behind him even though there was no fire to warm them at this time of the year. Rotenhausen looked as if he desperately needed warmth. He was a bloodless man, as pale as linen. He smiled coldly at Major Kelly. There was no threat in his smile; it was just that Rotenhausen was incapable, even in the best of times, of a smile that was not icy. "Well, Father Picard, you have a most pleasant home. It will serve splendidly as our overnight headquarters." His French was less than middling, but so far as Kelly was concerned his sentiment was absolutely perfect.

Kelly smiled and nodded, twisted his black felt hat in both hands. He wondered if a French priest would treat a German general as an equal or as a superior. The point was academic, really, because he was too terrified to be anything but obsequious and subservient. "I am pleased you like it, sir," he said.

"Standartenführer Beckmann and I will require the two largest upstairs rooms. My aides could be quartered in the small front room. And the Standartenführer's aides could sleep down here, in the bedroom by the kitchen." Rotenhausen turned to the black-uniformed SS colonel who sat on the bench sofa. He smiled, and this time he *did* put a threat into it. "Have you any objections to these arrangements, Standartenführer?"

The SS officer was even more the Aryan ideal than General Rotenhausen. He was six-three, two hundred and thirty pounds. Like the slim *Wehrmacht* general, he was in perfect condition; however, unlike Rotenhausen, Beckmann was muscular. His legs were strong and sturdy and looked as if they had been poured into his black trousers and knee-length leather jackboots. His hips and waist were flat. The Standartenführer's neck was a thick, bullish stem of gristle, hard muscle, and raised veins. His face was a sharply featured square with a long brow, deep-set eyes, a Roman nose, and lips as thin as pencil lines. He was perhaps forty years old, but he was not touched by age in any way; he looked as fresh and young as one of his aides. And as nasty. His face was pale like Rotenhausen's face, but his eyes were a lighter blue, so sharp and clear they seemed transparent.

Beckmann returned Rotenhausen's ugly smile. "I think the arrangements will be satisfactory. But I do wish you would drop the clumsy *Schutzstaffeln* title and call me 'Oberst' instead." Beckmann looked at Kelly and shook his head sadly. "General Rotenhausen is such a one for form. Since we left Stuttgart, he has insisted on using the clumsy title." Beckmann's French was no better than Rotenhausen's.

"Standartenführer Beckmann is correct," the general said, directing himself to Kelly. "I am a man who believes in forms, rules, and dignity. Being a man of the Holy Roman Church, you must sympathize with me, Father Picard."

"Yes, of course," Kelly said.

"The Church relies on rules and form quite as much as the *Wehrmacht*," Rotenhausen said.

"Certainly, certainly," Kelly said, nodding stupidly.

Major Kelly sensed the friction between the two officers and thought he understood at least part of the reason for it. In the last year the German army, the *Wehrmacht*, had begun to lose nearly all of its battles to superior Allied forces. Meanwhile, the *Waffen* SS, the independent army which the SS had built despite *Wehrmacht* objections to this usurpation of its role, was still winning battles. Therefore, Hitler had begun to trust more in the *Waffen* SS and less in the *Wehrmacht*. The traditional army lost power, while the

*Waffen* SS grew larger and more formidable. Hitler favored the *Waffen* SS in every case: officer promotions, weapons development, funds, weapons procurement, the requisitioning of supplies. . . . And now as the Allies pressed closer to the fatherland, Hitler had given the SS permission to observe and oversee selected *Wehrmacht* units. A contingent of these black-uniformed fanatics now often accompanied a traditional army unit into battle—not to help it fight the enemy, but to be sure it fought exactly according to the *Führer*'s orders. Naturally, the *Wehrmacht* hated the SS, and the SS hated the *Wehrmacht*. This was interservice rivalry carried to a dangerous extreme.

Kelly suspected that this institutionalized hatred was compounded by a deep personal antagonism between Rotenhausen and Beckmann. Indeed, he had the strong feeling that neither man would hesitate to kill the other if the time was ripe and the opportunity without peril. And that was no good. If the krauts were so insane that they were ready to kill each other, how much closer must they be to ruthlessly slaughtering innocent French villagers, priests, and nuns who got in their way?

Kelly twisted his hat more furiously, wringing it into a shapeless lump of sweat-stained felt.

"Too much attention to rules and form makes dull minds and witless soldiers," Beckmann said. He tried to make it sound like the prelude to a pleasant debate, but the goad was quite evident. "Wouldn't you say that is true, General?" Beckmann asked. He knew that, while Rotenhausen outranked him, the terror induced by the SS image would keep the other officer from responding as he might have to a subordinate officer in the *Wehrmacht*. "Don't you want to venture an opinion, *Kamerad* Rotenhausen?" He used the *Kamerad* only to taunt the General, who was not a member of the Nazi Party.

"*Gewiss, Sagen Sie mir aber, bekomme ich einen Preis, wenn meine Antworten richtig sind?*" The general's voice contained a note of sarcasm which even Kelly could hear.

The major had no idea what Rotenhausen had said. But the tone of voice had made Beckmann pale even more. His lips drew tight and curved in a vicious rictus as he fought to control his temper.

Kelly nearly tore his hat to shreds.

"*Nein,*" Beckmann told the general. He maintained his false serenity with a bit more ease now. "*Sie bekommen keinen Preis. . . .*"

Rotenhausen smiled slightly. Whatever the nature of the brief exchange, however meaningless it had been, the *Wehrmacht* officer plainly felt that he had gained the advantage.

But around Beckmann, the air seemed charged with a very real if well restrained violence.

The two *Wehrmacht* oberleutnants who were Rotenhausen's aides stood at attention by the door to the kitchen hallway. They exchanged angry looks with an SS Hauptsturmführer and an Obersturmführer, Beckmann's aides who stood stiffly by the front door.

Though he was unaware of the fine points of the situation, Major Kelly knew that he must change the subject, get the two men thinking about something besides each other. "Will there be more officers who will require quality lodging for the night?" he asked Rotenhausen.

The general seemed to be relieved to have an excuse to break off his staring match with Beckmann. "Other officers? But already we have put out the other priests who live here, rousted your housekeeper from her room. We would not want to inconvenience you even further."

"It would be no inconvenience," Kelly said. "And . . . will your men want shelter for the night in the homes of my people?"

"Not at all," Rotenhausen said, dismissing the suggestion with a wave of his hand. "We would not dispossess nuns and deaf-mutes for the convenience of soldiers. Besides, Father Picard, I am known as a tough commander. My men must be constantly battle-hardened. They've had too much good living in Stuttgart. It is time they slept out and endured a bit of hardship."

"If it should rain—" Kelly began.

"So much the better for them!" Rotenhausen said. He was, Kelly thought, putting on quite a show for the Standartenführer.

Trying not to pray, Kelly turned to Beckmann. "And your men, sir? Will they require lodging tonight?"

Beckmann's broad face was set like a lump of concrete. "You know little about the *Schutzstaffeln*, Father Picard. I have but fifteen men with me—however, each one is tougher, more dedicated, more battle-hardened than any five other troopers the Third Reich commands." He looked at Rotenhausen and cracked a concrete smile. "Present company excepted, of course." To Kelly, he said, "My men will sleep out by the side of the road with the rest of the convoy. If rain should come, it will not perturb them, Father."

Major Kelly twisted his hat and hoped that the meager light from the two large kerosene lanterns would not reveal the immense relief that must be evident in his face. Yesterday, he had decided that it would be best to offer the krauts shelter in order not to seem suspiciously secretive about the town's houses and schools. Of course, had either Rotenhausen or Beckmann accepted the offer, the hoax would have fallen down like a village of cards. In this respect, their personal feud and the interservice rivalry between the SS and the *Wehrmacht* had worked to Kelly's advantage. Neither wanted himself or his men to appear weak and soft in the other's eyes. And thus far, neither had mentioned the necessity for a building-to-building search. They were so involved in their reciprocal hatreds that they might actually blunder through this whole long night without even suspecting the secreted enemy around them.

Kelly almost smiled at this thought—and then realized that he was indulging in hope. The deadly disease. If you hoped, you died. It was that simple, but he had forgotten.

He began to tremble twice as badly as he had done, scared witless.

Rotenhausen took a pipe from his shirt pocket, a thin tin of tobacco from his trousers. As he prepared his pipe, he stared at the top of Beckmann's head and discussed the procedure for standing down the convoy until dawn. "The Panzers should be parked on both sides of the road, at least twenty feet between them. Likewise, the trucks and artillery wagons. Only the 88 mm guns and the antiaircraft kliegs should remain on the road where they have a good base for counterattack in the event of a raid. No vehicles will be pulled into St. Ignatius; there is no need to jeopardize nuns and deaf-mutes." He finished tamping the tobacco. "We will post guards at all the intersections. Two-hour watches. Would you care to commit any of your men to this enterprise, Standartenführer?"

"Certainly, *Kamerad*," Beckmann said. He propped his jackboots on a small table before the sofa. "We will take responsibility for the bridge."

"Good enough," Rotenhausen said. He looked past Kelly at the two *Wehrmacht* junior officers who waited by the hall door. In German, he gave them orders for the bedding down of the convoy.

Even while Rotenhausen was speaking, Beckmann gave his stone-faced aides their orders for the establishment of an all-night guard patrol on the bridge.

One *Wehrmacht* soldier left, and one remained.

One *Schutzstaffeln* man left, and one remained.

Major Kelly, standing in the middle of it all, sweating profusely and methodically destroying his hat, thought that this was like some complex game of chess in which real men were the pieces. Clearly, the rules were elaborate.

Having lighted his pipe, puffing calmly on it, the warm bowl gripped in one hand so tightly that it betrayed his studied nonchalance, General Rotenhausen said, "Father Picard, with your kind permission, I will have my aide start a fire in the kitchen stove and heat some water for my bath."

"Certainly! Be my guest, General, sir," Kelly said in mediocre French. "But first–" He sighed. He knew this might precipitate disaster, but he said, "My people will be wanting to get back to their beds. Could you tell me when you will want to search the village?"

Rotenhausen took his pipe from his mouth. Smoke rose between his lips. "Search the town, Father? But whatever for?"

Kelly cleared his throat. "I am quite aware that not all Frenchmen are as uncommitted in this war as those in St. Ignatius. I would understand if you wished to search for partisans."

"But you have no partisans here, do you?" Rotenhausen asked, taking a few short steps from the stone fireplace, halving the distance between them.

"This is chiefly a religious community," Kelly said. Remembering how convincing Maurice could be when he was lying, Kelly clutched at his heart. "God forbid that the Holy Church ever take sides in an earthly conflict of this sort."

Rotenhausen smiled, stuck his pipe between his teeth again. He spoke around the slender stem. "You call this village St. Ignatius?"

"Yes, sir," Kelly said.

"And how many people live here, did you say?"

Beckmann sat on the sofa, watching, face expressionless.

Major Kelly could not see the purpose in Rotenhausen's asking questions to which he already had the answers. But he responded anyway. "Less than two hundred souls, sir."

"And the town is built around a convent of some sort?" Rotenhausen asked, smiling and nodding encouragingly.

He did not *look* like a man who would lead a backwoods French priest into a deadly admission and then blow his head off with four shots from a Luger. Nevertheless, he must be dealt with cautiously.

"The convent was here first," Kelly said, cautiously. "The deaf came to be taught. Then the mute. Then deaf-mutes. Other sisterhoods established nunneries here to help with the work. The church was built. Then the store. A few of the laity moved in, built homes, seeking the calm and peacefulness of a religious community." Kelly felt that his knees were melting. In a minute he was going to be writhing helplessly on the floor.

Rotenhausen took his pipe from his mouth and thrust it at Major Kelly. "To tell you the truth, Father, I would like to search your village."

Kelly almost swayed, almost passed out.

"However," the general continued, "I believe it would be a waste of time and effort. My men are weary, Father Picard. And they will soon be expected to fight the Allies. They need what rest they can get." He put the pipe in his mouth and spoke around it. "Furthermore, the Reich is currently in no position to make an enemy of the Catholic Church. If we were to pry through nunneries and church schools looking for partisans, we would only help to force Rome into taking sides, and we would buy even more bad publicity for the German people."

Behind Rotenhausen, Standartenführer Beckmann had gotten to his feet. Lantern light caught the polish on his leather belt, glittered in the death's head insignia on his cap and shoulders. He was an evil, black Frankenstein, his white face slightly twisted, half cloaked in shadows.

Kelly felt sure that Beckmann was going to disagree with the general. He was going to say the search should be held. Then everyone would die. Bang. Bang, bang, bang. The end.

But that was not what Beckmann had in mind. "Perhaps General Rotenhausen has given you the impression that Germany has, in the past, done the wrong thing and that, as a consequence, our country now suffers from a poor image in the rest of the world. I must set you straight, Father. Germany follows the dictates of the *Führer*, and it makes no mistakes." He smiled at Rotenhausen. "There is no need to search St. Ignatius, because the Catholic Church is no enemy of the Reich. Oh, at times, a few of your bishops have acted unwisely. But for the most part, you people have remained neutral. Why, even Himmler is of your faith, Father. Did you know?"

"I didn't know," Kelly murmured.

Standartenführer Beckmann's voice rose as he spoke. "Whether or not a search of St. Ignatius would generate bad publicity for the Reich is purely academic. The main reason we need not hold a search is that—you are all *Catholics* here. Christians. And that means you are not Jews." Beckmann's voice had taken on a strange, chilling urgency. His face was strained, his eyes wild. "The Jews are Germany's only enemies, Father Picard. The Jews, *Mischlingen,* and subhumans are the threat to the race's perfection. When the world is *Judenrein,* then this war will end, and everyone will see that the *Führer* was correct!" He was breathing heavily now. "Free of Jews! How good the world will then be! And your great church recognizes this, Father Picard. It remains neutral. It is no ally of the Reich, but neither is it an enemy."

Clearly, Rotenhausen found Beckmann's mania offensive. He turned away from the Standartenführer and ordered his aide to heat the bath water.

"Father Picard," Beckmann said, even as Rotenhausen was speaking to his man, "how many griddles on the stove?"

"Four," Kelly said. He was aware that the danger had passed, but he was slightly confused.

"My aide will heat water for *my* bath on two of the griddles, if that is all right with you, *Kamerad,*" Beckmann told Rotenhausen.

The general did not like that. But Beckmann's display of Nazi psychosis was enough to make him wary and, in fact, somewhat afraid of the SS colonel. "I suppose that will be fine," he said.

The aides rushed for the kitchen, nearly colliding in the narrow hall.

"Dear Father Picard," Rotenhausen said, "I believe we will not need you any more tonight. You may sleep in your own room. Tomorrow, please offer my apologies to your junior priests for our having had to put them out."

"I will do that, General," Kelly said. "Sleep well," he said, nodding his head vigorously to both of them and bowing in an oriental fashion as he backed toward the stairs.

That was when he fell over the chair. When he backed into it, he thought he had somehow bumped into one of the soldiers, though there were no more men in the room. The knobs at the top of the backrest felt like gun barrels in his kidneys. He cried out, staggered forward, tripped, and fell.

Rotenhausen and Beckmann rushed over and helped him to his feet. "Are you hurt, Father?" the general asked, solicitously.

"No, no," Kelly said. He was so relieved to find that he had backed into a chair instead of into a gun that he could hardly control his tongue. "It was merely a chair. Nothing but a chair." He turned and looked at the chair. "It is one I have owned for years. A chair cannot hurt a man. A chair can do nothing to a man unless he wants it to." He knew he was babbling, and his French was not good enough to trust to babbling, but he could not stop. For a moment, he had been sure they saw through him and were going to shoot him. But it had just been the knobs on the back of the chair.

"Be careful," Beckmann said as Kelly backed away from them again. "You're walking right into it, Father."

Sheepishly, Kelly looked at the chair. "I'm so stupid," he said. He patted the chair. "But this is an old chair in which I have sat many times. It cannot hurt me, eh?" Shut up, you idiot, he told himself. He reached the stairs and started up.

"Father Picard," Beckmann said. "Your hat."

"My what?" What was a hat? The word seemed familiar. Hat? Hat?

Standartenführer Conrad Beckmann bent down, picked up the shapeless black hat, and brought it over to the steps. He handed it to Kelly. "You twist, tear, and rumple it so fiercely, Father. I hope we have not made you nervous?" He smiled.

Was it just an ordinary smile? Kelly wondered. Or was

there something sinister behind it? Had Beckmann become suspicious?

"Nervous?" Kelly asked. "Oh, not me." He looked at the ruined hat in his hands. "I twist it up because—well, because it is only a hat. It is only the hat which I have worn on my head for years. It cannot hurt me no matter how much I twist it up." He gripped the lump of felt in both hands and wrenched it violently. He grinned weakly at Beckmann. "You see? I twist it, but it cannot hurt me. Just like the chair, eh?" He laughed nervously. Babbling, babbling . . .

"Goodnight, Father," Beckmann said.

"Goodnight, sir. Goodnight, General Rotenhausen." He turned and fairly ran up the steps to the second floor, past the house altar, down the short corridor, and into his room. closing the door behind.

"Why are priests all such idiots?" Beckmann asked Rotenhausen, as the door closed overhead.

In his room, Kelly collapsed on the mattress and hugged himself. He was shaking so badly that the brass bed vibrated under him like a drumhead. His hands were so cold he could feel the chilly outline of his fingers through his suit coat and clerical vest. Yet he was slimy with perspiration.

Don't pray, don't pray, don't pray, he told himself. He was so terrified that he was on the brink of prayer, and he knew that weakness would be the end of him. He hugged himself until the tremors gradually seeped away.

The room was blacker than Danny Dew. The sound of booted feet, foreign voices, and banging pans echoed up from downstairs, but this room itself was quiet. In a while, the darkness and silence soothed Kelly and restored a bit of his self-confidence.

Thus far, the ruse *was* working. Thanks to an unknown and unforeseeable personal clash between Beckmann and Rotenhausen, and thanks to their interservice rivalry, and thanks also to the Third Reich's favored treatment of the Catholic Church, nothing would be searched. The bulk of convoy would not even spend the night in St. Ignatius, but would bivouac along the highway to the east. The long night was still ahead, and the crossing of the bridge in the morning, but it was beginning to look as if there were a good chance. . . .

No! that was the wrong way to think. Optimism was foolish. It was dangerous at best. At worst: deadly. Don't hatch your chickens before they're counted, he told himself. And don't put all their baskets in one egg. The thing was not to hope, but to let the fairy tale carry you. Drift along, play the role, hang on.

Fifteen minutes after he had flopped on the bed with a severe case of the shakes, Kelly heard boots echo on the stairs. The officers' aides carried up two bathtubs and put them in the large bedrooms. A minute later, the first of the boiling water was brought up in heavy pails, with the general and the colonel directing their subordinates. Kelly heard water splashing. More orders in German. The sound of booted feet thumping down the stairs. Boots coming back up again. More water. More orders given. Two young aides thumping down the steps again. And then right back up, *clump-clump-clump*, this time with buckets of cold water to temper the baths.

Finally, the only sound on the second floor was a faint musical splashing as the men soaped and rinsed in the privacy of their rooms, skinning off the film of dust that coated them after a long day on the road. The splashing slowly increased in volume, as if the officers were becoming intoxicated with cleanliness and were jumping about in drunken exuberance, then gradually began to decrease in volume, and faded out altogether. The second floor was silent. Downstairs, two German voices were raised in conversation as Beckmann's aides prepared for bed in the room by the kitchen. In a few seconds, even that noise was stilled.

Kelly waited.

Ten minutes later, when neither Beckmann nor Rotenhausen had made a sound since abandoning their tubs, the major was confident that they had retired for the night. They would both be sleeping contentedly. They would pose no real threat until dawn. Until the convoy began moving through St. Ignatius and across the bridge, Beckmann and Rotenhausen were the least of Kelly's worries.

The *most* of his worries, until the sun rose, were his own men. He did not trust them for a minute. They were crazy. You could not trust lunatics. In the hours before dawn, as the tensions grew more severe, one of those men would do something idiotic, childish, dangerous, and perhaps deadly. Instead of staying in his assigned building where he could not get into trouble, one of those men—maybe dozens of them—would venture out under the misapprehension that he was safer beyond the limitations imposed by four walls. When that happened, Major Kelly wanted to be there to salvage the hoax—and their lives. His duty, then, was not to remain in the rectory and listen to the officers snoring their heads off. Instead, he had to be outside in the fake town, troubleshooting.

Careful not to make a sound, Kelly got off the feather mattress. His back ached from the base of his spine to his neck, and he was glad he did not have to sleep in a bed with so little support. If this madman Beckmann discovered the hoax, he would probably make Kelly sleep on a bed like this for several days and *then* shoot his head off.

When he was certain no one had heard the readjustment of the goose and chicken feathers inside the coarse mattress case, Kelly walked quietly to the room's only window, which was discernible against the dark wall despite the blackout blind that was taped to the window frame. He peeled the tape away. He lifted the blind without rattling it, and slid noiselessly underneath.

Beyond the glass, at the back of the rectory, lay a quiet French religious community: small houses, a dusty street, a nunnery, a churchyard. . . . Kelly smiled, fond of his creation.

The window was well greased. It slid up with only a faint

rasp of wood on wood. Slight though it was, that whispered reluctance seemed like a scream on the calm night air.

Kelly froze, holding up the bottom half of the window, listening for the thud of jackboots in the hall outside his room.

Two minutes later, when no one had stirred, Kelly squeezed through the window and stepped onto the board-shingled roof over the back porch. He eased the window down, not quite closing it. Stepping softly to the corner of the roof where a rose-vine lattice had been built to serve as his ladder, he climbed down to the ground.

He crouched at the edge of the porch. The night wind chilled the back of his neck as he surveyed the rear lawn.

He was alone.

Aware that the rectory windows were covered by blackout blinds, convinced that the night was dark enough to hide him from any German soldier patrolling the streets, Kelly ran to the fence that marked the southern perimeter of the rectory property. A three-foot section of this shoulder-high barrier served as a hidden door. Kelly found the key panel, pressed on it, walked through. On the other side, he pushed the boards back into place and winced at the protracted squeak they made.

He was now on the southern half of the block. Four fake houses, a shrine to the Virgin, four outhouses, and one elm tree offered hiding places. He crept eastward along the fence, then left it for the less promising shelter of the second in a row of three outhouses. He pressed his back against the rough wall of the tiny building and tried to melt back into the purple-black shadows.

Beame was waiting as planned, his own back against the east wall, right around the corner from the major. In a trembling voice, Beame said, "Is that you, Major Kelly?"

"Beame?" Kelly whispered.

"Is that you, Kelly?"

"Beame?"

Beame did not move. Why wouldn't the man around the

corner answer his question? Was it because the man around the corner was not Major Kelly—was, instead, some kill-crazy, sten-gun-carrying Nazi monster? "Major Kelly, is that you?"

"Beame?"

"Kelly? Sir? That you?"

"Beame, is that you?" Kelly asked. He put his palms flat against the outhouse wall, ready to push off and run if this turned out to be anyone but Lieutenant Beame.

"Major Kelly, why won't you answer my question?" Beame was shaking violently. He was certain that a wild-eyed, bloodsucking, death-worshipping Nazi maniac was around the corner, ready to pounce on him.

"What question? Beame, is that you?"

"No," Beame said. "There's no one here."

"No one?"

It was hopeless, Beame knew. "There's no one here, so go away." Beame thought he was going to vomit any second now. He hoped that if he had to die he would be shot before he suffered the indignity of vomiting on himself.

Major Kelly risked a quick glance around the corner and saw Beame. The lieutenant was rigid, arms straight down at his sides, eyes squeezed shut, face contorted with a grimace of expected pain. Kelly slipped around the edge of the building and joined him. "Beame, what in the hell is the matter with you?"

The lieutenant opened his eyes and was so relieved to see Kelly that he nearly collapsed. Leaning against the outhouse, he said, "I didn't think it was you, sir."

"Who else would it be?" Kelly whispered.

"I thought you were a kraut." Beame wiped sweat from his face.

"But I was speaking English, Beame."

The lieutenant was surprised. "Hey, that's right! I never thought of that." He grinned happily, suddenly frowned, and scratched his head. "But why didn't you identify yourself at the start, when I first asked you?"

"I didn't know who you were," Kelly said, as if the answer must be obvious even to a moron.

"Who else would it be?" Beame asked.

"I thought you were a kraut."

"But I was speaking English—"

"Let's get down to basics," Kelly hissed. He crouched, forcing Beame to hunker beside him. He looked around at the backs of the fake houses in which his men were sheltered, at the other houses, at the dusty streets that he could see between the buildings. Lowering his voice even further, he said, "Have you checked on the men?"

"Yes," Beame said. "It wasn't easy with a kraut at every intersection. Thank God they didn't park the whole convoy in the clearing—or search the buildings. They *aren't* going to search, are they?"

"No," Kelly said. "Look, what about the men? They okay?"

"They're all in their assigned houses—except for Lieutenant Slade."

Kelly's stomach turned over and crawled around inside of him, hunting for a way out. "Slade?"

"He was supposed to be in one of the platform houses with Akers, Dew, and Richfield. None of them have seen him since early this evening."

"You mean he's on the loose?" Kelly asked.

Beame nodded.

"What's the sniveling little bastard up to?" Kelly wondered. "What does that rotten little son of a bitch have up his sleeve?"

For a while, they were both silent, trying to imagine the inside of Slade's sleeve. At last, Beame could not tolerate any more of that. "What will we do?"

"We have to find him," Kelly said. "Whatever he's got up his sleeve, it's rotten as month-old salami."

"Maybe he ran away," Beame said.

"Not Slade. He wants to fight, not run. He's somewhere in

the village—somewhere he shouldn't be." And we're all dead because of him, Kelly thought.

And then he thought: No, we're all dead because death is the theme of this fairy tale. Slade's a particularly ugly plot problem, that's all. What we have to do is go after him and play our roles and make ourselves small, please the crazy Aesop behind this so maybe he'll let us live. And then he also thought: Am I losing my mind?

"Won't be easy finding him," Beame said. "Every intersection has a sentry."

Kelly wiped one cold hand across his face, pulled at his clerical collar. "It doesn't matter how difficult it is. We *have* to find him." He stood and moved away from the outhouse. "Let's get away from this place. It smells like shit."

## 2/

Lieutenant Slade wished that his mother could see him now. For the first time since he had been assigned to Kelly's unit, he was getting a chance to act like a real soldier. Tonight, he had the opportunity to prove that he was as heroic as all the other men in his family had been.

He lay flat on the ground beside a fake stone well, watching the sentry who patrolled the Y-B intersection. The kraut walked twenty paces east, then twenty west, turning smartly on his heel at the end of each circuit. He did not seem to be interested in anything around him. Probably daydreaming. Just like half the other guards Slade had thus far observed. Fine. Good. They were not expecting danger from nuns, priests, and deaf-mutes. When it came, they would be overwhelmed.

Slade waited for the sentry to turn toward the west. The moment the man's back was to him, he pushed up and ran silently across Y Street into the darkness between two of the single-story platform houses. From there, he slithered westward on his stomach, over to the Y-A intersection where he made notes on yet another sentry.

Now was *almost* the time. He had very little reconnaissance left to do. He had noted each sentry, had discovered the weak points in the German positions. He was almost ready to lead a silent attack. In half an hour, he could go find Major Kelly and kill him. And then make heroes out of this whole pack of cowards.

## 3/

Hiding in shadows, crawling on their bellies, running tiptoe from one tree to the next and from one building to the next, Major Kelly and Lieutenant Beame went all over the village looking for Lieutenant Slade. They stopped in at every house, school, and nunnery, hoping that someone would have seen Slade during the night and could shed light on The Snot's intentions.

But no one had seen him since early in the evening. Not that anyone had been *looking* for him.

"You try *not* to notice The Snot," Lyle Fark told them as they stood with him and seven other men in one of the hollow two-story houses. "I mean, you don't *want* to know what he's doing, most of the time. But when he isn't there, you notice it right away. Everything's so tranquil. You get such a sense of well-being when he goes away."

"And when did you get this sense of well-being?" Kelly asked.

"Early this evening," Fark said. "Yeah, he must have disappeared around eight o'clock, because things seemed to pick up about then."

It was the same answer they got from everyone. Slade had not been seen for several hours; but although they could just about pinpoint the time of his departure, they could not discover where he had gone.

Shortly after two in the morning, they slipped past the sentry at the bridge road and A Street and crawled over to the hospital bunker steps. A one-story house had been thrown up atop the hospital. It was like most of the other fake houses, except that it had outside steps into the cellar. The steps, of course, lead into the bunker where Tooley, Kowalski, Liverwright, and Hagendorf were holed up for the duration. At the bottom of the steps, Major Kelly stood up and softly rapped out shave-and-a-haircut-two-bits on the wooden cellar door.

A minute passed. Slowly.

Down by the river, frogs were singing.

Another minute passed. Slower than the first.

"Come *on*, Tooley," Beame whispered. They were somewhat exposed on the steps, good targets for a *Wehrmacht* sharpshooter.

Kelly rapped on the door again. Even before he finished the tune, the portal scraped open a fraction of an inch, like the entrance to a crypt controlled by demonic forces.

"It's me, Tooley. Major Kelly."

"*Whew!*" the pacifist said. "I thought it was a German." He stepped out of the way, let them in. He was invisible in that lightless chamber.

When the door was closed again, Tooley switched on a flashlight, confident that none of its glow would escape the subterranean room. Liverwright, holding his wounded hip, loomed out of the darkness. And so did Maurice.

"What are *you* doing here?" Major Kelly asked.

"Dying," Liverwright said.

"Not you," Kelly said. "Maurice, you're supposed to stay

away from here. You told me you didn't dare show your face around General Rotenhausen."

Maurice nodded. "And I pray I will not have to." His face glistened in the flashlight's glow.

"We have big trouble, sir," Private Tooley said.

"Then you know about Slade?"

"Bigger trouble than that." The pacifist sounded as if he were on the brink of tears. "Blood's going to be spilled."

"Bigger trouble than Slade running around loose?" Kelly asked. He felt as if he might vomit.

Maurice moved forward, commanding attention with his hefty stomach and his low, tense voice. "Two hours ago, one of my contacts came from the west to tell me that an Allied tank division has broken through the German lines and is rolling rapidly your way. I have checked it out myself. The Allies are driving hard to capture this bridge of yours."

"Ah . . ." Major Kelly said. He wished that he had been born without his legs. If he had been a cripple since birth, he would never have been drafted. He would be at home right now, back in the States, reading pulp magazines and listening to radio and having his mother wheel him to the movies. How nice. Why hadn't he ever before realized the wonderful life a cripple could have?

"Allied tanks?" Lieutenant Beame asked. "But this is no trouble! Don't you see? Our own people are on the way. We're saved!"

Maurice looked at Kelly. "There's another good reason for him to stay away from my daughter. I won't have her marry a stupid man."

"What do you mean?" Beame asked, baffled. "Aren't we saved?"

"I'm afraid not," Maurice said.

"Well, when are the Allied tanks getting here?" Beame asked.

"They ought to arrive before the Panzers start across the bridge from this side," Maurice said. He looked knowingly at Kelly. "By dawn or shortly thereafter, Major."

"Even better!" Beame said. "I don't understand why you're unhappy."

Major Kelly sighed and rubbed his eyes with one fist. Maybe if he had been born with only one hand he could have avoided this mess. He would not have had to be really seriously crippled to stay out of the Army. "Think about it for a minute, Beame. In a couple of hours, you're going to have Allied tanks on the west bank of the river—and German tanks on the east bank. The Allies will control the land over there, and the Germans will control St. Ignatius. Neither the Allies nor the Germans are going to permit the enemy to cross that bridge."

"Stalemate!" Beame said, smiling at Maurice, Tooley, Liverwright, then at Kelly, gradually losing the smile as he went from one face to the next. "Oh, God," he said. "Oh, God, there's going to be a tank battle for the bridge!"

"Sure," Kelly said. "They'll sit on opposite shores and shoot at each other. And we'll be right in the middle."

Beame looked as if he were going to be sick on his own shoes.

"Don't be sick on your own shoes," Kelly said. "I couldn't stand that right now."

"Look," Beame said, "we don't have to wait around for this battle. We can slip away into the woods until it's over."

"Two hundred of us?" Kelly and Maurice exchanged a grim smile. "Even with darkness on our side, we've had trouble moving around town. That was just two of us. With two hundred—no chance."

Despite the changes which had taken place in him recently, Beame was much the same as he had always been: naive, full of hope. "Well . . . what if we sent someone west to meet these Allied tanks before they got here? If we told them that the Panzers were here, maybe we could persuade them to let the Germans cross and hold the battle elsewhere."

"This they will not do," Maurice said. "For one thing, the Allied tank commander would know that the Germans will blow up the bridge after themselves. They almost always do these days. And the Allies wouldn't want to lose the bridge."

"We can build them another bridge in a day!" Beame said.

Tooley nodded eagerly. "That's true."

"You forget that only Blade knows we're here," Kelly said. "The commander of those Allied tanks doesn't suspect there's a unit of engineers and laborers stranded behind the lines. Although, I suppose we could *tell* them. . . ."

Maurice shook his head sadly. "No good, *mon ami.* If it were any other Allied commander at the head of this force, he would help you. But this general will not even pause to listen to what you have to say. He's too caught up in the success of his one-unit campaign." The greasy, sweaty old man looked at each of them and delivered the final blow. "The Allied tanks coming this way are commanded by General Bobo Remlock."

"We're all dead," Kelly said.

"Well," Beame said, "I guess we are."

General Bobo Remlock was a Texan who called himself The Fighting General. He also called himself Latter-Day Sam Houston, Big Ball of Barbed Wire, Old Blood and Guts, and Last of the Two-Fisted Cowboys. They had all heard about Bobo Remlock when they were stationed in Britain prior to D-Day. The British and Americans who had served under Remlock could never get done complaining about him. Remlock encouraged his men to call him Big Tex and Old Blood-and-Guts, though not to his face. What he did not know was that everyone called him That Maniac and Blood Beast and Old Shit for Brains behind his back. If Bobo Remlock were leading the approaching force, he would not stop for anything. He would roll up to the other side of the gorge and utterly destroy St. Ignatius in the process of liberating it.

"We do have *one* chance," Maurice said.

"We do?" Beame asked, brightening.

"No, we don't," Major Kelly said.

Maurice smiled. He put his two pudgy hands together,

pressed them flat and tight, then threw them open as he whispered: "*Boom!*"

Kelly decided that Maurice had lost his mind, just like all the men in the unit had done.

"With the machines hidden in the convent," The Frog said, "you also have many sticks of dynamite. Many yards of wire. A plunger and battery. If we waste no more time, we might be able to plant the explosives under the bridge. In the morning, if the expected showdown between Generals Remlock and Rotenhausen comes, we will quite simply demolish the bridge. Neither commander will be able to take his tanks down a gorge as steep as this one. And because there will be nothing left to fight for once the bridge is gone, both the Allies and the Germans will have to seek elsewhere for a river crossing."

"Blow up our own bridge?" Kelly asked.

"That is right," Maurice said.

"Blow up the bridge that we've busted ass to keep in shape?"

"Yes."

"It's not a bad idea," Kelly admitted. "But even if it works, even if Bobo Remlock goes away to look for another crossing, we're still not out of the frying pan. The krauts will come down hard on us. They'll think partisans set off the explosions, and they'll search St. Ignatius."

Kelly had wisely decided not to assign any men to the fake house over the hospital bunker. He was doubly glad of that decision now. He had not wanted to put men in the house and then have them terrified out of their minds when Kowalski began to moan and mutter in one of his clairvoyant seizures. Even if they knew it was only Kowalski under them, any men in the house would have been scared silly by the sounds he made. Everyone was especially keyed up tonight. It would take very little to send them screaming into the streets. And if men had been upstairs right now, ears to the floorboards to listen to this conversation, they would have exploded like bombs with short fuses.

"Perhaps the Germans will not go looking for partisans," Maurice said. "This Rotenhausen is a dedicated soldier. The first priority, so far as he will be concerned, should be Remlock's tanks. If you get to him soon after the bridge goes up, and if you tell him where to find the nearest fordable stretch of river, he will be off like a flash, leaving St. Ignatius in peace."

"Maurice, you are a genuis!" Beame exclaimed.

The greasy mayor accepted the compliment with little grace, smiling and nodding as if to say that Beame was perfectly correct.

"One thing," Kelly said. "How much will you want for the dynamite and other equipment—which was once my property but, as you may recall, which I am now only holding for you until this present crisis passes."

"I want nothing more than what you have already given," Maurice assured him, raising two workworn hands, palms outward to placate Kelly. "Naturally, I will expect you to rebuild the bridge and put up the tollbooth according to your original agreement."

"And nothing new?"

"I am no monster, Major," Maurice said, putting one hand over his heart. "I do not always require payment. When my friends need me, I am always there."

## 4/

The young *Wehrmacht* Schütze at the intersection of A Street and Y Street took his twentieth step eastward, turned sharply, and paraded toward the river again.

The Schütze at the intersection of B and Y took his twentieth step *westward*, turned just as sharply as the first soldier had done, and marched toward the forest.

In the half minute when both sentries had their backs on the block between them, Major Kelly and Private Tooley burst from the north side of Y Street and ran quietly across to the back of the convent yard. Kelly located the hidden door in the eight-foot-high fence—which was exactly like the hidden door in the fence behind the rectory—and they passed through. Tooley pushed it gently into place behind them.

They both stood still for a moment, listening to the sentries' jackboots.

No alarm was raised.

They went across the convent yard to the small door in the back of the false structure. Kelly hesitated a moment, then softly knocked shave-and-a-haircut-two-bits.

Lily Kain opened the door. "What's wrong?"

"Plenty," Kelly said, slipping past her into the dark building.

When the door was closed, one of the other nuns struck a match. Two well-hooded kerosene lanterns sputtered up, the fuel feed turned as low as possible. They barely diluted the darkness.

The whole of the convent, with the exception of the foyer which had been finished toward the front, was one enormous room with a plain dirt floor. The walls soared up three stories to a jumble of wooden beams which supported the simple roof. There were no rooms laid off. There was no furniture. Only the phony nuns and the heavy machinery and various other supplies occupied these sacred quarters. The machines stood in two lines, one row against each of the longest walls. They looked like peacefully slumbering animals, oil and grease puddled under them instead of manure.

In the middle of the floor, between the machines, stood the other nuns. Fifteen of them in all. Kelly recognized Nathalie Jobert, and he smiled at her. She was a sweet little piece, all right. She was a good kid.

He also recognized Nurse Pullit, now Sister Pullit, but he did not smile and nod at the nurse. He tried to pretend Pullit was not even there.

"Have you found Slade?" Lily asked.

"How did you know he was missing?"

"David was around earlier, asking about him."

"We have a worse problem," he said. He told her about Bobo Remlock.

While he talked, he looked her over. If her face had not been so unwholesomely erotic, and if her big jugs had not molded to the bulky habit she wore like a knit sweater, Lily would have made a fine nun. Her winged cowl was neat and crisply starched. The rim of her cowl fitted tightly around her lovely face, holding her long hair out of sight. Her robe was black and fell to the floor, with a wide white vent down the left side. The Eisenhower women who had sewn the costumes really did know what a well-dressed nun should wear. Unless the nun was Lily Kain. If the nun was Lily Kain, the habit did not look good on her at all. If the nun was Lily Kain, she should wear pasties shaped like twin crosses over her nipples—and a G-string made out of rosary beads.

"Blow up our bridge?" Lily asked, when he finished telling her the plan. "Is that our only choice?"

"Seems to be," Kelly said. He looked at his watch. "Almost three. We have a whole lot to do before dawn."

He and Tooley located the T-plunger, a coil of wire, and a wooden case full of carefully packed dynamite which was wrapped in airtight plastic to keep the sticks from sweating. They lugged the stuff toward the door, anxious to get on with things.

"Major, wait!" Nathalie Jobert said, clutching his hand as he reached for the doorknob. "What about David?"

Kelly looked into her lovely black eyes and smiled. "He's fine. I'll keep him right beside me, safe and sound."

"Will you tell him I said–" She looked away, wiped at her pert nose with the back of one slender hand.

"Yes?"

"Tell him that I–"

"That you love him?" Kelly asked.

She blushed and nodded.

"I'll tell him," the major said. He leaned over and kissed her cool forehead below her winged white hood. "Now I have to go."

She raised his hand and kissed it, just as the lights went out. "You're a wonderful man." Then she was gone.

But Lily was there to detain him another minute when he opened the back door and stepped into the convent yard. She came outside with him and, while Tooley crossed the yard, threw both arms around him. "I don't love you," she said, kissing him.

Kelly put down the T-plunger and the wire. He embraced her, crushed her against him, inhaled the vaguely musky odor that always clung to her. "And I don't love you."

"I don't love you at all," Lily said. "Not even a teensy little bit."

"You make me so happy, Lily."

"Do you love me even a teensy little bit?" she asked, looking up into his face.

"No. You mean nothing whatsoever to me."

Lily shivered. "That's marvelous, darling."

"Yes, it is, darling."

"Kiss me again."

Kissing her, he lost control and slid his hands down her back and cupped her round buttocks and began to knead her firm flesh through the black gown. Abruptly, he pulled away from her. "I have to get moving. We have to get the explosives planted under the bridge."

Lily sighed. "Don't worry about anything, Kelly. As long as neither one of us loves the other even a teensy little bit, we'll be okay."

"You're right," he said.

He picked up the plunger and wire and left her. He crossed the convent yard, cracked the secret gate, and cautiously checked on the sentries at the nearby intersections. When both the Germans were facing away from him, he went out into St. Ignatius. Tooley followed him, carrying the box of dynamite.

Lieutenant Slade had just taken shelter at the base of an elm tree when he saw a gate open in the back of the convent fence. A second later, Major Kelly and that chickenshit pacifist, Tooley, came out and pushed the gate shut and ran silently across Y Street, taking shelter by the side of the house just as the sentries turned to face that block. Both men had their arms full. But full of *what?*

Major Kelly led the pacifist westward, dodging from shadow to shadow, and Slade followed them. At the intersection of Y Street and A Street, they knelt beside the nunnery and waited for the sentry to face away from them.

Slade crept as close to them as he could, but was unable to tell what they were carrying.

What was this? What was Kelly doing out of the rectory? What cowardly, yellow-bellied plot were they involved in now?

The sentry turned his back.

Kelly and Tooley went across the road, lugging the mysterious objects. They took just enough time so that Slade was unable to follow them until the sentry had made one more circuit. When he got over there, they were gone.

Which was too bad. After all, *now was the time.* Slade had finished his reconnaissance. All that was left was to murder Major Kelly, preferably in silence. Knife him in the back. . . . And then take a commando team into the rectory to slit the throats of the German officers. Soon, they would all be real heroes.

Smiling at the darkness, the lieutenant crept southward, trying to find where Major Kelly had gone.

# 5/

Maurice opened the bunker door and ushered them into the eerily lightless room, closed the door, and switched on a flashlight. He shone the beam on the plunger and the wire, then on the dynamite which Tooley set gently on the floor. "It looks like enough," he said.

"More than enough," Kelly said. "The bridge will drop like a rock down a well."

Shining the flashlight deeper into the bunker, Maurice said, "Everyone is here, all the men you requested."

Danny Dew, Vito Angelli, Sergeant Coombs, and Lieutenant Beame sat on the hospital cots, eyes gleaming with reflected light.

"You've heard the whole story?" he asked the three newcomers whom Beame had fetched during his absence.

"We heard," Danny said. "What a bitch of a night."

"I think we should use the dynamite on the krauts," Sergeants Coombs said. "Not on our own bridge."

Major Kelly had only one weapon he could use on Coombs. He used it. "I'm a major, and you're a sergeant. We'll do things my way."

Coombs scowled, grudgingly nodded agreement. In a pinch, he was a book man, a rule man, a regulations man, who would obey even a poor disciplinarian like Major Kelly.

"And what *is* your way?" Danny Dew asked, getting up from his cot and pacing in and out of the soft light.

"There will be seven of us," Kelly said. "Danny, Vito, Beame, Sergeant Coombs, Tooley, Maurice, and me." As quickly as possible, he told them how they would do the job. "Any questions?"

Danny Dew smacked his lips. "Yas, massah. Dumb ol' Danny have a question, suh. You really think we's gonna be able to do all this without makin' a noise them guards up on the bridge would hear?"

Kelly shrugged. "We can try to be perfectly quiet. That's all I can say. We can *try*."

"We can do it," Beame said, optimistic despite the way their situation had deteriorated.

"That reminds me," Kelly said. "One other thing. The SS is guarding the bridge. There won't be *Wehrmacht* privates above us, but about four or five of those black-uniformed crackpots. So you better be twice as quiet."

"Next," Danny Dew said, "he's going to tell us we have to pull off this operation blindfolded."

Maurice switched off the flashlight.

The darkness was so deep it seemed to pull at their eyes.

Kelly opened the door the whole way. For a while, they stood there, letting the lesser darkness of the night creep in. When their eyes adjusted, Danny Dew picked up the plunger and the wire. Tooley hefted the case of dynamite and held it close against his massive chest. Major Kelly led the way out of the hospital bunker, and they followed. Liverwright, who was dying, closed the door behind them.

## 6/

The clouds formed a thick roof from horizon to horizon. No stars shone. Only a hint of moonlight penetrated the black thunderheads.

Kelly and the others went south along the edge of the ravine, far enough back from A Street to be hidden from the German sentry at the intersection of A and Z. Well past the last of the fake houses, they made their way cautiously down the sloped ravine wall until they reached the riverbank.

A frog croaked in front of Kelly, startling him.

Recovering what little nerve he had left, the major looked upstream at the black framework of the bridge which was silhouetted against the blue-black sky. From this distance, it appeared deserted. The SS guards, in their black uniforms, blended perfectly with the night and the steel beams.

"Here's where we get wet," Kelly said. He looked at Tooley. "You sure you don't want someone to help you with those sticks?"

"No, sir," Tooley said. "I'm strong. I can handle them. We can't afford to lose any of them—or drop them and let them get wet. If we can't keep this stuff stable, we're all dead."

"We're all dead anyway," Kelly said.

"Major, we have—company," Lieutenant Beame whispered, behind them.

Kelly whirled, expecting to see hordes of Germans rushing down the ravine slope. Instead, he saw three nuns, their white-winged hoods glowing ghostily in the darkness. Lily. Nathalie. And Sister Pullit. "What in the hell—"

"We *had* to come," Lily said. "We'd have gone crazy wondering if you were dead or alive. Remember, each of us has a man out here."

Kelly looked at Pullit.

"She's right," the nurse said.

Kelly looked *away* from Pullit. The nurse resembled a nun too closely, so far as Kelly was concerned. Pullit was sweet, dimpled, innocent, with a freshly scrubbed look.

"We want to go along with you," Lily said.

"Are you crazy? You'll get us all killed!"

"We can help," Lily said. "Haven't you heard? Women have more endurance and strength than men."

The major was not yet able to cope with the situation. He

kept looking from the nuns to his men and back to the nuns again. He could not understand how his life had come to this, how so many years of experience could have funneled down to this absurdity.

"They'll drown in those bulky costumes," Tooley said.

"That's right!" Kelly said, seizing the argument. "You'll drown in those bulky costumes."

Before anyone could object, Lily tore open her habit and shrugged out of it. She peeled away her hood and cowl and dropped that on the robe. All she wore, now, was a flimsy two-piece dancer's costume out of which *everything* might pop at any moment.

Every man there drew a long, deep breath.

"Lily—" Kelly began.

Horrified by something he had seen out of the corner of his eye, Kelly turned and confronted Pullit. The nurse had stripped, too, and now stood there in bra and panties. Lily's bra, stuffed with paper. Kelly had no idea who had given Pullit the panties: large, white cotton things with a blue-bow trim.

"No," Kelly said. "No, I—"

"We have come this far," Nathalie said. "You can't send us back now. That would be more dangerous than if we went with you." She had taken off her own habit, stood there in panties and bra, giving Lily Kain a run for the money. Not a very serious run, so far as Kelly was concerned, but something of a run nonetheless.

Lieutenant Beame seemed to be whimpering.

"Major," Tooley said, "this dynamite is getting heavy. The longer we wait, the more time we waste—"

"Okay. It's insane, Lily, but you can come along."

She grabbed him and kissed him, her heavy jugs pressing into his chest and rising dangerously in the thin silken cups. "We're all in this together, anyway."

Kelly looked at Angelli, then at Pullit. "You two stay away from each other, you understand?"

They nodded sheepishly.

"Oh Christ," the major said, turning away from them.

"We'll be all right, darling," Lily said. "I don't love you."

"And I don't love you," he said.

"Good! I was afraid you were angry with me."

"What's the use?" Kelly asked. "It's a fairy tale. You aren't the one who makes up the plot twists. You're just another character."

The major went into the river first. He did not bother to remove his shoes or clothes, chiefly because there was no time left for that. The water swirled up to his knees, frothed around him like it frothed around the rocks which thrust up in the middle of it and the roots of the big trees that grew out over its eroded shore.

Speckled with white water, the river would do a fairly good job of hiding them while they approached the bridge. If they had walked north along the riverbank, they would surely have been seen. Any movement at all on the open land would catch a sentry's eye. But the river, constantly moving, concealed their progress and covered over the ordinary noises they might make.

And they would make a lot of ordinary noises, Kelly thought. There were too damned many of them. It was a fucking *parade!*

Kelly walked carefully. For every step, he tested the muddy bottom before committing his weight to it. He knew there were holes, drop-offs that could swallow him. Furthermore, he did not want to slip and fall on a water-washed stone or on a particularly slimy stretch of mud. The splash might not reach the SS men on the bridge. However, in falling, he might involuntarily cry out and bring the Germans down on them.

Behind the major, the others moved forward as cautiously as their chief. Nathalie watched where Kelly stepped, and still she tested every step of her own before taking it. Beame had trouble taking his eyes off Natalie's ass and the slim line of her back, but he somehow managed not to slip or stumble. Pullit followed Beame, gasping as the cold water swirled higher. Danny Dew followed Lily Kain, wondering how he could pretend to trip and grab hold of either her ass or her jugs to keep from falling; he was afraid the move would be painfully transparent. Behind Dew came Maurice, walking like a man balancing on raw eggs and trying not to crack the shells. He held the T-plunger and the wire over his head. Coombs followed cautiously but less gracefully than Maurice, then Angelli. Private Tooley came last, and he was the most careful of all. Now and then, he fell behind the others and forced them to wait for him. He was taking no chances with the explosives.

Kelly led them eight feet out from shore, until the water reached halfway up his chest. Any deeper, and Angelli or Nathalie, the smaller members of the troop, might be swept downstream.

The Germans were their greatest worry, naturally. However, they also had to be afraid of drowning. At least *Kelly* was afraid of drowning. He could swim well enough, but he did not know how far he could get in a water-soaked suit and a pair of heavy-soled shoes.

Not very far, he supposed. Maybe five feet.

He put his foot forward, put it down, and felt it slide over the edge of a drop-off. He pulled back so fast he bumped into Nathalie and Beame and almost knocked them off their feet. Nathalie not only had to keep standing, but she was modestly trying to conceal her belly button with one hand, as if that were the most obscene thing she could reveal to them. Her knees buckled, but she did not fall.

"What? What?" Lieutenant Beame asked, as if he thought Kelly had engineered the fall to get a feel of the French girl's excellent, slender body. Which was not a particularly bad idea. . . .

"Almost fell in a hole," Kelly said.

He did not know how deep the pit was, but he was somehow certain that it would have have sucked him down and away before anyone could help him. Moving them a little closer to the shore, he found a way around the drop-off and continued toward the bridge.

A hundred yards from the span . . . ninety-five, ninety . . .

The water gushed between Lily's long legs, foaming around the crotch of her panties. Which was, in fact, also her own crotch. The foam tickled, but it also—well, *aroused* her. She shivered and moaned softly as she followed the others upriver.

Eighty-five yards, eighty . . .

Overhead, the sky split open and let out a bolt of white lightning which danced a crooked jig across the night. Major Kelly felt exposed as a paramecium on a biology student's lab slide. In that brief glare, he clearly saw two of the guards on the bridge, and he was certain one of them had been looking his way.

For the first time, he realized that if they were seen and if the krauts opened fire, a single bullet could strike the case of explosives and blow them all the way south to Spain.

The lightning did not frighten Danny Dew. It pleased him. The white light shimmering on Lily Kain's sleek body was one of the most beautiful things he had ever seen in his life. It was so beautiful, in fact, that he did not care if the next bolt struck and killed him. He had already seen perfection. What was left?

Thunder followed the lightning. It slapped across the gorge like an explosion, reverberated between the sloped walls, reluctantly died away.

The sudden noise almost caused Angelli to fall. He had been leaning to the left, trying to look around the others and catch a glimpse of Nurse Pullit. The thunder startled him and put him off stride.

Cold, gray rain sliced across the river. Slanting in from the northwest, it made the water around them froth even more. It soaked the half of Kelly which he had thus far been able to keep out of the river.

Wonderful, he thought. Just great. A rainstorm. What next, Aesop?

He shuddered. If he had not already been an aethist, this latest trick of fate would have made him into one. Or would have convinced him that God was a nasty little boy.

Seventy yards to the bridge. Sixty-five . . . sixty . . .

Nathalie said, "Major!"

Kelly stopped, froze, looked at the looming bridgeworks, trying to see what she had seen. Was one of the guards even now leveling a submachine gun at them? A bazooka? A howitzer? A *cannon*?

"Major," she said, "Tooley wants to talk to you."

Relieved that they had not been spotted, Kelly turned around and crowded in with the others. They formed a circle which resembled a football huddle, leaning towards each other, the rain beating at their backs and the river sloshing at their hips and waists.

Tooley sheltered the case of dynamite against his chest, bending over it as if he were trying to protect it from the other team. The krauts? "Major, the sticks are going to get wet. If they start sweating, this stuff will go off even if you just breathe on it wrong."

"It's wrapped in airtight plastic," Kelly said.

"So says the U.S. Army." Tooley made a face. "You ever know the Army to do something right? You want to bet me there's not one little plastic seam that's split open? If one stick goes, it'll take the rest with it. . . ."

"What do you suggest?" Kelly asked.

"That we move faster."

"And drop down a hole in the riverbed."

"It's a risk we'll have to take," the pacifist said.

"We're doing all right so far," Lily said, with the enthusiasm of a cheerleader. Pullit and Nathalie joined in with her: "Yeah, we are! All right so far!"

"Tooley's right," Angelli said. Next to the weight lifter, he looked like a child and strangely out of place here in the middle of the river on a stormy night. "The longer we stay out here, the more dangerous it is—because of the Germans, the dynamite, because of everything." He smiled at Pullit and winked reassuringly.

"Okay," Kelly said. Let's move, then."

They fell back into single file, started upstream again, moving more wrecklessly than before. The rain stung their faces, pasted their hair down, glued their clothes to them, slopped into the boxful of plastic-wrapped explosives. The water frothed around them and excited Lily Kain, and the bridge grew nearer.

Fifty yards, forty, thirty-five . . .

Major Kelly had wondered earlier if he were losing his mind. Now he was sure of it. He had never played in a football game in his life. He was not sports-oriented. Now, in the dead of night, in a thunderstorm, in the middle of a river, under the guns of German maniacs, pursued by a man with a caseful of unstable dynamite, he was caught up in what amounted to a goddamned game. . . . The bridge piers loomed like goal posts.

Thirty yards, twenty-five . . .

The sky was branded by another lightning bolt, this one even brighter than the first. Major Kelly saw three SS sentries, two at the eastern end of the bridge and one just about in the middle.

He kept on moving forward.

No one cried out. There was no gunfire.

Twenty yards. Now fifteen. Ten . . .

They waded under the floor of the bridge without being seen. Major Kelly wanted to cry out in triumph as he crossed that all-important line. The rain on the bridge floor overhead was like the ovation rising from the stadium around them. It was glorious. But then he reminded himself that the job was not yet finished. The ball could fall to the other team any time now. They could still lose. *Would* lose. Did even a big league player dare hope for success?

# 7/

After having built all those bridges across the gorge, they were perfectly familiar with the topography of the riverbed in this area. There were no holes or drop-offs. The bottom was scarred and uneven from all the construction work and from bombed bridges collapsing on top of it, but it was nowhere deeper than the middle of Tooley's chest or the base of Angelli's neck.

According to plan, Sergeant Coombs took a long-bladed knife and waded ashore to stand guard under the eastern cantilever arm. Danny Dew tested a matching knife against the ball of his thumb, kissed Lily Kain—who kissed back with passion—grinned whitely, and waded off to the west to mount guard over there.

Kelly motioned to the pacifist.

Tooley waded forward, holding the box of explosives against his broad chest, and stood in front of the major. He looked down at the sticks and grimaced at the water caught in the folds of plastic.

Kelly reached into the box and took out four packages of dynamite, six sticks to the bundle. He held two in each hand.

Maurice Jobert, who had taken the T-plunger all the way up the river, said something to Nathalie, scowling fiercely at her immodesty and at the way Beame reveled in her immodesty. Then he waded quietly to the shore and set the device down on the bank not far from where Coombs stood.

Except for the brief, whispered exchange between Maurice and Nathalie, no one dared to speak. The rain drumming on the river and on the floor of the bridge overhead was sufficiently noisy to cover their movements. But a voice was distinctive and might carry up to the SS sentries despite the overlaying susurration of the storm.

Private Tooley turned away from Kelly and carried the rest of the explosives over to the farside bridge pier. Stalking about in the bridge shadows, naked from the waist up, his powerful body tense and glistening, he looked like a mythical creature, a super troll making plans to kidnap travelers who passed above him. . . . Angelli followed the big man, pushing through water that reached almost to his chin, holding the spool of copper wire over his head. Before Kelly could make known his objection, Pullit followed Angelli. The three of them, if the lovebirds could keep their hands off each other, would rig the sticks at the other pier.

Maurice came back into the water when he saw Beame and Nathalie were not going to be separated. His belly bobbled in the foam like a gigantic fishing lure.

Handing the four packages of dynamite to Beame, Kelly grabbed Lily and kissed her. She kissed back, with passion, as the water sloshed between her legs and foamed up her belly to her thinly sheathed jugs.

Revitalized by that kiss, Kelly worked his way over to the nearside pier and looked up the forty-foot-high column of stones and cement. Fortunately, their facilities here at the camp had precluded the construction of smooth, featureless bridge pillars. The stones protruded from the concrete and provided hand- and footholds. Kelly quickly judged the easiest route, hooked his fingers over an inch-wide ledge of fieldstone, and began to pull himself up.

In theory, it should have been a relief to get out of the cold water. His flesh was icy. His bones ached. And he was tired of resisting the river's steady pressure. But the theory was faulty. Clinging to the crude bridge pier, Kelly felt worse than ever. The rain lashed him. The growing wind chilled him to the bone. He had begun to delevop a severe headache behind the eyes, and now it stretched around and pounded in his temples as well.

He thought of Lily, standing below him in her skimpy costume, her silk halter pasted to her jugs, her hard nipples standing out nearly an inch. . . .

He kept on climbing. The cement was rough, and it chafed his hands. Each time he found a new grip, the sharp stones creased his fingers; and when he let his weight hang, the stone cut his fingers across the soft pads of flesh. The blood trickled down his hands and was sluiced away by the rain.

Three-quarters of the way up, thirty feet above the surging river, he stopped and pressed against the stone column, breathing quickly and shallowly. He could hear the thump of his heart above the rain and the thunder, and he wondered if the SS men overhead could also hear it. His toes were wedged onto a two-inch cleft in the pier. Above him, his bloodied fingers were curled over a concrete lip only half as wide as the one below. He did not see how he could regain his strength when all his resources were required to maintain his present position.

He looked down at Maurice, Beame, Nathalie, and Lily.

That was a mistake, even though he thought he could see Lily's nipples from clear up here. Dizziness enveloped him. The shimmering water, the white upturned faces, and the three stories of stone pillar falling away under him made him ill.

He thought of the brass bed at the rectory. Lily Kain. Putting it to her on a big brass bed. . . .

He pulled himself up, scrabbled for a new handhold, held on, went on.

Ten minutes later, he reached the top of the pier upon which the steel support beams were set. There was just enough room to pull himself up and in, off the sheer face. He still had to hold onto a girder, but the eight-foot-wide pillar provided a welcome resting place.

When he regained his breath, he fumbled in his coat pocket and found the ball of thin, strong nylon string which he had picked up from the supplies in the convent. He held onto the free end and threw the ball over the edge, let it unwind as it fell away into darkness, dropped down and down and down to the river and to Beame.

A minute passed, then another. Finally, Beame tugged three times on the other end of the cord.

For a moment, Major Kelly wondered if all of this was actually worth the effort. Even if they placed the explosives and got away from the damned bridge without being seen, would they be any closer to ultimate safety? Would this dangerous enterprise bring them one day closer to the end of the war and the end of violence? What about Slade running around loose in the camp? What about Hagendorf, now drunk and unconscious but maybe sober and screaming ten minutes from now? What about all the other men and all their neuroses that might at any minute trigger a situation that could ruin the hoax?

Lily Kain.

Hard nipples.

Brass beds.

*Baby, I don't love you at all.*

He reeled in the line and dragged two packages of dynamite over the edge of the pillar. He untied those from the cord and tucked them against his belly, dropped the nylon again.

Two minutes later, the tug was repeated. Kelly reeled in the last two packages and then began to place all four of them around the steel bridge supports.

Ten minutes passed in unbearable inactivity. The rain dripped through the floorboards of the bridge and found Kelly. It dribbled in his face no matter how often he eased himself into a new position. Every two minutes a pair of booted feet stomped past, inches from his head, right on the other side of those boards.

Where in the hell were Tooley and Angelli? How long did they need to finish the job on the farside pier and walk back with the spool of wire? Were Angelli and Pullit wasting time over there—necking, smooching . . . ? Or had they all been caught? Had everyone down there been apprehended? Was he waiting up here for people who had already been dragged off by SS guards?

Numerous paranoid fantasies raged through his mind, and he knew he had never been this lonely before in his life.

It was terribly dark and muggy up here. The rain striking the bridge floor inches away was no longer a reassuring cover-up for his own noises. It was a maddeningly relentless booming that would eventually deafen him. Muggy and cold . . . It should not be muggy and cold at the same time, should it? But it was. He was sweating and freezing all at once. He was—

Beame tugged at the other end of the cord.

Stiff and sore from lying in the narrow space between the bridge floor and the pier roof, the major cursed under his breath as he reeled in the line and fought the fiery ache in his shoulders and upper arms.

The end of the nylon cord was tied to the copper detonator wire. Kelly took the spool, which fed back to the explosives on the farside pier, and he began the tedious, tricky chore of wiring the detonators here without breaking the continuity of the line. The wire was wet and cold and slipped through his hands, but it did what he demanded of it.

Ten minutes later, fingers sliced even more than they had been, he was finished. The plastic packets had been holed only enough to allow him to attach the blowing caps, and now the copper wire was twisted tightly to the tiny initiators.

Kelly tossed the spool over the side and hoped Beame would see it coming. Then he started down to join the others.

The pillar was slippery, the concrete greased by the rain. Kelly lost his hold, almost fell, grabbed desperately for protruding stones, held on. But when he moved again, his shoes slipped off the ledges he had found for them. Over and over again, he lost half of his balance, teetering on the brink. When he was twenty feet down, with twenty more to go, his hands and feet slipped at the same moment, leaving him helpless. He fell.

He struck the water with an horrendous crash and went under. Water flowed in his mouth and nostrils, filling him up. Darkness pressed close. He could not tell for sure which way was up. He flailed, could not find air, tried to snort out the water he had swallowed, and succeeded only in swallowing more.

Then someone grabbed him and rolled him onto his back, put an arm under his chin in the familiar lifesaving hold. In a moment, he was safe again, on his feet against the pillar.

"Okay?" Lily whispered. It was she who had rescued him. She had lost her halter in the attempt. Her large, perfect breasts jutted up and out at him, all wet and shiny. The nipples were larger than he had ever seen them.

He spat out some water. "Okay," he whispered back. He looked up at the bridge, and looked questioningly at her.

She came closer. Her jugs squashed against his chest as she leaned over and whispered in his ear. "You didn't yell. They heard nothing."

"I don't love you," he whispered.

"Same here."

"Not at all," he said.

"Not the least little bit," she said.

They smiled at each other.

# 8/

Because he was the slimmest, darkest, and quickest man among them, Vito Angelli was given the job of taking the spool of wire and the T-plunger up the sloped ravine wall to the rear of the village store, which was the nearest cover he would find up there.

Major Kelly sent all the others out into the river, then drew the private close and risked a whisper. "Remember, there are two krauts guarding the eastern bridge approach. When you go over the crest, you'll be passing within ten feet of them."

Angelli nodded his head vigorously. He was drenched and shivering, and he looked like the classic drowned rat. He was badly frightened.

"If they see you and challenge you, don't play hero. Drop everything and run. To hell with blowing up the bridge. If you're seen, it won't matter any longer."

Angelli nodded his head. He understood. Or he had palsy.

"You see the T-plunger?" Kelly asked, pointing to the device where it stood on the shore.

"Yeah," Vito said, teeth chattering.

"Here's the wire." Kelly gave him the spool. "Make sure you hold it like this, so it continues to pay out. If you hold it wrong, it'll be jerked out of your hand, or you'll be tripped up."

Vito nodded and started for shore. Then he turned and came back, leaned close to the major. "If I buy the farm . . . tell Nurse Pullit my last thoughts were about her."

Kelly did not know what to say.

"Will you tell her, sir?"

"Vito—"

"Promise, Major."

Overhead, one of the SS guards laughed heartily at a *Kamerad's* joke, and jackboots thumped on the board floor.

Looking into Angelli's dark eyes, the major suddenly realized that the private's affair with Nurse Pullit was *his* method of hanging on. Kelly had his cheap philosophy, and Angelli had Nurse Pullit. One was no worse, no crazier than the other.

"I'll tell her," Kelly said.

"Thank you, sir."

Angelli went ashore. He picked up the T-plunger and started up the slope, sliding sideways in the mud.

Still shocked by his insight into Angelli's condition, Kelly turned away from the shore and the bridge and waded out into the river where the others waited. The men were so fascinated with Lily's bare, wet jugs that they did not even see him until he thumped each one on the shoulder. He lead them south again, the way they had come.

They had no time to waste. If Vito made it, then there was no use watching him go. If he failed, they would not be able to help him, and they would become targets themselves.

Lightning speared the earth and glazed the surface of the river and made them stand out like ink spots on a clean sheet of typewriter paper. Each of them waited for the chatter of guns, the bite of a bullet in the back. . . .

Major Kelly thought of brass beds.

# 9/

Six men and three nuns struggled out of the ravine at the same place where they had gone down nearly two hours ago. They were wet and muddy and worn out.

Major Kelly led them northward along the ravine crest until they came back to the hospital bunker. The others went down the steps and slipped inside when Liverwright opened the door to them. The major continued north toward the rear of the village store.

Angelli was waiting there. He had made it.

"Never mind giving my last words to Nurse Pullit," he whispered happily. "I'll tell her myself."

"Yeah," Kelly said. "Now let's get the job done."

# PART FIVE

# Hanging On

## Dawn—Dusk / July 22, 1944

# 1/

Dawn tinted the horizon even as Major Kelly and Vito Angelli were tying up the loose ends of the operation. And on his way back to the rectory, the major was forced to lie low while a *Wehrmacht* squad marched up and down St. Ignatius changing the sentries at the intersections. By the time he reached the churchyard, Kelly knew it was too light for him to return to his room by way of the rose lattice and the rear window. Even if Rotenhausen and Beckmann were not up yet—and they surely were—the chances of some guard on a nearby street spotting him on his climb to the porch roof were too great to be ignored.

The bold approach was called for.

Nearly half an hour after dawn, he entered the back of the church. He hurried through the sacristy, up onto the altar platform, down into the auditorium, and out the front door. He winced as the rain struck him anew. He paused only a second at the top of the church steps, then went down to the street.

The *Wehrmacht* sentry on duty at B Street and the bridge road was wearing a green rain slicker and a disgusted look. He hunched his shoulders against the rain and paraded back and forth, putting as little into the duty as he could. He gave Kelly a brief smile but did not stop him, for he had just been posted and did not know that the priest had never passed from the rectory *to* the church.

Kelly went up the porch steps, crossed the porch, went through the front door with the rain still stinging his back. In the rectory foyer, rivulets of water streamed from him onto the floorboards.

General Adolph Rotenhausen was just then coming down the steps from the second floor, tamping tobacco into his pipe. "Father Picard! Where have you been at this hour, in this terrible weather?"

"At the church, General," Kelly said.

"Oh, of course," Rotenhausen said. "I suppose you have to get ready for Mass each morning."

"For what?" Kelly asked.

"Mass, of course," Rotenhausen said.

Before Kelly could respond, the general's aides appeared at the top of the steps with the officer's belongings, which they brought down and took outside into the morning rain.

Rotenhausen came to the open door, looked across the porch at the raindrops bouncing on the street. "Miserable day for travel." He looked at his watch. "But Standartenführer Beckmann was out there an hour ago. . . . Sometimes, I think those madmen *deserve* the world." He glanced at Kelly and, for the first time, saw how wet the priest was. "You couldn't be so drenched just from crossing the street, Father!"

"Uh . . . I went for a walk," Kelly said.

"In the rain?"

"Rain is God's creation," Kelly improvised. "It is refreshing."

Rotenhausen looked at Kelly's dripping suit, shook his head. He turned and continued to watch the rain slash in sheets across the bridge road.

Also watching the storm, Kelly thought of Lily's wet breasts. For a moment, he was warm and happy . . . and then he realized he could not afford to love her. He had almost made a drastic mistake.

Rotenhausen puffed on his pipe.

Thunder rolled across the sky. Behind the steady drumming of the rain was the dinosaurian roar of Panzer engines as the convoy prepared to pull out.

"We don't have to worry about Allied bombers today," Rotenhausen said.

As he spoke, his aide ran up onto the porch. The man took a folded slicker from under his own raincoat, shook it out, and held it up for his chief. The general slipped his arms into the plastic sleeves and buttoned up, turned his collar high. He flipped his pipe upside down and tapped it against the door frame. Ashes fell on the wet porch floor.

"Good luck at the front, sir," Major Kelly said.

"Thank you, Father. You have been most gracious."

"Not at all." Which was true.

Rotenhausen smiled, nodded, and turned away. He and his aide went down the steps and east along the bridge road to the first tank in the long convoy.

The rain continued to fall.

A flash of lightning made shadows jump across the veranda floor.

The first tank, Rotenhausen's tank, lurched into the middle of the road, tracks churning up mud and gravel, and started toward the bridge two and a half blocks away.

Still, no alarm had been raised at the west end. Bobo Remlock had not yet arrived. Maybe the Panzers would all get across before Old Blood and Guts made the far side.

Kelly left the front door. He hurried through the deserted house, passed through the kitchen and out onto the rear lawn.

The cold rain hit him again, but he hardly noticed. He was too worried about getting his head blown off to be concerned also about catching a cold. His baggy trousers were sopping wet and hung on him like a pair of old-fashioned beach pantaloons for men.

He passed through the hidden gate in the fence, and ran between two fake houses in which his men huddled fearfully. He crossed B Street, ran the length of the cemetery, and crossed A Street to the rear of the village store.

Lieutenant Beame was watching for him and threw down a rope from the store roof. Kelly took hold of the rope, tested it, then climbed the fifteen feet of vertical wall to join the lieutenant in his observation post.

Beame was not alone, though he should have been. Lily was there, too, braless beneath her habit. Pullit and Nathalie were behind Lily. Maurice was there, watching over his daughter, and Angelli was watching over Pullit. Danny Dew was sitting by the T-plunger with a rifle over his knees.

"We couldn't let you face this alone," Angelli said.

"Of course not," Kelly said.

"We had to share the danger with you."

"What else?" Kelly asked. "Just keep down. Don't stand up, or someone on the street will see you."

"No sign of Old Blood and Guts," Beame said when Kelly knelt beside him.

The village store was the best observation post for the coming showdown. It was the only structure in St. Ignatius with a flat roof—not because French country shops had flat roofs, but because they had simply run out of the necessary beams and shingles and had been unable to give the place anything *but* a flat roof. Furthermore, the store faced the bridge road, where all the action, if there were any, would transpire; and it was close enough to the bridge to allow them to establish the detonator here.

Beside Beame, next to Danny Dew, the heavy T-plunger stood on the wet wood, waiting for its crossbar to be stroked down and the dynamite touched off beneath the nine-hundred-foot span.

And now they were prepared to do just that.

Kelly turned to Maurice. "You shouldn't be up here. You should be on the other side, waiting for Remlock."

Maurice hesitated, looked at Nathalie, then at Beame. "You will see that they are kept apart?"

"Yes, yes," Kelly said, impatiently.

"Very well." Maurice went down the rope ladder and disappeared.

Kelly wiped a hand over his face and looked east along the bridge road. Rotenhausen's convoy was pouring into the far end of the town. Already, the first Panzer was halfway past the convent, less than a block from their position and little more than a block from the bridge. Behind the first Panzer was another, and another—then two long-barreled Jagdpanthers, two heavily armored cars with 75 mm cannons, then a motorcycle with sidecar which was darting in and out of the convoy, working its way to the front where it belonged. Rotenhausen was starting slowly, but he would reach the bridge in less than two minutes.

Kelly saw that they would have to blow the span even if Bobo Remlock did not show up. If they took a chance and let Rotenhausen start across, and if Remlock showed up when *some* of the German tanks were already on the other side, there would be no way to avoid a battle that would level St. Ignatius—and kill everyone who pretended to live there.

He stooped low on the roof, trying not to be seen, and he placed both hands on the T-plunger.

"Already?" Lily asked.

He nodded.

"Just a minute, then." She took a rifle from beneath her voluminous habit. "I thought we all ought to be armed, if it comes down to that."

"You're going to fight tanks with rifles?" Kelly asked.

"Better than fighting them with rocks," she said.

"I guess so."

"I don't love you, Kelly."

He kissed her, quickly. "I don't love you."

To the east, the advance motorcycle escort weaved around the two leading tanks and shot out in front of the convoy with a loud growl. As Rotenhausen's Panzer churned by the last of the churchyard toward the A Street intersection, the motorcycle flashed past Kelly and the others, went over the bridge approach, and accelerated toward the west bank.

Over there, six German soldiers armed with automatic rifles stood guard over the farside approach. The cycle with its two *Wehrmacht* soldiers sped out of the bridge and blurred past them, roared toward the bend in the road—and braked suddenly when the first of General Bobo Remlock's tanks, a British Cromwell, hove into view, cruising at top speed.

"Here we go!" Danny Dew said, lying flat on his stomach and bringing his rifle up where he could use it.

Rotenhausen's Panzer, the first in the German convoy, was through the A-Street intersection and on the approach to the bridge when the general saw the enemy tank. The Panzer bit into the cracked macadam and held on, chugging to a stop at the brink of the bridge, at the corner of the village store. Looking over the edge of the roof, Kelly and the others could see the top of Adolph Rotenhausen's head just four feet below.

The rest of the German convoy slowed and stopped.

Even while Rotenhausen's tank was jerking to a standstill, Kelly looked westward again. Only a few seconds had passed since the cycle had taken the lead in the German line and zoomed across the bridge, though Kelly could have sworn it was more like two or three hours. Over there, the motorcycle was still bearing down on the cruising Cromwell and trying to come to a full stop on the wet pavement. Abruptly, the front wheel came up. The cycle rose like a dancing bear, then toppled onto its side. The monstrous, British-made tank slowed a bit, though not much, and ran right over the screaming *Wehrmacht* cyclists, grinding them into the mud.

Nathalie cried out.

"Sadistic bastard," Lily hissed, staring at the Cromwell as if she could vaporize it with a look of pure hatred.

"One guess who's commanding the Cromwell," Beame said.

"Old Blood and Guts," Kelly said.

"Yeah. Big Tex."

"The Last of the Two-Fisted Cowboys."

"The Big Ball of Barbed Wire himself."

"The Latter-Day Sam Houston," Kelly said.

"Yeah. The Fighting General."

"Old Shit for Brains," Kelly said. "No doubt about it." He could not understand how he could go on like this with

Beame. He had never been so terrified in his life. And he had a great many other terrors to stack this one up against.

The six German riflemen on the far side turned and ran when the Cromwell crushed the cyclists and kept on coming. They were halfway back across the bridge now, every one of them a religious man no matter what his beliefs had been a few minutes ago.

Behind the Cromwell, other Allied tanks loomed out of the curtain of gray rain: several Shermans, two British M-10s, another Cromwell, an armored car with twin cannon. . . . Some of these left the road and deployed southward, all turning to face across the ravine, mammoth guns trained on the village and on the part of the German convoy which they might be able to reach. The lead Cromwell and several other tanks remained on the road and stopped at the farside bridge approach, bottling it up.

"Massah Kelly," Danny Dew said, "I do wish I was back in Georgia. Even dat sorrowful ol' place do seem better than this."

It was an almost classic military problem. The Germans held the east bank of the river. The Allies held the west bank. And no one controlled the bridge between.

The showdown.

"If we get out of this," Beame whispered to Kelly. "I'm not going to take any of Maurice's guff. I'm going to ask Nathalie to marry me."

"He'll eat you alive," Kelly said.

"Once, he would have. Not now."

"Good luck."

"I won't need it," Beame said. "I know what I want now. Just so I live to have it."

The wind gusted across the roof, stirred the nuns' habits, pummeled them with thousands of tiny, watery fists.

To the south of the bridge on the other side of the gorge, one of the dark-brown M-10s elevated its blackened cannon to full boost. Kelly watched this without fully grasping the implications of the movement. A second later, one shell slammed out across the river. Just one. None of the other tanks opened fire, and the M-10 did not immediately follow through with a second round. The long shot arced high over the river and fell squarely into the building which was next to the store on A Street. The blast was a gigantic gong, then a compact ball of fire, and finally a violent wave of force that flung Kelly, Beame, and the others flat on their faces, even though they had already been kneeling. The armed T-plunger tipped over without setting off the dynamite under the bridge.

The house which had taken the shell was chewed into toothpicks and spewed in all directions. The burning floor collapsed down into the hospital bunker where Tooley, Liverwright, Hagendorf, and Kowalski did not have a chance. They probably did not even have time to look up and see it tumbling in on them, Kelly thought. Just a great noise, heat, a flash of pain, and endless darkness.

"No," Beame said. "No, no, no!" He stared in horror at the flames which licked up from the bottom of the hospital bunker. A jug of alcohol burst; blue flames spurted briefly skyward, dropped away.

Nathalie was crying, crossing herself, praying.

Lily was cursing the M-10 and giving it the same look of loathing she had directed against the Cromwell.

Major Kelly's first thoughts were insane. First, he decided that Hagendorf had at least been released from a world of chaos by the ultimate chaotic event. And Tooley would not have to witness any more violence. And Liverwright did not have to die slowly now; he was finished in an instant. And most insanely of all—Kowalski had been released from the compulsion to predict a future which he was powerless to change. It was even a bit funny . . . Kowalski had forecast every violent event which had plagued them—except his own demise. What good was it to see the future if you could not see and avoid the source of your own death? And if a genuine fortune-teller could not avoid his own grave, what chance did an ordinary, balding, middle-aged slob have of living to celebrate his next birthday?

Kelly began to cry.

He did not know if he were crying for the dead men or for himself. It did not matter very much.

Angelli and Pullit were also crying, comforting each other, hugging. Kelly did not bother to go over and separate them.

Without warning, the second shell from the M-10 plowed into the side of the gorge just short of the village store. The earth leaped up like a bronco under the buildings. Inside the store, canned goods and other merchandise fell from the shelves in a series of tinny explosions.

"Hey!" Beame said. "Hey, they're after us—not the Germans! They must think that we're up here spotting for the kraut artillery!"

"Nuns, spotting for the kraut artillery?" Kelly asked.

But he saw the M-10's cannon elevate a couple of degrees more and line up a new trajectory. The third shot would get them as surely as the first had accidentally slaughtered Tooley, Liverwright, Hagendorf, and Kowalski.

"Jesus Fucking Christ!" Kelly screamed, surely loud enough to be heard over the Panzer engines in the street below. He shoved clumsily to his feet and turned toward the T-plunger, took a single step, and was knocked to his knees by a tiny snapping sound off to his right. He looked down at his arm and saw blood running over his clerical suit. He had been shot.

But by whom?

Then he saw Lieutenant Slade coming onto the roof.

# 2/

All night long, Lieutenant Slade had prowled the fake town looking for Major Kelly. When he had first lost the bastard after following him and Tooley from the convent to the west side of A Street, Slade had been sure he would pick up the trail in no time. But minutes and then hours passed, and Kelly was nowhere to be found. And the longer Slade took to find him, the less chance there was that the coup could be pulled off and the Germans defeated by clever commando tactics.

Where was Kelly hiding?

Slade raced from one end of St. Ignatius to the other, looked in all the buildings, did everything but pry under the rocks. He never thought to look down in the gorge, out in the middle of the river, or up under the bridge, because he could not have conceived of Major Kelly doing anything as dangerous and brave as wiring the bridge with explosives.

Then, just minutes ago, he had been standing in the sacristy doorway at the back of the small church, staring out at the graveyard and trying to think if he had forgotten to look anywhere. To his great surprise, Kelly had come bounding down one of the aisles between the tombstones, wearing a muddy clerical suit. He had crossed A Street and gone up to the roof of the village store, leaving a convenient rope ladder dangling behind him.

Slade knew there was no longer any chance of killing Kelly *and* organizing the men into commando groups. He was going to have to settle for just the first half of his plan. Perhaps, after he had murdered the major and the Panzers had gone, he could shape the men into killer squads and prepare them to do battle with any other German force that happened through this way.

After Maurice Jobert came down from the store roof and disappeared into the ravine, Slade hurried across the churchyard and over to the west side of A Street. He reached the back of the village store just as a shell slammed into the hospital bunker on his left. He was thrown to the ground, knocked to the verge of unconsciousness.

When he finally got to his feet, he stared across the gorge and saw the Allied tanks for the first time. He did not understand how they could have arrived at this most propitious moment, but he did not stop to wonder about them. If the Allies were going to recapture this part of France today, it was more important than ever that he kill Major Kelly. When the liberation was completed, Slade wanted to be able to prove to the conquering troops and to all the American people and not least of all to his mother that he had done everything within his power to wreck Major Kelly's cowardly plans.

He went quickly up the ladder to the roof, stepped onto the slippery pine planks. Kelly was immediately in front of him, running across the roof. Slade pointed his .45-caliber revolver and pulled the trigger.

## 3/

Major Kelly was surprised that the revolver had made so little noise. Then he realized that the Panzer engines and the echoes of the exploding shell had blanketed the shot. And *then* he realized that it did not matter if the krauts heard the shot—because whether or not they heard it, he was dead.

Slade sighted in on him, holding the big gun in both hands as he lined up the second shot.

Looking into the muzzle, Kelly tried to think of brass beds.

"Major!" Beame shouted.

Before Kelly could tell the lieutenant that he was too late, Beame tackled Slade from the side. The two lieutenants went down hard enough to shake the hastily laid roof, and rolled over and over as they punched at each other. The gun clattered away from them.

"Little Snot!" Lily cried, and threw herself into the melee.

Suddenly, Kelly remembered the M-10 tank which had been preparing to fire a third round. He got off his knees and staggered over to the T-plunger. He turned it over, set it upright. Without checking to see if both copper wires were still wound to their terminals, he jammed the crossbar down.

The gorge filled with two simultaneous *cracks!* and then a pair of duller but more fundamental *whumps!* that chattered back from the low sky.

The bridge wrenched sideways on its moorings, steel squealing like pigs at the heading block. The anchor plates on both the nearside and the farside approaches buckled and popped loose. They flew into the air and rolled end for end, catching the morning sunlight. Then they fell like leaden birds back to the earth. One of the piers gave way. The concrete had been shattered by the dynamite, and now the pieces separated and fell away in different directions. They made big splashes in the river.

The bulk of the bridge shifted lazily westward toward the remaining pier, overpressured that weakened pillar, and broke it down into a dozen irregular slabs.

Beame knelt at Kelly's right side. "She's going down!" he cried, oblivious of his split and bloody lip.

Lily knelt on the left. "You okay?"

Kelly was holding his wounded arm. "Fine. Slade?"

"Knocked him out," Lily said.

"Look!" Beame said.

Four of the German riflemen were still on the bridge, only a few steps from the safety of the St. Ignatius shore. They had been thrown to the deck with tremendous force when the dynamite blew. As they struggled to their feet, dazed and bloody, their uniforms ripped and their pot helmets dented, the second pier crumbled. The bridge sluggishly parted company with the gorge walls and its anchors. Two of the four Germans, not yet recovered from the first blow, were pitched out into space as the long structure rolled like a mean horse. The remaining pair clung to the twisted steel beams and rode the bridge to its final resting place.

They did not have a chance.

The bridge dropped.

It bounced on the rocks below and broke up like a ship might, slewing sideways in the river, every part of it strained against every other part. Rivets popped from their fittings, deadly bullets that whined off the superstructure. Twenty-foot beams snapped loose, jumped up. They quivered momentarily in the gray rain. Lazily, they fell back into the body of the ruined span.

This was a slower death than the bridge had ever before suffered, but it expired just as completely, settling into a mass of useless materials.

"Christ, what a show," Danny Dew said.

Nathalie knelt beside Beame and put her arms around him, held tight to him. He kissed her cheek, leaving bloody lip prints.

Gradually, silence returned.

And after a moment of silence, Kelly became aware of the Panzer noise and the drumming rain.

On opposite sides of the gorge, the Allies and the Germans stared across the void at one another and wondered what in the name of God they were to do now.

# 4/

Dreadfully weary, Major Kelly walked around the village store, one hand against the wall to balance himself. Wet, muddy, bloody, he came out on the bridge road where the German convoy stretched eastward as far as he could see. He went looking for General Adolph Rotenhausen.

The general was standing in the hatch of his Panzer. He was fearlessly eyeballing General Bobo Remlock, who was standing up in his Cromwell turret nine hundred feet across the ravine. "Father Picard!" Rotenhausen cried when he saw Kelly standing ankle-deep in a mud puddle beside the tank. "This is a dangerous place right now. Go back to your church and–"

"No," Kelly said. He slopped through the mud, put one foot in the huge mud-clogged tread gears, and clambered up until he stood on the tank fender. "I am worried about my people, my village."

"There is nothing you can do now," Rotenhausen said. "You should have done something sooner. You should have stopped the partisans from blowing up the bridge."

"I knew nothing of that," Kelly said. "And I guarantee you, General, that no partisans take shelter in St. Ignatius. They must have come up the river from some other town."

Rotenhausen turned his aristocratic face to the sky. The rain stung it, rolled off his white cheeks onto his glistening slicker. "It doesn't matter whether I believe you or not. The deed is done."

Kelly wiped nervously at his face. When would Bobo Remlock get tired of sitting over there and lob another shell at them?

"There is no other bridge in the area wide enough to accommodate your Panzers," Kelly said, just as he and Maurice had planned for him to say. Right now, on the west bank, Maurice was imparting this same information to Bobo Remlock. "But ten miles to the north, near the base of the mountains, there is a place where the gorge becomes shallower and the river broadens. You could get over to the west if you went up there."

Rotenhausen perked up for a moment, then squinted suspiciously at Kelly. "Why do you tell me this?"

"I don't want my village destroyed," Kelly said. "Already, several of my people have died. And I have been injured myself."

For a long moment, Rotenhausen looked across the mist-bottomed gorge at the Cromwells, Shermans, and M-10s. Then, as the tanks on that side began to pull back, turn, and start north, the German made his decision. "I must get this convoy turned around," he told Kelly. "We'll reach that ford before they do, Father Picard."

"Good luck," Kelly said, jumping down from the tank. Holding his wounded arm, he walked over to the village store and leaned against the wall and watched the tanks move out.

## 5/

Danny Dew raised the sledgehammer over his head and brought it down on top of the shortwave radio. The metal casing bent, but nothing broke.

Major Kelly was standing beside Dew, his arm in a sling. The bullet wound was not serious, merely a crease; but it pained him too much to allow him to wield the hammer himself. "Again!" he shouted.

"Yes, Massah," Dew said. He swung the hammer a second time. One of the casing seams popped open.

"I don't understand why you have to destroy it," Lily said, looking mournfully at the shortwave set.

"Neither do I," Beame said. He was standing next to Nathalie and Maurice, though The Frog was glaring fiercely at him.

"I don't ever want to talk to Blade again," Kelly said. "Even if I gave the radio to Maurice, Blade would have a way of reaching me."

"*Mon ami*—" Maurice began.

"Again, Danny!" Kelly said.

Dew raised the sledgehammer. His hard black muscles rippled. He put his strength into the swing and broke the glass in the front of the radio. The blow echoed in the large, one-room convent building, whispered for a long time in the rafters overhead.

"But you *have* to talk to Blade," a handsome young soldier said, stepping up between Lily and Private Angelli. "He's your commanding officer."

Kelly could not remember ever having seen this young man, which was odd, since he prided himself in knowing all his men by their first names. "He isn't my commanding officer any longer," Kelly said.

Lily stamped one foot, a gesture that made her breasts jiggle in the velvet cups of her dancer's costume. "Kelly, I won't let you—"

"Danny, hit it again!"

Dew struck the radio another vicious blow. It crashed off the stand onto the floor.

"You simply can't fire your commanding officer," Vito Angelii said. He was standing beside one of the French girls who had been dressed like a nun. His arm was around her waist, one hand circling up to cup her full right breast. He no longer seemed to be such a one-woman man. Or, more accurately, a one-pervert man. Nurse Pullit was nowhere in sight. "You can't choose your commanding officers," Angelli insisted.

"Well, from now on that's exactly what I'm going to do," Kelly said. "I don't want another one like Blade. I don't think he ever did care about us the way a general is supposed to care for his men. He's been using us."

Lily frowned at him. "*Using* us?"

Kelly nodded. "I've been putting bits and pieces together. . . . You know we've thought there was a traitor in the camp. The Stukas always knew when the bridge was rebuilt, always returned to bomb it the day after it was completed. *Someone* had to tell them it was ready. I think that someone was General Blade."

"Bullshit!" Coombs said. He, too, was standing with a French girl. She was rather ugly.

Lily looked at Kelly as if he had gone mad. "That's ridiculous! Blade—"

"It makes sense to me," Kelly said. Perspiration trickled down his forehead and ran to the end of his nose, but he ignored it. "Keep in mind that Blade had his entire career staked on us. No one else thought this bridge was of any strategic importance. Blade said so himself. Yet he disagreed with the other generals. He secretly sent a whole unit of Army engineers behind German lines in order to keep the bridge open. What do you think would have happened to Blade if the bridge were never bombed, if we just sat here without anything to do?"

Lily thought about it. They all thought about it. She said, "He wouldn't be up for any promotions when his superiors found out about it."

"Exactly," Kelly said. "Once he sent us here, he had to establish proof that the Germans considered the bridge strategically important. And what better way than to get them to bomb it repeatedly?"

"Now, wait a minute, sir," the handsome young soldier said. "General Blade can't order Stukas to do his own dirty work!"

"That's right," Beame said. "He can't control the German army!"

Kelly frowned. "There are bits and pieces that maybe fit. . . . For example, Beame told me that General Blade probably dabbles in the black market. When we were in Britain, I heard the same thing about Bobo Remlock. That sounds terribly coincidental, doesn't it—that both our nemeses should be in the black market?"

"Hell," Angelli said, "probably every one of our generals is in it."

"Another thing," Kelly said, ignoring Angelli. "I've also heard that some of our officers are not against profiting from deals made with officers on the other side."

"*With Germans?*" Lily asked.

"I've heard that, too," Angelli said. "Hell, Eisenhower's investigative staff brought charges against two high-ranking officers while we were in Britain. But what does this sort of thing have to do with us?" He fondled the French girl's breast, and she giggled.

"Plenty," Kelly said. "If American and German officers fly to neutral territory to swap black market goods. . . . Well, suppose Blade gave a German air force officer a planeload of whiskey at one of these neutral ports—and didn't take any material goods in return. Suppose, instead, he asked his German opposite to see to the bombing of this bridge and help him establish his reputation among the Allied brass? Blade could inform this German officer each time the bridge was rebuilt—"

"You think Blade would engineer and go through with a wild scheme like this just to get a promotion?" Lily asked, incredulous.

"Either that, or he's syphilitic."

"Bullshit," Coombs said.

"This is paranoid," Lily said. "The world isn't as Machiavellian as you're making it out to be."

"Look," Beame said, "Blade's an idiot, but he can't be the kind of manipulator you're trying to say he is."

"I wonder . . ." Kelly said.

"Look," Lily said, "maybe the radio will still work."

"Hit it again, Dew!" Dew obliged. "If we don't destroy it, Blade will call us again tonight. He'll send in the DC-3 loaded with supplies, and he'll order us to rebuild the bridge. And as soon as the bridge is up, he'll call his German friend, get it bombed into rubble. You know . . . it's also possible that Blade somehow arranged for Rotenhausen's convoy to take this route, to come this roundabout back way just so the bridge would appear to have strategic importance and—"

"You can't *know* any of this!" Lily shouted. "This isn't some fantasy we're involved in. This is *real.* This is life!"

"Wrong," Kelly said. "It's all a fairy tale, grand in color—"

"Bullshit," Coombs said. His ugly French girl friend giggled and said, "Boolsheet."

"Kelly," Lily said, "if you destroy the radio, no one will know we're here. Blade will think we're dead. We won't get out of this place until the war is finished."

"I don't care," Kelly said. "Just so we get out alive."

"Well, *I* care!" Lily said. "I have a *career* to think of!" She turned and walked toward the front of the convent, her firm ass swinging in a blue velvet dancer's costume, her long legs scissoring gorgeously.

Major Kelly was tempted to run after her, grab her, peel her out of that skimpy suit, and desecrate this holy convent with unspeakable acts of carnal lust. But it was more important to oversee the destruction of the radio. . . .

"If you completely demolish this set," Maurice said, "you're going to have to find something else with which to pay me."

"I will," Kelly said. "Dew, hit it again."

Forty blows later, Dew dropped the hammer. Everyone

had wandered away except the handsome young soldier whose name Kelly could not recall. The three of them stood in silence for a moment, as if mourning the departed short-wave set.

"Major," the handsome soldier said, "I just came from a duty shift at the jail, watching over Lieutenant Slade. Lyle Fark took my place and. . . ."

"And?" Kelly asked.

The young soldier cleared his throat. "Well, Slade's demanding a trial, sir. He won't let up about it. Keeps wanting to know when he can have a trial. He says that a good court-martial will prove he was right all along. He expects to get medals, he says. But there has to be a trial first, you see. He's impossible to work around, sir. Fark asked me if you could give him a tentative trial date he can use to shut Slade up."

"Tell him after the war," Kelly said.

"That's all?"

"That's all. Just sometime after the war."

"He's really anxious to get those medals," the soldier said. "He isn't going to like your answer, but I'll tell him anyway." He left the convent by the back door.

"Gee," Kelly said, staring after him, "I always thought I knew everyone in the unit by sight and name. But I can't place that one."

"You're kidding," Danny Dew said. "That's Pullit."

"Pullit? Where's his nurse's uniform?"

"He doesn't need it anymore," Dew said. "At least, not for the moment, not until the pressure builds up again."

"The uniform—all of that was Pullit's way of hanging on," Kelly said, a man to whom a spiritual revelation had just come.

"I guess so," Danny Dew said.

Dew left by the back door, while Kelly went out and joined Lily Kain on the convent stoop. She was looking at St. Ignatius, at the quaint church and the rectory, the pleasant streets still damp with the morning's shower.

Kelly put one arm around her waist. "Pretty, isn't it?"

"It *doesn't* look half bad."

Overhead, the clouds were breaking up. Scattered pieces of blue sky shone down on the town.

"Well!" Kelly said, pointing east along the bridge road. "Look up there!"

Lieutenant Beame and Nathalie Jobert were walking hand-in-hand toward the edge of town. When they reached the trees, they ducked furtively into the undergrowth, out of sight.

"Good for them," Lily said. She leaned against Kelly and clasped his buttocks in one of her quick hands.

"I'm glad Dave's finally grown up," Kelly said.

"Who?"

"Dave. Dave Beame."

Lily tilted her head and smiled at him. She wrinkled her pug nose and ran all her freckles together into one brown spot. "I never heard you call him by his first name before."

Kelly shrugged. "Well, maybe it's safe enough for things like that now. Maybe first names are okay again." He turned her around until she was facing him, encircled her with his arms. She came against him, warm and pliant, hugged him back. "I even feel safe enough to tell you I was wrong before." He slid his good hand down her back and cupped her buttocks. "I *do* love you, I think."

"Me too," Lily said. "At least for a little while." She kissed him, licked inside of his mouth. "Say, how would you like to go back into this convent here and—"

"Desecrate it with acts of unspeakable carnal lust?"

Lily grinned. "Yeah." She opened the door for him. "Let's chase out all these religious spirits and have us a nice den of iniquity."

Kelly let go of her, stepped back, and appraised her with one frank look. "You know, everything might really be all right. And you know what I was just thinking when we were looking at the town? I think we could have a *real* village here, if we wanted. We could finish the insides of these houses. We could anchor them down, put basements under them. Dig some real wells."

"Whoa!" Lily said, still holding the convent door open. "Before you get wrapped up in that fantasy, remember that Maurice owns all of St. Ignatius. He also owns your tools, machines, supplies—and everyone's next paycheck."

"Yes," Kelly said. "But Maurice can be taken too." He glanced up the bridge road to the place where Beame and Nathalie had disappeared into the trees. "I'll have to speak to Dave about the kind of dowry he should demand from Maurice, when he marries Nathalie. He ought to get a good piece of money. A bulldozer. Maybe even a budding little town. . . ."

Lily laughed and grabbed his hand. "Spinning fairy tales again. I thought you wouldn't need those anymore."

"I thought so too," Kelly said. He looked back at St. Ignatius. And he began to realize that when the war ended he would still have to fight to hang on, to survive. It was not just the insane generals like Blade and the chaos of war which made hanging on his greatest, most time-consuming enterprise. It was *life.* The hanging on never ended. At times, the effort required to hang on was less than on other occasions; but the degree of difficulty was the only thing that changed.

"Come on," Lily said.

Numb, he followed her into the convent. The door closed behind them.

In the dark foyer, she pulled off her dancer's costume and moved up against him, kissed him, nibbled at his ear.

"Life *is* a fairy tale, Lily, grand in color but modest in design. It really, really *is.*"

"Ahhhh," she said, "shut up and put it to me."